GREEN HOUSE

near Loveville

9/8/17

To Arthur,
   Thank you for
stopping and talking.
I enjoyed hearing
about a slice of your
life. Hope you enjoy
the book.

Bill

William Crute

PAGE PUBLISHING, INC.
New York, NY

First originally published by Page Publishing, Inc. 2015

ISBN 978-1-68213-463-4 (pbk)
ISBN 978-1-68213-464-1 (digital)

Printed in the United States of America

Dedicated to:

My son

James Brandon Crute

and his wife

Danielle Giuffre Crute

The Guest House

This being human is a guest house.
Every morning a new arrival.

A joy, a depression, a meanness,
some momentary awareness comes
as an unexpected visitor.

Welcome and entertain them all!
Even if they're a crowd of sorrows,
who violently sweep your house
empty of its furniture,
still, treat each guest honorably.
He may be clearing you out
for some new delight.

The dark thought, the shame, the malice,
meet them at the door laughing,
and invite them in.

Be grateful for whoever comes,
because each has been sent
as a guide from beyond.

—Rumi

Acknowledgments

Paul Macrae Montgomery helped me with a character in this book, Bob, for which I will be forever grateful.

Barbara Trippe-Crute was my copilot on this adventurous flight. Without her, the wheels of our plane would never have touched back down on the ground safely.

With gratitude,
William Crute

PART I

Morgan Make$ Money

$

IT WAS STILL SPRING, but summer humidity had already taken over this southern town. A salesman was walking house to house trying to make his quota for the day and had stopped between the last house and the next one to wipe beads of sweat from his forehead. He pushed his wet handkerchief into his back pants' pocket as he walked up the sidewalk and the porch steps. He knocked on the storm door, and a woman appeared quickly behind the glass reaching for the door handle. When the door opened, he stepped back and said to the woman wearing white shorts and a V-neck t-shirt, "Good morning, ma'am, I'm Johnny Johnson with Armstrong Protection Systems—"

She cut him off. "I'm not interested," she blurted out and attempted to pull the storm door shut, but Johnny had the toe of his left shoe behind the bottom of the aluminum door, preventing it from closing. On the other side of the street, another salesman for Armstrong Protection Systems had made it over the first of multiple hurdles in door-to-door selling, having reached the living room of the home and was preparing to negotiate another hurdle—customer apathy and procrastination.

"Three break-ins just last week in your neighborhood—it's just a matter of time before they break into your home and clean you out," he said.

Farther down the street, Morgan Armstrong had already closed a sale with this homeowner and was walking down the sidewalk toward the street with a woman by his side. He routinely used this brief period of time to reassure customers, because it reduced the chances of them changing their minds later and canceling orders. Morgan said, "Very few people today are willing to face reality and do the wise thing. You, on the other hand, have selected the most advanced protection system we have and will enjoy its benefits while your neighbors live lives of quiet desperation. Criminals are running rampant from one end of our community to the other, unrestrained by conscience, morals, or even the police." He stopped at the curb and knocked on the passenger door of his new Volvo. "Solid as a rock. Yes, ma'am. I, too, believe in buying protection. My men will be here this afternoon, not tomorrow morning, to install your system. We do not want you to go another night without being absolutely SAFE."

"You don't have to rush, Mr. Armstrong," she said, as Morgan pulled out his iPhone.

"Getting it done today is not a problem. What's important is you and your husband sleeping soundly and safely tonight," Morgan responded as he entered information into his phone.

She smiled thinly, "No husband."

Morgan looked up and said, "But surely, there's a man around?"

She replied, "Nope—no man around."

"I'm surprised," he replied.

"But there is a WOMAN around," she added, cornering a smile.

Morgan mirrored his customer's smile, "Gone to the other side, have ya?"

"No fuss, no muss," she pertly replied.

Morgan chuckled, "I can appreciate your preference, shoot, you like what I like. Can't fault you for that!"

$

The designated hour in the afternoon had arrived. The two salesmen and Morgan pulled up in front of the park bench and got out of their cars. Both salesmen immediately held up an open hand indicating that they had sold five systems. Morgan placed his right foot on the seat of the bench quickly, admiring the shine on his new Clarks Bostonian shoe. "That's not bad, boys," he said, checking his watch, "BUT—my swimming pool needs a bubble, my kids want to go to sailing camp, and Cindy wants a new Lexus, so you two need to get back out there and sell one more system each before knocking off. It's just three thirty."

"Morgan?" they pleaded simultaneously.

Morgan pulled his handkerchief out and wiped off a slight film of dust on the toe of his shoe. "You aren't school teachers, you know. You're salesmen, and your day does not end in the middle of the afternoon."

"Are YOU going back out?" one salesman asked.

"No, I've made my SIX sales, now you need to make yours. After you get ONE more sale, come to the Doll House. Chicken wings and beer on me."

$

Morgan pulled into the Dream Cars, Ltd. lot and parked next to the sales office. A man opened the door and said to Morgan, "Big sales today, Boss—incredible sales!"

Morgan passed through the door and didn't stop walking. The sales manager caught up to him in the service area. A mechanic shouted to the sales manager, asking him where he wanted the mileage set, but he deferred to Morgan, who shouted out—3...6...2... 5...2. The mechanic gave him a thumbs-up and put his head back under the hood.

Outside, Morgan was eyeballing the rows of gleaming vintage cars. Pointing, he said, "Showcase the '53 vette tomorrow, and get me the keys to the Bird. I'll have it back before you open in the morning."

As Morgan drove off the lot with the top down on the '57 Thunderbird, the sun was setting, creating a pink-orange horizon over the river. He removed his necktie and unfastened the top button of his dress shirt, exposing a gold herringbone necklace. The diamond ring that adorned his left pinkie finger was catching the last golden rays of the sun. His eyes darted to his wrist and the hands of his Omega Constellation watch. He was right on schedule.

$

Morgan walked into the Doll House (an adult eatery) through the back door. It was happy hour. Waitresses were weaving their way through the crowd selling and delivering drinks. Bonnie, the manager, saw Morgan walking to the bar and joined him there. The bartender immediately slid a glass of orange juice to Morgan and shook out two vitamin C tablets into his outstretched hand. Morgan tossed the tablets into his mouth and washed them down with the juice. A customer standing next to Morgan asked, "You own this place, man—why don't you knock down some hard stuff?"

Morgan turned to him and replied, "Because I need to keep one step ahead of you." The customer stared blankly at Morgan then looked at Bonnie, who said to the customer, "Yep, that's Morgan— one step ahead of you, me, and everybody else!" Morgan smiled and walked away heading for the stage.

The Armstrong Protection Systems salesmen had arrived and were proudly indicating as they walked toward the bar that they had been successful selling the additional units. They snagged their cold mugs of beer off the bar and walked toward the stage where the mistress of ceremonies was introducing the wet t-shirt contestants so they could enjoy the show with Morgan and Bonnie. Before they got to the stage, the man who had asked Morgan earlier about drinking the hard stuff posed another question to him: "You ever get any from these chicks?"

Without hesitating, Morgan replied, "Why eat hamburger out when you've got steak at home!?"

The man who had asked the question cocked his head and replied smiling, "You got it all, man. Got it all," and walked away.

After the guy disappeared into the crowd, Bonnie looked up at Morgan and snarled, "Liar, liar pants on fire!"

The mistress of ceremonies was adjusting the brass nozzle on the shiny red plastic hose as she aimed it at the t-shirt contestants. The white cotton shirts were becoming transparent and were clinging to the women's bare breasts and hard nipples, allowing the audience to more fully enjoy the different shapes and sizes of the breasts that were competing for the five hundred dollar top award. The music grew louder and the crowd more raucous.

The MC shouted into the microphone, "Turn ladies!" and the contestants whirled around easily on the wet floor. The MC changed the spray setting from GENTLE SHOWER to FULL ACTION and pelted the contestants' backs, then their asses, and finally, their legs. "Voting time is coming up folks," she shouted. "Checkout these chicks and vote for the one who's got the hottest SET OF TITS! If there's a TIE ON TITS, we'll go to ASSES to break the tie—whew! Competition is tough tonight!"

Morgan was looking down at his phone catching the evening news and could hear the newscaster commenting on the governor's Prison Reform Initiative. "Taxpayers," he said quoting the governor, "will no longer have to shoulder the outrageous burden that comes from rehabilitating people who have chosen to break the laws of the Commonwealth."

"I hear you, Guv'na—make those som bitches work and pay for their own rehabilitation and NOT ME!" After Morgan uttered those words, he turned to see how many people were gathered behind him to watch the action on stage, and he saw a man he knew approaching him. When that man arrived at his side, Morgan withdrew a note from his coat pocket and handed it to him. "Hold tight for two weeks, Reggie, then do those on the list." After Reggie read the note, Morgan added, "Stick with the worthless stuff—get in and out quickly. We just want to scare them into doing the right thing—buying a security system."

After Reggie shook his head in agreement, Morgan handed him an envelope. While his employee counted the money in the envelope, Morgan explained why the payment was less than the normal amount. "Your adlibbing last week cost you two hundred bucks. Don't do it again!"

Morgan walked away from Reggie and entered the billiards area. One of the players looked over at him, "Let's play after I sink this ball. Which way should I go with it?" Morgan told him and he made the shot. "Got time to play?" he asked.

"You're still not ready for me," Morgan replied. "Take that money you just won and buy your kids some cool clothes."

In the office, Bonnie handed him the night deposit bag. "It's been a year, Morgan," she said, "and I've met and exceeded your sales goal."

Anticipating what she was leading up to, he said, "And you want a raise!"

"Yep," she said.

"Your raise is already in the computer, honey," he said. "You've done a great job!"

"Thanks for keeping your word," Bonnie said.

"What's wrong?" he asked, hearing a worrisome tone in her voice.

"Nothing," she replied, weakly.

"What?" Morgan asked.

"If I told you, you'd—"

"I'd what? Tell me."

She paused, turned, and obeyed, "I'm making a lot of money, but I don't want to do this anymore."

Morgan replied, "You're making FIFTY THOUSAND BUCKS a year, and you don't want to do this anymore!?"

"See, you're mad!" she said.

"What do you want?" he asked.

Bonnie looked up, then down, then up again. "I don't know," she said, frustrated.

"Well Bonnie," Morgan said calmly, "stay here and make money until you do know. Then quit, and I hope this—whatever it is—doesn't hurt your job performance. If it does—"

"You'll fire me," she said preemptively. "That's right!—nothing personal—it's just business."

"It's not going to hurt my performance," she said and paused, then said, "I want to be a veterinarian."

Morgan smiled, "Well good, you do know. That's better."

Bonnie's eyes brightened. "Yeah, but how am I ever going to become a veterinarian? I'm not sure I can even spell the word—V-E-T-E-R somethin' somethin' somethin'."

"That's a good racket," Morgan said. "Heck, they make more than fifty thousand dollars a year—a lot more. Maybe we could work out a partnership? Call it—*Bonnie's Little Darlin's Pet Spa*. We could make some SERIOUS MONEY—people spend more money on their pets than they do on their kids."

$

Inside Armstrong Detective Agency, Morgan watched Jimmy, the manager of his detective agency, withdraw a large envelope from a drawer and drop its contents out on the top of his desk. Morgan picked up one of the photographs and said, "Were you able to get audio?" Jimmy pushed the play button on the recorder, and the audio started. Morgan listened, and at the end of the recording, he said, "I think that'll do it. THIS, my long-time friend, is going to make me a member of that very exclusive country club. Gonna soon be GOLFING on the river, thanks to you, big boy!"

"Don't know why you want to belong to that place so badly, Morgan," Jimmy said.

"'Cause, like the mountain, it's there," Morgan replied. "Naw, that's baloney, Jimmy. I want to belong to that club, because the MONEY people are there—the BIG MONEY people!"

Jimmy let Morgan's response sink in, then replied, "When we were just kids on the other side of the tracks, you talked about being a member of that club, and you weren't thinking about BIG MONEY then."

Like Jimmy, Morgan let Jimmy's words sink in before responding. "You're right," he replied, as he pulled out his phone and placed a call. "I felt inferior to the kids who were members—the rich kids—and I didn't like that feeling, and I still have it, even though I'm rich." Morgan diverted his eyes away from Jimmy when he heard her voice. "Hi, sweetie, what's for dinner?"

His wife on the other end of the call opened the freezer door and ran her index finger across the Gourmet TV dinners lined up inside and stopped on one. She said, "fettuccini primavera with vegetables."

Morgan asked, "Dessert?"

Her finger moved and stopped. "Mrs. Smith's Deep Dish Apple Pie," she said.

"A real find there," Jimmy said after Morgan put his phone away. "Took you three tries, but you finally got a real jewel with Cindy."

$

Now that he was on the interstate, Morgan pulled out his radar detector and put it on the dashboard. He passed the car in front of him and saw no vehicles up ahead. He pressed the accelerator and watched the needle climb—75...85...95...105...when an alarm went off, he slowed down and took an exit ramp heading for the golf driving range.

The attendant saw Morgan coming, excused himself from a customer, and had Morgan's bag and a bucket of balls ready when he arrived at the counter. As Morgan headed to the practice tees, the attendant poked the arm of the person he had been talking to and told him to watch. They saw Morgan reach out and grab a handful of balls off the top of the last basket and stuff them into his coat pocket. "He does that every time he comes," the attendant said, shaking his head. "But he tips big, so what the hell do I care about a few extra balls?"

Once Morgan got to a practice tee, he started hitting balls with his driver. Intentionally, he hit some well and others not so well. Soon, he said to the guy next to him, "First one who hits the two-fifty marker wins a basket of balls—okay?" The guy accepted the challenge, and they started aiming for the sign. When the other guy hit the sign, Morgan immediately bought him a basket of balls. When Morgan got back to the practice tee, he said to the guy, "I think you got lucky on me. Let's increase the challenge—first one to hit the THREE-HUNDRED-YARD MARKER wins fifty bucks," Morgan proposed. The guy accepted the challenge and hit his first ball at the target and missed. Morgan placed a ball on a tee, took a few practice swings, and hit a line drive that nailed the three-hundred-yard marker. The guy looked at Morgan and said, "LESSON LEARNED."

When he finished practicing, Morgan returned his clubs to the attendant who remarked, "Doesn't your CONSCIENCE ever get to you, buddy?" Morgan laughed as he handed the attendant his clubs and a twenty-dollar bill. "Nope," he replied, smiling. "Never had one of those."

$

As the door reached its fully open position overhead, Morgan drove the Thunderbird into the garage and stopped next to Cindy's Lexus.

Morgan's three children were outside playing around the pool with some friends. When he entered the kitchen, he gave Cindy a kiss on her cheek and took her in his arms and started to slow dance across the kitchen floor. "I have to get dinner for you," Cindy said, as she tried to break free from his embrace. He pulled her back and waltzed her over to the microwave where she pushed the open button. The aroma of the fettuccine primavera escaped from the oven and filled the kitchen.

After they finished eating, Morgan hit a switch on the intercom and looked out the window at his kids in the pool and shouted, "Whose turn is it for dishes?" Standing in the shallow end of the pool, Raquel raised her hand. "Dishes are waiting," he said. He saw his daughter scrunch up her face, and she didn't move. "Whose MONEY built the pool?" Morgan asked. No response. "Whose MONEY sends you to private schools?" No response. "Whose MONEY buys your clothes?" After the last question, Raquel said dramatically—"YOURS, YOURS, and YOURS, DADDY!"

Heather had her back turned to the house with her hands cupped around her mouth and whispered to her friends, "It's almost THAT TIME. Want to listen in?"

Her friends giggled and went inside with Heather to help Raquel wash the dishes and to eavesdrop on the adults.

Cindy and Morgan had taken showers, turned up the AC, and were in their canopy bed under the comforter beginning foreplay. The kids were downstairs in the kitchen gathered around the intercom. Morgan was making his way down Cindy's body, kissing things, whispering sweet nothings. The kids heard Cindy start doing her thing: "YES—OH, OH…YES—OH—YES—YES… OHHHHHH—that's it, that's it, right there!" The kids were silently mouthing their stepmother's words and noises and suddenly became aware that the lovemaking sounds had stopped. They stepped closer to the speaker, but they knew what sounds would come next: the squeaking of a drawer opening and the steady buzz of a vibrator.

"He's done it again!" Heather whispered. "Daddy's fallen asleep in the saddle, and Cindy is settling for the designated hitter— THE VIBE."

$

It was Thursday, and Morgan was pushing his mother down the hall in her wheelchair toward the lobby and front doors of the nursing home. She no longer had to ask Morgan to stop at the birdcage to admire the finches. "They need a bigger cage," she said as soon as they stopped. "They're too crowded in there?"

Morgan agreed and left his mother at the birdcage and walked over to the reception desk where a woman was sitting reading *The Weekly Gazette*. He slipped a silver money clip off the folded bills and flicked up five of them with his thumb and dropped them on the newspaper. "You think five hundred dollars is enough to get a nice, big cage for the finches?" he asked.

"Should be," the receptionist replied without shifting her attention from the newspaper. After a brief silence, the receptionist picked up the five one-hundred-dollar bills and attempted to hand them back to Morgan, saying, "The director of this nursing home can take care of that. Buying birdcages isn't my job."

Morgan didn't take the five bills back. Instead, he flicked up two more hundred dollar bills and dropped them on the newspaper, saying, "Those two bills are for you, if you can make it your job," and watched her add the two new bills to the other five in her hand. For the first time, the receptionist looked up at Morgan and sighed, as she very deliberatively patted the seven bills into a neat stack. Morgan could feel her annoyance and knew the seven hundred dollars was coming back to him, which annoyed him. He flicked off three more hundred-dollar bills onto the newspaper and looked at her nameplate. "Mildred, I'd like to see the birds in their new home when I return next Thursday. Think you can do that for me?"

$

A week had passed and Morgan was checking in at the reception desk and noticed that the finches were still living in the overcrowded birdcage. He did not see Mildred, so he asked the woman filing her fingernails if Mildred was there, and the woman replied, "Mildred fills in here just every now and then, when we're in a lurch. I think she and Buster have gone to Canada for a short vacation—she might have played one of those Virginia Lottery Scratch things and won some funny money."

$

Cindy was instructing kids at the Ice Palace and noticed the owner standing across the rink motioning for her to come over to the railing. When she slid to a stop, the owner said, "This is Sergio—he'll be taking over basic instruction after you train him." Cindy extended her right hand to shake, but instead of shaking her hand, Sergio raised it to his lips and kissed it softly.

Cindy blushed. "Nice to meet you," she said, glancing over at the owner, who winked. Cindy skated back to her students to resume instruction. Out of the corner of her eye, she looked to see if Sergio was still standing at the railing watching her, and he was. She smiled at the kids, "Now, where were we?"

$

An Armstrong BUG OUT Company truck was parked at the curb, and the pest inspector was already under the house, but instead of inspecting for infestation, he was gluing termite tunnels to the foundation and floor joists and releasing hundreds of termites from a jar. After getting the tunnels and video equipment in place under the house and the video monitor set up on the porch, the inspector told the homeowner to look at the monitor. She looked, but she was standing too far back, so he asked her to step closer. Then the inspector zoomed in on the tunnels and said, "See how they're coming out of the ground, up the foundation and over to the joists?" She squinted and jutted her head forward. "Now look," he exhorted, shifting the camera and refocusing on another area. "Here! Look here!" he said excitedly. The woman shaded her eyes with one hand and covered her mouth with the other, as she watched termites running across the joists. "Look at 'em!" the inspector exclaimed slapping his thigh. "God made little green apples, but he didn't make them damn thangs—the DARK ANGEL made 'em—evil devils!"

Morgan had been eavesdropping on the bug out inspection while sitting in his car. Now that he'd gotten his cue, he started his engine and drove his Volvo around the corner where the inspection was taking place to close the deal. The inspector introduced Morgan, his boss, to the homeowner, who still had one hand over her mouth. Morgan looked at the inspector and said, "I can see she's upset—how much damage is there?"

The inspector replied, "They've been concentrating on building their tunnels, so, thank God, they haven't done no damage."

Morgan knew that the young man was a recent hire and therefore was not getting his lines exactly right. He should have said— they haven't done TOO MUCH damage instead of NO DAMAGE. "BUT," the young man quickly added realizing his error, "they're ready to start chomping at that wood now!" He felt better and kept going. "This house needs to be treated immediately. If not, it's going to be a pile of sawdust in no time."

Admiring the young man's newly invented dialog, Morgan said to the woman, "The work must be done ma'am. Delaying treatment will only make the situation and condition of your lovely house worse. Doing the treatment today might make the difference between your home STANDING UP or FALLING DOWN."

The woman walked, shuffled really, over to the glider. Morgan followed and helped her sit on the slatted seat. He turned to his inspector, "Is there MOISTURE DAMAGE too?" The inspector didn't remember this question being part of the sales scenario in the training manual, so Morgan silently coached him nodding his head. The young man got it and replied, "Yes sir, MOISTURE DAMAGE too." Morgan grimaced, "And I hate to ask it, but what about POWDER POST BEETLES and CARPENTER BEES?"

"They're under there too, sir!" the young man snapped out sharply.

"I'm sorry," Morgan said softly to the woman. "You've got bad, bad problems here, but they're not insurmountable. Just give me the word, and we will SAVE YOUR NICE LITTLE HOME."

$

Morgan was behind the wheel of a 1963 GTO Pontiac convertible watching three boys in the parking lot of an elementary school riding bicycles. They were trying to best one another with their acrobatics. Morgan shouted, "I will give you ten bucks—no, thirty bucks, if you will teach me in the next thirty minutes to do one good stunt."

The kids looked at one another, and one of them said, "We'll teach you a cool stunt just to ride in your car, mister!"

$

"Yes, Mr. Armstrong, how can I help you?" the attorney said.

Morgan replied, "I want you to help me with some divorce things that another lawyer has never resolved."

The attorney rose from his chair and replied, "I'm sorry, but I don't do that kind of work." He quickly added, "However, there are other lawyers in this firm who can ably serve your needs in that area."

Morgan remained seated and switched to the real reason for his visit. "As you probably know, since you're the chairman of the membership committee, I have applied for membership at your country club. Do you know if I've been accepted?"

The attorney replied, "I don't know, but if I did know, Mr. Armstrong, it wouldn't be proper for me to tell you. All applicants receive letters, advising them one way or the other." The attorney stepped to the side of his desk with intentions of walking Morgan to the door. Morgan, however, had no intentions of leaving. He withdrew a large envelope from his briefcase and slid it across the desk. "Please sit down and take a look, Mr. Askew," Morgan said politely. "I want very much to be a member of the country club, and I know that your support and vote will be necessary for that to happen."

Mr. Askew sat down, opened the envelope, and withdrew a banded stack of hundred-dollar bills. He fanned them, then placed the money back in the envelope and slid it back across the desk to Morgan who let it sit in front of him. Mr. Askew opened his top right desk drawer, withdrew a pistol, and offered it to Morgan who took it, as it was presented, by the handle. Mr. Askew said very deliberately,

"I'd rather be shot dead than vote in favor of accepting a sleaze ball, such as yourself, into my country club."

Morgan closed one eye and found himself looking directly down the pistol barrel at the attorney's forehead. He slowly lowered the gun to the desktop and left it there. He returned the envelope full of money to his briefcase, and pulled out another envelope and placed it before the attorney. "There's one more thing I'd like you to look at before I take my leave."

Mr. Askew snapped open the envelope and dumped its contents out. The photograph on the top of the pile showed the attorney nude in bed with another man. Morgan pushed the play button on a small recorder sitting in his briefcase, and the audio that was recorded when the pictures were taken started. "How's this for SLEAZE?" Morgan asked, noticing beads of sweat forming on the attorney's forehead. "I didn't want to do it this way, but will I get your support now?" After Mr. Askew silently nodded his head affirming that he would, Morgan put everything back in his briefcase, stood up, and headed for the door.

"What about the money?" Mr. Askew asked still seated behind his desk.

Morgan stopped and replied, "You'll get some of my low-class money when I'm a member of your high-class country club." After responding, Morgan looked at the four fox hunting engravings on the wall behind the attorney and said, "I've always liked *The Chase* the best. Which is your favorite, Mr. Askew?"

Mr. Askew replied, "The next one down—*The Kill*."

Morgan grinned, "Yeah, I can see how that might have real strong appeal to you—a lawyer."

$

Morgan was sitting on a bar stool eating a hamburger and reading a list of games to be played that night when the owner of the restaurant came up. "How are the condoms selling?" Morgan asked him.

Sammy said, "Okay."

Morgan looked up and said, "No they aren't, Sammy. You ought to be selling five times what you're selling." Morgan then walked over to the ladies' restroom, peeked in and came back to Sammy. "Why don't you have condoms in there? Didn't my salesman suggest that?"

Sammy shrugged his shoulders, "Didn't make sense to me. Thought it might even offend some of the women who come here."

Morgan shook his head and looked at the crowded tables and shouted. "Let me have your attention, please." He got no attention, so he hopped up on a table holding out a hundred-dollar bill. People stopped talking and looked at Morgan. "Ladies—and LADIES ONLY—the first woman to put a condom in this hand gets the hundred dollar bill!" As women scream and laugh excitedly searching their purses, Morgan looked over at Sammy and smiled, "You're old school, Sammy. Old school."

$

Morgan asked the man if he could check out his online catalogs. The salesman shrugged, "The computer is all screwed up—been screwed up for two days! Even the computer guy can't figure it out!"

"Show me," Morgan said.

The salesman turned the computer on but was unable to bring up the catalogs.

Morgan said, "Do you mind?" gesturing that he wanted to try to fix the problem, and the salesman stepped aside. Morgan typed in some codes and within minutes he had the catalogs up and the problem solved. "It's just a dumb machine," Morgan said. "You have to tell it to do everything, or it won't do anything."

The salesman said, "Hey, you're good. Look up anything you want."

Morgan went beyond looking up stuff; he ordered three stunt bikes (at wholesale) and requested that they be billed and shipped directly to his home address. That was Morgan's cardinal rule: NEVER PAY RETAIL.

$

He was wearing a Tommy Bahama shirt, white slacks, and deck shoes and was sipping orange juice through a straw, as he began his descent down the steps of his pool. His kids started pointing and laughing at him and that was the whole point of doing it for Morgan. He enjoyed making them laugh. He kept advancing toward them. "What do you want for dinner—steaks, seafood, what?" he asked holding his glass above his head. The water was up to his chin. "We're going to start celebrating tonight, because we're going to be new members of the country club, very soon."

"Both," his kids said, "Surf AND turf!"

"What kind of surf?"

"Lobsters!" they screamed.

"And dessert?" Morgan asked, knowing what their answer would be.

They laughed, because they knew their father already knew their answer. "Every kind!" they said together.

Once Morgan got his children's dinner request settled, he picked up the floating phone and called the Ice Palace to talk to Cindy about the time for dinner but was told that she had left early for a doctor's appointment.

$

Morgan went first to the produce section of Whole Foods and noticed immediately a curvaceous woman picking over the red seedless grapes. She was wearing sunglasses, leopard print polo shirt, yellow clam diggers, and international orange (trimmed with gemstones) flip flops. Morgan couldn't see any signs of or need for a bra. He took a position just down from her in the melon section. He grabbed a medium-size cantaloupe and shoved it up his shirt, then selected a second cantaloupe of comparable size, and shoved that one up his shirt giving himself boobs about the size of hers.

The woman turned in his direction and observed what he'd done. "Very funny!" she said.

"Imitation is the best form of flattery," he replied.

The woman dropped a bag of red seedless grapes in her basket and walked swiftly away into the deli section.

A short while later, Morgan was in the seafood section looking at the lobsters in the big saltwater tank. He heard her before he saw her: flip flop flip flop flip flop. Casually, he turned in the flip flop direction, and there she was standing about five feet away next to the iced down Alaskan king crab legs. She lowered her sunglasses and encouraged him with her eyes to look down at her crotch. He eagerly accepted her encouragement and saw what appeared to be a three- to four-inch long sausage sticking out of her front zippered clam diggers. He returned his eyes to hers.

"Is that about right, slick?" she asked, flipping her sunglasses back in place.

Morgan laughed. "Yeah," he replied, and playfully added, "and I really do know how to use it."

$

At home, Morgan had the kids helping him prepare dinner. In exchange for their help, he was allowing them to listen to THEIR MUSIC, and they were taking this opportunity to show him how to DANCE to THEIR MUSIC, and after just a few minutes of observing THEIR DANCING, Morgan said, "I learned those moves a long time ago, but we didn't call it dancing. We called it—" Before Morgan could finish his sentence, the door leading out to the garage opened, and Cindy came in with her gym bag slung over her shoulder. The kids and Morgan turned their attention to Cindy. "How was work today?" Morgan asked.

Cindy kept walking toward the living room and the stairs to the second floor. "It was exhausting—ten to five with only a thirty-minute lunch break!"

"Sorry, slip in the whirlpool and de-stress yourself, honey," Morgan said sympathetically, knowing she had lied.

The kids were gawking at the lobsters that were still alive in their water-filled plastic bags.

"Okay," Morgan said, "let's cook these babies."

His kids stared at him as they backed away from the kitchen sink.

"You do it, Daddy," they said in unison.

"You can slice up vegetables, but you can't put lobsters in a pot of boiling water?" he asked them.

They replied, "Vegetables don't have feelings like lobsters!"

"Oh yeah?" Morgan replied. "I think they're going to discover years from now that vegetables AND FRUITS have feelings."

"No they don't, Daddy!"

"Wait and see," Morgan said, as he lifted one of the lobster bags above the sink where he loosened the tie, and dropped the lobster into the pot of boiling water. The kids squealed and turned away.

"YOU ARE SO CRUEL!" they screamed, happily.

They had finished the celebratory dinner. The kids were inside the house watching TV, and Cindy and Morgan were sitting beside the pool enjoying the sunset. His phone rang, and he answered it.

The attorney, Mr. Askew, told Morgan to meet him later so they could make the exchange—membership acceptance letter from the country club for photographs, audio, and money.

Morgan slid his phone back into its case on his belt and lifted his glass to propose a toast to his wife. He clinked his glass of orange juice to her glass of pinot griggio and said, "To the country club."

$

Morgan was heading for the place the attorney had suggested. It was in an isolated part of the city—not much activity and not much chance to be spotted by anyone. He parked behind an abandoned building as agreed and waited. When he saw a car coming his way, he grabbed his briefcase and got out of his car. Then he saw that there were two cars coming down the road and then a third coming from the opposite direction. When they got closer, he saw that all three were police cars, and very quickly, they surrounded and illuminated him with their headlights. Six policemen walked up to Morgan and took him across the littered field where they found a body lying face down on the ground. Morgan saw who it was, Reggie, and also recognized the pistol next to his body.

A cop said, "We are arresting you for murder," and then slapped handcuffs over Morgan's wrists, and another cop took his briefcase and walked away with it. Morgan watched the cop give the briefcase to a man standing next to the abandoned building and walk away. The man receiving the briefcase raised his right arm, so that it was parallel to the ground and pointing straight at Morgan. The man's hand rocked back like it would if it were holding a pistol that had just fired a shot. The man slowly brought his right hand and index finger to his mouth and blew. Morgan now saw who it was, Robert Askew, the attorney, and he knew he'd been had. His hand and fingerprints were all over the murder weapon.

$

The Commonwealth Attorney was concluding his remarks to the jury, "I urge you to find this man guilty of murder, premeditated murder. The Commonwealth has established motive. We have the murder weapon that bares the defendant's fingerprints, and we have the dead body of a poor man who worked for Morgan Armstrong. To meet the needs of his family, Reginald Smithers burglarized homes, so Morgan Armstrong and his salesmen would have an easier time selling home security systems. Money, GREED really, has always motivated Mr. Armstrong. His pest control company even puts pests IN HOMES, and then gets people to pay him TO GET THEM OUT—now that's low, low as you go—UNCONSCIONABLE behavior. This time he went too far. He went beyond just greed and unethical behavior. This time he took a man's life, a loving husband and father, a man who had decided to turn his life around. Armstrong killed this poor man to keep him from spilling the beans—killed him, shot him, left him in a field of litter and weeds—not a field of dreams—to save his own sorry neck. I'm asking you to find Morgan Armstrong guilty, guilty of murder, without a doubt, he is guilty as charged by the Commonwealth. Our community will be a better and safer place with Morgan Armstrong sitting behind bars in the big house up river."

An hour and a half later, with Cindy, his children, and his mother sitting behind him, Morgan stood to hear the jury foreman announce the verdict: "Your Honor, the jury finds Mr. Armstrong GUILTY."

Morgan turned around and saw his mother rolling toward him in her wheelchair. He had never been this sad. She stopped in front of him and said, "I know you didn't kill that man, son."

"Thanks, mom," Morgan replied.

"Get Jimmy on it," she pleaded.

"He's on it already, and we know who set this up. Jimmy will get him."

$

Morgan was carrying a pillow, sheets, and a blanket. They stopped. The guard spoke into his phone and the cell door opened.

"Someone's in this one," Morgan said.

"You'll be sharing this cell with him until the new wing is completed," the guard said, motioning Morgan inside.

His cellmate was sitting at a table reading and taking notes. He didn't look up. Newspapers, magazines, notebooks, pens, and pencils were strewn all over the cell. The guard said, "Bob, this is Morgan Armstrong, your new cellmate." Bob did not respond to the introduction. The guard returned his attention to Morgan and pointed as he spoke, "Your cot, table, lamp, and chair, Armstrong, and you got your bedding in your arms. Any questions?"

Morgan nodded his head toward the far corner of the cell, "And that's where we TAKE a DUMP, huh!?"

The guard stared at Morgan briefly and responded, "That's a smartass comment! Have a nice stay."

Morgan glanced at Bob, then sat down on his cot. He heard the clanging of cell doors and the shouts of prisoners as they reverberated through the dimly lit, concrete, and metal facility. This, he was hoping, is a nightmare out of which I will awake. He heard gentle tapping and saw that Bob's fingers were running over his tabletop as if it were a piano keyboard. Morgan said, "What are you in here for?" Bob did not respond. Morgan then raised his voice and said, "Hey, are you deaf?" Bob still didn't respond. "SCREW YOU!" Morgan shouted angrily, then turned and hit his pillow with his fist and buried his face in the depression his fist had created.

$

"Over here, Armstrong," the nurse said. Morgan didn't hear her, because he was talking to the guy next to him in the infirmary line. "Armstrong!" she shouted in his direction. This time Morgan heard his name and turned. "Get over here—pay attention!" the nurse said snapping her fingers. Morgan disliked her snapping fingers more than the words she had spewed out. Before he moved, he looked around the room and saw that all of the prisoners were staring at him. Once he observed that he was the center of attention, he casually strolled across the floor and stood in front of the nurse who was patting her crepe-soled shoe on the concrete floor. "I've got lots of things to do today, besides this, Armstrong!"

Morgan quipped loud enough for all to hear, "WELL, I don't!"

"I wouldn't talk like that to a person who's getting ready to stick a huge needle in my arm. Clench your fist," she said. When he complied, she tied a rubber tube around his upper arm just above his elbow and picked up a syringe from the table. Morgan watched as she stuck the needle in his vein. As blood began to flow into the tube, he said quietly, "Doesn't this place scare you?"

"No," she replied.

"Being around criminals and murderers doesn't scare you?" he responded.

"No, not a bit," she said, flippantly, as she removed the needle from his arm. The nurse looked directly into Morgan's eyes. "You guys are just like everybody else. You just robbed somebody or killed somebody—that's all." Morgan sat speechless watching the nurse's fingers place a cotton ball and piece of tape over the puncture in his arm. Then he said just above a whisper, "Just between you and me, I didn't kill anyone—or should I say—*aye ain't killed no body?*"

The nurse smiled at him, and said, "I know you didn't, sweetheart. That's why being around you prisoners has never really bothered me. Everybody in here is INNOCENT. All the GUILTY people are on the outside."

Morgan leaned forward and whispered his response to her playful comment, "No, really, I was framed."

The nurse nodded her head and said, "I'm SO SORRY. Follow me."

Morgan stood up and walked behind her, and as he did, he noticed that she was wearing bikini panties, which shown through the white uniform as pink. When they arrived at the next station, she turned and told him to sit down, and then turned back around to check something on her clipboard. Morgan looked at the faces of other prisoners sitting quietly around the room, and communicated with his eyes, mouth, and hands how much he appreciated the nurse's ass. Some of the men began to chuckle. Inspired by their amusement, Morgan reached his hand out and pretended to rub the nurse's buttocks, which raised the chuckling to laughter and prompted him to actually place his hand on her ass. As soon as his hand touched her, she whirled around, caught his wrist, and wrapped his arm behind his back. "Cute, Armstrong!" she said, slamming him against a wall. "Rule number one around here is TOUCH NO ONE, especially staff." Morgan's initial grimace turned into a closed smile. She saw the smile and wrenched his arm upwards until his smile faded from his face, then she released his arm, "Sit down, you jerk, and grow up!"

$

The guy walked into the recreation room and went immediately to the TV and changed the channel, then walked over to the pool table and began racking the balls.

"You guys good with that?" Morgan asked the other prisoners sitting on the couch with him. They shrugged their shoulders, indicating that they were okay with it.

One of them said, "That's the way he is, and he'll whip your ass if you mess with him." Morgan immediately picked up the remote and switched the channel back to where it was.

The big guy saw what Morgan did. He propped his pool stick against the wall and started walking toward the TV. While the big guy was walking toward the TV on one side of the room, Morgan was walking toward the pool table on the other side. When the big guy got to the TV, he changed the channel back to where he had put it, and when Morgan got to the pool table, he broke the racked balls, sending them all over the table. When the big guy got back to the table, Morgan was chalking the tip of his pool stick getting ready *ostensibly* to make a shot, but what he was actually doing was getting ready to defend himself.

"Whatchudoin'?" the guy muttered.

Morgan replied, "I'm getting ready to sink a few balls. Wanna play?"

The guy replied, "Dis MY table."

Morgan stood more erect and got a good grip on the pool stick, then replied, "I thought you were watching TV?"

The guy replied, "Doin' both!"

Morgan took a deep breath through his nose and released it slowly through his mouth, then said, "You can do ONE, or THE OTHER, BUT NOT BOTH."

The guard stationed in the back of the room started walking toward them.

"Which will it be?" Morgan asked.

With the guard standing at his side, the big guy answered, reluctantly, "Pool."

After the big guy announced his decision to play pool, Morgan returned his pool stick to the rack and walked back to the couch and switched the channel back to the movie, he and the others were watching. An inmate sitting next to Morgan leaned closer and whispered, "You're going to pay for that."

$

Cindy was standing behind the auctioneer recording the selling prices of the cars, as they were auctioned off one by one at the Grand Liquidation Sale of Dream Cars, Ltd.

$

The prison psychiatrist, Dr. Morris, was sitting at her desk trying to pull up a file when her secretary entered the room announcing that her ten o'clock had arrived for a counseling session.

"Oh, I just hate this computer!" she said, exasperated. "Show him in."

Morgan was already rolling into her office in a wheelchair. He stopped at her desk. "Another computer, I see, is on the blink!" he said.

Dr. Morris hadn't turned or taken her eyes off of her computer screen, and therefore, had not seen that Morgan was sitting in a wheelchair when she said, "You may sit on the sofa."

Morgan thought it was strange that she wanted him to sit on the sofa, but he decided that he would comply with her directive, because he didn't want to appear oppositional. He engaged the break on his wheelchair and maneuvered himself onto the sofa.

Dr. Morris turned and finally saw the wheelchair and Morgan. "What happened to you, Armstrong?"

"I think it was something that I did last week in the recreation room that made him want to kill me," he answered. "Caught me by surprise this week in the laundry room."

Dr. Morris rolled her chair from her credenza to her desk and said, "This computer just keeps me exasperated. You would think they could hire someone to keep these things up—wouldn't you?"

"What's the problem? Is it the people operating the computers, or is it the computers?" he asked.

"Time is too precious to spend trying to answer that question right now. Why did you want to see me—the PRISON SHRINK?"

"I can probably fix your computer," Morgan said, thinking he might be able to soften her up by doing her a favor.

"No, no," she replied. "The tech guy's coming. Are you having some problems adjusting to prison life?"

"I want to be transferred to a psychiatric hospital," Morgan replied.

"What would qualify you for THAT?"

"I'm ready TO KILL MYSELF," he answered.

"Join the club, Armstrong."

"I don't belong here. I've been a little dishonest, here and there, but I'm not a criminal, a murderer. All the bars, locks, rules, criminals are driving me CRAZY. And Silent Bob, my roommate—cell-mate—is a MUTE. Might even be a MORON. Can't tell—he won't talk, and I need someone to talk to. He's a black hole. Stuff goes in, but absolutely nothing comes out!"

"I see," she said.

"Transfer me to a hospital. Maybe just for a month or two, while they get the real murderer back home."

"Armstrong, they do the investigating and gathering of evidence before the trial, not after someone has been found guilty."

"I was framed, and my private detective is working on it," Morgan replied. "Things could change in a heartbeat."

In the meantime," Dr. Morris said, "THIS PLACE will be your home."

Morgan jumped up, grabbing the back of the wheelchair for support, and said angrily, "A maniac has just nearly beaten me to death. My wife has robbed me of everything I own, and she's screwing a friggin' teenage ice skater from Romania, and my three kids are in foster homes eating Sugar Smacks for breakfast and Ding Dongs for dinner." He paused to gather himself. Tears started rolling down his cheeks. "I need help. I'm going crazy. I want out of here." He began sobbing, and in the midst of sobbing, he was wishing he had taken at least one drama class in high school. Throughout his adult life he had found that good acting is a skill that is much more valuable and useful than algebra, geography, or history.

Dr. Morris rose from her chair and walked around her desk to sit next to Morgan on the sofa. Morgan leaned forward and placed his face in his hands. Dr. Morris placed one of her hands on his back and gently massaged his shoulders. "It's okay, Armstrong," she said quietly. "Grieving is necessary for healing. Just let the pain out." Morgan was thinking that his "grieving" must have been fairly credible. He decided to show Dr. Morris that he was listening and taking her advice. He started WAILING. "Oh you poor man," she said and moved closer to Morgan; her thigh was now touching his. She whispered, "I'll scratch your back, if you'll scratch mine?"

Morgan was perplexed for a few seconds, but when he felt Dr. Morris's hand touch his thigh and slide over to his crotch, her message became crystal clear. Morgan looked down at her hand and said, "Are you saying that you will get me transferred out of here, if I SCRATCH YOUR BACK?"

Dr. Morris moaned softly, and whispered into his ear, "That's exactly what I said, baby!"

$

It had taken two weeks to get an appointment with the prison attorney. "I see," Ms. Spangler said.

Morgan waited for more, but it didn't come. "That's it—that's all you have to say—*I see?*"

"What do you want me to say?" Ms. Spangler asked.

"Say—she shouldn't have promised to transfer you to a psychiatric hospital in exchange for getting screwed—it's unprofessional and unethical."

"Okay, Armstrong, in the interest of time, let's just say that I said what you said."

Morgan hesitated and then said, "You know it's really unfair for anyone, much less a psychiatrist, to renege on a promise once the bribed party has delivered the goods."

"Well, Armstrong, I know I'm being picky here BUT—did you ever SCRATCH HER BACK?"

After Ms. Spangler asked her question, Morgan sprang out of his chair, "WHAT!?—you know she wasn't talking about scratching backs."

Ms. Spangler smiled. "Sit down, Morgan. Can't you take a joke?"

"Not in THIS PLACE!" Morgan replied.

Ms. Spangler sat up straighter in her chair and leaned forward showing some cleavage. "You're right, Dr. Morris shouldn't have done that, all three: the bribing, the screwing, and the reneging, but hey—maybe you should look at it differently—REFRAME IT!

She's a pretty hot ticket, and believe me, if I were in your shoes, living in this hell hole of a state prison, I'd consider myself lucky to have gotten laid by a hot chick like that! Think about it, Armstrong! Think buddy!"

Morgan looked at Ms. Spangler and smiled, "I see your point, Ms. Spangler. While I'm SCRATCHING BACKS—would you like me to SCRATCH YOUR BACK?"

Ms. Spangler laughed, "That's better, Armstrong. Keep a sense of humor. It works out better that way in here."

$

Morgan's three children had run away from their foster homes and had come back to their former home, which had just been sold at auction, to get some money they had hidden in a closet. They entered the dark house and walked immediately to the girls' bedroom and to a closet with a secret compartment in the floor. Heather found the loose board in the floor and lifted it up, so Raquel could retrieve the box. Unfortunately, Raquel discovered the box was not there. "Oh NO!" she exclaimed. "It's gone—now what!?"

$

Cindy was leaving work. After driving for a few minutes, Morgan's three children rose together. Matt reached over the front seat and grabbed Cindy's purse.

Totally surprised, Cindy shouted, "What are you doing?"

Raquel had Cindy's wallet and was searching it.

"We need some money," Matt said.

"She's got lots of money in here," Raquel said, counting it—"at least two thousand dollars!"

Cindy said, "Put that money back! It's not yours!"

"And it's not yours either," they screamed. "It's Daddy's."

When Raquel flipped Cindy's purse out the window, Cindy veered off the road onto the shoulder and shoved the gearshift into PARK. Then she jumped out of the car and ran back to find her purse.

Matt crawled over the front seat and got behind the steering wheel.

His sisters yelled—"Put it in DRIVE and floor it!"

Cindy was running down the side of a big drainage ditch. She tripped, fell, and rolled into the water.

The girls yelled, "Go Matt. Get out of here!"

Cindy was now out of the ditch waving her arms and shouting at them. All three children were beginning to panic, fearing that Cindy was going to get back to the car and call the cops.

Heather grabbed Cindy's gym bag and screamed, "Get up, Matt! Get your butt off the seat!" Matt complied and Heather stuffed the gym bag under his butt, elevating him high enough to see over the dashboard. "Now GO, brother!"

$

The three kids entered the front doors of Wal-Mart. The two girls went to Casual Wear, and Matt headed for Boys. Cutting through the Men's Department, Matt snatched a dark brown wig and matching mustache off a mannequin and stuffed them in his pocket.

$

The kids were heading west out of town and had stopped at a Wawa for gas. Matt was inside paying the cashier for candy, chips, drinks, and gas. The young cashier counted out his change and said, "The hair and mustache are cool."

"You're cool, too," he replied, as he accepted his bag of goodies and change. "How about one of those Scratch Lottery cards?" Matt asked, thinking he might get lucky.

The young cashier smiled widely at Matt and replied, "The wig and mustache makes you look OLDER, but not THAT OLD, dude."

$

Matt had gotten off the interstate and was doing eighty-five miles per hour on a country road. After passing a derelict silo, he saw in the rearview mirror the blue lights of a patrol car. His sisters heard the siren and looked back. "Don't let him catch us, Matt," they pleaded. "We can't go back—they'll put us in Juvenile Detention this time."

The Lexus lifted up and took off leaving the vintage black and white patrol car way behind.

$

It was late at night. Morgan had faked his way back into the infirmary and was searching computers for information. His visit with the prison psychiatrist had inspired the idea, and the records search he was conducting would give him the information he needed to make the proposal to the director of human resources.

$

"I've noticed since my arrival that your computers are often on the blink and that most of the prison staff are computer illiterates," he said to Mrs. Halperin, HR director. "So I've been thinking that I could put my knowledge and skills to better use. Instead of working in the laundry room, I could work on computers and teach your staff how to use them better—and it won't cost you a dime!" Mrs. Halperin nodded approvingly. "Not only that," Morgan rushed to add, "since this is a progressive prison, dedicated to rehabbing prisoners, so they can get out and do something with their lives, I can set up a computer lab and teach them how to do information technology—IT stuff." Morgan stopped talking to assess things and decided, based on Mrs. Halperin's body language, that more selling was needed. "Technology jobs are plentiful. In fact, there aren't enough trained people to fill the jobs we have right here in Virginia. Every day this prison is sending prisoners out of here unequipped to find or fill good-paying jobs. They leave out one gate and come back in another—it's a revolving door, as they say. While prisoners are in here, I can teach them skills that they can trade for high-paying jobs when they get out."

As Mrs. Halperin reached for a file resting on her desk, Morgan said, "I'm sure you have read my file and know my background. This is a progressive prison, let's see what we can do to make life better for individuals and families, Mrs. Halperin. Let someone else DO LAUNDRY—let me EDUCATE PEOPLE."

"It makes sense to me, Armstrong. I'll see what the warden thinks about your proposal."

"I have one small request to make this all happen," Morgan said. "I'll need a computer in my cell and ten to twelve computers for a computer lab—that's it, and we'll be in business!—AND, I'll need INTERNET ACCESS."

$

Lights were out, but Morgan couldn't wait until morning to check out the computer that Mrs. Halperin had provided. He quietly rolled off his cot and hit the switch. The monitor screen turned blue.

Bob rolled off his cot as well and retrieved a flashlight from a drawer and started reading a newspaper and taking notes at his table.

$

Cindy and Sergio were skating with other contestants under the discerning eye of the ICE Age talent scout. When the music stopped, the talent scout started calling names of contestants who had made the cut. Their names were not called.

$

The car was winding its way up the dusty gravel road. They initially overshot their mailbox but returned to it and followed the overgrown driveway to the cabin. It had been a long time since their last visit, which was just before Cindy came onboard as wife number three. The yard was now nothing but weeds and briars; vines had grown up the walls and onto the roof of the small cabin. The kids did not find the key in the buried tin can next to the porch, where they had always kept it, but then they discovered that they didn't need a key.

The door had been busted in years ago. Once inside, Matt yelled, "Give me a barf bag!" Mattresses from the bunk beds were scattered on the floor with stuffing hanging out the sides. What remained of the wooden bedframes was in the fireplace. Fast food wrappers, paper cups, beer cans, and whiskey bottles lay in piles on the squeaking trampoline floor.

Heather said, "Look up there," pointing at the ceiling. In the corner was a gigantic wasp nest. "We need to call FEMA. This place is a disaster!"

"And it STINKS!" Matt added, walking over to the bathroom. He peeked around the door and jumped back holding his hands over his nose and mouth. "Oh boy," he said into his cupped hands. "I think a bear crapped in the toilet!"

$

Morgan had set a small goal for himself that day: get Bob to say one or two words. He knew Bob could speak, because he would occasionally talk in his sleep. He wanted to accomplish this very modest goal that evening. Morgan looked over at Bob and asked, "What do you want to know, Bob? You read, read, and read and make notes—you've got to want to know something that you can't find in those newspapers? Ask me a question, any question, and I'll get you the answer—right now."

Surprising him, Bob looked up and said, "What was the rainfall last month in Uruguay?"

Bob's unexpected and quick response to his question shocked him. He looked at Bob, then at the keyboard, and for a few seconds couldn't remember what Bob wanted to know. Then he remembered and started typing.

"How do you spell *Uruguay*, Bob?" Morgan asked.

"Capital U…r…u…g…u…a…y," Bob replied.

Within seconds, the rainfall information appeared on Morgan's monitor, and he read it to Bob, and Bob wrote it down in his notebook.

"What else do you want to know?" Morgan asked.

When Bob didn't respond, Morgan switched off his computer and crawled onto his cot, happy to have achieved his goal for that day.

When Morgan heard Bob starting to put his stuff away, he said, "Your flashlight and paper rattling won't bother me tonight, Bob. Work as long as you want."

Bob got back to his table and unfolded a weeks-old newspaper from the prison library. Morgan turned over on his stomach and nestled his head into his pillow. He was smiling. Silent Bob had spoken.

$

The inmate next to Morgan pressed his elbow into Morgan's side and pointed his fork across the cafeteria. "Look at your cellmate Bob. He's moved up the table, and that's significant, brother, 'cause Bob has sat in the chair at the end of that table for the last ten years or more. Since I've known him. Never anywhere else. What's with Bob?"

$

The music started. Cindy and Sergio were skating, auditioning for a touring show. Unfortunately, Cindy slipped and fell face down on the ice, and before she could get back on her feet, the talent scout made a mark on his clipboard and shouted, "Thank you, NEXT!"

$

Heather and Raquel were lying on a blanket sunbathing. Raquel turned to face her sister and said, "School starts in two weeks."

"Not for us," Heather replied.

Raquel asked, "How is this going to work?"

"What?" Heather asked.

"Dad's in prison, no one knows where mom is, Cindy has all of dad's money and doesn't give a crap about us, we're living in a mountain cabin, winter's coming, we can't go to school without parents—THAT'S WHAT! Are we going to live like this until we're adults?"

"No, Raquel," Heather replied. "This is temporary. Don't worry."

They heard footsteps. "Good morning," the man in a park ranger uniform said.

"Hi," the girls replied.

"Haven't seen you before," he said. "Just up for the day?"

Raquel shook her head up and down, affirming that they were. Heather, however, told him they had a cabin that used to have a sign saying *The Armstrong's*.

The ranger smiled, "Where's your cabin?"

The girls pointed in opposite directions—UP the road and DOWN the road. Then Heather observed, cleverly, "My sister couldn't find her way out of a wet paper bag. Our cabin is the next driveway UP the road from here." After her comment, Heather looked up at the ranger to see if he was buying it, and she wasn't sure, so she continued, "Our dad always used that phrase—*couldn' find her way out of a wet paper bag* to describe my sister—so that's why I used it even though I really don't know how that phrase means that she often doesn't know where she is."

The ranger smirked and replied, "Yeah, it's an old saying, but you seem to understand its meaning."

"Thanks," Heather said, and watched the ranger walk over to Matt who was sitting next to the stream nervously holding a fishing rod he had found in the cabin. The ranger looked in the bucket next to Matt and saw a rainbow trout, "Got a license, young man?"

"No sir," Matt responded, without looking at the ranger.

"Then you're breaking the law," the ranger replied. "AND that trout is TOO SMALL. Where are your parents?"

Matt looked over at his sisters who were both mouthing words and pointing UP the road and once he understood what they were telling him, he said, "Our parents MIGHT be up the road in our cabin, or they may be down the mountain getting some groceries."

The ranger looked at Matt and said sternly, "Put the trout back in the stream young man, and get your father to buy you a license."

"Yes, sir," Matt replied.

The ranger walked away from Matt, and as he walked by the girls, he said, "You got sunscreen on?"

Together they looked up and replied, "You're just like OUR PARENTS—always on our backs!"

$

Morgan and another prisoner were unloading a couple of carts stacked with computers when they saw a woman walking down the hall toward them, and as she neared their position, Morgan and the other guy could see that a parrot was perched on her left shoulder. When the woman was close enough, Morgan looked at the woman and commented, "What a beautiful creature."

The woman stopped and replied, "Handsome, HANDSOME creature. It's a male."

Morgan immediately replied, "I wasn't talking about the bird," which caused the other guy to roll his eyes skyward.

The woman remained silent while she dipped her head slightly quickly sizing up Morgan over her glasses. Without commenting, she turned and walked away.

Morgan followed her with his eyes and soon said to his work-mate, "Who is she?"

"That, my buddy, is THE WARDEN," he replied grinning.

Morgan's eyes lit up and quipped jokingly, "If I'd known SHE was here, I would have killed someone sooner!"

The guy smiled and said, "Yeah, that's Catherine Sinclair, daughter of the infamous hanging judge—James Sinclair."

"You're kidding?" Morgan said.

"No, she is the warden, but I don't know that her father was *the infamous hanging judge*—but he was a judge. I threw those other words in just to impress you."

$

Morgan was sitting in front of his computer in his cell, and Bob was on his cot reading a month-old *Barons* newspaper.

"Come on over here, Bob," Morgan said. "Come on. Take a look at this curriculum." Bob didn't respond. "I want you to take my computer class. Will you do that?" No response from Bob. "Once you take my class and join the computer support group, you'll have access to THE WORLD." Bob kept reading. "This machine, Bob, is like having ten thousand clerks working for you. More maybe— heck, if you wanted to know the monthly rainfall in Hong Kong, or the annual amount of methane gas produced by cows in India, you could." Bob brought his newspaper down to his chest and looked over silently at Morgan. "You don't know it, Bob, but I'm talking— communicating—with someone in England—right now. What do you want to know about England?"

Bob leaned forward and said, "Nothing—can you get someone in China?"

Morgan smiled and typed as he whispered, "China, here we come."

Bob stood up and dragged his chair over to the computer and sat down.

Morgan looked over at Bob and said, "What do you do with all that information you jot down?"

Bob had his eyes fixed on the monitor, but responded, "Nothing really. It's just something I do for amusement." He looked over at the stacks of spiral notebooks, and added, "There's years of amusement."

The screen indicated that Morgan had found a chat-mate in China. "There we go," Morgan said, excitedly. "We have a friend in Beijing, China." Bob scooted closer to the screen. Morgan looked at Bob, "What's so amusing about pouring over newspapers and magazines and filling up spiral notebooks with notes?"

Bob looked at Morgan, "I play the world markets, on paper, of course. It's an endless mental challenge sprinkled with fleeting moments of cerebral ecstasy."

$

As he began to dismiss the class, Warden Sinclair walked through the door. "Don't mind me, Armstrong," she said. "Carry on."

"Okay, that's it for today. Good job. Tomorrow we'll learn more about those little symbols at the top of your screens and how to save and retrieve information. It will get more exciting as we go along—Hacking 101 starts Friday—naw, just kidding, Warden."

The prisoners filed out of the room, leaving just the warden and Morgan in the room.

"Well, how'd the first day go?" she asked.

Morgan answered, "Fine. But I thought we'd have more people sign up."

The warden smiled, "Small steps first, then bigger ones."

"Yeah, yeah," he said. "But they really do want to know how to HACK into places."

"No doubt," the warden said.

"By the way, Warden," Morgan said with excitement, "my cell-mate Bob is a stock market genius."

The warden pulled her head back and replied, "That's interesting. How so?"

"He's been keeping track of stocks for as long as he has been here. You've seen the notebooks and newspapers stacked up in his and now OUR cell—right?" The warden shook her head affirming that she had noticed his cluttered cell many times. "He's made a fortune!"

The warden snickered, "Made a fortune, Morgan!?"

Morgan quickly responded, "On paper, of course, it's all on paper—pretend trades, but he knows what he's doing, Warden, believe me. I got him to open up some—I saw his books!"

"Well, good for him," she concluded.

Morgan looked directly into her eyes, "Bob could make us a bunch of money."

"US—you and me—how?" she asked.

"I get the information from Bob. You buy the stocks or whatever he says to buy, and WE SPLIT THE PROFIT?"

The warden replied, "How would we split the profit?"

"TWO ways," Morgan said quickly. "YOU and ME—fifty-fifty."

"What about Bob?"

Morgan grinned, "Bob's a lifer. He doesn't need money."

The warden said, "I'd like to know Bob's investment strategy… GENIUS that he is. My husband's a stockbroker and, likewise, a GENIUS."

$

Bob and Morgan were sitting in the warden's office looking at the framed photographic portrait of a man dressed in a black robe hanging on the wall behind her desk. In the far corner was a green, red-headed parrot sitting on a perch surrounded by a plethora of tropical plants.

"Armstrong tells me that you are a stock market whiz—a genius—is that right?" the warden asked.

Bob scanned the office nervously and licked his lips before responding, "That's Morgan's proclivity for hyperbole. What I can do with a fairly high degree of accuracy is predict the ups and downs of market sectors and, sometimes, I can actually predict a spectacular rise of a particular stock."

Morgan quickly reacted to Bob's response. "Bob is too modest. He's got graphs and charts that show patterns in the market that not another person on the face of the earth would see."

"Can you explain what you do, Bob?" the warden asked.

"I've been able to watch, even from here, obvious things like world markets, wars, new leaders, governments, corporations, patents, and less obvious things like weather, rainfall, hemlines, hit movies, TIME magazine covers, et cetera for a long time, and it turns out to be more CORRELATION than CAUSE and EFFECT—"

The warden interrupted him. "Can you tell me or anyone, with one hundred percent certainty, if a stock is going up or down within a very narrow window?"

Bob didn't hesitate with giving his answer, "No."

The warden looked at Morgan who said, assertively, to her, "Yes he can!" Then Morgan quickly turned his attention to Bob. "What do you mean—NO? You just did it the other day?"

Bob calmly replied, "The warden said with one hundred percent certainty but it's more like NINETY-EIGHT PERCENT."

Morgan laughed. "Yep, there you go. He can't do it one hundred percent of the time, Warden, he's right just NINETY-EIGHT PERCENT of the time!"

$

The older of the two girls, Heather, was in the living area of the cabin and saw the park ranger walking up the porch steps. He knocked on the screen door.

"Hi," she said.

"May I come in?"

She opened the door. "What can I do for you?" she asked. Matt and Raquel were in the girls' bedroom listening.

"Oh, I just came by to introduce myself to your parents," he replied. "Are they here?"

Heather straightened a blanket resting on the back of a chair, "Welllll," she began, drawing the word out to increase the amount of time she had to think of a good response. But before she started her explanation, she and the ranger heard heavy breathing coming from the bedroom.

Heather pretended to be embarrassed, then said, cocking her head toward the room and the noise on the other side of the wall, "I'm sure they would like to meet you but…" When Heather hesitated, the ranger nodded, getting her point, and backed up to the screen door. Heather continued, "They do THAT a lot up here." The ranger pushed the screen door open and stepped out of the cabin onto the porch letting the screen door snap shut. "Goodbye, Mr. Ranger," Heather said sweetly, adding, "THIS is SO EMBARRASSING, sorry."

$

He was reading when Catherine walked into his study. "Hi, sweetie," he said.

Catherine smiled, "Hi, Dad." She leaned over him and gave him a kiss on his forehead. She then walked a few steps and sat down in the bay window and looked at her father's flower garden.

He said, "I keep reading about you and the governor's prison reforms in the newspaper. How's it really going?"

Catherine turned, grinning, "Real well, Dad. Truly—the prisoners are learning new trades, business skills, and they're making money."

The judge placed his book on his knee and said, "Maybe this and the educational reforms in the schools will get him into the White House—and you too?"

Catherine moved from the bay window to the wingback chair across from her father. "Who knows? POLITICS is a nasty and tricky game," Catherine replied and then looked at her father having decided to change the subject. "I've got a new prisoner. More than one actually, obviously, but this one's in on murder—"

Before she could finish her sentence, her father said, "Armstrong?"

Surprised, Catherine replied, "Good golly, Judge James Sinclair, you are still staying up with who's killing whom in the great state of Virginia."

He replied soberly, "Once a judge, always a judge."

Catherine stood up and walked back to the bay window and stared at the Delphiniums and said, "They have the most exquisite color." She turned and switched back to her new prisoner. "Armstrong's sharing a cell with the guy who killed his wife's lover and her twenty years ago—"

Catherine's father said, "Robert Wheeler."

"Correct—Pass Go and collect two hundred dollars," Catherine said with a flourish, "and Wheeler hasn't talked to anybody since he came in the place. Other prisoners call him Silent Bob."

"How's that working out?" her father asked.

"Armstrong has Wheeler talking, and swears that his cellmate Wheeler is a STOCK MARKET GENIUS!"

"The Stock Market GURU Who Slew Two—maybe he could pass on a few tips to your husband," her father replied.

Catherine laughed and said, "Armstrong suggested that the two of us, He and I, team up and make some money—GET RICH—on Bob's stock predictions—here's the deal according to Armstrong—he gets the PICKS from Bob, I buy the stock with MY money—then we split the profits FIFTY-FIFTY."

Catherine's father asked, "What about Bob?"

"That's what I said to Armstrong, and you want to know what Armstrong said?"

"What?"

"He said—Bob's a LIFER, so he doesn't need money."

"Does Bob have a family?" her father asked.

"No," Catherine responded.

"Then he's got a point, but Armstrong's got a long haul himself. Does Armstrong have a family?"

"Yes," she said. "Third wife has taken everything and split. His kids have run away from foster homes, and the biological mother has been gone."

Her father sighed, "All the grownups have screwed up."

"Morgan says he's innocent and that he'll be out soon—when his detective friend gets the goods on the guy who really did the murder."

"They're all con artists, Catherine, you know that."

She laughed quickly, "Right! I read his file—Armstrong's quite a hustler!"

Her father replied, "A Wheeler Dealer in this case!"

Catherine grinned, "Always playing with words aren't you? Just one of the things that I love about you, Dad."

Her father replied, "I know getting rich has never interested you, Catherine, a fact that has always made me wonder why you fell in love with and married a stockbroker."

"Who knows why we fall in love with someone, and I surely fell in love with Anthony."

"Any regrets?"

"Not really," she answered.

"Does that mean you have things that almost qualify for regrets?"

"Maybe, but who doesn't?"

Both of them remained silent for a moment, then she said, "Armstrong's motives, ethics, and morals were certainly undesirable in the business world—maybe even DISGUSTING—but he's done a good thing getting Bob out of his self-imposed isolation, brought him back to life really. I think there's great promise in what they might be able to do together."

"Cutting Bob out of the profits tells me that Armstrong's got a long ways to go with his motives, ethics, and morals, dear daughter."

Catherine thought about what her father said, then replied, "I think Armstrong's got POTENTIAL."

"And that's one of the things I love about you," her father said. "You see the good in people, and you have a way of bringing light out of darkness."

$

Cindy looked at Sergio and said, "I have lots of money now, and I can do whatever I want, but I'm still not happy...isn't that weird?"

Sergio looked over at her and replied, "You have lots of money; you can do whatever you want, AND you have me, and you're still not happy—yes, that's weird."

$

Catherine was hitting balls on her personal tennis court outside her office as they were being shot over the net by a ball machine. The gate opened and Morgan walked out into the court area. A ball shot across the net, and as she hit it, she said, "I think you're right, Armstrong. I told my husband some of what Bob said the other day, and he said that Bob could be a genius or he could be just a loony jailbird."

Morgan smiled, "Okay?"

Catherine continued. "I'm going with GENIUS, and I know you are a salesman—a marketer, so let's get going with this thing!" She turned and walked off the court. Pointing to the balls that kept shooting out of the machine and landing in the empty court, she said, "I'm never going to hit those balls, and you may never get out of here. The challenge for you now is to make these days meaningful, and you can do that by helping some of these prisoners learn skills that will increase their chances of becoming productive citizens when they get out."

Morgan countered, "Making a bunch of money will make these days meaningful."

Catherine replied, "I want you to help me DO GOOD."

Morgan laughed, "I'm not interested in DOING GOOD. I'm only interested in MAKING MONEY."

Catherine acquired a determined expression and said, "Perhaps a compromise is in order. What's it going to take?"

Morgan calmly replied, "I get half the profits, and since you're not interested in making money, your half will go into a fund for parolees."

She smiled, "No, you and Bob and the website staff will split half of the profits and the other half goes into a parolee fund, deal?"

Morgan replied quickly, "Bob's never getting out of here. He doesn't need money?"

"HE HAS FAMILY, Armstrong," she said (knowing she was lying).

Morgan shot back, "You would never know it. Nobody ever visits him."

"Who would know you have family?" Catherine replied. Morgan remained silent. Catherine continued, knowing she had hurt him with that comment. "Let's hope there will be PROFITS."

Morgan nodded, agreeing.

Catherine looked at Morgan compassionately, "This is a good thing, Morgan, and you're a good man. Make it work."

$

Cindy had an AAA triptych in her hands tracing out their route with her index finger. She said suddenly, "Sergio, take this exit!" Sergio started to take the exit and then didn't.

Cindy blurted, "You should have turned off there!"

Sergio looked at her and said, "I don't think so."

Slapping her leg, she countered, "I've got the map, and you should have turned back there!"

"I know who has the map," Sergio said. "But—"

Cindy cut him off, "BUT you screwed up, now get off this road, and GO BACK!"

Sergio stared at Cindy and started counting to a hundred silently—first in Romanian and then in English. When his anger had subsided, he said, "We need to invest in a GPS—wouldn't you agree?"

$

The woman said, "Oh, you look just like your pictures!" Cindy smiled as she shook hands with the owner of the ice skating center. The woman turned to Sergio and said, "And you are so handsome." She put out her hand to shake, but Sergio lifted it to his lips instead. She blushed, as she looked over at the man next to her. "My husband," she said. Sergio extended his hand to her husband who kept his arms wrapped tightly across his chest.

The woman's husband quipped, "Oh no. You're not going to kiss my hand."

They all laughed. The woman said to Cindy, "You have a couple of hours before the workshop starts."

$

Cindy was driving on an interstate highway heading for another town and another workshop. She looked at the windshield and the GPS that was mounted there and said to Sergio, "I can't wait to hear that cute woman's voice tell me to GET READY TO TURN."

Sergio looked up from the map he was holding in his lap and replied, "Looks like that might be a hundred miles down the road."

"Darn," Cindy said, then switched topics, "I'd like to have a dog. Wouldn't it be nice to have a dog with us? Maybe a Pomeranian."

"Oh my God," Sergio exclaimed.

"What's wrong with a Pomeranian? How about a poodle?"

"If we're going to get a dog, I'd like to have a REAL dog—a Russian wolfhound would be nice."

They drove not speaking for fifty some miles, and that was when Cindy saw a billboard advertising a mall. "Let's get off at the next exit and see if they have a pet shop in there."

$

"Aren't they adorable?" Cindy said, looking at the poodles. Sergio's facial expression indicated that he didn't think they were adorable. Cindy turned to the salesman and told him that she wanted to hold one of the poodle puppies.

Sergio looked at the salesman and said, "Do you have a ROMANIAN wolfhound—mistakenly referred to sometimes as RUSSIAN wolfhound?"

The salesman said they didn't, but that they could get one from another store across town.

"How much is my poodle?" Cindy asked.

"Seven fifty," the salesman said.

"And how much would the wolfhound be?"

"A thousand," the salesman answered.

Sergio looked at Cindy, shaking his head disappointedly. "I can't afford to spend that much money."

Cindy quickly replied, "I'll buy it for you, honey." He looked at her and shook his head side to side silently declining her offer. "It's just money, baby," she added.

"No, maybe I try SPCA," he replied.

Cindy looked at the salesman and told him that she wanted both—the ROMANIAN wolfhound and the poodle for fourteen hundred and he accepted her offer.

$

It was now fall and the leaves were beginning to turn in the National Forest. Morgan's kids were walking down the gravel road toward a house. Heather knocked, the door opened, and they entered.

Two girls were standing in the living room. Their brother, Austin, was standing next to a gun cabinet putting on his coat. With his coat on he opened the cabinet and took two rifles out handing one to Matt. Austin slung his rifle over his shoulder, pulled a flash-light out of his jacket pocket, checked to see if it was working, and then said to Matt, "Let's go."

Raquel said, "If you kill Bambi, Matt, I'll never speak to you again."

$

On top of a huge boulder on the bank of the rocky stream a mile or more from his home, Austin was ready to demonstrate how to cross the stream without getting wet. He had done it many times. Austin said, "Watch me," as he gripped the vine tightly and backed up as far as he could on the top of the boulder, took a breath, lifted his feet and started swinging forward, downward at first, and then out and upward over the stream. That was the easiest and most exciting part. The hardest and scariest part was letting go of the vine on the other side of the stream. Austin watched for the point where he needed to drop off the vine, and when he reached that point, he opened his hands and became airborne. Like he had done many times before, he landed on top of the boulder and just needed two small steps to get his balance. Austin could feel his heart beating against his chest and had to remain still for a few seconds to catch his breath, and once he got oxygen into his lungs, he yelled, "Your turn, Matt!"

Matt was holding the end of the cord that was tied to the end of the knotted end of the vine, which was now dangling straight down from a high limb above the stream. He started pulling in the cord and watched the rope start moving to his side of the stream. Once the end of the vine got to him, Matt copied Austin's preparations, said a quick prayer, and lifted his feet off the boulder. He began the swing across the stream flying fast over the white water and rocks. When he got close to the release point, he heard Austin yell GET READY TO DROP, which made Matt tighten his grip on the vine and look for the boulder he wanted to land on. Then he heard Austin yell—DROP! Matt wanted to release his grip, but his hands wouldn't open. Matt found himself swinging back toward the other side. Austin knew Matt would end up swinging back and forth across the stream if he didn't release immediately. He yelled DROP again, but Matt still didn't let go of the vine. Austin watched Matt sail back across the stream, and he knew Matt would not reach the launch point where he could get off safely. Austin looked at the small rocks and boulders that Matt might reach on his second trip across the stream and found one that wasn't too far from the bank. As Matt was swinging back across the stream, Austin yelled, "You have to drop off that vine when I tell you to Matt!"

Matt yelled back as he swung back toward Austin, "Okay, but I'm afraid, I'm going to fall into the water!"

"You're going to be okay. Get ready," Austin yelled and watched for the release point thinking that Matt had a good chance to land on a boulder and stay out of the water. If he missed it, Austin knew that Matt would end up in the stream and would be in BIG TROUBLE— the water was rushing fast and was freezing cold. Austin watched Matt nearing the release point and yelled—"DROP! DROP NOW!"

Matt did release the vine and landed on the boulder that Matt had selected, but he lost his balance and fell off the backside.

Austin leapt from rock to rock out to the boulder Matt had landed on and found him sandwiched between the boulder he had selected and another one behind it. He tried to pull Matt up and out of the water, but couldn't. Matt said, "My feet are stuck between these rocks."

Austin said, "Wiggle your feet. Wiggle your leg."

Staring straight up stream at the white water rushing toward them, Matt said, "I'm going to freeze to death or drown if I don't get out of here."

Austin replied, "I'll cut your feet off or your leg off before I'll let you drown!"

"YOU ARE NUTS, Austin!" Matt shouted. "Go get your dad!"

Austin pulled the flashlight out of his coat pocket and handed it to Matt. "You hold onto this. It's going to be dark before we get back. Shine it straight up, so we can find you."

Once Austin found a spot to cross the stream hopping rock to rock, he started running and never stopped running until he got home, and luckily found his father pulling out of their driveway heading to work.

Austin's father, Ray, ran into a tool shed and got a coiled up rope and slung it over his shoulder. Then he and Matt ran into the woods and when they reached the stream, they followed it looking for the familiar boulder and vine and the narrow column of light that would be marking the two boulders that Matt was sandwiched between. Austin saw the column of light first and pointed to it. When they got closer, they could see that there were no rocks they could use to reach the boulders where Matt was trapped. The water had risen too high.

Austin's father looked up at the tree limbs and tried to figure out what he was going to do. Once he had decided, he told Austin what he was going to do and started climbing. When he got out on the limb that hung out far over the stream and over the boulders trapping Matt, Austin's father took the coiled rope hanging over his shoulder and fastened one end of it to the limb and released the coil, letting it uncoil as it fell. He grabbed the rope and twisted it around his arm and wrapped it around his leg, and started lowering himself toward the stream. When he got to the end of the rope, he looked down and saw that he was going to have a long fall. He let his feet slide off the knot and slowly worked his way down the rope with his hands. He gripped the knot and looked down again. Matt was holding the flashlight with two hands. Water was up to his neck. "I'm going to get you out," Austin's father said and dropped and landed on the boulder. Matt was screaming and coughing water out of his mouth. The flashlight fell out of his hands, no light.

Austin's father went underwater and slid his knife blade under one shoe lace and pulled up. The blade cut the lace successfully and then he did the same thing with the second shoe. After cutting the second lace, he had to come up for air. After catching his breath, he went back down and pulled Matt's shoes off and was then able to pull Matt's feet and legs free.

Austin's father lifted Matt out of his position between the boulders and held him in his arms as he dropped off the boulder into the stream. Once he was in the water, he carried Matt to the bank followed by his son who was holding onto one of his father's arms. When Austin's father got to the bank, he laid Matt on the ground. Austin looked at Matt, then at his father and asked, "Is he alive?"

Austin's father leaned down to Matt's head and listened. "He's unconscious," Austin's father said. "He was in that cold water too long. Let's run. I hope I can do it—I'm too fat!"

$

Morgan said to Bob, "You're going to do just what you've been doing all these years, but now, other people and computers are going to make it easier." Morgan looked at Bob to see if he understood what he had said. Bob said nothing. "You won't have to do the grunt work anymore." Pointing to the prisoners standing in the doorway and hall, he added, "They and the computers are going to do it."

Morgan shouted across the room to the line of prisoners, "When I give the word, walk through that door, take a test, sit down, and wait for further instructions." Once the prisoners were in the room and seated, Morgan said, "This is a test, gentlemen. If you want to work on the website and make some money—show me by doing your best on this test. If you can't read or write and do math, it's going to show up here, and if it does show up here, you won't be hired. It's the same in here as it is out there in the world. Any questions?"

Bob and Morgan were checking and sorting completed tests putting them in two stacks: PASS and FAIL. Morgan said, as he dropped a test onto a stack resting on his desk, "See Sally run."

Looking at Morgan, Bob responded, "I thought it was Spot—see Spot run?"

"Maybe you're right, Bob," Morgan replied. "That makes more sense."

Prisoners who passed the test were given *Windows for Dummies* and were later seen reading them in the cafeteria, gym, laundry room, bathrooms, and in their cells trying to stay up with Morgan's syllabus.

$

Their dogs were watching them from the sidelines. Cindy's poodle was wearing a red cap and leggings and the wolfhound was sporting a black Nike visor. A young couple skated up to Cindy and Sergio.

The woman said, "Thanks for the lesson. Before you go can we show you something we've been working on?"

Cindy and Sergio agreed to stay and watched them go to the center of the ice. When the young couple finished, they skated over to Cindy and Sergio who were politely applauding their performance.

"Do you think there's a market for that?" the young woman asked.

Cindy replied, laughing, "What would you call it—Dirty Dancing on Ice?"

"Maybe—can you help us develop it into a touring show? It'd be hot!"

"How much money do you think it would take?" Cindy asked.

The young woman replied, "I don't know—a million dollars?"

"Who's got a million dollars?" Sergio asked looking at the young woman's partner.

"We thought you would," he answered.

Cindy shook her head, "Sorry, we don't have a million dollars."

"Got a half million?" he asked.

Cindy replied, "Do you really believe the public is ready for—for—" Cindy was searching for a good showbiz word, and then found one, "for SEXCAPADES!"

"Heck yeah!" the two of them said in unison.

"We don't have that kind of money," Cindy said. "Sorry, but give me your cards just in case I find a goldmine or kick up an oil well out west."

$

They were sitting in the Winnebago cooling down. Cindy said, "I do have a half million dollars and some change."

"I'm glad," Sergio replied.

She continued, "I think there might be an audience, a niche, for what they were doing, and I think SEXCAPADES is a good name for it—SEX SELLS EVERYWHERE ELSE!"

They were both silent for a while, then she said, "I've always dreamed of going to Las Vegas and betting my life's savings at the roulette table. Just ONE bet on RED. With one turn of the wheel—

and one fall of that little white ball, my life savings disappear or DOUBLE! And it's always RED!"

Sergio nodded his head up and down, then said, "If I doubled my life's savings, I would have about two hundred dollars."

Cindy was only half listening to what Sergio was saying. She was thinking about Las Vegas, roulette, and doubling her money. "The way I'm figuring it—I have nothing to lose, if I win, I'd have a million dollars and enough money to do the SEXCAPADES thing, and if I lose, I'd just be back to where I was before I stole Morgan's life's savings, which he wasn't going to need anyway sitting in prison."

"Oh boy," Sergio said with a heavy hint of negativity in his voice. He then walked to the front of the Winnebago and sat in the driver's seat. He withdrew the keys from the glove compartment and cranked the engine. Looking back, he said, "This is the express bus to Las Vegas—all aboard!"

$

A social worker was driving up the road and waved to Mrs. Stewart, Austin's mother, on her way to Morgan's cabin. Raquel opened the door. The social worker explained who she was and why she was there: to check on Matt's condition. She also wanted to speak to THE PARENTS.

"They aren't home right now," Raquel said.

"Hmmmmm," she said. "Your parents never came to the hospital to see Matt, did they?"

"No, they had to work," Raquel answered.

Before the social worker could ask another question, Mrs. Stewart walked up, and said, "Good morning, Raquel," then she nodded hello to the social worker and added, "These kids have the nicest parents."

After the social worker drove away, Mrs. Stewart looked at Raquel and said, "Now, young lady, I've lied for you kids more than once, but how long do you think we can get away with this?"

$

All ten of the prisoners who were selected to work on the website were sitting in front of computer monitors gathering information for Bob. One of the prisoners had brought a boom box and was playing rap music. Bob entered the room and immediately shouted, "Cut that crap off!"

The prisoner closest to the boom box scooted off his chair and pushed the OFF button.

Morgan looked at Bob and said, "What's the problem?"

Bob replied, "That music is ANTITHETICAL to THINKING."

One of the prisoners turned to face Bob and said, "What!?"

Bob explained to the whole group, "Playing the stock market is like playing a game of chess. It requires thought, reflection, meditation, and listening—ultimately a quiet, relaxed, open mind must be attained. Only CLASSICAL or OPERATIC music is suitable for this room."

All of the prisoners stopped looking at their screens and stared at Bob. Morgan looked at Bob, and said, "You mean operatic stuff like Figueroa—Figueroa—Figueroa!?"

"Yes, OPERA—and CLASSICAL MUSIC—" Bob answered.

"Well, Bob," Morgan said, "Music is very personal, you know. YOU like opera." Pointing, he said, "He likes RAP. Maybe he likes JAZZ. I like ROCK AND ROLL. Maybe we could take turns—each of us gets a turn to play what we like?"

Bob shook his head, "Absolutely NOT!"

The prisoner who had brought the boom box into the computer room grabbed his machine and said assertively, "I'll just take my BOOM BOX back to my CELL!"

All of the website workers yelled at the same time, "NO, NO, Noooo—don't do that!"

Bob shouted back, "Leave your boom box where it is, but don't put any of that GOD AWFUL MUSIC in it! We're not on the FRIGGIN' STREET you know."

Morgan looked at Bob, "Yeah Bob—we're in a FRIGGIN' PRISON! I don't like OPERA. I don't like CLASSICAL. I don't like SYMPHONIES, and I never will—I LIKE ROCK AND ROLL! If we can't reach an understanding, and if we can't give some to get some—maybe we can't do the website!"

$

Catherine was on the tennis court practicing overheads. The ball machine was shooting ball after ball across the net, and she was solidly smashing each one of them. Beside the court stood a perch on which Catherine's parrot was resting.

Morgan came out of the building unescorted and said, "Warden, I need your help."

After smashing a ball, she said, "How's that?"

Morgan shouted, "I've got a personnel problem."

Catherine was waiting for a ball to come down into hitting range.

While he waited, Morgan looked at her parrot. Then he said, "Aren't you afraid he'll fly away?"

Catherine hit the ball into the net. "DON'T TALK when I'm preparing to hit a ball."

Morgan chuckled, "Hell, I'd never speak if I followed that advice."

Catherine stared at Morgan and blurted, "THAT wasn't ADVICE—THAT was a DIRECTIVE!"

Morgan quickly reminded himself of his place in the scheme of things, "Sorry, Warden."

Catherine walked over to the ball machine and turned it off, and on the way back across the court, Catherine realized that she had been rude, because of a situation in her life outside of the prison. When she reached Morgan, she said, "Please accept my apology, Morgan. My remark was way out of line, I'm sorry."

Morgan felt relieved. "An apology wasn't necessary, but thank you anyway."

Catherine looked at Morgan and said, "I think you asked me why I wasn't afraid that my parrot would fly away—is that right?"

"Yes," Morgan replied.

Catherine replied, "Maybe he will one day, his wings aren't clipped, but why would he want to leave? He has all he wants and needs right here."

"You gotta point there," Morgan said, then he changed the subject. "We've got a personnel problem, and I need you to get some things to help fix it."

$

Morgan and Bob were standing together looking at the prisoners sitting in front of their computers. All of them were wearing headsets. As they started to walk behind the prisoners, Morgan pointed to each man and told Bob what kind of music was loaded on his device—country, rap, blues, rock and roll, or jazz. At the end of the line there was a headset resting on a tabletop. Morgan picked it up and handed it to Bob. "This is your headset, and your device is loaded with classical and operatic music. Hope you approve of the selections."

$

Morning sunlight was streaming through the window into the hotel room. Sergio had just awakened and was looking at his watch. He leaned over and kissed Cindy on the cheek, "You have to call your bank." One of Cindy's eyes opened and then the other. She rolled out of bed and walked to her purse to get her cellphone. Sergio said from the bed, "Do you want to reconsider?"

"No honey," she replied. "I'm going to get my bank to transfer the money today—no turning back!"

$

Cindy walked up to the cashier window and gave the woman her ID and answered some questions. In exchange, the woman gave her TEN chips—each one valued at $50,000. As they walked away, Cindy very deliberately placed the ten chips in her small red-beaded purse. Sergio watched her check the fastener twice, making sure it was securely closed. When Cindy looked up, he asked, "Don't you want to have dinner before—"

"Nope," she said before he could finish his question. "I wouldn't be able to eat anything right now, or if I did eat, I'd THROW UP."

They edged their way through the crowd, through the aisles of slot machines, and into the roulette area and after looking at individual roulette tables, Cindy found one that she liked and sat down, but she did not take the chips out of her purse. Eventually, the dealer asked Cindy if she was going to play.

"I'm not ready to play yet," she replied.

Sergio leaned down and whispered, "You have TO PLAY if you want TO SIT at the table."

Cindy looked at the dealer and pulled her seat closer to the table and leaned forward slightly, intentionally showing off her breasts to the dealer. Then she asked in a quiet sexy voice, "I've never played this game before. Is it okay to sit here for a few minutes while I get my courage up?"

The dealer smiled and said, "Certainly. Relax. Play when you are ready, madam."

Sergio stopped a cocktail waitress and took two glasses of wine off her tray and offered one of them to Cindy, but she pushed the glass away, "Not now, I'm too nervous."

Sergio said, "Okay," and quickly downed one of the glasses, and then the other one. He was more nervous than Cindy.

Cindy reached into her purse and pulled out the chips. She counted the chips one at a time to make sure she had a total of ten. Once she had them counted, she stacked them making sure they were in perfect alignment, and once that was accomplished, she looked up at the dealer and smiled. The dealer gave her a wink and a nod, "Ready?" he asked.

Cindy nodded affirming that she was ready.

The dealer spun the wheel and said, "Place your bets ladies and gentlemen."

After the dealer released the ball and it started falling toward the slots in the trough, Cindy picked up ALL TEN of her chips—the whole stack—and placed them on the RED rectangle.

The dealer immediately leaned forward and removed Cindy's stack of chips from the RED rectangle saying, "You can't bet that amount there, madam."

Cindy wasn't paying close attention to what the dealer was doing or saying—she was silently saying a prayer—so when she saw the dealer pick her chips up and put them back in front of her, she put them back on the RED rectangle. The white ball was still hopping in and out of slots. The dealer removed Cindy's chips again and said, "ILLEGAL BET," and put her chips back on the table in front of her.

Cindy looked up at the dealer, puzzled, and starting to panic, as she watched the ball bouncing in and out of slots—black, red, black, red and when she saw the white ball fall into a GREEN slot, she did panic, because she had never considered that the ball could land in a GREEN slot, because she didn't know there were GREEN SLOTS. Cindy quickly picked up her chips and placed them back on the RED rectangle, and held them there. With the last bit of energy left in that white ball, it jumped once more and settled in a RED slot.

The dealer looked at Cindy who was now jumping up and down screaming, "I WON, I WON!" and he said in a polite, calm voice, "I am sorry, madam. You made an illegal bet. YOU DID NOT WIN."

Cindy stopped jumping and shouted at the dealer, "You moved my bet, I WON, GIVE ME MY MONEY!"

The dealer tried to explain, but Cindy kept protesting. "The HECK you say!"

People started gathering around her table. The dealer looked back at the four men standing behind him then back at Cindy. "It's just the rule—you can't place a bet that large on RED or BLACK."

She stood more erect and restated her position in a calmer manner, "I placed my bet THREE TIMES on RED and I WON—GIVE ME MY MONEY!"

The dealer shook his head side to side. "I'm sorry, madam. You'll have to talk to the gentlemen behind me," he said, as he gestured for the four men to come forward. "People are waiting to play."

Cindy looked at the other people sitting at the table and said, "Look...look at these guys—it seems to me that a big, fancy, glitzy place like this could pay up when it loses."

One of the security men behind the dealer stepped forward and tried to grab Cindy's arm, she recoiled and shouted, "NO, you aren't going to get me out of this place until you pay me!" The man dropped his hand by his side and looked up at the ceiling and the window where other security people were watching. Cindy then looked at the crowd and said in a loud, assertive voice, "I don't think you should play here if THEY CHEAT like this!"

People in the crowd started nodding in agreement, which made the dealer and the people upstairs nervous. More nervous when they saw all the other players at the table stand up and leave their seats. Cindy looked at the men and women who walked away from the table, and thanked them for their support, and then returned her attention to the dealer and the security team. "Go talk to your people up there in the window," she said pointing, "You owe me a HALF MILLION DOLLARS!"

The crowd standing behind her had grown even larger, and they were beginning to shout, "Pay the lady! Pay the lady! She won the bet!"

A casino man dressed in a tuxedo walked up to the table and said very calmly, "There's a misunderstanding."

"MISUNDERSTANDING MY PETUNIA!" Cindy said loudly. "I placed a half million dollar bet and won—and you don't want to pay me. There is no MISUNDERSTANDING—the meaning of this is quite clear! People should STAY AWAY from this place!"

The crowd continued the refrain—"PAY THE LADY—PAY THE LADY!"

The man in the tuxedo looked nervously around and replied, "It was an ILLEGAL BET, madam." The crowd booed. "BUT…we will make AN EXCEPTION FOR YOU, if it will make you happy." He paused. "We will allow you to place your half million dollar bet AGAIN on RED or BLACK. This time, if you accept our offer, your bet will be LEGAL."

People in the crowd close enough to hear the conversation started repeating what they heard to other people in the crowd, so the noise level was getting higher and higher and the higher it went the more confident Cindy became. She smiled at the man and took a deep breath, "Nice try, buster. I have already placed a bet—THREE TIMES I PLACED MY BET—and I won that bet. Now you're asking me to place that bet again, which means I have to be right AGAIN to get what you already owe me—that's not fair."

The casino man listened to the instructions coming into his ear. "Okay, madam, you drive a hard bargain. We are willing to GIVE you FIVE HUNDRED THOUSAND DOLLARS for winning your previous bet—even though it was ILLEGAL—if you will add the five hundred thousand dollars you are presently holding in your hands and make a ONE-TIME BET of ONE MILLION DOLLARS on RED or BLACK."

"Great! Great!" Cindy screamed. "Thank you, thank you! I'm a MILLIONAIRE!"

"If you agree to the deal," the man said. "You will have one million dollars in your casino account, and if you win your million dollar bet, you will have TWO MILLION DOLLARS making you a MULTIMILLIONAIRE."

The DEAL the casino was offering was being repeated through the crowd, and soon the crowd was shouting—"Take the deal, Cindy!"

Cindy looked at Sergio who was nodding approval.

Cindy looked at the casino man and said, "Okay, I accept the deal! Let's go."

The casino man smiled, "Not tonight. We've had enough excitement for one evening," he said looking at the crowd. Then he added, "How about next Friday night—does that work for you and your friend?"

Cindy hooked her arm around Sergio, and replied, "My partner's name is Sergio."

"All right," the casino man said. "We'll expect to see you and Sergio at the same table next Friday night at 9:00 p.m."

"Wait, wait," Cindy said raising her hand. "I'm expecting the casino to pick up expenses for our room, food, and bar tabs through Friday night...COOL?"

The casino man stuck out his right fist and she met his with hers.

When the casino man walked away, a reporter stepped out of the crowd followed by a camera man with lights and hot microphone,

"What are you going to do with the TWO MILLION DOLLARS if you win the bet?"

She smiled, and replied, "I'm going to put it into a new ice skating tour show."

"That's great," the reporter replied. "What's the name?"

Cindy's eyes sparkled as she smiled at Sergio, "I—WE can't say right now."

The reporter responded, "Will you do the premiere right here in Las Vegas?"

Cindy replied, "Maybe," and looked directly into the camera. "First things first. America, be here next Friday night and cheer me on." She looked at Sergio who was standing by her side. "I should say—cheer US on. This is SERGIO my partner."

Sergio took two glasses of champagne from a tray that was placed in front of them and handed one to Cindy who lifted it above her head saying, "Here's to MONEY...LOVE...SEX and LUCK!"

$

Matt and Austin were playing Mortal Combat on Austin's laptop computer when Austin's mother walked up a said to her son, "After you get your butt kicked, Austin, go out and get us a chicken for dinner."

"Okay, Mom," Austin replied without taking his eyes off the screen.

Mrs. Stewart added, "Take Matt out there with you and show him how to kill and dress out a chicken." She grinned and winked at her son, "I sharpened the hatchet this morning. Oughta take just one chop."

"No way!" Matt exclaimed. "I'm not watching—that's gross!"

"Come on, Matt," Austin pleaded. "After I ring its neck, it doesn't feel a thing!"

Matt stuck his index finger into his mouth and pretended to gag. Then he retracted his finger, "Naw—naw, I'll stay right here, thanks. You go kill the chicken!"

$

Catherine was sitting at a table with five men and two women. "The governor," a man said, "has received numerous inquiries and objections to the new entrepreneurial venture—Morgan Make$ Money website."

Catherine replied, "I would think that the governor would be pleased about all the publicity and interest that's being generated by the group."

The board member replied, "The public seems to like the idea that the money prisoners are making goes to pay for their incarceration, lessening the burden on taxpayers, but they don't seem to like the idea that prisoners can actually make money for themselves."

Catherine smiled, then responded. "The governor won the right to serve as the leader of this state primarily because he said he was going to RE-INVENT the prison system, and he is carrying out that promise and doing a fine job. Yes, prisoners are personally benefitting from their entrepreneurial endeavors and they should, but we aren't talking about great sums of money. That will most likely be true for this new venture as well. Some of the revenue from Morgan Make$ Money will go to the new Parolee Relief Fund, which will provide money to prisoners who are paroled, making it easier for them to transition back into society. This, of course, will certainly reduce the recidivism rate. It's a win-win situation. The State and taxpayers will be saving money and people down on their luck will become successful, tax-paying residents of our state—everybody wins." Catherine looked around the table and said, "What's the problem?"

Another board member said, "Well, Warden, quite frankly, none of us thought this thing would get very far off the ground to begin with, but now that it has—especially with the play that this new venture is getting in the media—people are objecting, because it looks like criminals are being rewarded, not punished for their crimes."

Catherine smiled, "As I said previously, the governor promised the voters prior to being elected that he would reinvent the prison system, and he's doing it. He and WE should be okay with this, because it's the right and honorable thing to do. The prisoners are in prison to pay their debt to society, and we are paying our debt to them—prisoners are entitled to live in an environment in which they can learn and better themselves, so they can return to society ready to make a contribution and enjoy, hopefully, the prosperity that will come from their newly acquired skills, knowledge, and confidence."

Catherine surveyed the faces around the table. "I think we are done, ladies and gentlemen. Thank you for your understanding, patience, and support. Everybody feels better when they earn money—and that's especially true for this population. Feel good that you're part of this. See you next month."

$

They were walking through the flower garden pulling weeds and deadheading plants. Both of them were wearing straw hats and shades.

"All of the publicity the Morgan Make$ Money website has gained has served to enliven all the other business ventures within the prison," Catherine said. "They've all become more creative in their promotions and they're all contributing to the Parolee Relief Fund that Morgan initiated."

After snipping off a few seed pods, her father said, "Perhaps your horticulture group could use some seeds."

"Anything you want to donate, I'll take it," Catherine replied, putting out her hand. Her father dropped the seed pods in her outstretched hand.

"How did Armstrong get the Wheeler fellow to come out of his shell?" her father asked.

Catherine put the seed pods in her jacket pocket and swept her hand clean. "I think calling Bob a genius and believing that he was a genius was the beginning of it. Morgan is a man who won't be denied, a natural self-promoter—what's the name of the website?--MORGAN Make$ Money—He's a supreme manipulator with lots of energy and that energy invigorates other people. People feel better, want to be better, and definitely want to PLEASE him. Even though there might also be times when they would like to kill him."

"Interesting," her father replied.

"Morgan IS SPECIAL," Catherine said, smiling.

Her father snipped off another dead flower and put it in a bag with others. He stopped walking and looked at his daughter. "Are you ATTRACTED to this man?"

"Intrigued."

$

Cindy and Sergio were dressing up for the big evening at the casino and caught a little snippet on a TV news program reminding people to watch the Cindy-versus-Casino showdown. It was the talk of the town.

When they walked out of the elevator with their two dogs, Cindy and Sergio were dressed to the nines, which would be expected, but their dogs were also decked out compliments of a local pet shop. TV lights came on and questions spewed out of the crowd of reporters and photographers.

At the cashier window, Cindy asked for her million dollars in chips, and the cashier handed her ONE chip.

"ONE CHIP," Cindy exclaimed, and laughed. "A million dollar chip! I can't believe it," she said to Sergio.

The cashier said, "We made it just for you, hon, Good Luck!"

When Cindy turned around, a security guard walked up to her and introduced himself. She told him that she wanted to pose for the photographers. She held up the million dollar chip, then she lowered it to her lips and kissed it. When she looked at the chip, she saw the bright, red imprint of her lips on the chip. Excited, she flipped the chip around so the crowd of photographers could take pictures of the chip that she had tattooed with her lips. She looked at Sergio and asked him the time, and he told her that it was eight fifty-five. Once she heard the time, she announced to the crowd of photographers and reporters that they had five minutes to get to the roulette table.

"Wish us luck!" she said, waving at the photographers with one hand and grabbing Sergio's hand with the other.

The security man led them through a roped off walkway and arrived at the roulette table at precisely nine o'clock. The dealer smiled and said, "Are you ready?"

Cindy took a deep breath and said, "Yep."

The dealer turned and made eye contact with the security team and the hotel owner who stepped forward and thanked the crowd in the casino for attending the special event and the millions of people who were watching on TVs around the world.

Cindy looked at the dealer and when he nodded, she sat down and placed her million dollar chip on the table in front of her. "Good luck, madam," he said. "Here we go." He put his hand on the wheel and spun it.

Cindy watched the wheel spin, blurring the slots and numbers and colors as they sped by. What was most conspicuous and clearly defined, however, were the TWO GREEN slots—ZERO and DOUBLE ZERO—that the white ball could easily settle in instead of RED or BLACK. How much that reduced her odds from fifty-fifty, she didn't know, but that was neither here nor there, at that very moment, she had to choose RED or BLACK. All of her adult life, she had dreamed of playing RED as she had told Sergio, and last time for real, the ball settled in a RED slot. She was thinking what are the odds of the white ball settling in RED again? Will it be BLACK this time? Or GREEN? Damn them! The dealer had delayed dropping the ball to give Cindy time to make her decision and place her bet. The dealer placed his hand on the wheel and spun it faster.

"Are you ready to place your bet?" he asked. Cindy didn't respond. "Are you ready for me to drop the ball?"

"Yes," she replied.

The dealer immediately dropped the ball and the sound of it rolling across and dropping on the smooth surface of the wheel filled the air. Cindy still had her million dollar chip in her hand. The dealer said, "Place your bet, madam."

Cindy looked back at Sergio. "I'm getting mixed messages—I'm confused—ambivalent—I've known it would be RED all my life, and IT WAS RED last time, but what will it be this time—what will it be NOW?"

Sergio didn't answer. She turned back to face the dealer.

The dealer said, "Madam?"

Cindy moved her hand forward and placed the chip on the BLACK rectangle and the crowd cheered.

The ball started bouncing in and out of slots. Cindy couldn't remain seated. She stood up and picked up her chip, and moved it to the RED rectangle, and the crowd cheered even louder than it did when she put her chip on BLACK which made Cindy gloriously happy. The sound of the ball hopping in and out of the slots was becoming less loud now, and when Cindy looked down, the ball was less lively, and she suddenly had a premonition that the white ball was going to land and settle in a BLACK slot, so she very quickly picked up her chip and placed it back on the BLACK rectangle. The ball was still hopping in and out of slots—red, black, black red, green, and then BLACK, and it appeared that the ball might remain there. Cindy grabbed the edge of the table hoping her grip would reduce vibrations in the wheel and increase the chances that the ball would stay in that BLACK slot, but it didn't. Somehow the ball contained enough energy to pop up and out of the BLACK slot and into the RED slot next to it.

Cindy closed her eyes and dipped her head. She released her grip on the table. The dealer took her million dollar chip. The crowd groaned. The TV lights went dark, and the crowd drifted away.

$

Morgan was watching the TV special—Ice Queen versus Vegas Casino in the recreation room. "That woman's crazy," a prisoner exclaimed. "A million dollars gone—pissed away!"

Another prisoner said excitedly, "The bitch had some tits!"

His buddy said, "Keep rappin', brother!"

The brother complied, "*The bitch had som' tits like som' ho, put her life's savings on Black, when she shoulda stayed on Red, now she's gonna have to make a hard livin' bangin' bubbas in bed. Yeah, yeah, the bitch had som' tits!*"

The prisoners sitting on the sofa with Morgan were laughing at the guy's spontaneous rap, but Morgan wasn't.

"What's the matter, man?" One of the prisoners asked Morgan. "That bitch lost a million dollars, don't you find that entertaining? Looking at your face, you'd think it was your money she lost."

"They had that wheel rigged, man. No way that woman was gonna win…didn't matter which way she played it—that ball was going where they wanted it to go. They had little levers in the bottoms of them slots. If that ball goes in the WRONG SLOT—they surely gonna BLIP IT OUT."

Morgan replied, "Covering the bet was nothing—they got TEN MILLION DOLLARS worth of advertising for free."

The guy looked at him and said, "Yeah, sure did. And what da hell did she get out of it?"

Morgan smiled, "She was famous for fifteen minutes."

The guy shook his head, "Good God All mighty—cost her a million dollars to be famous for fifteen minutes—wow man, she shoulda settled for being famous for seven and a half minutes and kept a half million in the bank! Now, she's screwed!"

$

When they got to their cell, Bob said to Morgan, "Was she your wife?"

Morgan replied, "She was and that WAS my money."

$

They were still in bed when the phone rang. He handed the receiver to Cindy. She listened and said a total of three words to the caller: great, great, and okay. After Cindy handed the receiver back to Sergio, he asked, "What was that?"

Cindy replied, "Some guy wants to talk to us about the new ice skating show WE WERE GOING TO DO in Vegas."

"Oh," Sergio uttered.

"We have to be down stairs in forty-five minutes for the limo," she said excitedly. "Get happy!"

They and the dogs walked out of the hotel to the limousine that was waiting at the curb. They drove through town to get to the office building, and when they got there a doorman took the two dogs. "Don't worry about your dogs, they'll be in the pet lounge while you are upstairs meeting with The Mann."

"We're going to be meeting with The Man, are we?" Cindy asked playfully to their escort.

"Yes, indeed," he replied.

After they stepped out of the elevator (equipped with slot machine), they were met by a very nice-looking, well-dressed man. He said, "You're even more attractive in person. Thanks for coming over on such short notice. I'm The Mann."

Cindy extended her hand and they shook. Before Sergio got his hand extended to shake the guy's hand, Cindy said, "I know you're THE MAN, but what's your name?"

The Mann laughed, "The Mann really is my name."

Cindy smiled, "You're kidding me."

"No, I'm not, " he responded. "Mann was our last name, and my parents were weird. They thought giving me THE as a first name would be fun."

"FUN for others maybe. What was it like in first, second, third grade when the teachers called roll—where's The Mann?"

My classmates laughed the first day or two then everybody got used to it, and it was no different than having a name like John Smith. " He paused and then proposed that they talk about the ice skating show. "Do you or DID you have a name for it?"

Cindy looked at Sergio, then looked back at The Mann. "Yes, we do. It's SEXCAPADES."

$

Heather had an envelope in front of her. "If we send this, they're going to know where we are."

"Look," one of the Stewart girls said. "This has to stop some time. You can't stay here in the woods forever. Mom and Dad want you to live with us—send it and let's get things rolling—you need some parents."

$

Morgan was standing off to the side of the court. Catherine was practicing her ground strokes. She asked him, "How many hits are you getting on the website?"

"We get more each day," Morgan said.

Catherine asked him to increase the trajectory, so the balls would land deeper in the court. The adjustment Morgan made worked for the next few balls, but then the balls started landing short again. Catherine dropped her racket on the court and stood with her hands on her hips, frustrated. She and Morgan met at the ball machine. Morgan turned it off and looked inside to see what was causing the problem.

"This machine is on its last leg," she said.

"I see the problem," Morgan said.

"It just needs to last another month," Catherine said. "After that, it'll be too cold to practice out here." She watched him fiddle with a wheel inside the machine. "Never mind, Morgan. Don't bother with it now. I sent for you, so I could tell you that I've been receiving phone calls from TV people." Morgan stood up and looked at her. "They all want you and Bob on their shows."

Morgan smiled, "*Ellen?*"

"Not *Ellen,*" Catherine replied. "Right now, it's the financial shows, but if you want me to, I'll contact the *Ellen* people and see if they want to book you and Bob on their show."

"Good, I like *Ellen,*" Morgan said and waved as he headed back inside the prison.

$

Bob was explaining a chart to Morgan when Catherine entered the room. She said, "It's confirmed, Morgan. I just finished talking with a CNBC producer, and she wants you and Bob to come on the show next week."

Morgan said, "Fantastic!"

Bob remained silent.

Catherine looked at Bob and asked excitedly, "Are you ready to go to New York, Bob?"

"No," Bob replied.

Morgan turned and stared at Bob. "What do you mean, No? Appearing on TV shows means MONEY! We're going to make some money!" After Morgan got those words out of his mouth, he looked at Catherine and said, "Bob's going to New York!"

"I'm not going, Morgan," Bob said. "Makes me sick just thinking about it."

Catherine looked at both men, "Well now, isn't this a pretty picture!?"

Morgan and Bob had their arms folded across their chests staring down at the floor.

Catherine folded her arms across her chest and said, "I think it's kind of weird, but the producer told me that she'd throw in a couple of tickets to the Met, but who would want to see an opera!?"

Morgan looked at Catherine with disbelief.

"I'll GO!" Bob said quickly.

Catherine winked and smiled coyly at Morgan.

$

Catherine was on the phone with the CNBC producer, "I know you have agreed to cover—airfare, hotel, clothes, limousine, and food," Catherine said and paused, then added, "I'd like to add one more thing—BOX SEATS at the Met?"

$

A prison sedan pulled up in front of a men's clothing store and stopped. Bob, Morgan, and two security men walked out of the store carrying garment bags over their shoulders.

$

Morgan, Bob, and the same two security men were standing in line to board a plane. All four were dressed stylishly. As the four of them walked onto the plane, flight attendants greeted them with polite smiles. Morgan said to one of them, "I'd like some orange juice, please."

"Yes, sir," she replied. "I'll get that for you after take-off."

"Thanks, sweetheart," he replied.

"Like they say at Chick-fil-A, it will be MY PLEASURE!"

$

Just off the set, a staffer was attaching a microphone to Bob's lapel, but before she could get it attached, Bob told her to hold up. "I have to use the bathroom."

"But you have to start the interview in SIXTY SECONDS," she replied.

Bob looked at her and said, "I have to throw up—where do you want me to do it?"

She handed Bob a trash can.

The woman said looking into the camera, "If you haven't heard about the Morgan Make$ Money website and its right-on predictions, you need to stay tuned! It is a fascinating story. Today, right now, we have the two gentlemen who created the Morgan Make$ Money website—Morgan Armstrong and Bob Wheeler." She turned in her chair to face them. "Thank you for coming to our studios today. I'm sure our audience is anxious to meet you two—the principals behind the website. Of course, what makes this so interesting is the fact that you are prisoners—CONVICTS. Just how did you two CONVICTS get so knowledgeable about stocks, about WALL STREET?"

Morgan sat up straighter and pointed to Bob, "Bob's the stock market GENIUS—I'm just the IT—Information Technology guy."

The host looked at Bob and asked, "How did you acquire so much knowledge about buying and selling stocks?" Bob was battling nerves. He looked at Morgan who gave him a very confident nod. The host didn't want to let the silence go on too long, so she asked, "What's the secret to picking STOCK WINNERS?"

Bob cleared his throat, "Excuse me, I just finished throwing up in the trash can over there." He paused. "It's more CORRELATION than CAUSE and EFFECT, more ELIMINATION than SELECTION."

The host replied, "Uh-huh."

Bob continued with a modest increase in comfort and confidence. "It takes a while to explain."

"We have the time," the host said, "please tell us how you predicted such BIG WINNERS?"

"Well, I've been in prison for the best part of twenty years and for most of that time I have been following stocks, because there's not much to do in prison to occupy one's mind."

The host said, "Okay, okay."

Bob continued, "After years of recording data, I started noticing how things went in cycles. How one thing happened here and was followed consistently by another thing happening over there with nothing at least on the surface that connected them. There was never a direct cause and effect relationship that I could see, but they were nevertheless connected in some significant and relevant way. There was a CONTINUUM."

The host was impressed by what Bob had said but was worried that the show's audience might appreciate something that might be more NUTS and BOLTS. She turned her attention to Morgan. "How does Bob pick winners, so accurately?"

Morgan replied, "For two decades he has read every magazine, newspaper, and journal that has come into the prison and from the reading and his notes, his brain picks up patterns and in time spits out WINNERS—just like slot machines spit out quarters, half dollars, or whatever when things line up." Morgan paused, then summed it up, "Bob's a GENIUS."

The host responded, "Yes, I think we are beginning to see that. What specific stocks has he—"

Morgan started to respond but Bob started talking first. "It was the Bio-Med sector's time and, within that sector, there had always been a history of advances and declines—"

The host interrupted Bob because of time constraints, "Fascinating, just fascinating," she said.

Bob went on, however, "In the field of bio-medicine, it's important to keep up with grants, research reports, journals, papers, congresses because advances are made here and there around the world and soon they add up to mean something. Because of my incarceration, I've been able to follow the research and the researchers. I know them—not personally, of course, but I know their work. I've read everything in print which has enabled me—"

The host interrupted him again. "Thanks, Bob. Time has run out—let me ask you one last question—how were you able to predict this recent advance in the Bio-Med sector when all the stock gurus were predicting the opposite, and how did you know that that one particular stock was going through the roof? It's just so—unbelievable!?"

Bob looked over at Morgan, then back at the host, and said, "How can one explain the child Mozart writing complete symphonies and operas without revision—they just came to him. Just like these things come to me now—would that I were a child."

$

Morgan, Bob, and the security men were decked out in Speedo swimwear. As Morgan walked toward the diving board, a woman in a group of women looked at him and said, "Didn't I just see you on TV?"

Morgan smiled widely and said, "Yes, you did."

The woman looked around at her friends and said pointing, "And that's Bob over there—he's SUCH A GENIUS!"

Morgan snapped his Speedo goggles over his eyes and said, "Excuse me, ladies. Watch this double pike turnout."

"You and Bob are so cute," she exclaimed. "What did you do to get in prison?"

Morgan stopped his dive preparations to answer, "We were both convicted of MURDER," he said and paused. "BUT both of us were and ARE INNOCENT."

The woman who had initiated the conversation immediately replied, "Of course, ya'll are INNOCENT, DARLIN'."

$

The orchestra had warmed up. The lights went down, and the curtain rose. They're looking through opera glasses. Bob had the man's face dialed in close enough to see the whites of his eyes. Morgan had chosen to zoom in on the lead soprano, specifically on her breasts, where beads of sweat were glistening like drops of morning dew on ripe summer melons.

$

They had gone directly from the opera to the Ginger Man restaurant for dinner. Morgan was making eye contact with one of the women in a party of four just sitting down at the next table, and walked over. "Did you ladies attend the opera at the Met this evening?" he asked.

All four of the women nodded their heads affirming that they had.

"It was wuuunnnnderful, wasn't it?" Morgan asked and turned to look at Bob. Morgan raised his voice, "Maaagnificent costumes weren't they Bob?"

Bob nodded his head, "They were SPLENDID, Morgan."

Morgan made quick eye contact with all four women, and asked, "Won't you beautiful ladies join me and these three handsome gentlemen for dinner? My treat!?"

$

Morgan was surprised with the ease with which he was able to persuade the security men into having the women over to their hotel suite to discuss the opera.

$

It was now morning, and the eight people who came together the evening before are now waking up as FOUR COUPLES. One of the security men was checking his watch and saw that there was a good chance that he and the other three men were going to miss their flight back home—back to the state prison—if they didn't get outside and catch a cab. With hurried hugs and kisses the men said good-bye to the women and rushed out the door of their hotel suite for the elevators.

$

At least a week had passed and Catherine was talking on the phone to a CNBC accounts person who informed her of the expenses that were incurred at the Times Square Marriott. She heard—twelve bottles of champagne and twenty pounds of seafood: shrimp, scallops, oysters, crab—after hearing CRAB, Catherine stopped listening.

$

Morgan saw that he had a letter in his snail mail inbox and he recognized the handwriting. Heather told him that they were in their cabin and that the Stewart family down the road wanted to adopt them. She wanted to know if he would consider it.

He was relieved to know where his kids were, and he was thankful—even though he didn't know the family—that they wanted to adopt three kids. It was good news but good news that brought greater sadness. He was re-reading the letter when a runner from the warden's office showed up in the website room.

"She wants to see you, Morgan," he said.

Catherine raised her head when Morgan entered her office and watched him approach her desk. Her parrot over in the corner fluttered its feathers and pecked at the apple stuck on the end of a stick next to its perch. "Oh my!" the parrot screamed, "WHAT A BAD BOY!"

Morgan chuckled.

"Well," Catherine said with the slightest of smiles, "How did it go last week?"

Morgan motioned that he would like to sit down.

Catherine said curtly, "YES, SIT."

Morgan sat down knowing that something wasn't right. "Bob was great," he said. "Didn't you watch the shows?"

Catherine replied, "I watched and recorded all of them."

"How about the governor?" Morgan asked.

"I sent him the BEST ONE," she replied. "He's a busy man." After she replied, she was silent and Morgan was also silent, which made the moment pregnant with implications. "What about the rest of the time. The off-camera time? How did all that go—the Met, dinner at the Ginger Man—tell me all about it?"

Morgan shifted his position in the chair suddenly feeling even more awkward and nervous. "Oh," he said. "The hotel was first class, and the limo was out of sight: TV, phone, bar—no alcohol of course—we felt like MOVIE STARS."

"How did Bob like the Met—wasn't it FAUST?"

"Bob was in heaven. The guy sold his soul to the devil, I think, couldn't understand what the heck they were saying most of the time, so it was hard to follow the story, but I'll tell you one thing—there were no small-breasted women in the show."

Catherine leaned back in her chair and said sarcastically, "Then it wasn't a total loss for you. Tell me more."

"Not too much more to tell, Catherine—Warden," Morgan replied. "We left the opera, had a nice dinner, returned to the hotel, and came back here in the morning."

Catherine stared at Morgan, and said, "Tell me more about the Ginger Man."

Morgan pushed his butt to the back of his chair and sat up perfectly straight before answering her question. "I had a NEW YORK STRIP STEAK, some mixed vegetables, and a fancy French dessert. I can't remember what the others had. What's with all the questions?"

Catherine replied calmly, "You obviously aren't going to tell me on your own. The restaurant sent the accounts payable guy at CNBC an invoice for EIGHT dinners, not FOUR, and the hotel sent them an invoice not only for the SUITE, but also for room service which included—twelve bottles of champagne and twenty pounds of seafood—do I need to go on?"

Morgan started to reply but stopped when Catherine jumped up and slapped a packet of papers down on her desk and screamed, "EXPLAIN ARMSTRONG!"

Morgan said as calmly as he could, "There were four lonely looking women—"

Catherine cut him off, "Stop it, Morgan! Just tell me the damn truth, you IDIOT!"

After silently digesting the word IDIOT, he continued, "Four women sat down next to us in the restaurant, just after we had been seated, and I found myself—no, I didn't FIND myself going over there. I PURPOSEFULLY WENT over to their table and invited them to have dinner with us, because I wanted to be with SOME WOMEN—and I was willing to take the consequences."

Catherine sat back down in her chair and said, "Well, how nice, Morgan. You were such a GENTLEMAN. Then YOU—NO DOUBT—INVITED the LOVELY LADIES to your SUITE at the MARRIOTT!"

"Yes, I did," he answered.

"ALL of this—on TAXPAYER MONEY," she added, calmly.

"I guess that's right…I hadn't given that much thought, I guess," Morgan said, quietly.

Catherine leaned forward and in a deliberate, but angry voice, she said with the volume escalating as she spoke, "I am upset, embarrassed, dismayed, disappointed, alarmed, and pissed off—Armstrong! You took four sluts—HOOKERS—back to your hotel, GORGED yourselves on EXPENSIVE FOOD, and SLEPT with them!"

Morgan stood up, and replied, "THEY WEREN'T HOOKERS! We had dinner at one of the finest, most expensive restaurants in New York City—they wouldn't have been HOOKERS, not in there, and THEY NEVER ASKED FOR MONEY!"

Catherine sat back down and laced her fingers together. "Then they were just SLUTS. All kinds of people frequent upscale New York restaurants—look at who they picked up—TWO CONVICTS—TWO MURDERERS and TWO INCOMPETENT security BOZOS! You could be HIV POSITIVE right now! How STUPID!"

Morgan didn't say anything and neither did Catherine. It was the parrot that broke the silence, "OH MY," the bird said.

Morgan quickly turned and said, "Shut up bird!"

After a period of awkward silence, Morgan looked at Catherine and quietly said, "I am not a murderer."

Catherine calmly replied, "A jury of your peers said you were."

"May I leave now?" Morgan asked.

"Please do," Catherine answered.

$

The prison attorney, Ms. Spangler, looked at Morgan and asked. "Are you sure you want them adopted?"

"What other options do I have?"

Ms. Spangler replied, "Foster homes, group homes—"

"No, adoption is what they want, and it's what I want. I'll sign when the paperwork is ready."

$

Inside their cell, Bob was working on his laptop computer, and Morgan was lying on his cot. Bob didn't take his eyes off the screen when he asked, "Being in here is harder now, isn't it?"

Morgan didn't respond.

Bob stopped looking at the screen and peered over at Morgan. It was unusual for Morgan to be lying around doing nothing. It was also unusual for Morgan not to be talking. Bob said, "That night in New York, Morgan, was the most wonderful experience in my entire life." Bob waited for Morgan to say something, but he didn't.

$

A week had gone by since her heated conversation and confrontation with Morgan. Her phone rang. She lifted the receiver, gave her name, and listened to the voice of the caller as she removed her glasses. "Yes, I have your letter in front of me, but I have a few questions."

$

"SHE wants to see you, Morgan," the runner said. Morgan went to the warden's office and was told that she was on the tennis court. "She's the TENNIS QUEEN, isn't she?" he said to Catherine's secretary, not expecting an answer.

Catherine was hitting, but unlike other times, she said, "Please, shut that thing off," pointing to the ball machine. Once he had it shutdown, she invited him to the net, and said, "I owe you an apology." Morgan was totally surprised by her first words. "Under no circumstances should I have said what I said the other day. I was disappointed, hurt, and scared, when I called you an idiot and then a murderer."

Morgan started his reply but stopped when Catherine kept talking. "I was angry and definitely wrong in more than one way." She paused and looked down at the court. Morgan remained quiet. She swallowed, then said, "I learned this morning that a confession in your hometown has been validated and accepted by the court. As you have said all along, Morgan, someone else killed that man, not you. Morgan's eyes glistened. He blinked. "My runner will help you process out. You should be able to leave the prison by tomorrow afternoon," she said.

"I'm free?" Morgan asked quietly.

Just as quietly, she responded, "Yes."

He looked at her and said, "This is such a surprise. Is this a GOOD thing?"

"What?" she asked, perplexed by his question.

"You're always talking—asking whether something is GOOD—is this a GOOD thing?"

"You know it's a GOOD thing, Morgan—you are going back out into the world and live a FREE LIFE!"

"If it is a GOOD thing, why don't I feel good?"

"Well," she replied. "I don't know. Maybe it's the SUDDENNESS of it. Suddenness screws us up for a while."

Morgan thought for a few seconds and monitored his physical responses, then replied, "Maybe I'm feeling like most of us feel when we lose something, something important. Maybe I'm feeling this way, because I'll be leaving Bob and the other guys, the website?"

"That could well be, Morgan, you've created something IMPORTANT, and you've established a meaningful relationship—relationships."

"Maybe I want you to teach me how to play tennis," Morgan replied.

Catherine responded, "You can learn how to play tennis on the outside."

Morgan replied, "I've never played a game where LOVE is a part of scoring."

Catherine answered, "Yes, tennis is unique that way. It's the only time in life when LOVE means NOTHING."

After a long, nervous pause, Morgan said, "When I learn the game well enough, may I come back and play with you?"

She smiled and said, "I would like that. I haven't played a match in a long time." She became silent as did he for a while, then she continued. "On a different note, what are you going to do now?"

He answered, "Start over. Everything's gone."

"Remember," she said, tilting her head. "You'll be eligible to receive money from the Parolee Relief Fund. I guess you'd qualify even though you won't actually be a PAROLEE and that's—a very GOOD THING!"

"I'll keep that in mind," Morgan replied. "What's your next step—the White House?"

She thought, then said with a modest but cute smile, "Sainthood."

Morgan's eyes twinkled. "Don't you have to be DEAD first?"

"Yeah, that's right," she answered.

"So what are you going to do between now and then?" he asked.

"GOOD THINGS, of course," she replied and walked over to her parrot. Morgan followed her to the perch, and when he got there, he said, "I understand better now why your bird doesn't fly away."

Catherine looked at her parrot. "Say—goodbye to Morgan."

The parrot bobbed its head a few times and then said, "*Adios, amigo.*"

Morgan chuckled, and then stared into Catherine's eyes, smiling as he was remembering the first time he saw Catherine, and repeated what he had said that day—*What a beautiful creature.*

Catherine's eyes sparkled, "Thanks, Morgan," she said. "It's just as enjoyable to hear those words, today, as it was the first time."

"Then you knew at the time that I wasn't talking about the parrot?"

Catherine smiled, "Yes, and I saved your words to a special file."

Morgan was surprised that his words had meant anything to her. "What file was that?" he asked, smiling.

"COMPLIMENTS, we can never get too many," she replied.

PART II

The GREEN HOUSE

When Morgan walked out of the main gate of the prison, he got in his best friend's car and headed south on interstate 64. An hour later, they arrived at Jimmy's home in Poquoson. Morgan no longer had a home there nor were any of his businesses still existent in the metropolitan area. His home, the Armstrong Detective Agency, the Doll House, Dream Cars Ltd, Bug Out Exterminating, Condom World, and Armstrong Protection Systems had been auctioned off by his third wife who pocketed all the money and run off with a young Romanian ice skater for parts unknown. Morgan did have fifteen hundred dollars in his wallet—thanks to the Parolee Relief Fund—which saved him from being totally broke.

Once they got inside the small brick rancher, Jimmy's wife served up tuna salad sandwiches to Morgan and her husband. After lunch, Jimmy took Morgan out the back door of his house to his garage for a surprise. Jimmy reached down and grabbed the handle on the old, wooden garage door and yanked. The door moved up about a foot where it got stuck. Jimmy moved his feet closer to the door and yanked again. This time the door moved more freely, but as it moved up the metal channel, it created a sharp screeching sound until it reached its final overhead destination inside the garage.

"Your garage door is in dire need of lubricant, Jimmy," Morgan said as he rubbed down the hair that had been raised on his arms by the screeching door. Suddenly, he noticed the classic car license plate on the bumper of the VW bus.

"Do you remember selling this vehicle to me, Morgan?" Jimmy asked.

"Yep, I do," Morgan replied as he slowly and carefully walked beside the vehicle feeling the smooth, shiny paint with his fingertips.

"As you can see, it's still in mint condition," Jimmy said, "but it's older now, so check the engine oil and air pressure in the tires frequently, and keep a good coat of wax on the paint. I'm going to loan it to you for a while, because you're going to need it."

Morgan looked at his friend, "No, Jimmy, I can't take this vehicle from you. I don't want to put a lot of mileage on her."

Jimmy's wife, Mary, walked up to her husband's side smiling, "Jimmy hardly drives the bus anymore, Morgan, and I suspect you can't afford to buy a vehicle right now. So take these," she said, dangling a set of keys in front of her. Morgan took the keys and dropped them in his pocket.

Later, Morgan drove the bus to see his mother who was still staying at the assisted living facility just fifteen minutes from Jimmy's home. When he walked through the entrance, he saw the bird cage and noticed that there were significantly fewer finches in the cage. He wondered what had happened to them as he continued down the hall.

"Mr. Armstrong, so nice to see you," a woman said excitedly from an alcove.

"Hi, Roberta, I'm here to see, my mom," Morgan said.

Roberta smiled and walked toward him. "She's not in her room. I'll take you to her. She likes to sit in the solarium." When they turned the corner, Roberta pointed down the hall. "There she is," she said.

Morgan saw his mother and replied, "I see she's still keeping her hands busy doing needlepoint."

"Yes," Roberta replied, then added. "Your mother gave me one of her needlepoints not long ago, and I had it stretched, but I framed it myself and hung it on my dining room wall."

When they reached the solarium, Morgan stooped over behind his mother and whispered, "Hi, Mom."

His mother looked up over her shoulder and saw her son. Roberta smiled widely at Morgan's mother and said, "It's a wonderful day, isn't it?"

Mrs. Armstrong put her needlepoint aside and stood up unsteadily from her wheelchair. She was totally flummoxed seeing him in front of her. Morgan had not called to let her know that he was being released from prison. Roberta watched them hug and then excused herself, saying to Morgan, "This is a very happy day for your mother; she hasn't had very many visitors—just Jimmy, every now and then."

Morgan spent some of the afternoon with his mother describing prison life and explaining why he had been released. Jimmy and

Mary had taken her to the prison in Richmond to visit him once, but she never went again, not because Jimmy hadn't offered to take her. He had offered, but she had always declined his invitations saying she would write letters but, unfortunately, she never did, nor did he.

At three o'clock, Morgan went down the hall for his appointment with the facility director who informed Morgan that the date requiring another annual commitment was looming on the horizon. "If you can't commit to paying the whole yearly amount or monthly installments," the director said, "your mother will have to give up her room and move out, there's a waiting list."

After his meeting with the director, Morgan went to his mother's room and rolled her down the hall in her wheelchair to the lobby and told the associate at the desk that they were leaving the facility for a few hours. As he had always done, Morgan stopped at the bird cage to let his mother enjoy watching the finches for a few minutes. "It seems, Mom," he said, "that there aren't as many as there were six months ago. What happened?"

"I don't think they're being taken care of properly, Son," his mother replied, "and when they die, they're not replaced. I was here one day looking at them flit from place to place in there when one of them just dropped from its perch and fell to the bottom and never moved. The bird was flying one moment and then it was lying lifeless in a pile of seed husks and poop," she said looking up at her son. She raised her eyebrows and smirked, "Kind of like some of us old birds in this place—here today, gone tomorrow."

¤

Morgan had plenty of time to think about his mother's situation, and the reality that she wasn't going to be in that facility much longer. It was going to take him about four hours to drive from his hometown to his cabin in the George Washington National Forest, which was just up the mountain from Loveville, a small place where cars and trucks slowed down before crossing a narrow bridge over the Tye River. Once across, there were three places where people might stop—a convenience store with two gas pumps, a diner that served decent coffee and a good breakfast, and an antique shop that sold mostly secondhand furniture.

Once he crossed the bridge, Morgan recognized the convenience store that he had frequented decades earlier and turned right onto a road that ran parallel to the Tye River for a couple of miles and then gradually started an upward climb into the Blue Ridge Mountains. He saw random snowflakes fall out of a grey sky and, as his vehicle rose in elevation, the snowflakes increased in number and size. Soon, Morgan had to speed up the oscillation of the small wiper blades, because the icy mixture was building up on the windshield to the point where Morgan was having trouble seeing clearly where he needed to point his vehicle.

As the gravel road continued its winding route up the mountain, the angle of attack at times was so severe going up, then down, and around, that Morgan crossed his fingers hoping that there wasn't another vehicle around the bend coming his way. When he did finally meet other vehicles coming down the mountain, the other vehicles had to pull over and wait as close to the side of the mountain as possible, while he passed them on the outer edge of the road. Morgan got to pass first, but he also had the riskier task—a miscalculation of an inch or two of road width would send the VW bus plummeting hundreds of feet to the rocky riverbed below. There was a chance, however, Morgan reminded himself as he looked over the side that there were numerous thick, tall, old forest trees that might halt or, at least, slow the vehicle's descent. Either way, a complete or partial fall would be a terrible death for a classic VW bus. Climbing the mountain would have always been a challenge for the bus, because it had a standard sixty-eight horsepower engine, but on this day, the challenge was even greater—the engine was over forty years old, and the gravel road was covered with a fresh coating of snow. Regardless of all the challenges, and the different shades of white that his knuckles turned, Morgan guided the old bus up the mountain without accident and found his cabin.

Once he engaged the emergency brake, took a deep breath, and gathered his thoughts, he opened the car door and hopped out of his vehicle. As he walked toward the cabin, he looked at the steps leading up to the porch and concluded that no one had gone up or down those steps that morning, because they were covered with an inch of unblemished snow. Without looking up at the front window, he could see with peripheral vision a curtain being pulled back, and it made his heart beat faster knowing that his children were peering out and discovering that their father was out of prison.

He knocked on the door and could hear their footsteps and quiet chatter. The door opened, and he stepped inside. He smiled and hugged his children—Heather, Raquel, and Matt.

"This place looks great!" Morgan exclaimed looking around. "Where did you get all of this furniture?"

"From all over, Dad," Raquel replied.

Then Heather added, "From the Stewart's, actually." Raquel nodded in agreement with her older sister.

Matt's face brightened as he started to speak, "You should have seen this place, Dad!" After getting those words out, Matt started laughing, which made his sisters start laughing. Matt added, "I think a bear was living in here—a bear or some animal crapped all over the place!"

Morgan laughed with his children, then said, "It must have taken a miracle to get this place looking like this!"

"No, Dad," Raquel said. "It took rakes, shovels, brooms, sponges, and lots of Pine Sol and rubber gloves!"

Morgan said, "You did a great job. Did you take before-and-after pictures?"

"Yes, we did," Heather said and reached for a box of photographs. "Mrs. Stewart let us take pictures with her camera and paid for the prints. She's been so kind. Mr. Stewart took some pictures too with his phone. Maybe he'll show them to you."

Morgan started lifting up some of the pictures and shook his head in disbelief. As they watched their father go through the photographs, all three of his kids were wondering about what had happened—why he was there and not in prison. Eventually, Heather actually blurted out—"Dad, did you escape from prison!?"

Morgan smiled, and said, "No, the real murderer confessed."

Heather then hurriedly replied, "Then you are out of there for good?"

Morgan nodded, "Yep, for good."

All four of them were quiet briefly. Then Raquel asked, "Are we going to live here, or in a REAL HOUSE somewhere?"

Morgan replied, "Yes, we're going to live here, because there's no other place to live."

Heather responded, "Dad, we know Cindy sold our house and everything else."

"Yes, she did," Morgan said. "Regrettably, she did sell everything and kept the money, so we're temporarily in bad shape, financially, but we'll be okay."

"Did you see Cindy's Lexus parked outback?" Heather asked.

"No I didn't," Morgan answered.

Heather continued, "We took it from her, and all the money she had in her purse—close to two thousand dollars—which was probably your money—not hers—anyway. That's how we got up here. Matt drove the Lexus!"

Matt was beaming, "Yes! And I outran a cop too."

"We fooled Mrs. Stewart with Cindy's car for a while, and later fooled the park ranger, and the Child Protection people, telling them that we were up here with our parents. The Lexus kind of proved that we weren't living up here by ourselves."

"Maybe you could sell the Lexus, Dad, and get some more money that way, and we still have most of the money we got from her," Raquel said.

"The title to the Lexus is in Cindy's name, so I can't sell the car, legally, without her signature on the title."

"Ask her to sign it, Dad," Raquel said.

Heather looked at Raquel and rolled her eyes, "Oh yeah, like that's really going to happen!"

"Forge her signature," Matt suggested.

Heather looked at him and said, "That, my dear brother, might get our dad back in prison."

The following morning, Heather peered through the window above the sink and admired the blue shadows that trees were casting over the glistening, white snow. Two crows were sitting in different trees, taking turns squawking. They sounded upset about something, Heather thought, and leaned closer to the window and looked around thinking that there might be a deer or fox or even a bear close by. She didn't see any animals, not even squirrels. She lifted her shoulders acknowledging to herself that she didn't know what was disturbing the crows. Then it occurred to her that the crows weren't really upset at anything—that was just her interpretation of the noise (squawking) they were making. They were just being crows. She filled a pot with water and placed it on the hot plate. She then opened a cabinet door and pulled out a Quaker Oats canister and a loaf of sliced bread. Matt was behind her, putting an extra place setting at the table for their father. Morgan's children weren't rushing around that morning as they usually did, because they knew the school van wouldn't be coming up the mountain to get them. The early snow had cancelled school for that day.

Heather told Morgan over breakfast that the family down the road, the Stewart's, had looked after them since the time they arrived at the cabin in late summer. "The pots, pans, toaster, utensils, dishes that we are using now," she said, "came from them." She paused, then added, "They're the family that wanted to adopt us."

Matt looked at his father and decided to change the subject, "Let me tell you about what happened to me."

"Oh no," Raquel said and moaned.

"What happened to you, Matt?" Morgan asked looking over at Raquel.

"If it wasn't for Mr. Stewart," Matt said excitedly, "I'd be dead!"

Matt did describe in detail how he became stuck between two boulders in a stream and how Mr. Stewart rescued him.

"Getting in that jam served Matt right," Raquel said at the end of Matt's story. "He and Mr. Stewart's son Austin were out there in the woods trying to kill Bambi—a baby deer."

After breakfast, Morgan and his children walked down the road to visit the Stewarts. Once the introductions were done, the kids pulled off to themselves, which gave Morgan a chance to thank the Stewart's for helping his children and to express immediate concerns about their situation. He also told them what he had not told his kids. "In the near future, I'm going to bring my mother to the cabin to live, because I don't have the money to pay for the assisted living place anymore."

"Anymore? How much does that place cost you?"

"Thirty-six thousand dollars a year," Morgan replied, looking at Mr. Stewart's face scrunch-up.

"My Lord!?" Mr. Stewart grunted.

"That's right, and it wasn't a problem before, but it is now, because I'm broke."

"You could have built a house for your mother with thirty-six thousand dollars, Morgan," Mr. Stewart offered.

"I didn't put her in the assisted living place, because she needed a roof over her head. She had that. She needed someone to provide care—assistance with everyday things. I didn't have time to do that stuff!"

"Oh," Mr. Stewart responded. "I SEE."

Judging from the tone of Mr. Stewart's I SEE, Morgan sensed that Mr. Stewart wasn't favorably impressed by Morgan's admission that he didn't have time to take care of his mother, but he didn't try to defend himself...*there is no defense*, Morgan said to himself. "So," Morgan said, "living conditions in the cabin are going to be more cramped than they already are. As it is now, I'm sleeping on the couch and using stacked cardboard boxes for a chest of drawers."

"Could be worse," Mr. Stewart said.

Morgan looked at Mr. Stewart and said, "It was worse in prison—much worse! So I'm not complaining." The three of them were quiet for a few seconds, then Morgan continued. "Mr. Stewart, do you know where I can get lumber and building materials at bargain prices—and a handyman who works cheap?"

Mr. Stewart replied, "Call me Ray. Call her Ethel. Yes, I know where you can get building materials at reasonable prices, and I'm a good handyman who can work cheap, if I have to. What size addition do you want to put on that cabin?"

Morgan smiled, "Right now the girls have a room and so does Matt. I'd like bedrooms for me and my mother, maybe another bathroom and some additional storage space."

"Okay," Mr. Stewart said. "How reasonable does the lumber have to be and how much for labor?"

"All I've got at this moment is fifteen hundred dollars—"

"Holy moly!" Mr. Stewart exclaimed interrupting Morgan.

"I might be able to borrow some money once I have a job," Morgan responded. "How much do you think I'll need?"

"Eight to ten thousand dollars—minimum, and that's a low ball number."

Morgan was silent for a moment. "Okay. Maybe it'll have to be a couple of cots for mom and me and some more cardboard boxes. The addition will have to come later."

Mr. Stewart stared at Morgan and said apologetically, "I'd offer you some rooms here—temporarily, but we're plum out of rooms."

▯

A couple of days later, Morgan called Social Services in his hometown and told them that he was out of prison and living just outside of Loveville. He also gave them his post office box address and cell phone number just in case they needed to reach him. The Social Services person suggested that he contact Child Protective Services and let them know that he and his children were now together and living in another community in the state.

Within two weeks, Morgan pulled out a letter from his post office box from the IRS, which told him that he owed $100,000 in back taxes on the proceeds from the sale of his businesses. Morgan later explained over the phone to the IRS person that his wife was the one who liquidated everything and had taken all the money. "That's too bad," the woman said. "You and your wife owe the taxes. We don't care who did what—the taxes must be paid."

Morgan already knew that Cindy had lost all his money, because he had watched it on TV while in prison, but he called her anyway, because he had Googled her and learned that she and Sergio were launching SEXCAPADES with a high roller in Las Vegas named The Mann. Sergio answered the call and immediately handed the phone to Cindy. Morgan told her that he was out of prison and had been notified by the IRS that THEY owed $100,000 in back taxes and asked her to pay it since she had liquidated everything and taken off with all of the money. Cindy responded in a sweet voice, "Oh baby, that money is long gone!"

Morgan replied, "You owe me half a million dollars, and I'm willing to call things even, if you will pay the hundred grand—that's a good deal—and it looks like you can probably afford it with all the money you and Sergio will be pulling in from SEXCAPADES."

"Sue me, Morgan!" Cindy shouted and hung up.

◻

Morgan parked the bus in the prison parking lot and scanned the old, dark brick outer wall, as he walked toward the main gate—a gate that he had gone through in the opposite direction just a few weeks before. The guard at the gate told Morgan that he would get another guard to escort him to the warden's office, but Morgan declined, saying he knew the way and started walking toward the entry doors.

"You might know the way, Mr. Armstrong, but you can't just walk in there by yourself," the guard responded.

Morgan stopped and looked back at the guard and asked, "Why?"

"Because that's the rule," the guard replied. "This ain't Wal-Mart!"

When Morgan entered Catherine's office escorted by a guard, he saw her right away, standing by her secretary's desk. "Hey, Morgan," she said. "What brings you back to this place so soon?"

"A few things," he replied. "I want to see if the prison attorney, Ms. Spangler, can help me with some legal problems, and I'd like to say hello to Bob."

"Okay," she said. "First come into my office, and I'll bring you up to date on Bob and the website, and my secretary will check with Ms. Spangler to see if she has a few minutes to talk to you."

Catherine told Morgan that another prisoner had joined the staff who knew a lot about computers and websites and had, she thought, established a good working relationship with Bob.

"What about advertising revenues?" he inquired.

"Now that, Morgan, is where there's definite slippage."

"How much slippage?"

"No one in the group has your skills at that—getting advertisers. So the slippage has been considerable—75 percent. Do you think you can restore some of that?" she asked.

"Maybe, but I don't know how much time I could afford to devote to it," Morgan responded.

Catherine pushed a button and asked her secretary if she had spoken to Ms. Spangler and then she returned her attention to Morgan.

"She's ready to meet with you right now, Morgan." Catherine said and then withdrew a file from her desk drawer. Looking inside the file, she said, "I believe we have enough money in the Entrepreneurial Fund to pay you for general oversight of the website. Are you interested?"

"How much are you willing to pay me?" Morgan asked with a smile.

"Starting out I think you should come here once every two weeks for five hours of butt-busting telephone calls, e-mails, staff development, et cetera. Two fifty sound okay?"

"Plus travel expenses?"

"Yes, okay, that's fair—fifty dollars for travel—total of three hundred dollars, okay?"

"I'm driving an old VW bus which is going to break down with all the miles I'll be putting on it. Plus the price of gas is getting ridiculous—how about a hundred dollars for travel?"

"Seventy-five. A total of three hundred twenty-five per trip. Deal?" Catherine asked.

"You are tough as nails, Catherine," Morgan replied. Then quickly added, "Deal."

"I'll get a guard to escort you to Ms. Spangler's office," Catherine said.

Morgan looked at her with a half-smile. "Catherine, you know that I know where Ms. Spangler's office is. I don't need an escort."

Catherine cocked her head back and looked at Morgan. "Yes, you do," she said, then added, "But since you're going to be on the payroll, I'll get a badge made up for you. In the future, you'll be able to walk around by yourself all you want to. But for today, you're going to need an escort."

□

Ms. Spangler told Morgan after he had explained the situation that he and his wife did owe the taxes to the federal government and that they would have to pay them in full or in part. "Settlements, however, are always possible," Ms. Spangler said and volunteered to contact the IRS to explore that possibility.

"The accountability can't be divided fifty-fifty?" Morgan asked, but Ms. Spangler's head was shaking side to side before his words had gotten out of his mouth. "Well, that's a bunch of crap!" Morgan snapped.

Ms. Spangler just smiled at him, then she surprised him by asking, "How's your love life?" She had not forgotten about Morgan's "interlude" with Dr. Rosemary Morris, the prison psychiatrist.

Morgan smiled and replied, "Nonexistent right now, Ms. Spangler. How's yours?"

"Could be better," she said, flipping hair back off her shoulder.

Morgan glanced mischievously at Ms. Spangler, "I'll be back in a couple of weeks," he said arching his eyebrows. "See you then?"

Ms. Spangler picked up her ballpoint pen and clicked it open by tapping it on her desk calendar. "What day and time will that be, Mr. Armstrong?" she asked very professionally.

Morgan replied, "Let's just say I'll be back here two weeks from today noon to five."

"Drop in that day and I'll let you know about the IRS stuff, and maybe *we can play it by ear* after that?" Ms. Spangler said and stood up offering a handshake.

Morgan joined his hand with hers, and said, "It's going to be a long two weeks, Ms. Spangler."

She smiled, "That's one of the best parts—ANTICIPATING."

After his session with Ms. Spangler, Morgan walked down to the website room without calling for his escort. After meeting with Bob and some of the staff, he and Bob went over to a corner where they could talk privately.

"What's going on, Bob?" Morgan asked.

"In the past, there was no pressure," Bob said. "Now, of course, there's pressure to produce big stock winners all the time."

"No doubt," Morgan said.

"But Morgan," Bob said. "I can't predict winners every week. It takes time for things to line up. Before you came here I had all the time in the world. Now I don't. Now things are harder."

Morgan remained silent, thinking of what he could say to Bob, and Bob had said all he wanted to say about his predicament, so there was silence in their corner of the room. After a while, though, Bob turned to Morgan and asked, "How are things on the outside?"

Morgan smiled at Bob, remembering when he had thought that Bob was a mute or moron. "I'm living with my children in a small mountain cabin with financial challenges, but I'm happy...no, let me take that back—like you, the pressure is on. I'm broke, unemployed, responsible for three children, and my mother will soon be joining us in the cabin that's way too small for five people. But—I'm very glad to be living THERE and not HERE."

◻

Back in Loveville, Morgan stopped at the convenience store to get gas and was returning the nozzle to the pump when a pickup truck pulled up in front of him and backed up fast. Morgan was ready for the pickup truck to crash into the bus when it stopped just inches from the VW's bumper. When the driver hopped out of the truck, Morgan said to her, "Thought I was going to have to place a call to my insurance company for a moment there."

The woman replied, "Me and my truck are one. You had nothing to worry about, mister."

Morgan left her lifting the nozzle from the pump and went into the store to pay for his gas. Returning to his vehicle, he looked at the woman who was wearing a plaid flannel shirt, jeans, and cowboy boots and determined—what he hadn't previously—that she was gorgeous! "What do you do for a living?" he asked her.

Putting the nozzle back on the pump, she replied, "Landscaping," and walked away toward the store.

"Nice meeting you," Morgan shouted.

The woman didn't respond to his comment. He followed her with his eyes admiring her ass, as she walked hurriedly toward the store. When she got closer to the building, she skipped up onto the sidewalk and sassily pushed open the glass door and scooted inside out of sight.

◻

When Morgan got home, all three of his children were in the front room looking at an animated video. Morgan started wondering right then why he had agreed to spend money for satellite TV. Morgan leaned in and watched. What he saw were two dogs sitting in mom and pop loungers watching TV. The dog on the right turned its head toward the other dog and said, "What would you like to watch tonight, honey? SOFT PORN or HARD PORN?" As that dialog advanced, Morgan's children began scrunching down in their chairs.

"Okay, children," Morgan said authoritatively, "I can see that homework is done, dinner started, and daily chores are complete—right!?"

Heather reached forward and turned off the television. "No, Daddy, but almost."

Morgan stared at Heather, "No more of THAT and anything like THAT, agreed, Heather?"

"Sorry, Daddy," she replied.

Morgan noticed that Matt was still in his chair staring at a black screen, which seemed odd. "Matt?" he said. "HELLO?"

Matt turned his head slowly toward his father and smiled thinly. "Hi, Dad," he said meekly.

Morgan lowered his head more to the right, so he could see both of Matt's eyes. When Morgan made that adjustment, his son turned slightly away from his father, but not far enough. Morgan reached out and turned the left side of Matt's face toward his position.

Raquel blurted out, "Some dick-guy at school punched him. Eighth grader dude!"

Morgan looked at Matt, "Tell me more, Son."

"It was an eighth grader, and he shouldn't have been on our hall to begin with," Matt responded. "And he shouldn't have been pushing and teasing this guy. So I went up to him and told him to cut it out. That's when he clobbered me."

Morgan replied, "Did you learn anything from this?"

Matt looked at his father, "Yes, like a good boy scout—I should have been PREPARED."

"Good answer, Matt," Morgan said as he gently lifted his son's chin and looked more closely at his son's swollen and bruised eye. "Heather, get—"

Heather knew what her dad wanted, "Ice pack coming up, Dad."

The following day, Morgan went to the school and met with the principal. In that meeting, Morgan told her what his children had told him and asked her to check it out. While there he asked about their computers, and whether they needed help with them.

"Do we ever!" she replied. "Something goes wrong all the time, and when we put a request in to fix these problems, the company in Charlottesville is slow to respond."

Morgan was glad to hear that from the principal. "Mrs. Collier, years ago I was in the Army where I learned a lot about computers, and I've been working with them ever since. I live just up the road, so I could provide you with immediate and excellent service. Give me a try, and I'm sure you'll be pleased."

Mrs. Collier smiled. "Mr. Armstrong, I have to tell you up front that what the school system pays isn't all that great."

Morgan responded, "I'd like it to be great, but that's okay—let's give it a try. You want and need good service, and I can use some extra money—school clothes for three children, doctor visits, you know."

"Yes, I know, Mr. Armstrong," she said. Then Mrs. Collier turned her head to the side and held it there for a moment, obviously thinking. Then she asked, "Would you also consider subbing—we need subs all the time?"

"Yes, sure," Morgan replied. Images of substitute teachers he had had as a kid flashed through his mind. *Money is money*—he said to himself.

"You could be subbing for core classes or you might be subbing for the computer lab instructor who is pregnant and routinely sick once or twice a week."

□

On the way home that day, Morgan stopped at the convenience store and, as luck would have it, the young, gorgeous woman he had met there previously came barreling off the hard surface road and came to a tire-squealing stop in the parking space next to his vehicle. When he heard the first piece of gravel hit the side of the bus, his hands clenched tightly around the steering wheel and his shoulders hunched up around his ears and stayed there until there were no more metallic pings. He silently guessed that the bus no longer had pristine paint on its right back panel. He opened his door and stepped out onto the gravel. Morgan looked over at the truck and saw that the pretty young woman was talking on her cellphone. He was deciding whether to address the issue of damaged paint on his VW bus immediately, or after she concluded her phone conversation. He decided he would wait and went inside the store where he found the items he needed and went to the checkout counter to pay for them. While he waited in line, the young woman came through the front door and went directly to the back of the store. The two customers in front of him had only one item each, so they quickly processed their purchases, leaving him face to face with the cashier, Molly. "Hi, Mr. Armstrong," she said as she grabbed one of his items to ring up.

Morgan muttered a quick hello as he turned slowly toward the young woman falling in line behind him with a gallon of milk dangling from her left hand.

"Hello," he said when she came to a stop. "I met you the other day out there at the gas pumps."

The woman gave him a quick look and replied, "Yes, I remember," and handed money to the cashier. Morgan cradled his bag of grocery items against his chest and walked toward the front door. As he walked, he was thinking about the gravel that had sprayed against the back panel of the VW bus and thought that he had better get outside and check to see if there actually was damage, but when he opened the door, the woman was right in front of him, so he nodded his head indicating that he wanted her to exit first, which she did. Outside, Morgan focused on the gallon jug of milk and the young woman's ring finger and didn't see a ring. Influenced, undoubtedly, by the sexy good looks of the young woman, Morgan decided not to address the possible paint damage on the bus. He could get that fixed pretty easily if it was actually there.

"Do you have time for a cup of coffee at the diner just down the road?" he said loudly, as she neared her truck.

"No thanks, I don't drink coffee," she replied stepping into the space between her truck and Morgan's bus.

Morgan smiled and replied as he entered the space between the two vehicles, "I don't either, how about tea?"

She stopped at the driver's door, turned, and found herself facing Morgan. "Look, I've got a cold jug of milk in my hand, and I want it to get home that way—COLD," she said.

"My name is Morgan. What's your name?"

"Christine. My friends call me Christy—being an honest kind of person, I should say—my one and only FRIEND calls me Christy," saying that, she swung open the cab door and settled in behind the steering wheel.

Morgan looked at her through the window and gestured for her to roll the window down, which she did. "Yep!" she snapped.

Morgan assessed the tone of the *yep!* as—I'm in a hurry—rather than—I'm annoyed with your persistence. "Okay, Christy," Morgan said with a smile, "what would you like to drink the next time we end up here together?"

Lifting the gallon container of milk, she replied, "MILK."

◻

While Morgan was driving up the mountain, he was thinking of Christy and imagining her naked, which gave him an erection that triggered a memory of New York when he and Bob and the two security men spent the night with "the ladies of the night" in the Times Square Marriott Hotel. A loud bang at the back of the bus brought Morgan out of his thoughts of getting laid. The bus rolled to a stop. Morgan turned the key to OFF and turned it back ON and tried to start the engine, but nothing happened. He took out his cellphone and punched in Mr. Stewart's phone number to see if he could tow the bus to the cabin.

After Ray got Morgan's bus parked in his backyard and unhitched from his truck, he said, "If you have to go somewhere tomorrow, Morgan, we've got some wheels for you. Won't be a spiffy ride, like this VW bus, but it'll get you where you want to go."

◻

The next morning, Morgan did not have to go anywhere, so after his children boarded the school van, he walked down to the river and watched the water flow in, around, and over the rocks, eventually forming a deep pool the surface of which gleamed and sparkled with morning sunlight. He sat down on a large boulder and leaned back supporting himself with his forearms and elbows. He breathed deeply and felt the cool air fill his lungs and slowly released it, and as he did, he heard a voice inside his head say—*this is where you're supposed to be.* He picked up a small rock and tossed it out to the middle of the pool where it broke the smooth surface sending ripples out from the point of entry. Somehow he could feel himself in the pool of water with the small ripples softly rolling up to and through his body, as if he had no substance—as if he were a spirit, or ghost, not flesh and bone. The experience actually scared him. He looked around and tested his arms and legs to make sure he wasn't dreaming or dead. Within minutes though, Morgan had settled back into his reclined position and was shielding his eyes partially from the brilliant sunlight sifting through the branches overhead. In that very quiet, still moment, Morgan experienced an intense sense of aloneness and awareness. Then the same inner voice that he had heard a few minutes earlier whispered:

> *You are a human being. Your origin and the origin of all things can be traced back to stardust. It has taken billions of years for you to appear here in this configuration, and you will have a very small sliver of time to enjoy life on this planet. Make the most of it. Do no harm. Attempt to do good things—you know innately which is which.*

¤

Later that morning, Morgan found the cellphone number of the former head mechanic at Dream Cars Ltd. and called him to see what the best course of action would be regarding the VW bus. Larry, the mechanic, told him that a first-class rebuilt engine would be selling for three to five thousand dollars depending on the source. Morgan told Larry that he didn't have that kind of money anymore. "Maybe, in that case," Larry said, "you might want to fix just what you have to and see how far that gets you down the road."

"And how would we do that?" Morgan asked.

Larry told Morgan that he could come up to Loveville on a weekend and break the engine down and see what has to be done. "For you, Morgan, I'd just bill you $250 net, no charge for the travel and all that shit."

"And that's just for determining what has to be fixed, right?" Morgan asked.

"Right," Larry replied.

"Using your best guess, Larry, what's the least amount it could be to get this vehicle back on the road?"

"Probably a thousand to fifteen hundred—parts and labor," Larry answered.

"Let me lean on you a little, Larry, you know Cindy took everything I had while I was in prison and left town. So I'm up here in the George Washington National Forest living in a cabin with my three children with two part-time jobs."

"Uh-huh," Larry replied.

"That means I don't have a thousand to fifteen hundred dollars laying around. Can I pay it off in installments?"

"I'm kind of bumping across bottom financially, too, Morgan, but sure, I can accept installments. I know you are good for it."

Larry did drive up to the cabin and broke the engine down and ordered the parts needed from a distributor in California. The parts were delivered in the next week, and Larry came back and completed the work in an afternoon. The bill totaled out at $1,350.

□

"Being broke and looking for a job is not fun," Morgan muttered as he handed the stack of envelopes to the postal worker behind the counter.

"You're right, brother," the postal worker said as he took the envelopes. "Been there, good luck."

□

It was just after the dismissal bell that afternoon when a sixth grade teacher walked into the computer lab.

"I'm Mrs. Kaufman, Raquel's teacher, Mr. Armstrong, welcome aboard."

Morgan shut the filing drawer and shook her hand. "Thank you," he said.

Mrs. Kaufman cleared her throat, "I thought I should let you know that Raquel had to leave class today to go to the clinic." When Morgan heard those words, his attention to what she was saying became more focused. "Raquel did return to class and stayed afterward to talk with me. She said she was experiencing her first period. The nurse in the clinic provided her with a tampon. You might want to stop at a store on the way home to get a box of them." Morgan thanked her for the heads up and walked to the office and put his notes for the day in the lab teacher's mailbox.

On the way home, Morgan stopped at the convenience store, as Raquel's teacher had suggested. He had to hunt for the tampons but eventually found them. When the cashier asked him if he wanted a bag, he waved it off saying, "No thanks, Molly—doing what I can to save trees."

When Morgan got outside, he saw Christy walking straight toward him. He smiled at her and didn't move away from the door, which forced her to stop. He noticed Christy's eyes. She was looking at the box of tampons he was carrying. "For my daughter," he said, lifting the box. "She just got her first period while in school today."

Christy replied, "Let the fun begin!"

"Do you have children?" Morgan asked and maintained his position in front of the entrance to the store.

"Yes, one boy," Christy answered and gestured with her hand that she wanted to get by him and get into the store.

"Sorry," he said and moved partially out of her path. Her answer disappointed Morgan, because it was likely that there was a husband around, but he decided not to make any assumptions. "I don't see a ring?"

Christy reached around Morgan and grabbed the door handle and held the door open while she responded to Morgan's statement. "I am married, but my husband and I are separated, so I no longer wear the ring," she said.

Morgan was relieved and decided to continue, "Are you available?"

Christy replied, "WE are in the process of DIVORCING."

Morgan said to himself—she didn't say NO. "Okay," Morgan replied. "I take that to mean that you ARE AVAILABLE."

Christy saw that a customer inside the store was approaching the door, so she gestured for Morgan to step out of the way of the door that was going to be opening. After the customer had gotten out of range of hearing their conversation, Christy replied to Morgan's question, "AVAILABLE for what?"

Morgan didn't reply immediately because he was thinking of an appropriate answer. Then he said, "Available for having some fun together."

Christy looked around to see if there was anyone nearby before answering. She saw that they were alone on the sidewalk and that no one was approaching the front door of the store on either side. "Look Morgan, the truth is—I haven't made love in a long time, and I'm thinking you haven't made love in a long time either. So I'm looking for more than fun. I'm looking for a man who can make great love and keep it to himself. Can you do that?"

Without hesitating, Morgan replied, "I can do that."

Christy replied, "I've got to scoot into the store and get some things, then I've got to meet a customer down the road in fifteen minutes."

"Can I call you?" Morgan asked, wanting to make plans for getting together.

"We'll meet up again," she replied with a quick smile and entered the store.

When Morgan got home, he stuck the box of tampons under his coat before entering the cabin. He saw Matt and Heather, but he didn't see Raquel. Heather pointed silently to her bedroom. Hers and Matt's faces told the story. Morgan knocked on the bedroom door, hesitated, and then entered the room. Inside, Morgan removed the box of tampons from under his coat and placed it on the bed next to Raquel without explanation.

"Thanks, Dad," Raquel said quietly.

◻

A couple of mornings later, Ray walked up to Morgan's cabin with a cup of coffee in his hand. Morgan was outside looking at an exterior wall. When he heard footsteps behind him, he turned.

"Hey, Morgan," Ray said. "What are you looking at?"

"I'm just trying to figure out where to start with this addition, or how to start it," Morgan replied.

Ray took a sip of coffee, then said, "You ever MADE anything, Morgan?"

Morgan stared at Ray, then grinned, "I used to MAKE MONEY!"

"Have you ever BUILT anything—built a house, remodeled a house, made an addition to a house, tiled a floor—stuff like that?"

"No," was Morgan's answer. "I paid people to do that stuff for me."

"Okay, nothing wrong with that, but what that tells me is that figuring out this addition by rights shouldn't come easy to you."

"You're right, Ray. It's not coming easy," Morgan replied.

"I think I've got some good news for you," Ray said and took another sip of coffee. "A couple years ago in April or May, just after they stocked the river with trout, I met a man who was standing on a big rock in the river just down the way here hoping he'd catch one of them hatchery trout. After talking a while I found out that he was a professor at the university—school of architecture. Since then when he comes up here to fish, he always drops by our place for a cup of coffee, lunch and maybe dinner. Delightful guy and he has always kept me up to date on what's happening at the university. That's the intro to the good news, Morgan." Ray took another sip of coffee. "So yesterday I called him, his name is Madison, and told him about your situation thinking that he might be able to help you in some way—he's got lots of connections. The architectural students are always doing projects. He said he had a group of students who had won a grant to build a GREEN HOUSE that would incorporate the most advanced systems available—solar, waste, electrical, wind, geo and so on. But the professor said there was one hitch in building the GREEN HOUSE, which was—not having a piece of land to build it on. You see where I'm going, Morgan?"

Morgan's eyes opened wide. "What are you saying, Ray?"

"You've got land—nice property," Ray replied, "and they have a GREEN HOUSE they want to build. It's a marriage made in heaven, my man!"

Morgan shook his head and stared silently at Ray. He was thinking of all the things that Ray and Ethel, his wife, had already done for his children. "You saved my son from drowning, Ray. You and your wife took care of my children while I was in prison. Now, it appears that you might be responsible for THIS—a new house."

Ray smiled, "Don't count your chickens before they hatch, as they say. Let's take just one step at a time, and see what happens."

◻

After Ray left, Morgan left a note for his children, telling them that he might be late getting back from Richmond. Then he got in his bus and headed down the mountain, and as he was winding his way to the interstate, he saw Christy's truck at a plant nursery. He turned in and found her in the back putting potted plants on a wagon. He told her he was heading to Richmond and stopped just to say hello, and he was also hoping to make some plans for getting together. She swiped back strands of hair that were hanging over her eyes. "Could you meet me at the convenience store around five?" she asked with a quirky smile.

"I should be back here around that time," he said and asked for her cell number just in case he needed to contact her.

Christy replied, "I'm not ready to give you my cell number, just yet. If you aren't there by five-fifteen, I'll take it that you've had a problem, and I'll move on with no hard feelings."

Morgan leaned closer to Christy, and she quickly leaned away thinking he was going to kiss her on her cheek. "Not here—too many eyes," she warned.

"I was just going to say, quietly, how much I was looking forward to getting to know you," Morgan offered.

"Oh," Christy said. "I thought you were going to kiss me, and that would have gotten the rumor mill going!"

"Small town thing," Morgan replied, remembering Christy's earlier remark about Loveville.

"Yeah," Christy said. "But think about our rendezvous all day long. Let your imagination run wild—you won't be disappointed."

◻

Morgan couldn't help thinking about Christy and making love to her as he sat across from the prison attorney, Ms. Spangler, who had spoken to the IRS regarding Morgan's back taxes.

"Well Morgan," she said, "This is a very interesting web that has been woven."

"I'm sure," Morgan replied.

"Cindy was your wife when she hired an auctioneer to sell everything that you owned. Not only was she your wife, but you had VERY GENEROUSLY given her power of attorney as well."

"I've never disputed her legal right to sell everything," Morgan said impatiently.

"I know," Ms. Spangler said. "I'm just setting the stage. When Cindy and Sergio arrived in Las Vegas, the first thing she did was to divorce you. Before doing that Cindy was your wife with $500,000 belonging to the two of you. After divorcing you she was just Cindy, not your wife, with $500,000 that belonged to both of you."

"Okay," Morgan said.

"After divorcing you, she ultimately lost the $500,000 at a roulette table. Now, who is responsible for the back taxes? You or Cindy? The answer is BOTH of YOU. There's a second question—can you sue her for the money she lost at the roulette table? NO—you gave Cindy power of attorney to handle your affairs."

"Couldn't I sue her for the $250,000 that was legally mine?"

"You're thinking that in Virginia husband and wife split things fifty-fifty—right?"

"Yes."

"Not true, but many people think that's true. Husbands and wives divorcing in Virginia have to determine who gets what and, if they can't make that determination, the court will do that for them."

"SOOOO, you are saying, Ms. Spangler, I'm screwed!"

"Precisely," she responded.

"What did you find out about Cindy and the IRS?"

"Here's what I got from them: The Mann, what a name. THE is his legal first name, and MANN is his legal last name. He is the money behind SEXCAPADES. Contractually, he obligated himself to provide Cindy and Sergio the following—a fabulous house, two sedans (Mercedes and Lexus), an SUV (Porsche), credit cards with monthly limits for food, clothing, gasoline, and entertainment. The Mann committed himself to pay for all operating expenses—everything—ALL EXPENSES related to SEXCAPADES, and in return he got artistic rights to everything and operating control: x-number of shows per week, all revenue from ticket and merchandise sales, TV money—you name it—he wanted it and got it."

"Wow! What about salary—bonuses—percentage of profits?" Morgan asked.

"Modest salaries for talent and crew and a little better for them. They were broke and desperate to see their names in lights. Sadly, they are little more than slaves. They have no assets—they own nothing—and if they quit, they can't work in Las Vegas or anywhere close to Las Vegas for three years. After three years of being out of the public eye in show business, you're dead!"

"You're saying I'm not going to get any help from Cindy regarding back taxes."

"That's right, Morgan. That's why the IRS has its site set squarely on you and your assets."

"Ha! I don't have any assets either. No, that's not exactly true—I own a cabin in the woods and the land it sits on."

"There you go. That's more than what Cindy has," Ms. Spangler replied. "Don't volunteer that information to the FEDS."

Morgan smiled quietly while he was thinking about the deal that might happen—deeding his cabin and property over to the university. That deal was looking better and better by the minute. "Thank you for checking this out with the IRS," Morgan said as he stood up.

Ms. Spangler stood up as well and walked around her desk to stand in front of him. "I'm glad I could help you, Morgan. Even though I'm not sure that I have actually helped you. I just clarified things for you."

"You have, and I appreciate it," Morgan said.

Ms. Spangler looked into Morgan's eyes, "I'm not married, and I'm between boyfriends—what do you think?"

Morgan looked into Ms. Spangler's eyes. "I think it would be steamy, Ms. Spangler."

Ms. Spangler stepped forward pressing her breasts against Morgan's chest. "Let's do it right here. Nobody's going to open that door."

Morgan grinned widely thinking she was joking. "Actually, I'd like to, but I have to meet with Bob and his staff over at the website and work for four or five hours on getting advertisers. Can we get into bed together on my next visit?"

"Zorba held that the only sin for a man is when he doesn't go to a woman's bed when she calls him there," Ms. Spangler said coyly.

"Maybe I haven't sinned," Morgan replied, amused. "Technically, there's no bed here."

Ms. Spangler's lips opened into a bright smile, "I'm not going to pull it out right now, since you're declining my invitation, but for future reference, there is a camping mattress—a bed—in that closet over there with an air pump that fully inflates the mattress in two minutes and thirty-eight seconds."

Morgan laughed, "You are kidding!?"

"No, I'm not."

"Are these walls soundproof?" Morgan asked.

"I can be quiet if I have to," Ms. Spangler responded. "BUT when I don't have restrictions, I can be quite noisy!"

Morgan put his arms around Ms. Spangler and grabbed her buttocks pulling her tightly against his body. He gave her a quick kiss on her lips, "See you in two weeks."

◻

Before going to the website room, Morgan walked to Catherine's office to say hello and to find out how things were going. Catherine's secretary was on the phone and just nodded toward the tennis court. Morgan kept walking and waved to Catherine when he got outside.

"Hi, I just wanted to let you know that I'll be working with Bob and the website staff this afternoon."

"That's fine," Catherine said as she tossed a ball up. She waited and then launched herself up and drove the ball into the corner of the service box.

Morgan shouted, "You killed it!"

She walked over to him, "That's what SEPARATING and DIVORCING can do for a weak serve."

It would be an understatement to say that Morgan was surprised by the news. "I want to say you're kidding, but I know you wouldn't kid about something like that."

"No, I wouldn't. It's happening."

◻

Driving home, Morgan stopped at a 7-Eleven store to purchase condoms. Being a former wholesale distributor of condoms, he looked for his favorite brands. He bought a half dozen not thinking he was going to need that many that night, but it was looking like he was going to need to keep a supply of condoms on hand in the glove compartment of the bus. Things were looking up with Christy in Loveville and Ms. Spangler at the prison.

It was already dark when he got to the convenience store in Loveville, and Christy was there waiting in her truck. He didn't park next to her, nor did he do anything that would indicate that they knew each other. Following her advice, he went in the store, bought something, and came back out to his vehicle. Christy then backed up and drove out of the parking lot and headed up the mountain. Morgan waited, letting Christy get up the road then pulled out of the parking lot and followed her staying well behind her truck. He kept checking his rearview mirror looking for a vehicle that might be tailing him, or her, but he never saw one.

A few miles past the point where the road turned from paved to gravel, Christy turned off and followed a narrower dirt road to where it dead ended in a thicket. From there he and Christy walked assisted by a flashlight farther into the woods along a path, which eventually led to a small open area where an army surplus tent awaited them.

Morgan looked at Christy, eyes wide, smiling, "You put this here!?"

"Well, of course, we wouldn't be able to go to my house, your house, or any motel within a hundred miles without somebody knowing it—that's country living for you. Besides, I think I'll like getting it on in an army tent deep in the boonies."

Christy unzipped the entrance to the tent and stepped inside followed by Morgan. Christy shined the flashlight beam around the tent until she found the lantern. Once she turned the lantern on, she switched off the flashlight. The lantern filled the tent with a rich, warm, golden light. "I want you to see my body, as I take my clothes off. I have a very good one."

"Yes, you do have a beautiful body," Morgan replied.

"And I want to see your body as you undress, Morgan," Christy added. "If you're not hard already, I want to see *Franklin* get hard. We'll take off one piece of clothing at a time."

"Can we take off more than one piece at a time?" Morgan asked.

"No, the slower we go the more excited I get."

"In case you are wondering," Morgan said. "I have condoms."

"I HATE CONDOMS!" she replied.

"I thought you might not want to run the risk of getting a disease or pregnant," Morgan said removing his jacket.

"Do you have a disease?" She asked as she unbuttoned her shirt.

"No," Morgan answered quickly.

"How do you know?" She inquired removing her shirt exposing her breasts.

Seeing her breasts took Morgan's breath away. After getting some air back in his lungs, he answered Christy's question. "I haven't had sex with anyone since my last blood test which showed that I was GOOD TO GO," he responded, removing his shirt.

"Do you think I might have a disease?" Christy asked as she removed her boots.

"There's no way for me to know that—YOU MIGHT?" he said, then he removed his shoes and socks.

"One item at a time, Morgan!" Christy warned him. "I haven't had sex since my husband and I separated," she said, and pulled off her jeans. "And my latest blood test showed that I too was GOOD TO GO."

"Okay," Morgan said excitedly, "Condoms are not needed." He stepped out of his trousers leaving no doubt about the level of excitement he was enjoying. Calvin Klein would have been proud of the elasticity of his briefs.

"Now for the final item," Christy said. "Off come my panties."

Still standing, Morgan grabbed the elastic waistband of his briefs and slid them down his legs stepping out of them one foot at a time.

Christy clapped her hands rapidly, and remarked, "Oh my, baby, I like the way *Franklin* stands at attention!"

Morgan laughed, enjoying Christy's comment. They were both ready, more than ready, to kiss, lick, and touch each other's body, but that desire quickly diminished when they heard four gun shots not far away.

"Oh my God!" Christy exclaimed immediately. "That's Mike, I know that's Mike, my crazy husband. He has just shot out four tires—two of yours and two of mine!"

"How could you know that?" Morgan asked stepping back into his trousers.

"Because I KNOW that crazy man and that's just what he would do."

"Tell me this, Christy," Morgan said. "Is your crazy husband coming down the path right now to shoot us!?"

"No, that wouldn't be like him. He's already had his fun."

"So why don't we just keep on going here?" Morgan asked, beginning to step back out of his trousers.

"Because we need to call Triple A for Off the Beaten Path Assistance," Christy answered sarcastically. "Besides, soldier boy *Franklin* there, has gone to Parade Rest!"

When they went back to their vehicles, they saw that Christy was correct—both vehicles had two flat tires each. As Christy walked closer to her truck, she shined her flashlight on one of the flat tires and she noticed something gleaming in the grass. She bent over and picked up four .45 caliber brass casings and, as she straightened up, she coughed out, "Mike, Mike, Mike...CRAZY MIKE!"

"Was he crazy before you married him?" Morgan asked.

"YEP," she said. "Before marriage, CRAZY was FUN. After marriage, CRAZY was frustrating, maddening, and physically brutal at times."

"You lived in fear?"

"Yes."

"Have you ever gotten a restraining order against him?"

"Yes."

"How did he know you were here?"

"I don't know. We never came here—NEVER!"

◻

Morgan pulled out a letter from his post office box and saw that it was from a company in Roanoke. One of the companies he had sent resumes to. He opened the letter while he was standing in front of his box and read it. The human resources director wanted Morgan to call him to set up a day and time for an interview. Morgan called him right then and arranged the interview for the following Friday at 3:00 p.m.

On that day, Morgan was in Roanoke at two o'clock and found the company at 2:45. At 2:55, he was being introduced to Howard Ross, HR director. Mr. Ross told Morgan that he had already interviewed two candidates and that he would be the third and final candidate. Mr. Ross retrieved Morgan's resume from its folder and looked at it for a few seconds.

"I see that you served in the Army Security Agency for four years and then got out. Why didn't you stay in the ASA for twenty or thirty years and then get out? Great training, great work, great security, great retirement?"

"Good question, Mr. Ross," Morgan responded. "After high school, I went to Washington, D.C., to work for the FBI and to attend George Washington University at night—the FBI paid for the classes—but after a year, I decided to join the ASA, because I wanted to learn more about computers and communications."

"I see," Mr. Ross said. "So then after serving four years in the ASA, you left the army, because you wanted to go to college, but it appears that you never attended college. Is that right?"

"That's not quite right, actually. I attended college for one semester after leaving the ASA."

"Then you must have started businesses—about five, no, six of them—Armstrong Protection Systems, Bug Out Exterminating, Condom World, Dream Cars, Ltd., Armstrong Detective Agency, and the Doll House—that's quite an impressive and diverse group of businesses, Mr. Armstrong."

Morgan nodded and said, "It was."

"Why didn't you complete your college education before starting your entrepreneurial ventures?"

"College wasn't for me, as it turned out. It drove me crazy sitting there through some of the required courses—even the business courses were boring. So I just jumped out into the world and started the pest control company—Bug Out Exterminating—which made good money—enough money to start the next business—Armstrong Protection Systems."

"Did your businesses make you rich?" Mr. Ross asked.

"One man's RICH might not be another man's RICH, but I can say that I was making a lot of money, and my assets easily exceeded a million dollars," Morgan replied.

"That must have made you feel very accomplished, yes?"

Morgan thought about Mr. Ross's assessment and replied, "Yes and no."

Mr. Ross smiled, "I think I understand your answer. Entrepreneurs, I've read, are rarely satisfied with their accomplishments, which drives them to take more risks or different risks in search of—" Mr. Ross paused to find the right word or words to complete his thought. When he found them, he said, "In search of something MORE or something ELSE—am I right?"

Morgan sat there determining his answer to Mr. Ross's question and, at the same time, he was trying to figure out how best to respond considering that he was interviewing for a job. He thought he could see where Mr. Ross was going. After three or four seconds, Morgan replied, "Mr. Ross, there are *entrepreneurs* like Steve Jobs and the Google guys and then you have *entrepreneurs* like me, and I can tell you we're not the same kind of animal. I started my businesses TO MAKE MONEY. There was no other reason. With Jobs and the Google guys, I think they were FOLLOWING THEIR DREAMS. To be honest, I didn't and don't have any GRAND DREAMS. Today, I just want to use the skills and knowledge that I possess, make a decent living, and provide a good life for my children."

Mr. Ross thanked Morgan for his answer and cleared his throat. "I see that all of your businesses are now closed. What happened?"

"The quick answer, Mr. Ross, I was convicted of a murder—I didn't commit—and was sent to prison. Within months, however, the real murderer confessed. When that happened, of course, I was released from prison but, unfortunately, my wife had already liquidated everything and taken off with all of my money."

"So here you are looking for an IT position?"

"Yes," Morgan answered.

"And you have kids—three, and they are with you and not your wife. I take it?"

"Former wife now, and yes they're with me."

"If you were to get this position, which is a relatively low-level IT position—I have to tell you—it's not going to make you wealthy or rich."

"I know and I'm okay with that."

"Even if you stay here and advance up the ladder until retirement, you aren't going to be rich."

"I learned something while I was in prison, Mr. Ross. I made a lot of money while I had my businesses, but I wasn't happy, and I mistakenly thought that if I could make more money, I would be happy. I was pursuing money, not happiness."

"So what's the secret to happiness?" Mr. Ross asked smiling.

"I've learned that the secret to happiness is NOT MONEY," Morgan responded.

Mr. Ross replied, "I've heard that before."

A thought flashed through Morgan's mind, and he immediately expressed it, "Happiness is a STATE of MIND." It was a new thought for Morgan, so he added, "Don't you think so, Mr. Ross?"

"No doubt," Mr. Ross quipped and remained silent.

Morgan paused to quickly evaluate where things were going in the discussion, and he decided that things were getting off track, but he felt compelled to provide Mr. Ross with a good answer to his question. "I'm beginning to believe that the PURSUIT of MONEY or ANYTHING—even the pursuit of happiness—is the thing that brings UNHAPPINESS into our lives."

"That's interesting," Mr. Ross said. "So if PURSUING something brings UNHAPPINESS into our lives, what brings HAPPINESS into our lives?"

Morgan was wondering how he had gotten himself into this discussion, and his mind was searching for a good way out. "Soooo," Morgan said, cautiously, "I don't PURSUE ANYTHING, because it ultimately results in UNHAPPINESS."

Mr. Ross smiled and adjusted his sitting position. "Aren't you PURSUING a job with this company, right now?"

Morgan knew he was in over his head and searched his mind for a good response. "I'm APPLYING for a job here, but I'm not PURSUING a job. I'm just doing what needs to be done and whatever happens, happens, and I move on—no evaluation, no judgment, no disappointment, NO UNHAPPINESS."

"Mr. Ross replied, "That's very ZEN-LIKE."

"Is that a good thing?"

"It could be a good thing," Mr. Ross replied.

Both of them were silent, then Mr. Ross stood up and said, "This has been enlightening, Mr. Armstrong. I have asked all the questions I needed to, so now I want to turn you over to the IT department people so you can ask them questions about the position you wish to fill, and they will also administer a short-answer instrument. Once that is done, we will be able to make a decision next week. Whichever way it goes you will receive a letter."

"You said—they will administer a short-answer INSTRUMENT—what is that?"

"It's a set of questions that determines an applicant's job suitability."

"Oh," Morgan replied and smiled. "How SUITABLE do you think I am?"

Mr. Ross cocked his head and smiled thinly and replied, "I think you would handle this IT position very well, Morgan."

Morgan was silent for a few seconds, deciding whether to address what he thought was Mr. Ross's unexpressed concern, then he sat up straighter in his chair and said—as convincingly as he could—"If I get this job, I'll be a long-term, loyal employee, Mr. Ross."

Morgan completed his interview around five o'clock and started driving back home on interstate 81. During the drive, he went over the questions that the IT people had asked him and his answers. Then Morgan started thinking about what he was going to have to do if he got the job, such as—moving to Roanoke, taking his children out of one school system and placing them in another, his responsibilities at the prison (the website), and how he would handle his commitment to the GREEN HOUSE project.

Between Roanoke and Staunton, Morgan's bus coasted to a stop on the shoulder of the interstate highway. The engine had stopped running. Morgan knew he had not run out of gasoline because he had just filled it. He cranked the engine, but there wasn't even a hint that the engine was going to start. Triple A sent a tow truck which took him into a nearby small town that had a garage that could work on VW buses, but the garage had closed at 6:00 p.m. Morgan wrote a note to the service manager on an envelope explaining that he would be back early in the morning and dropped it through a slot in the door.

The tow truck driver drove Morgan to the Mountain View Motel on 81. The neon sign outside read—VACANCY. Morgan paid the driver and thanked him for the ride. Before entering the office, Morgan called his kids and told them the bus had broken down again and that he would not be able to get it fixed until the morning. Then, he called Christy to see if she could pick him up in the morning at the motel and drive him back to the garage. Christy knew exactly where Morgan was and suggested that she not wait until morning to meet up with him.

"If I come tonight," she said, "I could save you from paying for a motel room, and we'll get an earlier start in the morning."

"Yeah," Morgan said, "but where are we going to sleep?"

"There's a KOA Campground very close to where you are," she said. "Just go into the motel and tell the person at the desk your situation and ask if you can just wait inside until I get there. They're good people."

Morgan said with disbelief, "We're going to camp out? It's freezing cold."

Christy replied, "Darn right! and the KOA better damned well be more secure than the other place—if you know what I mean!?"

Morgan did wait inside the motel office until Christy pulled up in her pickup truck. From there, they drove to the KOA Campground and paid for a tent space (winter rate $26). The woman at the counter told them that they could pick almost any spot they wanted.

"Right now, as you can see, we have two RVs and another tenter out there, and I don't think we're going to get any more people tonight."

Christy selected a spot way away from the RVs and the other tenter. After backing her truck into their tent space, Christy turned to Morgan, "I make a lot of noise when I'm making love, and I don't want anyone but you enjoying it."

It took them less than twenty-five minutes to get the tent set up with mattress inflated and covered with flannel sheets and blankets. Christy told Morgan to turn off the lantern. "It's too damned cold to do the disrobing thing like we did last time. Let's take our clothes off under the covers."

Morgan wanted to see her beautiful body again but was willing to wait for another time for that. They slipped under the blankets and undressed quickly. Once undressed, they held each other and started kissing. Thirty seconds after their lips touched, the first fireball hit the side of their tent, making a bright flash and a loud smacking sound. Then seconds later, another ball of fire hit the tent. Both fireballs slid down the side of the tent to the ground where they started burning the dry grass. Morgan dashed out of the tent naked and started beating down the fire with a blanket. A fireball hit Morgan's back, making him YELP, and the next one popped him on his butt. Christy came out with another blanket and saw that the fireballs were coming from the hill behind the campground.

"I think it's a Roman Candle," Morgan said, realizing for the first time that he was naked. "Is this Crazy Mike!?"

"Could be, could be, but I don't know how he knew we were here."

When they had put out the burning brush and the fireballs were no longer being launched from the hill, Morgan and Christy turned and saw that the KOA counter person, the RVers, and the other tenter were standing together looking at them.

"Good job, good job!" they shouted and applauded.

Morgan and Christy wrapped their naked bodies with the blankets they had battled the fires with. Morgan bowed, then Christy.

"Thanks for your support!" Morgan shouted.

The RVERs and the tenter started walking away, but the KOA counter person walked up to Morgan and Christy. "What was all that about?"

"We're not sure," Morgan answered. "Has that ever happened before?"

"Not hardly," she responded.

"You need some ointment on those places where you got tagged. On your back and buttocks—we have a first-class first aid kit."

"No, I'm okay," Morgan said.

"How 'bout you, hon?" the woman asked Christy. "I don't think you even got hit—you moved real good!"

Christy looked at the woman and smiled, "Ma'am, we saw some FIREWORKS tonight, didn't we?"

"Yes we did," the woman said. "And I haven't seen FIREWORKS in a long time."

The two women laughed as they patted each other on their backs. The KOA woman walked away but within a few steps turned around. "Folks, I'm going to refund your money. Have a blessed night."

❑

In the morning, Christy drove Morgan to the garage where they quickly determined that the fuel pump was the culprit and that they could get a replacement within an hour and would have Morgan on the road within two hours. Christy told Morgan that she would ordinarily wait and accompany him back to Loveville but would not this time, because she was going to have to haul ass back home to meet with a client. "See ya!" Christy said and kissed Morgan on his cheek. "Maybe next time we'll git er done, dude!" she said. "Never had so much trouble getting laid before!"

Morgan put his hand on her arm, "When I get back to Loveville, I want to inspect your truck when you have a minute. I think Crazy Mike has planted a bug on it and his GPS lets him know where you are at all times."

❑

On the way back to his cabin, Morgan stopped at the post office and found a letter from his mother's assisted living facility requesting a deposit to reserve her stay for the next year. They advised him that if they didn't receive payment within two weeks, they would assign his mother's room to the next person on the waiting list. A year earlier, paying them thirty-six thousand dollars in one lump sum wouldn't have been a problem for Morgan. This time, of course, it was a problem, and that's why he had already decided that his mother would be living with him and his children, regardless of where they were living—cabin, GREEN HOUSE, or a house in Roanoke.

When Morgan got home, he called Ethel, Ray's wife, to ask her if Ray had said anything about the GREEN HOUSE. Ethel said that Ray hadn't mentioned it to her. Later that day, Ray called Morgan and told him that he had just spoken to the professor and learned that a decision would be made soon. "You should know this week, Morgan," Ray said. "The professor thinks it's a go."

For the next few days, Morgan substituted for the seventh grade history teacher, math teacher, and then filled in for the computer lab instructor, which was going to provide him with a significantly bigger check at the end of the month, but he was looking forward to the day when he would have a permanent full-time position. Every day after school Morgan drove to the post office to check his box hoping to find a letter from Mr. Ross telling him that he had been selected for the IT position. On Friday, the letter was there. The third line down delivered his fate—we offered the position to another candidate and it was accepted. He didn't read the rest of the letter. He stared at the wall of boxes and breathed. *Don't let this bring you down, Morgan,* he said to himself. *Don't let this make you unhappy—just do what needs to be done.*

Morgan called Christy who had already arranged a time to search her truck at a Jiffy Lube. Once he got to the shop, it took him less than fifteen minutes to find the bug and remove it.

¤

Under cover of darkness, armed with a flashlight, screwdriver and wrench, Christy and Morgan crept up on her husband's car on 123 Cow Turd Lane and attached a bug on his car. When they returned to Christy's truck, they turned on her GPS.

"Well," Morgan said. "He'll probably know in the morning that we found HIS BUG. Let's see how long it takes him to figure out that he's riding around with OUR BUG on his little Honda hotrod."

¤

Ray and the professor visited Morgan a few days after Morgan got the bad news on the IT job and gave him the good news on the GREEN HOUSE. The professor explained what the university needed Morgan to do to protect himself and the university.

Morgan looked at the professor and said, "That's great! When will you get started?"

"Next week," the professor replied. "I've got the papers down at Ray's place. Come down and sign them, and we'll get this project rolling."

"How long will it take to build the GREEN HOUSE?" Morgan asked.

"Depends," the professor answered. "The weather, delivery of materials and equipment, and how many hands are helping are all factors."

Morgan looked at the professor. "What's the worst-case scenario, Madison?"

"We'll be popping champagne bottles in April," Madison replied, "beginning of spring, around the time that the river gets stocked with lots of RAINBOW TROUT."

□

Morgan knew he still had resumes out there, and he knew that any one of them might get him a job, but he couldn't be sure about getting a well-paying, full-time position. One accident, one trip to the hospital, one more serious car problem was going to do him in. He decided he would look for an additional part-time job that paid well. One of the businesses that he once owned, The Doll House, gave him some experience with operating a business providing food, drink, and entertainment to the public, so he thought he would look for a job as a waiter.

He and Christy went over to Charlottesville the next weekend and found a few restaurants that he thought would cater to people who would tip big and filled out employment applications. On the way back to Loveville, they went up to Crabtree Falls Campground and rented a tent site intending to use it just for a few hours (*to finally get er done dude*). On the way up the mountain, Christy turned on her GPS and looked at the screen. She pointed as she looked at Morgan, "Look, Crazy Mike is at home, probably playing video games."

"Yeah," Morgan replied. "Video games or porn?"

"Naw, Mike didn't do porn. I did, but his VIDEO addiction led to my PORN addiction. The more he played VIDEO games, the more I did PORN. Sometimes when he took a break from the joysticks, he didn't know what hit him—I was on him like a hornet from hell—*sting me baby!* I'd say, and he'd just walk away, drained from all the video."

Christy and Morgan knew that Crazy Mike's car was parked in his yard, but what they didn't know was that Crazy Mike had been tailing them the whole day in a friend's car and had followed them up the mountain to Crabtree Falls. Once he saw them turn into the campground, he did a U-turn and went back down the mountain to a general store and bought ten round steaks and had them cut up in smaller pieces and loaded into three plastic bags. When Crazy Mike returned to the campground, Christy and Morgan had pitched Christy's army surplus tent and were inside it with the lantern on. The sun had gone down below the mountain range, but it was still moderately warm for that time of year, which encouraged Christy to bring out her deck of playing cards.

Inside the tent, Christy and Morgan felt safe, because there were only two other tents set up in the whole campground, and they knew (thought) Crazy Mike was at home. Christy pushed the deck of cards closer to Morgan and said, "Cut them, babe." Morgan made a deep cut, and Christy put the deck back together and started deal-ing cards.

While they played Christy's version of strip-poker, Crazy Mike parked his borrowed car down the road and came back to the camp-ground carrying the plastic bags filled with bloody beef. He was wearing only hunting socks on his feet, no shoes or boots, to keep his movement quiet. Starting from across the road, he dropped little squares of beef every two or three feet until he got to the campground trash cans where he turned right and continued to drop pieces of beef all the way down to Christy's tent. At that point Crazy Mike heard them laughing as they played cards and disrobed. He placed the last pieces of meat around the tent and retreated to the woods off to the left of the campground. Once he was in the woods, he opened his jacket and pulled out a pistol and checked the clip. It was loaded.

Christy and Morgan were still playing cards when Crazy Mike heard the bears messing with the trash cans. Then he saw two cubs fol-lowed by momma bear. All three of them were picking up the pieces of meat and eating them as they got closer and closer to the tent.

Inside the tent, both Christy and Morgan were within a couple of pieces of clothing to being totally naked but had paused the card game, because they had heard some unusual noises outside the tent.

"Oh Jesus, what's that!?" Christy exclaimed, but she was pretty sure what was making those noises.

"Dogs!?" Morgan guessed.

"No, Morgan," Christy said. "Bears!"

Morgan grabbed his trousers and started slipping his feet into the legs while sitting on the mattress.

"What now?" Christy asked, as she got to her feet.

The cubs were scampering around the tent chasing each other and every now and then jumped up on the sides of the tent and clawed the surface of the rough canvas. Momma was close to the tent snorting and farting as they found and gobbled up the pieces of bloody meat. Between pieces of meat, one or both of them would go over to the tent and whack it with their paws in celebration of such a feast.

"Put your clothes on, Christy," Morgan said. "And your shoes. Once we're dressed you're going to hit the alarm button on your truck key which should scare the hell out of the bears making them run away and back into the woods. We're going to sprint out of here and get into your truck—you take the driver's side and I'll take the passenger side—don't forget to UNLOCK the doors!"

"I'm not ready! " Christy said.

Morgan looked at her, "Forget about the bra and shirt! Just throw the jacket on and let's go!"

Christy quickly put on her jacket and found her keys, and said, "I'm ready, babe!"

"Hit the alarm!" Morgan said putting his hand on the tent flap.

Christy pressed the alarm button and it went off. They dashed out of the tent with Christy going to the passenger side where she ran into Morgan realizing just then that she had gone to the wrong side. She started to reverse direction, but Morgan gestured for her to stay where she was. When he pulled on the door handle, he lost his grip, because the door was still locked. "Unlock the doors, Christy!" Morgan shouted, and looked around. Momma bear was charging.

When Morgan heard the doors unlock, he opened the passenger door and shoved Christy up and into the cab and turned his head to see where momma bear was. She was just about close enough to rip him a new anus. Morgan jumped in behind Christy and slammed the door shut.

"Damn his crazy ass!" Christy shouted. "That bastard's not home playing video games. He's here."

"And you've still got a bug on this truck! Who said there would only be ONE BUG—why not two or three!? I'm such a dumb ass!" Morgan exclaimed.

"Mike is CRAZY, but he's also very CLEVER!" Christy added.

"Do we dare get out of this truck and gather up our stuff?" Christy asked.

"You stay in the truck, Christy," Morgan said. "Back up to the tent, and I'll throw the stuff in the back. Just let me know if you see the bears coming back."

Morgan threw everything onto the bed of the truck and hopped back into the cab.

Crazy Mike watched the whole thing from the tree line across the road. "Crazygirl Christy," he said out loud. "No guy's gonna get up in you, but me!" Then Crazy Mike looked behind him and saw the three bears heading for him. He pulled his pistol out of its holster and shot up in the air, which made the bears reverse direction and scamper away.

◻

When Morgan got through the gates, he went directly to Catherine's office to sign in, but the real reason he wanted to go there was to find out more about her separation from her husband. Catherine's secretary was on the phone and indicated with her head that he should keep on going through the office out to the tennis court.

"Hi, Morgan," Catherine shouted and then walked over to his position just off the court.

"Great ground strokes," he said.

"Thanks," she replied.

"I'm going to work with Bob today and the guy who took my place. The website has to look better, and we've got to get more free publicity too—people forget about you quickly."

"Good," she said. "I think you're right on target." Catherine leaned to her left and sniffed her armpit. "Do I smell funky?"

Morgan leaned closer and sniffed. "No, you smell just fine—wonderful in fact (he was stretching the truth)."

"Let's sit down here by the court and talk for just a minute. Then I'm going to take a shower and return to work," Catherine said.

Morgan lifted Catherine's jacket off the back of one of the chairs and handed it to her. "You better put this on. If you're not moving you're going to get cold."

Catherine cleared her throat, and drank some water. "The website has got to start making money again for at least two reasons—first, it's a business and like every business it has to support itself. Second, if the website isn't making any money, the staff's morale will go down, and we don't need that. No telling what kind of evil that might bring."

"I understand," Morgan said. "Perhaps the new guy and Bob aren't jelling."

They are both silent for a few seconds, then Morgan asked, "Are you doing okay?"

"Yeah, I'm fine. Never thought I'd be divorced, but we've worked out the details of who gets what and that's usually the hardest part."

"Good. My wives and I didn't have any trouble with that—they usually got almost everything—and Cindy, the last one—got EVERYTHING."

"Yes, I remember that, Morgan. How are your children?"

"They're doing fine and things are getting better—slowly getting better. I'm getting some money from here, as you know. Some from subbing at the middle school, and I'll start waiting tables next week in Charlottesville."

"Well, that should be very interesting," Catherine said.

"The big news is—the university's school of architecture is going to build a GREEN HOUSE with the latest green design and technology on my property and refurbish my cabin."

"What!?" Catherine exclaimed.

"Yeah, yeah," Morgan said laughing. "All I have to do is give my property to the university and once the place is completed, live there RENT FREE and let visitors look around."

"Are you sure you want to do that, Morgan?"

"Yes, I'll have a ninety-nine-year lease and the university takes care of all expenses—electricity, heating, cooling—everything."

"You were once rich, now you're LUCKY."

"Ray Stewart, my neighbor down the road, got this deal going with the school."

"This is unbelievable, Morgan." Catherine said.

"I know, I know. If I don't do this deal, the IRS might take my property."

"May I come see your cabin in the woods and kids sometime?" Catherine asked.

Morgan was surprised by her request. "Sure, any time. I'll give your secretary my cell number and directions to my place before I leave tonight. According to the professor, the GREEN HOUSE might be finished by early spring."

□

Morgan was trained to be a waiter over three days at Thus Spoke the Raven. He noticed over those three days that he was considerably older than the other waiters and waitresses he saw on duty in the afternoon. Perhaps, he thought, the waiters were older at night (the shift he would be working). They weren't. They were all in their early twenties. Most of them were undergraduates at the university or college dropouts from other schools around the state.

On Morgan's first night as a waiter, he had Bayard (a sophomore at the university) assigned to him as his go to person if he needed help. The restaurant was beginning to fill up. Jacklyn, the hostess, looked at Morgan as she escorted a family to a table in his area and nodded, indicating that these guests were his—husband, wife, and three children. Morgan looked at Bayard, who was standing close by. "Okay Morgan, no problem," Bayard said quietly while thinking that Jacklyn could have given Morgan a lesser challenge on his maiden voyage as a waiter.

Once the family was seated and menus distributed, Morgan walked over to their table and introduced himself and welcomed them to the restaurant. The daughter who must have been seven or eight looked at her father and said, "Why do we have to have an OLD MAN WAITER when everybody else has cool young people waiting on them?"

Morgan smiled at the girl and then looked at the young girl's father. The father looked up from his menu and replied, "I don't know, honey. Be nice."

"I don't want to be nice, Daddy. I want a waiter like him." The man's daughter was pointing to Bayard.

Morgan cleared his throat before speaking. "May I get—" Morgan said but stopped, because the girl's father had raised his right arm and put the palm of his hand in front of Morgan's face, like a cop directing traffic, clearly indicating that he wanted Morgan to be silent. Then the man leaned forward, "Sweetie," he said, "if this waiter doesn't do a good job, we'll request another waiter, a YOUNGER one."

"Okay, Daddy," the daughter said, nodding impishly at her brothers.

The father leaned back against his chair and looked at Morgan. "You were going to say something weren't you—what was your name again?"

"Morgan."

"Yes, of course," the man said. "What were you going to say when I stopped you, Morgan?"

"May I take your drink orders?"

"Yes you may," replied the wife. "I'll have a martini, neat."

"Onion or olive?" asked Morgan.

"Neither."

"Vodka or gin?"

"Vodka."

Morgan noted it on his pad. "And you, sir?"

The man replied, "Bourbon straight up."

"Do you have a preference on the bourbon?"

"Stay with the SIR," the man said.

"Got it," Morgan replied. "Do you have a preference on the bourbon—SIR?"

"You catch on quick," the man said, cutting his eyes over at his wife, and then announced his preference, "Wild Turkey."

"*Wild Turkey* it is. Now how about you, kids? What would you like?"

The older of the two boys (ten or eleven) looked up at Morgan. "I am not—and neither are my siblings—KIDS. We are children or young people. I prefer YOUNG PERSON."

The other two children added, "We like that APPELLATION too."

Morgan smiled. "Yes, excuse me. KIDS are YOUNG GOATS, aren't they?"

"Yes, they are," they replied.

The daughter looked at her father, "Can we get a younger waiter now? This one isn't doing so well."

"What do you think, MORGAN? What's your assessment thus far on your job performance?"

Morgan was at a loss for words, but he quickly gathered himself and his honest thoughts. "I think I have failed as a waiter tonight, and I also think that you and your wife started failing as parents some time ago."

The man jumped up breaking toward Morgan who reached back and grabbed an empty chair and placed it between himself and the man charging his position. He saw Bayard rushing his way and held his ground.

"Don't let that rude waiter get away with that nasty remark, Harry!" His wife exclaimed. "Shove that chair up his rectum!"

Bayard stepped between Harry and the chair. "Calm down, SIR!" Bayard said, but the man pushed Bayard out of his way and moved forward. A man at an adjacent table got up and put his arms around Harry and restrained him from any further advancement toward Morgan.

Morgan looked at the man who was restraining Harry and thanked him for his help. Bayard gestured to Morgan to leave the area and he did.

Harry turned his head and said to the man restraining him, "You can let me go now. The object of my scorn has left the area." Bayard looked at the man providing the restraint and quietly told him that he could release the man, and then he added, "Your dinners tonight, sir, are on the house—and if you would like to enjoy after-dinner drinks, please do, compliments of Thus Spoke the Raven and accept our apologies for ruining your dining experience."

Once Bayard had gotten things settled down, he looked at the family and said, "Sorry about that, SIR, MADAM, and CHILDREN. I will be your waiter now. You SIR, I believe, would like a Wild Turkey straight up and you MADAM requested a Martini neat— no onion or olive—vodka not gin. And for you YOUNG PEOPLE what will it be?"

The older boy replied, "Peppermint flavored Perrier with a packet of Truvia on the side."

The younger boy sat up straighter in his chair, "Slices of peach and tangerine immersed in Perrier chilled—with ice on the side."

"And you, Miss—might I suggest a *Shirley Temple?*"

"You can suggest it, but I don't want a *Shirley Temple*. I'd like a *Jennifer Lopez*."

"Oh, I see," Bayard said as he jotted it down. (That was a new one on Bayard.)

While handing the drink order to the bartender, Bayard said, "Got an order for a *Jennifer Lopez*—are you up on that?"

"Yeah," she responded, "It's coconut milk, Hersey's chocolate syrup, a pinch of nutmeg, a pinch of cinnamon, and a half teaspoon of vanilla on the rocks."

"Great," Bayard said. "I'll be back. I'm going to talk to Morgan for a few minutes."

Morgan was sitting on a stack of boxes in the back room still wearing his waiter's apron. "Tough luck, OLD MAN," Bayard said, smiling. He patted Morgan on the back. "Don't worry about it. Baptism by fire—my father calls it. Things will get better. Stay back here until that ALL AMERICAN FAMILY leaves, then go back out there and give it another try."

"Thanks, Dad!" Morgan replied, smiling.

Sure enough, the rest of the night went just fine and the next week even better than Morgan had expected. For four nights work, he raked in $400 in tips.

¤

Weeks after Morgan had started working at the restaurant, a computer lab student called him over to her computer. She first asked him about the class assignment, and then she said very quietly, "I want to tell you something that you should know."

Morgan looked at her, "Sure, what is it?"

"On the nights you work at the restaurant in Charlottesville, there's a boy in this school who goes to your house and plays games with your children. Do you know that?"

"No, I don't know that," Morgan replied.

"I think he and Heather have a boyfriend-girlfriend thing going on," the girl said.

"I see."

"It might even be MORE than just a boyfriend-girlfriend thing," the girl said.

Morgan looked at the student feeling his concern rise to a higher level. "What kind of relationship is it?"

The girl was silent and took a small step forward dipping her head slightly, and whispered, "They're having sex."

Morgan knew what the girl was going to say before she said it, but when the words came out he took a long, deep breath and let it out slowly. "Are you sure about that?"

The girl replied, "Yes, they leave the house to GO FOR A WALK, but they really go straight to the Lexus and have sex."

"How do you know this?" Morgan asked.

"The guy blabs about it."

"What's his name?"

The girl was now getting very nervous. She saw a notepad on a desk and wrote the name of the boy on the top sheet of the Post it notepad and handed the pad to Morgan. "I really feel bad about squealing on Heather, but it's for her own good, don't you think?"

"Yes, you've done the right thing," Morgan replied and removed the top sheet from the notepad and put it in his shirt pocket.

❑

After dinner, but while they were still at the table, Morgan brought the first issue up for discussion.

"I was told today that a boy has been coming over here on nights that I work at the restaurant. Is that right?"

His children were surprised by his question. They were silent while scanning each other's faces. Then Heather responded. "That's right, Daddy."

"I was disappointed when I heard this today. Why didn't you tell me about it, and why didn't you ask permission?"

"It was fun having someone to play games with, and we didn't ask permission, because we were sure you would say no," Heather said looking at Raquel and Matt.

"I'm disappointed with all three of you," Morgan said, and then focused his attention on Raquel and Matt. "I want you two to clean things up, while Heather and I go to her bedroom to talk, but before we leave the table, do you have anything to say?"

Raquel looked at Matt, then said, "We are sorry for not asking permission and for not telling you."

"Thank you for saying that you are sorry, Raquel," Morgan said and then looked at Matt. "Raquel just said WE ARE SORRY—does that include you?"

Matt looked at his father, "Yes, sir, it does."

Morgan looked at his children and said, "What does that mean—WE ARE SORRY?"

After no one answered, Raquel looked at her brother and sister and replied, "I think it means that we did something that we shouldn't have done."

Morgan nodded his head and shifted his attention to Matt who said, "I agree with Raquel—we did something we shouldn't have done."

When Morgan made eye contact with Heather, she said, "I agree with them, but I also want to add—that by doing something that we shouldn't have done, we have disappointed and hurt you and may have even hurt ourselves—we have hurt the whole family."

"Okay, good answer," Morgan said. "By saying WE ARE SORRY, you are admitting that you have done something that I wouldn't have wanted you to do, but Heather took it further saying that your behavior was WRONG and may have been HARMFUL to you AND the whole family."

Raquel answered, "I thought that's what saying WE ARE SORRY meant?"

Morgan replied, "It might mean that, and it might not. For example, someone could say—WE ARE SORRY that our school's football team lost. They just REGRET that their school team lost indicating rightly that they weren't responsible for the loss. There's another word that we can use that takes care of taking responsibility for a loss or injury and that word is—APOLOGY. When you said WE ARE SORRY, it shows that you were aware that you had done something that you shouldn't have done, but it didn't say anything about TAKING RESPONSIBILITY for the harm it may have caused. That's why using the word APOLOGY is so important. It shows that you are taking responsibility for doing something wrong, but it also shows that you are aware that you have HARMED someone—in this case, you could have said—We WERE WRONG. WE APOLOGIZE for hurting you, our family, and perhaps ourselves."

Morgan looked at his children and added, "That's long-winded, but I hope you get the point: APOLOGIZE when you become aware that you have done something that may have HARMED someone and ASK FOR FORGIVENESS." When Morgan's children did not say anything, he added, "Here at my age, I'm just now learning how to use these words. I took this time to give them to you, because you might find them useful as you go through your lives." His children were motionless and quiet. Morgan looked at Heather and nodded his head toward her bedroom.

Sitting on Raquel's bed, Morgan could tell that Heather was about to cry but decided that he would get right into it. "Have you been having sex with this boy, Charles, who has been coming over here?"

"No," she said.

There was a short period of silence after her answer, but it seemed like a very long silence to both of them. Heather knew she had lied and she couldn't stand the feelings she was experiencing. She looked up and said, "Yes, Daddy, we have had sex."

More silence, then another question, "How many times?"

"Twice," Heather replied.

More silence.

"THREE TIMES," she said, "if a premature ejaculation counts?"

"Did he wear condoms?"

"No, but it was safe—WE were safe. No chance of getting pregnant—I counted the days."

More silence.

"Heather," Morgan said. "We'll talk about the fertilization issue later, but what about STDs—sexually transmitted diseases—did you think about that? You've learned about that in health classes—haven't you?"

"Yes."

"When did you last have sex?"

"Two nights ago."

"Where?"

"In the Lexus."

More silence.

"When was the first time?"

"About two or three weeks ago or it might have been longer than that. We've done some heavy petting out in the Lexus too."

"I will buy a home pregnancy kit tomorrow, and we'll see if you and he have escaped the consequences of using very bad judgment."

"Yes, sir," Heather said holding her hands over her face.

Morgan stood up and sat down next to his daughter. He put his arm around her back and hugged her gently.

"You are a wonderful daughter who has made a mistake. You will make more mistakes as you live your life, but this one could be—"

Heather filled in the blank—"HORRENDOUS!"

Tears rolled down her cheeks. She put her head against Morgan's shoulder and wept.

◻

Morgan did go to the foot of the mountain the next morning and purchased a pregnancy kit and used it that night. Heather was pregnant, fifteen and pregnant. He got the boy's home phone number from Heather and called. The boy's mother answered, and Morgan introduced himself and asked if he could meet with her and her husband as soon as possible. She asked why he wanted to meet—AS SOON AS POSSIBLE—so Morgan downplayed it saying that he didn't mean to imply that it was URGENT that they meet.

"Is there a problem, Mr. Armstrong?"

Morgan didn't want to get into "the problem" over the phone so he just said, "Your son has been over to our place a couple of times, so I thought we should meet—get to know one another."

Two days later Morgan went to the boy's home. After the initial introductions and cordial comments, Morgan got to the issue—the problem.

"Your son, Charles, and my daughter, Heather, have been having sex and Heather is now pregnant."

The boy's parents were surprised, of course, and replied, "Are you sure?"

Morgan told them he was sure.

"SURE that she's pregnant," the father said. "AND SURE that our son is the father?"

"Both," Morgan replied, but added, "My daughter told me that your son was the father."

Mr. Applewhite excused himself and came back accompanied by his son. Once seated, the father looked at his son and said, "Mr.

Armstrong has just told us that you and his daughter, Heather, have been having sex and that she is now pregnant. Is that true, son?"

Charles replied, "Heather and I have had sex, and she might be pregnant, but I might not be the father."

There was an uncomfortable moment of silence. "Heather has told me, Charles, that you two have had sex together—three times— and it's been UNPROTECTED SEX. Is that right?"

"Yes, sir," Charles replied. "But I think she has had sex with others or another and that's why I might not be the father."

Morgan's stomach was beginning to burn. He took a deep breath, then said, "Do you know who OTHERS or ANOTHER might be?"

"This is very difficult," Charles said swallowing. "A couple of guys have claimed that they had sex with Heather. I don't know if they were telling the truth, and there is a rumor that Heather had sex with a teacher."

Morgan got up and walked around in the room trying to calm himself. Charles's parents were frozen in their positions on the couch not knowing what to do or say.

"A TEACHER!?" Morgan said loudly.

"That's a rumor, Mr. Armstrong," Charles said softly.

"Charles?" his mother said.

"I'm sorry, Mom, Dad."

"Do you have any symptoms down there, son?" Charles's father asked.

"No, Dad," Charles replied, shaking his head.

"She's obviously been sleeping around, son, she might have—"

Morgan stared at the father. "Watch yourself!"

"Sorry," the father replied. "I'm just shocked by all this."

"Heather told me that you, Charles, are the father of the child. That's why I'm here. Now, I've got to go back and ask Heather about the other boys and the teacher. Ultimately, we are going to have to have a DNA test done to see if there's a match. If there is a match, we will have to get together again to go over our options."

"I'm sorry, sir," Charles replied.

◻

The following day, Morgan met with Heather alone and told her what Charles had said—that there were rumors that she had had sex with other boys.

She paused briefly before answering, "Heavy making out, that's all. Neither of those boys would have impregnated me."

"Their penises never entered your body?" Morgan inquired.

Heather answered, "Their penises entered my body BUT NOT MY VAGINA."

Morgan raised his eyebrows and stared at his daughter. "This is difficult, Heather. Where did they enter your body?"

"They entered my mouth," she said and started sobbing.

Morgan remained silent for a while. Then said, "This is unbelievable, Heather!?"

"I can imagine how difficult this must be, Dad."

"Okay, okay, Heather. One more thing that Charles told me was that there was a rumor that you had sex with a teacher. Is that true?"

"There's no turning away from the truth now, Dad. It's true, but not intercourse."

"Where and when?"

"In his office after school last week."

"In his office? I didn't know teachers had offices?"

"They don't. He's a coach and a teacher and coaches have offices."

"How did this come about?"

"One day he pulled me aside in a hall and told me that he had seen me running laps on the track during PE and thought that I should try out for the track team. I don't know what I said, but I was pleased that he noticed me. He's twenty something and handsome. So that's when he asked me to come to his office after the last bell to talk about it."

"How did it get from talking about the track team to sex?"

"Dad, do you really want me to describe all this?"

"You are eventually going to have to tell this to the police and the principal, so let's go through it now."

"I was so flattered that this man noticed me, and the thought of making the track team made me ecstatic, really, really happy. He told me I could sit on top of his desk, so I did, and we talked for a while about track. Then he put his hand on my knee and squeezed. He said as he did that, 'You have great legs, very muscular, not to mention very beautiful. You would be a great runner—A STAR!' It was thrilling to hear him say those things."

"Then what?"

"He lifted my skirt and asked me if he could feel my thigh muscles—my quadriceps—and as he asked that question his hand moved up my leg, and massaged those muscles. Then his hand moved farther up and touched my vagina. By this time I was breathing hard, and I could feel my panties, and everything getting wet. He was breathing hard too and shaking, trembling—he was so excited. He asked me to lay back on his desk and I did. Then he told me that he was going to pull my panties off and give me the most incredible pleasure of my life. I didn't know what to think or say. He put his face between my legs and licked me everywhere. No boy had ever done that for me. It had always been one sided."

"Was that it?"

"No," Heather answered. "I think I had an orgasm, and once that happened, he asked me to turn over on my stomach and scoot down so that my feet touched the floor. As I did that, he unbuckled his belt, unzipped his fly, and dropped his trousers and briefs to the floor. I glanced back and saw his penis standing straight up. He reached in the top drawer of his desk and pulled out a blue bottle, opened it, poured some oil into his hand and then put the bottle in my hand. He said, 'Rub some oil in and around your anus.' While I did that he rubbed oil on his penis and testicles. Then he said he was going to give me even more pleasure, more pleasure than I could imagine. I did as he said, and then I asked for the cap, and he handed it to me. As I screwed the cap back on the bottle, I felt the head of his penis enter and it hurt. He went up into me slowly, at first, then he started moaning and groaning and I did too, not because it was pleasurable. It was hurting, but I wanted him to think I was enjoying it. He climaxed very quickly, and withdrew. As we were putting our clothes back on, he said that he wanted to make love with me again, and he asked me if I wanted to make love with him again, and I said yes, but I really wasn't sure about it. I was confused and scared, and could feel stuff coming out of me as I ran out of his office to catch the activities bus."

"You know that this man has committed a vile, despicable crime, don't you, Heather?"

"And what I did must be DESPICABLE too."

"No, what you did WAS NOT despicable. I know you don't consider yourself a child or even an adolescent. You probably feel that you are an adult—but you aren't. He took advantage of you. You were a victim—you are the victim."

◻

The following morning, Morgan took Heather to a regional health clinic to have a doctor examine her. The doctor found evidence that she had been penetrated by an object that caused tears in her rectal membrane. The doctor told Morgan that an official report would be mailed to him.

That afternoon, Morgan arrived at Heather's school just following the departure of the school buses and found his way to the coach's office. The coach was talking with a PE teacher but stopped the conversation when Morgan entered and introduced himself. When the coach heard Morgan's last name, Armstrong, his eyes opened wider and with a quirky smile said hello and put out his right hand, but Morgan ignored the coach's gesture and focused his attention on the top right drawer of the coach's desk. He reached out and opened the drawer and saw a blue bottle. He pulled it out of the drawer and shook it, and as he shook it, Morgan looked at the coach and said, "I'm Heather's father, and I would like to rip you apart right now, but I'm not going to do that, because with our screwed up criminal justice system, I might be the one who goes to jail." Morgan turned and looked at the PE teacher, asked his name, and got it. "Remember what you just saw me do—pull this blue bottle of oil out of the coach's desk drawer. You will be called to testify to that in court."

◻

Morgan handed the blue bottle of oil to the sheriff and told him to get the fingerprints off of it. He then explained to the sheriff what had happened and filed a criminal charge against the coach.

◻

A few days later, Morgan drove to the prison to work with Bob even though it wasn't a scheduled visit, and ruefully he wouldn't be paid for it. Decisions had to be made, and they could not be put off to the following week. As was his custom, he went to Catherine's office to sign in and, hopefully, to have the opportunity to talk with her. When Catherine's secretary, Sylvia, saw Morgan, she smiled and handed him his sign-in sheet and pen. Morgan signed his name and asked, "Does she have a minute to talk?"

Sylvia immediately lifted her phone and told Catherine that Morgan was in the office and listened. "Okay," she said and hung up the phone. Looking up, she said, "Catherine has someone with her right now, but go right in. She wants you to meet him."

"It's not the governor, is it?" Morgan asked.

"No," Sylvia responded, "but the governor did pay us a visit last week."

"That must have been interesting," Morgan said as he walked toward Catherine's office.

"It was interesting," Sylvia commented as Morgan stopped at the closed door. "Go in, Morgan. They're waiting for you."

When he entered Catherine's office, he saw a man sitting in front of Catherine's desk. He was imposingly large and well-dressed—a dark blue sport coat, white shirt, bow tie and charcoal, cuffed slacks. Morgan nodded hello to the man and then looked at Catherine who was getting up out of her chair. Morgan's eyes then went to the photograph on the wall behind her desk, which he had seen many times before. The face in the photograph matched that of the man sitting in front of Catherine's desk.

"Hi, Morgan," Catherine said and then looked at the man getting out of his chair in front of her. "This is my father James Sinclair. Dad, this is Morgan."

The two men shook hands, and as they did, Morgan was remembering that her father was a judge. After the handshake, her father grabbed a chair next to the wall and offered it to Morgan. "Please sit down and visit with us a while," the judge said. Morgan remained standing while the judge stepped back toward his chair. "My daughter," he said, as he began lowering himself into his chair, "has told me a lot about you over the last few months. I'm glad things have turned out so well for you."

Morgan smiled. "Thank you judge, me too, and Catherine has told me a lot about you, and the one thing that I like the most is your passion for plants and flowers—*horticulture*, I guess is the word to use here."

"Yes, *horticulture*—the art or practice of garden cultivation and management. What I do is not ART and my garden MANAGEMENT is questionable," the judge replied.

Catherine looked at Morgan and said, "My Dad is being modest. He's very creative and his greenhouse and garden are immaculate."

Catherine's father thanked her for the compliments and turned his attention back to Morgan. "If it hadn't been for my love and passion for the law, I might have become a botanist. As it has turned out, I've been able to enjoy both."

Catherine quickly added, "Yes he has, and Morgan, you will have to visit my dad's home and take a tour of the greenhouse and the gardens. You won't believe what this man has done while working a full schedule on the bench, and now that he's retired—who knows what beauty he will create."

"I'd like that," Morgan replied. "Speaking of horticulture—how's the Horticulture Group doing here in prison? Are they making any money?"

"Yes," Catherine said. "In fact, BUSINESS IS BLOOMING and BOOMING!"

"Good, and hearing that reminds me that business is not booming at the Morgan Make$ Money website—maybe we need to change the name to Morgan USED TO Make Money."

The judge looked at Catherine and said, "Sweetie, I've got to go home. Thanks for the time and the chit chat." The judge stood up and shook hands again with Morgan and walked over to his daughter's parrot. Catherine walked over to her father and gave him a one-arm hug.

"Julius Caesar has been quiet today, hasn't he, Dad?" she said.

"Yes," her father replied. "AND I see why—you gave him a juicy chicken leg to keep him quiet—thank goodness," her father replied and looked at Morgan. "Julius Caesar can WAKE UP THE DEAD with his outrageously loud and off-the-wall comments. Do you know what I'm talking about, Morgan?"

"Yes, I do," Morgan replied.

Looking at the parrot, the judge said, "Say something before I go, Julius." The parrot stopped nibbling on the chicken leg and looked around nervously. The judge leaned his head closer to the parrot, and the parrot dropped the chicken leg and stepped closer to the judge. "What do you have to say today, Julius?"

The parrot did a little quick dance on its perch, then said, "*Et tu, Brute?*"

The judge laughed and looked at his daughter. "That's a crazy bird, Catherine. CRAZY!"

After her father left, Catherine gestured for Morgan to sit down. Shutting the door, she said, "All is not lost even if the Morgan Make$ Money website doesn't make a dime, you know?"

"Really?" Morgan replied.

"The staff, the prisoners, are working and learning and retraining themselves and will eventually return to society better equipped to compete and succeed."

"Perhaps?" Morgan replied.

"You sound down, Morgan. Are you down?"

"Yes, I am."

"I'm having my tough times too, as you can imagine," Catherine said. "There's no fun to be had in DIVORCING."

Morgan went to see Bob who quickly revealed that he didn't have time as he once did to do sufficient research and didn't have enough time to think about the information that came out of the research. "Now," Bob said, "I've become just like the other stock gurus on TV—they just make their best guesses and hope for the best."

"So just do your best, Bob. Your predictions or even guesses are probably better than all of the others."

"They're not, Morgan. Not now. Besides, let's face it, our viewership will not and are not the COUNTRY CLUB SET, and even if it was, I don't want to serve them. I want to help people who are in prisons or people who are going to be in prisons, if they don't get some help."

"What are you saying, Bob?"

"Our website can still offer advice on stocks and investing, but we need to do more than that. You, Morgan, can probably see that in your life right now. Right?"

"Yes," Morgan replied.

"Have you found a GOOD JOB yet?"

"No."

"If your friend hadn't given you a car, would you be here today?"

Morgan thought about it. Then answered, "Maybe—maybe not—I don't know."

Bob replied, "I think not. If you hadn't had a cabin in the woods, would you and your kids be living together today?"

"Probably not. I get it, Bob. I've had some luck, some advantages."

"Yes, you have. Let's have a website that's more universal and practical. Let's provide information that will help people make decisions and take actions that will lead them to better lives, better living, and thus—better outcomes."

"Okay."

"For example, Morgan, we see now and then people who win lotteries and have great sums of money, but still don't know how to live well and are soon back where they started—BROKE, and if you are broke, you're most likely UNHAPPY, and if you are UNHAPPY, you're NOT LIVING WELL. We need to address this. Our approach to helping people who are ON THE ROAD TO PRISON or IN PRISON is LIMITED—totally INSUFFICIENT."

"Well, I can't argue with you, Bob. I'll take this to the warden and see what she has to say. She'll be the one who has to sell this idea to the Prison Advisory Committee."

"I'm never getting out of here," Bob said. "I just want to help others get out of here and stay out of here. I can keep doing the stock stuff, but I want us to do more than that."

"Catherine said in a conversation we had the other day that you have become another person."

Bob looked at Morgan, "How's that?"

Morgan took some time to think about his answer while sitting down in a chair across from Bob. "You've gone from a man who spoke to no other inmate in this prison for two decades to a man who now CARES about other people and WANTS TO HELP people who need to be helped."

"I think that's true."

Morgan smiled. "Bob, can you describe how or what it was that brought on the change? What has made you a different and better person?"

"I think I was a good person or at least a decent, law-abiding citizen, before I killed my wife and her lover. That sounds ODD, doesn't it? I didn't plan to kill them. It was a spontaneous, rageful act. When I got here and was put in a cage, surrounded by other people living in cages, I withdrew—went inside—because I was scared— scared of everybody in this place. I felt safe in my cage and safer still when I started delving into stocks—equity markets around the world. As my knowledge increased and my ability to predict the ups and downs of stocks and markets—I felt better—safer. I had some control. When I had to leave my cell for meals and recreation, I slid back into fearfulness and resisted any interactions with other prisoners or prison staff. The longer that went on, the more impossible it became to turn back. In time, no one tried to interact with me."

"I see," Morgan said.

"When you were placed in my cell, as you know, my safe environment changed in a significant way—my cell was no longer a sanctuary, and I was thrown back to feeling scared in a space that once provided autonomy and comfort, BUT YOU wanted and needed someone to talk with, relate to, because doing that, I believe now, reduced your fear. Your efforts, however, to reduce your fear increased my fear. But in time, you found something in me or about me that you considered valuable—financially valuable. And you also soon discovered that you possessed something that I would recognize as potentially valuable to me—computer and Internet knowledge. My selfish interest broke my silence and brought us together—but not with a common purpose: you wanted to make money, and I wanted to make more accurate predictions on market movements. Once we started talking and working together, making more accurate predictions became easier, and I felt smart and accomplished." Bob paused and looked at Morgan. Then he laughed quietly and said, "Because of you, I began to believe that I HAD VALUE that I was WORTH SOMETHING, and that BELIEF brought about the change that you and the warden have witnessed."

"All right," Morgan said. "Let's change things up, like you say, Bob. What will we call the new website?"

"I'll leave that up to you and the warden," Bob replied.

◻

Morgan was heading for the front doors when the prison attorney appeared ahead of him in the hallway.

"Hi, Morgan," Ms. Spangler said. "I heard you were in the building working over and above contractual hours—just can't stay out of this place—can ya?"

"With a beautiful woman like you here, how can I stay away?" Morgan responded.

"I think at the tail end of your last visit, I offered to show you my stow-away camping mattress. Do you remember it that way?"

Morgan smiled and while he was smiling he started wondering about the coincidence of two women in his life (Christy and Ms.

Spangler) having inflatable camping mattresses. Then he said, "Do you have time to show it to me now?"

"I do," Ms. Spangler replied. "There's something about BLOWING THAT THING UP that gets me all excited!"

Immediately, after entering her office, Ms. Spangler went to her closet and pulled out the mattress and small pump, which she hooked up to the air intake spout on the mattress and started inflating it. She looked at Morgan. "Please go over to the door and lock it. Last time, I know I said that no one would open that door, but I could be wrong." When the mattress was fully inflated, Ms. Spangler disconnected the pump and inserted the plug to keep the air from escaping.

Morgan was amazed that Ms. Spangler was serious about having sex in her office, and she wasn't wasting any time getting to it. She walked over to Morgan and slipped her arms and shoulders out of her blouse letting the silky material slip down and gather in folds around her waist.

"Unfasten my bra and take a look at these babies," Ms. Spangler whispered, and Morgan unfastened her bra and dropped it on the floor. He leaned his head back and gazed at her *babies*, and they were gorgeous. Both Morgan and Ms. Spangler were suddenly surprised and startled when they heard high heels clacking on the terra cotta floor in the hallway. They were familiar footsteps to Ms. Spangler. "That's Catherine, Morgan," she said. "Shove the mattress back into the closet while I get myself and my babies back where they belong."

Morgan did what he was told, while Ms. Spangler got her blouse back on and moved over to the door. After she quickly surveyed the scene, checking that the mattress and her babies had been stowed away, she saw her bra on the floor. Morgan saw Ms. Spangler staring at her bright red bra with wide open, frightened eyes and sprang across the floor and quickly picked the bra up and jammed it into his right trouser pocket. Ms. Spangler nodded a thank you to Morgan, unlocked the door, and waited for the knock. When it came, she waited for a couple of seconds and opened the door.

When Catherine stepped into the office, Ms. Spangler gave her a sweet, relaxed smile. Morgan nodded hello and slowly initiated a deep breath through his nose. "Oh," Catherine said with a look of surprise on her face. "I didn't know YOU TWO were meeting, sorry."

"No problem, Catherine," Ms. Spangler said calmly.

"We were finished anyway," Morgan said, "and I have to get going."

Catherine looked at Morgan and saw parts of a red bra hanging out of his pocket, which put a puzzled expression on her face. Ms. Spangler could see exactly what Catherine was seeing, and Morgan became aware of what the two women were staring at and scrambled mentally to find an explanation. He looked down at the red strap and looked up at the two women as he pulled the bra out of his pocket with a feigned embarrassed grin.

"Now, how long have I been walking around with this hanging out of my pocket!?" he said, shrugging his shoulders.

The two women looked at one another and rolled their eyes. Ms. Spangler turned her attention back to Morgan. "Okay, Mr. Armstrong, you've now given me a better understanding of what you meant a few minutes ago when you responded to my question— How's it going?—with—I've got my hands full...looks like 36D cups from here."

Morgan looked at Ms. Spangler and Catherine. "What can I say!?"

The women looked at one another again and said simultaneously—MEN!?

Morgan gave them a wide grin and headed for the door. "I've got to get back to Loveville," he said as he passed the two women. It didn't go unnoticed by Ms. Spangler that Morgan was leaving the premises with her new Victoria's Secret Revolutionary bra, and it didn't go unnoticed by Catherine that Ms. Spangler's breasts were not as VOLUPTUOUS as they were earlier in the day.

□

While driving home, he was thinking about his sex life. He had never experienced so much attention and opportunities for sex with beautiful women and gotten so little. All of that attention and nearness to "the gates of heaven" without actually getting through THE GATES were increasing his horniness. Morgan's thoughts left women's bodies and his horniness and went to his daughter Heather and her pregnancy. He wondered if abortion was even a legal option for her. Catherine would know, he thought. Ms. Spangler would certainly know. Perhaps, having two adolescent daughters, Mrs. Stewart would know. Morgan was realizing that he had many people to turn to for information and advice. None, however, were men, with one exception—Ray might know something about abortion. When Morgan crossed the narrow bridge leading into Loveville, he remembered that he needed to pick up bread, eggs, and milk at the convenience store.

After getting the total for his purchases, he pulled out bills from his wallet and handed them to Molly. She took the money and said, "The sheriff arrested Coach Kolster today."

"That news didn't take very long to get here, did it?" Morgan replied without a hint of emotion.

"No it didn't, and rumor has it that he raped YOUR DAUGHTER, HEATHER—is that true?" Molly asked as she gave Morgan his change. He wasn't shocked that Molly knew about the rape. The convenience store was the hub for rumors. He was shocked that she was insensitive enough to bring that subject up in a check-out line.

"That's kind of personal, Molly."

"Rumor has it that it was ANAL—is that true?"

"Molly! That's enough," he replied and stared into her eyes daring her to ask another question.

"I understand," Molly replied. "You don't want to talk about it."

"That's right, I don't."

After concluding the conversation, Morgan lifted the bag containing his purchases and walked away from the checkout counter.

"You never know, do you?" Molly said raising her voice. Morgan continued walking toward the front door and made no reply. When he got in his vehicle, his cellphone rang, and it was Christy.

◻

His children had dinner ready when he got home, but there was little conversation while they ate. After dinner, Morgan put a couple of pieces of wood in the Buck Stove, because the cabin had become chilly. While he was attending to the stove, Morgan was deciding whether to bring up Heather's situation or not to, and by the time that the pieces of wood had caught fire and were beginning to warm the room, he had made up his mind. He was sure that his kids had already talked about "the situation" among themselves, and thought that it would be good for him—the adult—to become a part of the conversation.

His kids were doing different things in the front room of the cabin, so Morgan asked them to gather around him so they could talk. At that point, the kids knew what was coming.

"I'm guessing that you have heard the rumors," Morgan said, looking at them. They nodded their heads. Morgan glanced over at Heather and said, "You know we have to talk about THIS?"

Heather tossed her bangs back from around her eyes and nodded. "To make a long story short: I am pregnant. Charles is the father, and I had sex with Coach Kolster."

Morgan looked at Matt and Raquel for some kind of response. They avoided eye contact with him. Neither did they make eye contact with Heather.

"Raquel and Matt, you already knew about this, before the rumors, didn't you?" Morgan asked.

Both of them nodded their heads YES. Raquel said, "We knew about Charles, but we didn't know about the coach part."

Heather looked at Morgan. "I just couldn't tell them THAT."

"What are your thoughts?" Morgan asked them.

Raquel looked at Matt, who was gesturing for her to respond. Raquel looked at her father and replied, "Heather is too young to have a child."

"Thank you Raquel," Morgan replied. "How about you, Matt?"

Matt looked at Heather. "I agree with Raquel. BUT IT'S TOO LATE—she's pregnant."

"Heather, what are your thoughts, right now?" Morgan asked.

"Even if the DNA test proves to Charles and his parents that he is the father, he's not going to take responsibility."

"Meaning, what?" Morgan asked.

Heather paused before answering. "If I go through with this and actually have a baby, he's not going to be around. Everything's going to be on me."

"How do you feel about that?" Morgan asked.

Again, Heather paused before answering. "Like Charles, I don't want the responsibility of a child, because it's going to screw up my future."

"Sounds like neither you nor Charles wants to have a child, so what are our options?" Morgan asked.

"MY options," Heather responded quickly.

Morgan looked at Heather, silently debating what he should say. "What are YOUR OPTIONS, but remember that I am responsible for you until you reach the age of eighteen."

"MY OPTIONS are: have an abortion, induce a miscarriage, go through to term, or put the child up for adoption," Heather replied.

"You've thought this thing through, haven't you?"

"Yes, multiple times," Heather replied.

☐

It was 6:30 a.m. on a Saturday that people from the university showed up at Morgan's cabin in cars and trucks, and shortly after those people arrived, a bulldozer and backhoe came up the driveway and parked up close to the tree line. Morgan had been told by Ray that work would start that day, but Ray didn't say that the work would start so early. The early starting time was scheduled, because snow had been predicted for the afternoon. They didn't want to be removing trees and rocks from Morgan's property with snow coming down. Besides removing trees and rocks, they also wanted to dig—blast if necessary—a sizeable hole in the ground that would eventually be the basement where some of the advanced mechanical systems would be located.

Ray followed on the heels of the university workforce having watched them pass his house on the way up the mountain. He smiled when he saw Morgan outside on his porch in his bathrobe. "Hi, Morgan, you didn't expect them so early, did you buddy?"

"No, Ray, I didn't, but we'll be ready to pitch in and help shortly. As soon as we find our gloves, boots, and jackets. Want some coffee, Ray?"

Ray lifted his thermos, "No thanks, got it right here."

Both Ray and Morgan saw Madison, the university professor, when he hopped out of the cab of his Dodge truck. He went over to the work crew standing around the backhoe and bulldozer and handed out rolls of yellow ribbon and explained what areas needed to be marked. Madison then walked over to Morgan and Ray. "We'll get that area cleared and get the hole blasted out today, regardless of snow, and next week the rock for the foundation, the wall units, and the bales will be delivered. They'll put everything right over there in the area the students are ribboning off right now."

Morgan looked at the professor. "When we first talked, professor, you referred to this house as a BALE house, and I didn't know what a BALE HOUSE was, so I later Googled it and found out that you were referring to HAY BALES. Is that right?"

The professor smiled. "Yes, I think the most successful bale houses were built in the southwest where it is hot and dry. Hay Bale houses have also been built in the EAST—but they have had problems, because our climate is different—cool, cold, wet, humid, hot—which creates moisture, rot, and vermin problems. So this bale house will be different from the ones that have been built out West. This house will not be built with hay bales actually. It will have bale-like units made of plastic—recycled plastic bottles that have been placed in a mold—the size of hay bales—and flash-heated, so that they melt and stick together, forming rectangular blocks with lots of air spaces, thereby, making them very light, rigid, efficient insulators, high R values, not subject to moisture, rot, and vermin problems. COOL, huh?"

"Yes, very cool," Morgan replied as his children walked up all decked out in their hats, coats, jeans, and boots. "Professor, these are my children—Heather, Raquel, and Matt."

The professor started shaking their hands. "You kids are going to love this house."

Heather looked at the professor. "Do you think we can help too?"

The professor replied, "Definitely! You can work with the university students."

Ray and Morgan went over to the bulldozer and backhoe guys and started talking and exploring the heavy duty workhorses of the construction industry. While he was checking out the equipment, Morgan received a call from Christy. She had seen the university work crew heading up the mountain earlier and wanted to see if it would be okay for her to come up to see what was going on. When she got there, Morgan showed her around. When they got to the professor, Morgan said, "If you have money in the grant, professor, for landscaping and plants, Christy can take care of it. She's a good friend and does excellent work."

"You know," the professor replied. "I'd love for her to do the job, but the university has a whole Landscape Architecture department. It's likely that those students will do the landscaping work, BUT there might be something I could send her way."

Christy looked at Morgan. "Good try, babe. I appreciate the thought."

The professor looked at Christy and said, "I do some work outside the university, commercial and residential, and maybe you could help out with some of those projects, Christy."

"I'd appreciate that," she replied and handed him her business card.

When Morgan's kids stepped out of the work area, Morgan took Christy over and introduced her to them. As he did that, his kids looked at him in a way that said—who is this woman? Which was understandable to Morgan, because he had not previously mentioned her to them and there was some significant age difference.

"How do you know our Dad?" Heather asked.

"I met him at the convenience store at the foot of the mountain—pumping gas. I scared him to death when I backed up TOO FAST (for him) to the pump in front of his classic VW bus."

"I like your Ford 150," Matt said.

"Thanks, Matt," Christy replied. "It does whatever I ask it to do!"

The two girls had been quietly and individually guessing Christy's age. Raquel thought she might be thirty-two, and Heather placed her at thirty-six. Both girls were wrong but they definitely knew that she was much younger than their father and even younger than Cindy.

"Do you have any children?" Raquel asked.

"One," Christy replied. "A boy, eight."

"You'll have to bring him over," Raquel said. "Matt's just a little bit older."

Matt quickly corrected his sister. "Quite a bit older, three years, but I'd like to meet him. Maybe we could go fishing together in the spring."

"He'd like that, Matt. He likes to fish and so do I," Christy said.

The kids excused themselves from Christy and their father, because they saw the university students waving for them to come over to the worksite.

Walking up to the cabin alone, Christy looked at Morgan and said with a twinkle in her eye, "They think you are robbing the cradle, darlin'."

"Yeah, I caught that, but I haven't even gotten to first base yet, honey."

"Shoot, Morgan, you've gotten to at least SECOND BASE—not safely—but you got there. Maybe next time, you'll get to THIRD BASE, then HOME PLATE. You know I want you to SCORE."

□

It was no more than five minutes after Christy's departure that afternoon that a Subaru pulled up into the yard. Morgan didn't have any idea who it was until Catherine stepped out of the shiny sedan.

Morgan walked over to Catherine and motioned to Heather to come over to meet the woman who had just arrived. Heather left her work group and gathered up Matt and Raquel, and crossed the field. When they reached their father, he introduced Catherine. "This lady surprised me today by coming here, and I'm glad she did, because now she can meet you—this is Catherine Sinclair, the warden of the prison where I stayed for a while. Catherine, these are my three children: Heather, Raquel, and Matt."

Right away, Raquel asked her, "Do you have children?"

"No, not yet," Catherine responded.

"Are you married?" Heather asked.

"Wow," Catherine said, chuckling. "Am I getting the third degree?"

"What's THE THIRD DEGREE?" Matt inquired.

"It's a phrase that means lots of pointed questions," Catherine replied.

"And what does POINTED QUESTIONS mean?"

Catherine turned to Morgan and said, "Your children have very inquiring minds," and as soon as she said *inquiring* minds, she knew she had another word to define, which was fine with her, because she was just realizing that she was avoiding answering the—*are you married*—question. She turned back to Matt and said, "POINTED QUESTIONS are a string of questions designed to get important and usually personal information from someone. You've probably watched shows on TV where police are INTERROGATING someone—asking a lot of questions. In this case, I'm the SOMEONE who's getting asked a lot of questions."

Matt replied quickly, "I'm sorry," Matt said, and looked at his father, and added proudly, "I APOLOGIZE." Morgan and his son enjoyed the moment.

Catherine looked at the two of them and said, "Matt, you only asked a couple of questions—not a problem—and it's a sign of HIGH INTELLIGENCE."

Matt smiled.

Catherine looked at Heather and said, "Heather, getting back to your question—yes, I am married."

Once Morgan's children had gone back to work, Catherine and Morgan walked down the hill to the gravel road and walked away from the cabin and work group.

"Well Catherine," Morgan said taking a deep breath, "Glad you could come, but I had no idea that you were coming today."

Catherine sighed. "Sorry, I didn't give you notice. I just had some time open up, so I decided to invest it in getting to know you and your family better."

"I'm glad you came. I have a situation you can probably help me with." He paused, then said, "Heather is pregnant."

"Oh," Catherine replied, quickly. "Pretty early is it?"

"Yes, I think so," Morgan responded.

"Has she been seen by a gynecologist?"

"Not yet," Morgan replied. "I've been busy with other things," Morgan said as he began to feel negligent.

"What other things?" Catherine asked.

"I have had a conversation with the boy's parents and him."

"How did that go?" she asked.

"They aren't convinced that their son is the father."

"Well, that's to be expected. The boy doesn't want to believe it and neither do his parents."

"Especially," Morgan said with emphasis, "when rumor has it that Heather has been having sex with other boys—and a COACH."

Catherine stopped walking and looked straight at Morgan. "I can understand better now how you have been delayed in finding a gynecologist. What does Heather say about the rumors?"

"Heather told me that the boy, Charles, is the father. She said that she's had vaginal sex with him only."

"Okay, she qualified it. No vaginal sex with anybody else. So there's been some other kind of sex with others?"

"Yes, anal sex with the coach. I took out a warrant for his arrest, and he's out on bail."

"ANAL SEX!?"

"Hard to believe, isn't it?"

"Was there damage?" Catherine asked.

"I had her examined at a public health center and they said there was some damage," Morgan replied.

"Disease?" Catherine said.

"No disease."

"She'll need an ultrasound test to determine how far along she is, and you're going to need a paternity test?"

"I know," Morgan said.

"She might be far enough along to determine that. You just need to locate a nearby blood collection point. When she's nine to ten weeks into her pregnancy, the child's blood is in her blood. The DNA will tell you what's what—if Charles is the father. It'll take about a week," Catherine said. "Have you and Heather talked about her options?"

"We've had one conversation," Morgan responded.

"What options does she think she has?"

"Have the baby, abort the baby, put the baby up for adoption, and induce a miscarriage," Morgan replied.

"Is she leaning in one of those directions?"

"She knows she's too young to be responsible for a child. That's where it stands, right now."

"Hard choices," Catherine said. Here's some information for you, Morgan. "Fifteen to twenty percent of pregnancies end with a miscarriage, natural or induced, so the three other outcomes may never materialize."

"That would be a blessing, wouldn't it?" Morgan said

"I think so," Catherine answered, "and there are safe and simple ways to cause a miscarriage, if they are used early in the pregnancy—so the clock is ticking and decisions have to be made."

"How do you know so much about this stuff?"

"I'm a woman," she replied.

When Morgan and Catherine returned to the construction zone, the crew was taking a break. His kids had prepared a spread of things—sandwiches, cookies, veggies, fruits—and were eating right beside the university students. Morgan looked at Catherine and asked, "Can you see the awe in my children's eyes?"

Catherine agreed that she could see the awe and asked, "Did you ever visit a college campus when you were a teenager?"

"Once, when my aunt and uncle took me with them to visit their son at VMI for parents' weekend. When we walked into my cousin's room, the first words I heard were from his roommates—DON'T COME HERE!"

"Yeah but, if you asked VMI alumni today, if they could go back in time, would they go back to VMI, they'd all say—HELL YES!"

"Really?"

"Yes, my husband went to VMI."

"I attended a military high school, and I loved it for two reasons—first, because I was out of my home, and second, because I wanted to go to West Point."

"I think I can see you going to military school, because you might have been one of those BAD BOYS in high school, but I can't see you WANTING to attend West Point. Explain that."

"I liked the uniforms, and I knew I would be getting a very good education for free," Morgan replied.

"I didn't see in your records that you attended West Point. What happened?"

"In the summer between my junior and senior year at the military school, I came back home after a date and found my parents drunk, and I'm embarrassed to say even now, my father had my mother on the couch pounding her body and face with his fists, and I got involved."

"How so?"

"I pulled him away from her and threw him on the floor," Morgan replied.

"I'm sorry, Morgan. I can't even imagine that," Catherine said shaking her head.

"Unfortunately," Morgan continued, "he didn't just hit the floor. He bounced off the coffee table first, then he hit the floor."

"Why—UNFORTUNATELY?" Catherine asked.

"Unfortunately, because the edges of the table broke some of his ribs."

"Oh boy!?" Catherine sighed. "Then what?"

"I don't know what my father or mother said to the people at the hospital, but the next day a couple of men showed up at our house—"

"Social Services?" Catherine asked.

"Yes, and they took me to the juvenile detention center and locked me up."

"Your mother didn't stand up for you?" Catherine asked.

"I don't know," Morgan responded.

"Did you talk about that with your mother, later?" Catherine asked touching his arm.

"No," Morgan replied.

"Why not?" Catherine asked.

"Because the day after I got out of the juvenile detention center, I attached a wagon to my bicycle and put practically everything I owned on it—clothes, shoes, toiletries, tent, sleeping bag, knife, lantern, towels and headed south."

"I can't believe this, Morgan. You're making this up!" Catherine said laughing.

"No, I'm not. I camped out and worked in restaurants sometimes just for food. Some restaurant owners would also give me money, especially when I was heading back out on the road making my way to Florida. They were scared for me. I was too young to be scared."

"You didn't get to Florida, did you?"

"I did." Morgan said and laughed. "I even got to Key West. I pedaled to the very end of US 1—the most southern point of the continental United States. It was a wild place! I made money helping out on sailboats that took tourists out for snorkeling and scuba dives. I stayed at a campground, which didn't charge me, because I did some work around the grounds—painting, cutting grass, cleaning bathrooms."

"Well, how long did this wild adventure last? Did anyone ever come looking for you?"

"Yes, toward the end of summer some guys showed up from Child Protective Services or some name like that and took me to a juvenile facility in Miami, and from there, they shipped me back to Virginia. I was dreading going back to my home, and I wouldn't have stayed there. A deal had already been worked out. My aunt and uncle, the ones who took me to VMI, let me stay with them through my senior year in public high school. Motivation for working hard and getting good grades wasn't there."

"There went WEST POINT!" Catherine said.

"AND COLLEGE, because my parents weren't going to help me with tuition or anything—room and board—nothing!"

"So that's why you enlisted in the army—the Army Security Agency?"

"No, my high school guidance counselor told me about a special program at the FBI for high school graduates leading to the position of special agent, so I applied and was accepted."

"My God, Morgan, you wanted to be a special agent?"

"Yes, absolutely. I thought that would be very exciting," Morgan replied. "The Army Security Agency came later."

"So at the age of eighteen, you went up to Washington, D.C., all by yourself!?"

"Yes, and I lived in a boarding house, and don't let that term mislead you. The office and dining hall were at twenty-first and P Streets, and the row houses that lined two or three streets had rooms that people rented. There must have been hundreds of people living there and most of them were students from other countries studying at universities in D.C.—American University, George Washington, Georgetown, and others. I had a room with a refrigerator and a bathroom and a window with a view of nothing but brick walls and a very small patch of grass and weeds. Pretty stark, but I could raise my window and get some fresh air moving in my room when temperatures and humidity rose into the '90s."

"No car, I guess?"

"No car. I walked or rode the bus every place. For the monthly rent I got breakfast and dinner five days a week in the dining hall. Lunch was on my own at the FBI cafeteria. On the weekends, the boarding house dining room was closed, so we had to eat elsewhere— expensive for a GS3. Toward the end of months money was tight. Sometimes instead of taking the bus home, I'd walk. Going without food was no fun."

◻

After it was determined that Heather was beyond the ninth week of pregnancy, Morgan contacted Charles's parents and told them that a paternity test could and should be used to determine if their son was the father of Heather's baby.

Mr. Applewhite's response was, "Charles told us that he pulled out before ejaculating and therefore he believes he's not the person who got Heather pregnant. His mother and I believe him."

"And Charles may be right," Morgan said. "So let's get that settled with a DNA test. It's very quick, not invasive, and not expensive. But if Charles is the father, we will have to talk."

"Look, Mr. Armstrong," Mr. Applewhite said. "We don't want any part of this. If my son and your daughter had sex, it was because she lured him into it. Just get an abortion or put the baby up for adoption. We aren't going to allow this kind of burden to derail our son from getting a good education, a good job, and a happy marriage and family."

Morgan took a deep breath and released it before answering. "Mr. Applewhite, I hear you. Now hear me, you and your son can cooperate in this, or I will take out a warrant for your son's arrest on a charge of rape. Which do you want?" A week later, the DNA test was completed showing that Charles was the father.

◻

Morgan was sure that enough time had passed, so he went to the sheriff's office to see the report. The sheriff was there and he told Morgan that there were two sets of fingerprints on the bottle that matched those he had attained from Mr. Kolster, the coach, and Heather. The sheriff told Morgan two other things: the first was that Mr. Kolster had retained an attorney, and that he (Morgan) had made a mistake when he took the blue bottle from the coach's desk and left with it.

"How's that?" Morgan asked.

"No one can prove now whether Heather's fingerprints were put on that bottle in the coach's office or someplace else—like your home for instance. You see?"

"Throwing out the fingerprints, it might be his word against hers," the sheriff added.

◻

The very next week, Morgan was notified by the sheriff's office that coach Kolster had apparently moved out of his apartment and was nowhere to be found. When the coach's attorney was asked about his client's whereabouts, he said he hadn't heard from him. "If he has skipped out," the attorney said, "he used poor judgment."

◻

It was afternoon when Christy dropped by Morgan's place to see him and the progress that was being made on the GREEN HOUSE. The basement floor had been poured and the stone foundation was very close to being finished. The work crew was ready to install the first-level flooring and walls. When Christy got close to the structure, the professor, Madison, suddenly appeared and approached her.

"Glad I wasn't here when your crew had to haul all those rocks up from the riverbed to build the foundation," Christy said jokingly.

The professor smiled. "No, no," he said. "Wish we could claim credit for that. The stones came here by truck from a place out in the county."

Christy replied, pointing down, "Why didn't you get them out of the river down there?"

"Time, labor," the professor replied. "We couldn't afford the time it would have taken, nor the backs it would have broken."

"You had more money than you had time, you're saying?"

"We're very blessed with wealthy alumni who wanted this project to be completed before the competition deadline. Universities across the country are building GREEN HOUSES, which will be visited by members of very distinguished architectural review groups, and through those visits, certain houses will be selected for Awards of Excellence. Getting one of those awards is or could be very beneficial to the university. So, yes, we had more money than time."

"What kind of GREEN features will this house have?"

"The biggest innovative feature is the thick walls, which isn't a new thing, because BALE houses have been constructed for over four or five decades using HAY bales. This house will have PLASTIC bales."

"Dasani bottles—drink bottles?"

"Yes, PLASTIC bottles put to good use. The bottles will form PLASTIC BALES, which will be placed into the very thick empty walls of houses providing super R values."

"That's COOL!"

"In addition, this house will have a sod roof, not so new, but much more efficient than previous systems, windows that allow a lot of sunlight to enter the living space or block it. You can't see it right now, but the house will have multiple floors and a vaulted ceiling that goes three stories up. Like any house that has vaulted ceilings, heat that is provided on the lower floors travels up to the ceiling and stays there, which is wasteful and therefore inefficient. This house will have collection tubes all the way up to the ceiling that will capture the heat and channel it back to the basement where it will filter back up, heating the living spaces again."

"Sounds like NEW technology and EXPENSIVE technology."

"New and expensive, but the prices will come down. The newest technology involved here is advanced cistern, well, electrical and septic systems," the professor said. Then asked, "Do you have any of those old systems in your house?"

"All of my house's systems are old!" Christy replied.

"The septic system in this house is revolutionary. Historically, septic systems have provided owners with problems—smell, clogging, drainage, maintenance throughout the years of its use. This system will have advanced chemicals to treat the sewage, better mechanical design, and better sludge storage and removal. The sludge will periodically be zapped with lasers reducing its water content, leaving a dry, easily removable granular mixture that can be used as fertilizer or soil enrichment. If people accidentally or stupidly flush things, like condoms, down the toilets, they can be removed easily."

"Gee whiz," Christy remarked, excitedly. "That's very interesting. Especially the CONDOM PART. It's funny that people would flush those things into a septic tank. What else, professor?"

"Call me, Madison, " the professor said.

"Okay, Madison, what else will this house have?" Christy asked.

"That's all I have time for right now, Christy, and what I've described is just about it. I know you and Morgan were interested in getting some landscaping projects for you, and I think I've got some projects coming up that you might be able to help me with. Why don't we have some drinks and dinner some place and talk about it?"

Christy didn't know if the professor was just a nice older man, or if that invitation meant something more. "Thanks for the offer, Madison, but I have other plans tonight."

The professor replied, "It doesn't have to be tonight. Pick a night that works for you. These projects could mean thousands of dollars to you."

Christy said with a hint of annoyance, "I have to PASS."

The professor gave her a quick smile and cocked his head slightly, "You know, Christy, in the BUSINESS WORLD, you have to take advantage of opportunities that can really pay off."

"I do that now, professor," Christy replied.

"How 'bout a hug before you go?" the professor asked.

The professor had crossed a line, and there was no doubt in her mind what he was trolling for. She stepped forward to go around him, but he moved in front of her and slipped an arm around her waist and pulled her against his body.

"Professor!?" she said, reaching for his hand that was gripping her buttocks. She couldn't remove his hand, so she stomped on his right foot and that sprang her loose.

The professor grabbed his boot and did some one-legged hopping around while he massaged his toes. "Sorry, Christy," he said releasing his foot and placing it on the ground. "I just couldn't control myself. You have such a beautiful YOUNG ASS!"

"But you had no right to GRAB MY ASS!" she replied angrily.

"I know, I know," he said. "Please, forgive me."

Christy looked up and saw the work crew standing in and around the construction site watching. The professor also looked up at the students. He tipped his baseball cap and shrugged his shoulders. "You WIN some, and you LOSE some," he muttered, then raised his voice and shouted, "It's getting too dark to work, boys and girls, let's go home."

□

"Wasn't there someone called Solomon in the Bible?" Morgan asked. "King Solomon?"

"Yes, Mr. Armstrong," Mrs. Applewhite replied.

"My grandmother used to talk about King Solomon. About how wise he was. What do you think he would say about our situation?"

"I have no idea what King Solomon would think and say. He lived a long time ago, in a place far away, in a culture very different from ours. What do you think we need to do HERE and NOW, Mr. Armstrong?"

Morgan was thinking about his response when Mrs. Applewhite said, "Tell me what you would be in favor of: ABORT the baby?"

Morgan remained silent too long, prompting Mrs. Applewhite to use another word: "KILL the baby—Mr. Armstrong!?" she asked.

"NO," Morgan quickly answered.

"How about—Heather has the baby and raises the baby without Charles's involvement?"

"I think YOU and your HUSBAND have already selected that option, Mrs. Applewhite," Morgan replied.

"Yes, my husband and I would prefer that Charles not be involved, but could you accept that?"

"If I had to accept that, I could, but…"

When Morgan hesitated, Mrs. Applewhite said, "BUT what?"

Morgan replied, "BUT I'd be mad as hell about it."

Mrs. Applewhite paused, then said, "You'd be *mad as hell about it*…what's IT?"

Morgan was getting irritated with Mrs. Applewhite's questions, but he didn't want to show it, and he had to dig through his thoughts and feelings to discover what IT was. Mrs. Applewhite patiently waited for his answer.

Seconds went by while he thought, but the seconds felt like minutes, which made Morgan scramble around in his thoughts to find the answer. Once he found it, he said, "IT is this: it appears that you and your husband are not going to require your son to accept responsibility for the pregnancy and to make every effort possible to resolve things fairly, and in the best interests of all parties."

Mrs. Applewhite smiled and said, "I thank you for your honesty. Would you be in favor of ADOPTION?"

"I would," Morgan replied, "but Heather has already let me know that this decision is HERS, not mine."

Looking directly into Morgan's eyes, Mrs. Applewhite said, "Just remember, Mr. Armstrong, Heather is a child, and Charles is a child, and CHILDREN shouldn't be asked or allowed to make ADULT decisions. This has to be YOUR DECISION, OUR DECISION—NOT HERS or CHARLES' DECISION!"

◻

A few days after Morgan had that conversation with Mrs. Applewhite, he received a call from Catherine, who was just checking to see how things were going. Morgan told her how the conversation had gone with Charles's mother. Catherine admitted that she was not a mother and had never dealt with a situation like the one he was dealing with, but she volunteered to help out.

"Heather," Morgan said, "hasn't had a mother around for a long time; I'm sure she would appreciate your shoulder and advice."

Once Catherine got Morgan's consent on helping out, she said cheerfully, "Now, how's it going with finding a fulltime, career position?"

"I have had a few more interviews but no luck. I think all of them have Googled my name before reading my letter and resume, and saw that I was convicted of murdering someone, which ditched my chances of getting an interview or a job."

"Probably," she replied. "What, Morgan, would you most want to do if a fairy godmother could make your wish come true with regards to a career, a job, a means by which you could make a good living?"

"That's a tough question," Morgan replied.

"Yes, it is. What do you most enjoy doing?"

"I don't think I can get paid for that!" he said.

"Get serious, Morgan," Catherine said.

"I like hitting golf balls," Morgan said.

Catherine chuckled, "Now, I can relate to that. I like, as you know, to hit tennis balls. How could you turn your passion for hitting golf balls into a job and not just a job, but a delightful way to make good money and a great way to spend your days and life?"

"I have no idea, Catherine."

"Think, Morgan, let's do some brainstorming," she said.

"I'd like to be a professional golfer," Morgan quickly responded.

"That's not going to happen," Catherine replied.

"Hey, you're not supposed to pooh, pooh things like that when you're brainstorming," Morgan replied.

"You're right," Catherine answered. "Sorry. Let's take a close look at this—back in your other life, how much golf did you play?"

"Actually, it was rare that I played a round of golf. I was too busy working—making money."

"Now we're getting somewhere. Tell me more," Catherine said.

"My greatest enjoyment came from practicing—hitting balls with different clubs, trying new shots, sharpening my skills, learning how to control the ball and even putting—PRACTICING was what I loved."

"Okay, how could you earn a decent living knowing what you know now?"

"I could operate—manage a golf range."

"Where you could—?" Catherine said, encouraging him to supply the answer.

"MAKE MONEY and hit a lot of balls—FREE!"

"What else?"

"Maybe I could make MORE MONEY if I gave lessons," Morgan replied.

"If you could teach people to be better golfers, what would that give you?"

"Catherine, come on—"

"What would that provide you? You need to get more than money out of your time and effort."

"A sense of accomplishment," Morgan replied.

"Yeah. Now, what might your career goal be?"

"To manage a golf driving range where I could give golf lessons," Morgan responded.

"Question—do you really believe you would be happy for long JUST MANAGING a golf driving range that was not your own?"

Morgan smiled, "No, I think I NEED TO BE THE BOSS—the owner."

"I do, too," Catherine said. "NOW, can you give me your career goal?"

"I'd like to OWN and MANAGE a golf driving range where I could help people become better golfers."

"Yes, that's precisely your career goal. Now, what's the first step in achieving that goal?"

"Look for and find the money to buy property, buildings, tractor, and so on."

"That's not the first step. You must first develop an authentic and BURNING DESIRE to achieve your goal, and then you start doing those things you just mentioned—find money, look for property, et cetera. Lastly, you must make a commitment to never say—I QUIT!"

Morgan became quiet and distracted by extraneous thoughts. "This is off topic, Catherine, but did you make a commitment to your husband when you two got married?"

She was initially silent and unsettled by Morgan's question, and she saw the connection. "Yes, I took a vow, and now I am breaking my vow—my husband and I are breaking our vows. Now, back to business—"

Morgan asked, "Did you want your marriage enough?"

"Morgan!?" Catherine said.

"What was missing?"

Catherine saw there was no getting back to the previous conversation. "FIDELITY for starters," she said. "Then world view, heart, genuineness."

"Do you think you will find a man with FIDELITY, the right WORLD VIEW, HEART, and GENUINENESS?"

"I think the stars will have to be aligned just right," she answered.

"And where would you find him?"

"The only opportunity I'll have to meet this man will be on Saturdays between the hours of ten and twelve in Trader Joes or Whole Foods. That's it. All the rest of my time is booked."

Morgan laughed. "Maybe you need to do some introspection—like what you just put me through—are you doing what you most want to do?"

"I was doing that, but I don't know now."

"Why—because of the divorce?"

"Maybe—divorcing rocks one's foundation."

Morgan felt disappointed with himself, because he wasn't asking the question that he really wanted to ask, so he asked it, "Would I have a chance with you?"

Catherine was pleased that Morgan had asked the question, because she knew they had a mutual attraction to one another, but she also knew she had to get off the phone. She looked at her watch and said, "I have to go, Morgan. I have a meeting, and it can't start without me, but here's my answer for now—I feel certain that if our personal information were fed into eHarmony's database, we would not MATCH UP AS SOULMATES, but I do find you fascinating, and please understand that I am just exiting a marriage."

◻

It was after dismissal when the principal met him as he was leaving the building for the parking lot and told him that the sheriff had come by and told her that Coach Kolster had been seen in Angel Fire, New Mexico.

Morgan cocked his head and replied, "I'm not glad he got out of here without being tried and sent to prison, but I am glad that we didn't have to go through a trial and like so many cases the sexual predator walks, because of a technicality of some kind. At least, he's out of here!"

"Yes," she said. "He's out of here, but will he end up in another state—in another school system? That's what we don't want. As it stands now, nothing is on his record. Nothing that would be picked up by another school system."

"Is that right?" Morgan asked.

"He has been arrested for sodomizing a child, but he has not been convicted of that crime, and without a conviction, a school system won't know about it."

"Well, sooner or later, I believe the authorities will find him and send him back here for trial, which will include his crime and running away. That should keep him behind bars for a good while."

"I hope so, Mr. Armstrong. Up to now, I haven't offered an apology for this incident. So please accept my apology."

Morgan accepted her apology and started to walk away when she asked him to wait. "Mr. Armstrong, Heather is going to start showing long before school is out, and for her own good and the good of other kids, teachers, administrators in the school, she should stop attending—withdraw soon."

Morgan walked back closer to the principal. "Where would she attend school?"

"I believe there are several sites in the region. If you would like, I can provide that information to you. The next time you come in to sub, just check your box. I'll put it in an envelope with your name on it—marked CONFIDENTIAL."

"Is there anyone in this school who doesn't know about THIS!?"

"To be perfectly honest—probably not, and I'm sincerely sorry."

Morgan walked to his vehicle where his kids were waiting and drove home. The kids went inside the cabin, and Morgan walked over to the GREEN HOUSE. The first floor walls were up and nearly filled with the plastic bales. He watched some of the university students cut some of the plastic bales with hot wires, so they would fit nicely around windows and doors. When he walked out of the enclosed space to what would be a wrap-around porch, he found the professor taking some measurements. When the professor saw Morgan, he walked over to him.

"Mr. Armstrong. I can call you Morgan, right?"

"Sure," Morgan replied.

"The other day, Christy came by here while we were working and asked some questions about the house, so I took her around and explained the technology involved and how things would work. Is she your girlfriend?" he asked.

Wanting to protect Christy's privacy concerns, Morgan replied, "No. She's a good friend."

"Good, I thought you introduced her the other day as a friend," the professor said. "I don't have to tell you, I'm sure, that Christy is a looker. Even the young university studs working on this place are gawking at her even though she's much older than they are. Regrettably, perhaps, I'm somewhat of a lecher, and my lecherousness got the better of me that day." The professor paused, grimacing. "Has Christy already told you about this?"

"No."

"When she was ready to leave, she walked over and hugged me. Before she stepped away from me, I put my arms around her and pulled her closer and grabbed her ass. When she heard the clapping coming from various places on the construction site, she withdrew. I think she might have been okay with my overture had it not been seen and applauded by the students. If Christy brings this up to you, she might have a different version of what happened that day, but you know now what happened."

"Professor, I now have your side of the story, and I don't know if Christy will provide me with hers. I also know that you consider yourself a lecher, so what you perceived might have been WHAT YOU WANTED TO SEE, and you did WHAT YOU WANTED TO DO, and now you might be COVERING YOUR ASS."

"Well said, Mr. Armstrong."

"Like it or not, professor, SHE gets to decide who touches her ass. Got it!?"

◻

Whatever Morgan was doing for over a week or more, he kept hearing the conversation he had had with Catherine regarding what he really wanted to do with his life. One day, Morgan wrote the following on a piece of paper:

1. Is there a golf driving range in the Loveville area?
2. How much land is needed?
3. What about buildings?
4. Lighting?
5. Employees/payroll?
6. Vehicles?
7. Operational expenses?
8. Insurance?
9. Business license?
10. Utilities?

Before he could go to banks to apply for a loan, he knew he would have to show them a business plan and document his net worth. He was confident that he could develop a comprehensive and acceptable business plan, because he had had to create multiple plans when he was starting his businesses decades earlier, but the document detailing and revealing his net worth would surely scuttle his chances of getting a loan. The only thing he owned was an agreement between him and the university giving him free occupancy of the GREEN HOUSE and cabin for ninety-nine years.

So as Morgan stared at his list of questions, he had to acknowledge there was no way a bank would lend him the money needed when he had no real assets. Added to that sad financial position, which he had temporarily forgotten, was the money ($100,000) he owed to the IRS.

This is ridiculous, he said to himself. Then he launched into a skit playing both roles:

Morgan: *Yes sir, Mr. Loan Officer, I want to borrow a million dollars.*

Loan Officer: *Yes, I see here that you live month to month on income you derive from subbing at a middle school, waiting tables, and part-time work at a prison—and you have no assets—is that right?*

Morgan: *Yes, sir. But I do have a place to live FREE for the next ninety-nine years. That's got to be worth close to two million dollars.*

Loan Officer: *Yes, that's very interesting. I'll get back to you, Mr. Armstrong, thank you very much for your loan application. We will give it serious consideration. Good day.*

Morgan knew he had no chance of getting a loan for any amount, because he was INSOLVENT. He thought back to the time when he started his first business, which followed his four years in the ASA, and his half semester in college. He may have had $1,400 in the bank. He decided to start a pest control business first, because every home and building needed protection from pests, and he wouldn't have to invest a lot of money to get into business. In just one day, he went to Lowes and bought pest control chemicals, a sprayer, goggles, gloves, hat, respirator, and coveralls. He already had a car that was paid for which he traded for a late model white Chevy van that Earl Scheib painted orange for just $29.95. An artist friend then painted frightening-looking pests all over the van for $50. He bought a few sheets of cardstock and cut them up into 2 x 3 ½ inch pieces and typed on each one of them BUG OUT EXTERMINATING, with the tag line PESTS HATE TO SEE US COMING, his name, and phone number. A month after starting his company, Morgan paid a local sign painter who was good with his hands to make a large termite sculpture that he bolted to the top of the van. Once the orange van with a large termite on its roof started running around town, it got noticed by a photographer at the newspaper who took a photograph of it and got it in the local interest section of the paper. The photographer's name was Jimmy, and he later came to work for Morgan as the manager of the Armstrong Detective Agency. From that first photograph that appeared in the newspaper, Morgan and Jimmy were friends and covered each other's backs.

□

Morgan's attention to things at home had to be suspended for one or two days because the day had arrived for moving his mother out of her assisted living facility. Jimmy met him at the facility and helped him move his mother's furniture into the U-HAUL truck. There were a few pieces of furniture and a couple of suitcases. She had downsized before moving to the assisted living facility. By noon, Morgan, his mother, and Jimmy were having lunch at the Golden Coral. After that, Jimmy went home, and Morgan and his mother went up Interstate 64 to Charlottesville and then took Route 29 and small back roads to Loveville. Morgan got some of the work crew at the GREEN HOUSE to carry his mother's furniture into the cabin and place it in the front room, because there was no other place to put it. She was going to have to live in that front room until the GREEN HOUSE was finished. Morgan, who had been sleeping on the couch in the front room, would now be taking up residency outside in Christy's army surplus tent. It was winter and cold, but he had a sleeping bag and could run inside the cabin when he needed to eat, bathe, use the toilet, or get dressed.

□

The following day, Morgan went to Charlottesville where he bought his mother a cellphone so she could call him or the Stewart's if she had an emergency or when she just needed something. When he was returning from Charlottesville, he heard an ad on the radio by a company that was giving emergency medical assistance devices to seniors who were eligible for Medicare or Medicaid, and he immediately gave them a call and ordered one. Within a week, one of the devices was delivered to his cabin—absolutely FREE—no charge for the device, no charge for shipping, no charge for processing—IT COST NOTHING. Morgan was sure that every taxpayer in the country was paying for the FREE emergency medical devices just like tax-payers had paid for the SCOOTERS FOR SENIORS a couple of years earlier. If he was paying for those devices, he thought he should get one even though it seemed unnecessary having just purchased a cellphone for her.

On the evening after the emergency medical device was deliv-ered to the cabin, Morgan and Christy told his mother and children good night and braced themselves for the cold night air. When they opened the front door, they dashed across the porch, down the steps, and into the tent where they removed their coats and shoes only and slipped under the flannel sheet and pile of blankets covering the inflatable mattress. In just a few minutes, both of them real-ized that the mattress was not inflated optimally, but neither of them was willing to put their coats and shoes back on, crawl out from under the blankets, find the air intake valve, hook up the pump, add air, remove the pump, re-make the bed, and crawl back in it. The underinflated mattress would have to do. Just thinking about all that effort had elevated their core body temperatures, which introduced additional heat to their space beneath the blankets, making things toastier, allowing them to remove clothing. Once that happened, foreplay began and they were finally on their way to consummating their relationship.

Suddenly, their enjoyment of the first moments of foreplay was diminished by the sound of a distant siren. A fire truck or rescue vehicle rarely came up the mountain, and even rarer still was a res-cue vehicle coming up the mountain at 10:30 p.m. The siren got louder and louder and eventually the ear-popping, mind-boggling sound of the siren put an end to foreplay. Both of them sat straight up when the rescue vehicle seemed to be on top of them. Whirling flashes of red light lit up the sides of the tent, and tires skidded to a stop just a few feet from the tent. When the ETMs opened the doors of the rescue vehicle, a wave of country music blasted through the canvas walls of the tent. Morgan and Christy threw off the pile of blankets and started putting their clothes back on. The ETMs ran toward the cabin and up the steps to the porch. The rescuer at the front of the line knocked on the door but didn't wait for anyone to open it. He turned the knob and pushed the door open and rushed into the front room of the cabin, shooting a column of light around the walls searching for light switches and someone in trouble. Other ETMs followed, and what they spotted first with their flashlights were four people huddled together on a sofa—an elderly woman and three children. One of the ETMs found the switch controlling the ceiling light and flicked it up, which allowed them to clearly see the frightened faces of the elderly woman and the children. The woman, it appeared to the rescuers, was clutching her chest, which motivated one ETM to open the defibrillator and shout—CLEAR THE AREA—and sprinted toward the sofa. Following the ETMs command, the children quickly retreated from their positions on the sofa, leaving their grandmother by herself.

"I'm sorry!" Mrs. Armstrong exclaimed in a frightened voice. She grabbed the emergency medical device hanging on a cord around her neck and shook it frantically in front of the ETM standing over her opening the defibrillator. She looked up into his flushed face and other faces now staring at her and said in a trembling, frustrated voice, "I must have set this THING OFF while I was sleeping. I don't know what I did. I think I was dreaming, and I was reaching for something in the dream—I don't know boys—IT SUCKS TO GET OLD! Sorry you had to come all the way up here—FOR NOTHING. I'm not having a heart attack!"

◻

In the morning, Christy drove Morgan around the county showing him land that might be suitable for a golf-driving range. Morgan had previously determined that there wasn't a golf-driving range within a twenty-mile radius of Loveville, which in Morgan's mind could be a good thing or a bad thing—good thing meaning there's a NEED for one, and a bad thing meaning there's NO NEED for one. He had also checked out a couple of golf courses in the area to see what they offered and found that what they offered was standard fare—practice tees and putting green. He started thinking that his driving range would offer the standard practice tees with spiffier targets, multiple putting greens, sand traps, various kinds of rough, and amenities such as nice healthy food choices served outside on tables shaded by umbrellas and a bar featuring wine and beer. Other things that might add appeal, he thought, would be a pro shop, gift shop, lounge, and video game room. In addition to taking golf lessons from Morgan, customers could learn things by watching professionally made videos on every aspect of the game. When Morgan thought about that idea, he realized he could videotape his lessons with customers and sell them to customers so they could run through the lessons as many times as they wanted at their homes. All the while these thoughts and images were going through his mind, he was also seeing and hearing the sound of a cash register ringing up the cost of those items. The possibilities were endless and thinking of them had gotten him excited. He turned his attention to Christy and asked, "Do you have a PIPEDREAM?"

"No, I have WET DREAMS," she replied, cutting her eyes toward him.

Morgan chuckled, "That's funny, Christy. Seriously, have you ever had a PIPEDREAM?"

Christy replied, "SERIOUSLY, Morgan. What's a PIPEDREAM?"

He thought for a couple of seconds before answering. "A pipedream is something people might think about, dream about having, but most likely will never have."

"In that case," Christy replied, "I have had a pipedream. As you know, I do landscaping for a living, which means I design yards and gardens for people or companies, and I eventually buy trees, plants, rocks, and other things from greenhouses and nurseries to put into my designs. I've never been satisfied with vendors around here. They don't provide a good selection of stuff, and they don't keep enough stuff. They keep their inventories low to save money. In my pipedream, I would have a beautiful building or buildings sitting on rolling land that was beautiful to start with, and then I'd enhance the whole place with a great variety of plants, trees, shrubs, flowers that are native to this area and show people what can be done with my designs. Just as PRESENTATION of FOOD heightens its enjoyment—professionally designed and installed landscaping heightens the enjoyment of plants, homes, and offices it surrounds."

Morgan replied, "Maybe we can turn your pipedream into reality one day!"

Christy responded, "Maybe? I see ponds, lakes, streams, and manmade things like walkways, bridges, and sculptures—that would add even more beauty to the natural environment—like some artist did years ago over in France. I think his name was Monet. I see intimate picnic areas for customers and visitors who could bring their own picnic lunches or order them from a menu and enjoy them on site. I want to inspire people to create gardens—LITTLE HEAVENS for themselves, using what God has given us—plants, flowers, trees, dirt, bees, sunlight, air, wind, and water, and I'd have a huge inventory. That's my PIPEDREAM!"

"Nice, Christy. Not too long ago, I could have financed that for you. Now, I don't have enough money to finance my own pipedream. Let me back up and phrase that correctly. Saying that I don't have enough money sounds like I have some money to finance my pipedream when the truth is—I DON'T HAVE ANY MONEY to finance my pipedream."

"I have saved some money, Morgan," Christy said. "But I didn't save it to finance a pipedream. I've been saving money for a down payment on a house."

Without commenting on Christy's remark, Morgan went straight to a sore subject. "Even if I somehow got the money I need, the IRS would swoop in and snatch it away, because of back taxes."

"Meet with them, Morgan. Agree to pay it off over ten years or twenty years and see if they will accept your proposal. You can't live with that financial threat hanging over your head—pipedream or not. Maybe you should go for thirty or forty years. You never know what they will accept—sometimes I think those IRS people get just as sick of us as we get sick of them and will accept just about anything, so they can get us out of their life."

Morgan smiled. "Okay, maybe I'll try that."

Christy focused on the road up ahead and got lost in her thoughts for a few minutes and so did Morgan. Then suddenly,

Christy asked, "I guess you loved that woman who robbed you blind. What did you love?"

Morgan replied, "I loved her looks. I loved the sex. I loved seeing her excitement when I gave her nice things."

Christy stared quietly at the narrow two-lane road as it twisted its way over the rolling terrain, and then she said, "I'm sitting here thinking about my husband, soon to be ex-husband, and what it was that I loved about him. I guess I loved his WILDNESS. It excited me and I loved making love to him—with him. So you and I loved someone enough to marry them, and neither of our marriages worked out. Does that teach us anything?"

"Well, to be honest Christy, not one of my THREE marriages worked out."

"Maybe I should have looked for a SUGAR DADDY. Plenty of women do that, you know," Christy said. "But not me. I'd live under a bridge before I'd do that!"

"I'm glad you feel that way, but you know—I might be old enough to be YOUR SUGAR DADDY," Morgan said, jesting.

Christy replied, "You might be old enough, but you're missing one key component—MONEY!"

Both of them laughed. Then Christy said, "Hey, let's take a day off and go to Charlottesville, check into a room at the Omni, and FINALLY have sex." She turned her head and looked at Morgan who was smiling. Then she added, "Can you believe we have known each other only a short time and LOVE EACH OTHER SO MUCH and—"

Christy stopped her comment right there to watch Morgan's reaction to her words—LOVE EACH OTHER SO MUCH—because she knew or thought she knew that neither of them was READY TO BE IN LOVE.

When Morgan saw her face morph into a smirky kind of smile, he smiled and felt relieved that she wasn't serious. "Let's do exactly that—go to the Omni, have sex, and then I'll take you to dinner at Thus Spoke the Raven—my treat!"

"What an odd name for a restaurant," Christy said.

"I think it has something to do with some guy named Edgar Allen Poe."

"Oh yeah, we read something by him in Senior English. Poet, I believe. Kind of creepy, but he was a Virginian!"

"I don't remember him," Morgan confessed. "The only poet I recall reading in high school was W. H. Auden—*On an Athlete Dying Young*—and I'm remembering now another poet—E. E. Cummings. The lower case letters were different—COOL."

▯

Later in the day when they were finished driving around the county and were heading back to Morgan's cabin, Christy asked, "When and where did you first GET LAID?"

Morgan replied, "It's going to take some time to answer your question—want to hear it?"

"Yep, we've got all the way back to your place—plenty of time," Christy replied.

"If you get bored, I'll cut to the chase."

"Oky-Doky," Christy answered.

"When I moved to Washington, D. C., after high school, I lived in a very ethnically diverse neighborhood, and one of the most 'diverse' people in it was a guy named Tony, and I don't know how he would have been classified in D.C. with regard to race or ethnicity. In my hometown, I'm sure he would have been classified as black, and would have lived in the black part of town. He wouldn't have been a good fit anywhere else. But there at that intersection in the heart of D.C., Tony fit in like a charm."

"What was he?" Christy asked.

"I didn't know what he was. Now, I might say a mix of black, Arab, Indian. I still don't know. What I do know is that he had something that attracted women, white women, Asian women, Black women, and all of them were PRETTY WOMEN. Every time he showed up on the sidewalk outside the dining hall, women hooked their arms through his and smiled at him adoringly. They hugged and kissed him on his cheeks, smiled and laughed at whatever he said. Tony was—average height, average weight, caramel skin, black slick-backed wavy hair, black eyes, some teeth were solid gold, and others were just trimmed with gold. When he smiled on a sunny day the street lit up, everything turned golden and happy. His shirts and trousers were always black and tight fitting, and YES he was well-hung judging from his bulging crotch. The heels of his shoes were an inch and a half high. Maybe he wasn't of average height after all. And his shoes were black and shiny with silver trim on the pointy toes."

"Were they shoes or boots?" Christy asked. "I've seen some boots like that."

"I'm not sure," Morgan replied. "I thought they were shoes, but they could have been boots."

"One Saturday morning, Tony and another guy were having breakfast in the neighborhood restaurant, and I could see them from the counter where I was sitting. The front door opened and a very exotic sexy woman walked in by herself and sat down in a booth. Tony immediately signaled the waitress to come over to his booth and whispered something in her ear; then she walked over to the sexy woman and whispered something in her ear. The woman looked over at the man the waitress was pointing to (Tony) and waved. She must have known him. Tony said good-bye to his friend and walked over to the woman's booth and sat down. After they gave the waitress their breakfast order, they talked, and she laughed a lot as women always did with Tony. He must have had a great personality. The waitress soon brought them their breakfast, and they started eating. When they finished, Tony picked up the check, slid dollar bills under his plate, paid the cashier and opened the door for the woman he had just treated to breakfast. From the counter, I watched them walk away from the restaurant. Tony had his arm around her back and his hand on her hip, which slid over to her ass as they made their way up the street."

"You watched all this?" Christy asked.

"Yeah, I had nothing else to do. Saturdays could be long days," Morgan answered and noticed that Christy was masking a yawn. "Is this boring you?"

"No, not really, I'm just kidding you," Christy replied. "But the story better get more interesting—still kidding."

"The story gets better or worse depending on how you look at it," Morgan replied.

"Good," Christy said, "I just love to hear stories about exotic, erotic, sexy women!"

"You asked me how I first got laid, didn't you?"

"Yes, I did—go on."

"Weeks later I was in that same restaurant getting ready to order breakfast at the counter when the same sexy woman came through the door and sat down in the very same booth as before, and I looked around for Tony, but I didn't see him. I don't know what made me do it...yes, I do—LUST made me do it. I heard a quiet voice in my head say—*Do what Tony did. Offer to buy her breakfast.* Then another quiet voice in my head said—*Don't be stupid! You aren't Tony, you're just a kid!* While my mind was vacillating, I found myself motioning to the waitress, and when she arrived at my side, it was too late to chicken out. I told her what I wanted her to do, and she smiled, 'You really want me to do that, sweetie?' she asked. No backing down now, I thought. While the waitress walked over to the woman, my nervousness increased, and I couldn't look. I thought about crawling or running out of the place."

Christy commented, "You were just eighteen, Morgan, but you had BALLS the size of grapefruits!"

"When I peeked over, I saw the waitress waving me over to the woman's booth. I walked over there with my head held high, chest out, and sat down in her booth. I slid across the slick, red plastic upholstery covering the bench seat and stopped midway across and looked directly into her face. This is what I saw—green eyes, shiny black hair cascading over her shoulders, dangling sparkling earrings, full red lips, beautiful white teeth, smooth blemish-free olive skin, and a low-cut, tight-fitting black sweater showing plenty of cleavage." Morgan paused.

"I'll bet you, she was Colombian—they are all like that—BEAUTIFUL and SEXY!"

"Why do you say that?" Morgan asked.

"I met a bunch of Colombian girls over at the university. They looked like that—dark, sexy, well-dressed—they had the total package! Should be a law against letting women like that into this country!—too much competition!"

Morgan didn't respond to Christy's comment.

"Just kidding," Christy said.

Morgan got back to his story. "While we ate, I asked questions, and fortunately, we finished eating before I ran out of questions to ask her. After I paid the cashier, we walked outside and she really surprised me when she said, 'Would you like to go to my apartment or would you like me to come to yours?' I didn't think she would be willing to spend another minute with such a boring person—boy… man…what was I? Mustering up as much confidence as I could, I answered—yes, definitely. Then she smiled and said, 'My apartment or yours?' That's when I realized that I had not made a choice, and I immediately said, let's go to YOUR APARTMENT, sheepishly knowing that I lived in a room—not an apartment."

"You were a boy growing up fast in a big city," Christy said.

"Walking up the street," Morgan said, "I wanted to put my arm around her back, as Tony had done, but I couldn't get my arm to go there. I was too scared, I guess."

Christy said, "You were young and exploring a whole new frigging world, Morgan."

"When we got to DuPont Circle, she took my hand and pulled it around her back and placed it on her hip, very, very close to her ass. My thoughts were: gonna get laid…might get laid…I hope I get laid."

"Were you a virgin, Morgan?" Christy asked disbelievingly.

"Yep," Morgan replied.

Christy stared at Morgan with a very perplexed expression on her face and said, assertively, "You should have gotten laid in high school, Morgan! Just about every girl and boy I went to school with got laid before graduating, for sure, and quite a few got laid before they got to high school. Someone as good looking as you should have had girls lined up."

"Thanks, but it just didn't happen," Morgan said. "Now, we're getting to the best or worst part of the story. Inside her apartment, she took off her jacket, and laid it on the sofa. Then she took my jacket and laid it on top of hers. When she turned to face me, I looked at her beautiful face: eyes, nose, lips, teeth, and then my attention went to the treasure that lay beneath her beautiful face and under her black, cashmere sweater—HER BREASTS. She stepped forward and ran her hands around my waist to the small of my back and then down to my ass. I kissed her and kept kissing her, but soon learned that I was doing TOO MUCH KISSING. Pulling back, she said in a tone I hadn't heard earlier, 'I've only got an hour for this. Do you want TO KISS or WHAT?' "

"I watched her shake her hair back from off her forehead and stare at me. I told her that I wanted to kiss, but quickly added, that I wanted to make love too. My answer didn't satisfy her. She stared and looked puzzled and could probably tell that I was puzzled. She then said, 'YOU KNOW THAT I'M A PROSTITUTE, don't you?' "

"NO—before, but—YES—now, I answered, flustered and embarrassed. She stepped back from me and grabbed the bottom of her sweater with both hands and pulled it over her head and flung it onto the sofa next to our jackets. My knees buckled as I looked at her big rounded beautiful breasts with nipples the size of marshmallows—MINIATURE marshmallows."

"My God, Morgan!" Christy exclaimed laughing. "The way you are describing things is HILARIOUS! I'm glad you requalified the SIZE of her nipples. LOVE IS IN THE DETAILS!"

"My lungs started sending messages to my heart for more OXYGEN. She asked with intensity—'Don't you want to make love to me!?' "

"I had just enough air in my lungs to respond, YES—absolutely!"

" 'Do you have THE MONEY!?' she said excitedly."

"Saliva began to collect on the back of my tongue. I swallowed and said, HOW MUCH do I need? But I already knew that any amount was going to be too much. When she told me, my head dropped. She placed her fingers under my chin immediately and lifted my head. 'I'm sorry, Morgan,' she said in a soft, sympathetic voice, 'I can't do this for FREE.' "

"Morgan was silent now. Christy was waiting for more, but Morgan remained silent.

"Is that it, Morgan?" Christy asked.

"Yes, that's it. I didn't get laid."

Christy laughed for a few seconds. Then she shook her head looking at Morgan and said, "I asked you when and where you first got laid? And you told me a LONG story, but you didn't answer my question!?"

"I know, but it was a FUNNY STORY, wasn't it? Much funnier than the one that would have answered your question. And that one would have been a VERY SHORT STORY!"

Christy laughed loudly and then asked another question—"Did she, whoever it was, say something like this—IS THAT IT!?"

Morgan nodded affirming that SHE had.

Christy smiled, "Do you want to know when and where I first got laid?"

Without any hesitation, Morgan replied, "No, I don't!"

◻

After Christy dropped him off, Morgan walked around the GREEN HOUSE, which now had a foundation, walls, and the structural beginnings of a sod roof. He walked through the front entrance and looked up three stories at the skylight openings where sunlight was streaming through silhouetting the finned tubes crossing the width of the vaulted ceiling. Each floor had balconies that overlooked the ground floor, which was a large circular patch of dirt surrounded by concrete. The dirt area would eventually be a garden containing flowers, vegetables, and even trees. His mind conjured up images of butterflies of various sizes and colors flying lazily above the trees and around the heat-collecting finned tubes. He couldn't believe his luck. When the light grew dim, he left the GREEN HOUSE and went to the cabin where he found his mother alone. Heather, Matt, and Raquel had gone down to the river. His mother asked him to sit with her. He took a position on the sofa and sighed. "It's been a long day, but seeing the progress on the GREEN HOUSE lifts me up."

Morgan's mother didn't comment on what he said. She was anxious to get on with a more important topic. "Heather and I had a conversation about her pregnancy and her wishes."

Morgan was surprised that his mother and Heather had had such a conversation. "Good," he replied.

"She wants TO HAVE the child, and she wants to RAISE the child," his mother said and paused.

Morgan looked at his mother and said, "That's news to me. I've never heard her say that. Did you say something to influence that decision?"

"No," his mother responded.

"What did you say during your conversation?"

"After she told me of her decision, I told her that she would face major challenges—just taking care of the child as a single parent, I told her, would be challenging enough, but on top of that, she might not even be able to finish high school, which assures her of minimum-wage jobs and leading and sharing an impoverished life with her child. I didn't sugarcoat anything."

Morgan didn't respond to what his mother had said, because he heard footsteps on the front porch. The three children came through the front door making sounds that indicated that they were cold. Morgan's cellphone started vibrating, so he pulled it out of his jacket pocket saw that it was Christy calling. She wanted him to know that a man had left a message on her phone identifying himself to be a friend of one of her former clients who had heard that she and Morgan were interested in a sizeable piece of land. After listening to her awhile longer, Morgan said, "What's the price?"

Christy kept talking and Morgan kept listening, then said, "What's the price?"

Christy then replied, "Listen, Morgan, he's a golfer and my intuition tells me that he might be willing to let you use this property FREE—if he LIKES YOU and YOUR PLAN."

"Christy!?" Morgan said emphatically intending to tell her to get realistic but she cut him off.

"This guy is a smart businessman," Christy said. "Before he called me he had already Googled you and knew everything about your VACATION in the penitentiary and your DUBIOUS business ventures in Newport News—DUBIOUS isn't flattering, is it?"

"No, probably not," Morgan answered.

"Regardless of that, he wants to meet with us on the property tomorrow at 10:00 a.m.—can you do that?"

Morgan told her he could, but then said, "Something doesn't ring right. Anytime someone tells me something is FREE, I put my fists deep down in my pockets, so they can't get their hands in there and pull my money out."

"My guess, Morgan," Christy replied, "is he owns some property, maybe lots of property, and for whatever reason, isn't interested in selling the piece of property we will see tomorrow. He's RICH—I already checked him out, so he doesn't need more money. Maybe this is KARMA working for you, Babe, maybe you get the use of this property for some buckets of balls and golf lessons. You can't predict what country people will do. WE'RE DIFFERENT!"

◻

The two of them did meet Ralph Tolbert on his property the following morning. They walked the rolling terrain despite the strong wind and snow flurries. Ralph asked lots of questions about Morgan's VISION for the driving range. Morgan was honest with Ralph, admitting that he would never have enough money to build it the way he would want it. Ralph responded, "I hear you Morgan, but describe your vision as if you had plenty of money."

Morgan explained his vision to Ralph and waited for Ralph's response as he wiped snowflakes off his forehead.

"Look, Morgan," Ralph said. "I've got some age on me. I refuse to say I'm old—so I just say what I just said—I've got some age on me."

Morgan replied, "I understand, Ralph. I don't plan to say I'm old when I get old either. I like your expression much better—I've got some age on me."

Ralph said, "I'm at a stage now, thank God, that I can help people out financially when they have a good idea and when that idea might benefit this town, this community." Ralph paused and looked at Morgan and Christy. They were standing side by side, still, and snow was sticking to their hair and clothes. "Do you two DESERVE to be helped out?"

Christy quickly responded, "Mr. Tolbert, this is Morgan's baby, not mine."

"I see," Ralph replied. "That's all right. Morgan, are you a man who DESERVES to be helped? Can I trust you to carry out YOUR VISION if I underwrite the project?"

Morgan answered, "Ralph you can trust me to ATTEMPT to carry out my vision, but you never know how things will go with a new business. If it doesn't go well, carrying out my vision might not happen."

Ralph stared at Morgan. Then he said, cornering a smile, "I'm going to back you."

¤

Before Catherine met with the Prison Advisory Committee, she anticipated that she would have to do a lot of explaining with regards to the expansion of programming and the cost. So she came prepared with a written statement that she read to them:

> Good afternoon committee members. Thank you for inviting me to speak with you about the expansion of our website offerings. The original idea with Morgan Make$ Money website was to provide qualified prisoners with the opportunity to acquire high tech knowledge and skills that would allow them to return to society better able to compete in today's job market. In just a few months, we have a website that is providing important information and advice to a substantial number of viewers—an audience large enough to attract advertisers and substantial advertising

fees. Now that a successful foundation has been laid, we want to step things up by expanding our offerings and prisoner participation. The website will now be called BCoolBSmartBFree. The new website will still provide advice on equity trading but, in addition, it will offer a broader range of subjects that will inform, educate, and entertain a wider mix of viewers. We envision segments that would deal with cooking, exercise, art, music, literature, acting, dance, health, bodybuilding, and more. The broader range of subjects will be viewed by our prison population and by people outside the prison. These subjects make life worth living. Exploring the things that make life worth living while in prison will allow our prisoners to re-enter society more able to APPRECIATE and ENJOY LIFE. They will become more participatory and more successful members of the web— the WEB of HUMANITY. Our viewers on the outside will learn as well and, through the learning, we see a good chance that they will be more able and motivated to make positive changes. Their life journey may well be different and better, because our programming will have provided them with new eyes, new ears, new imagination, new thoughts, new appetites and greater wellness. After going through many years of formal education, earning terminal degrees, working my way through various positions (leadership and nonleadership), I have found that once people become motivated to achieve a goal, NO ONE can stop them from achieving it. Should motivation not exist, there is very little that can be done from the outside. FAILURE is assured. So, members of this very important and vital committee, what we—the prison staff and our governor—

are all about is finding ways to INSPIRE and MOTIVATE people who have found their way into our prison. We also, most assuredly, want to inspire and motivate people on the outside who are leaning in this direction. We want them to stay out of prison. We want them to

BCoolBSmartBFree

That's what Catherine read to the Prison Advisory Committee. Some of the members smiled while others rolled their eyes, but they all came together at the end to approve the budget and the plan.

Before adjourning the meeting, one of the committee members asked the chairperson for permission to ask Ms. Sinclair a question. The committee member prefaced his question by saying that he should have taken the time to review Catherine's curriculum vitae but hadn't and offered his apology. Then he asked his question, "What degrees do you hold and from what institutions?"

Catherine smiled, "My undergraduate degree was a BS in psychology (University of Virginia), my masters DEGREES were in anthropology and philosophy (Vanderbilt), and my doctorate was in astrophysics (UC Berkeley)."

"No degrees in criminal justice?" the member asked.

"No, but I did spend some jail time in Berkeley," Catherine responded with a subtle smile.

The committee member who asked the question nodded his head without smiling. The other members of the committee leaned left and right whispering comments to one another and a few of them laughed quietly.

Another member said, "Very impressive, Dr. Sinclair."

Catherine quickly asked, "My degrees or the JAIL TIME?"

"Both!" the woman replied.

Another committee member asked, "How old were you when you got your first real job in the work-a-day world?"

"Thirty-four…thirty-five, I think."

"And what was it?"

"An investment bank on Wall Street hired me."

The committee member who asked that question shook his head, befuddled by Catherine's answer. "After all of that education, with advanced degrees in nonfinancial areas of study, why did you want to work for an investment bank and why did the bank want you!?"

"That's a very good question…Two things motivated me to go to work for an investment bank—I thought the work would be very interesting, and the money that they were offering me was simply irresistible, considering the debt I had amassed while getting my education."

"And why did the investment bank want to hire someone who didn't have any education or work experience in banking or finance?"

"They wanted to put a smart NON-MARTIAL ARTIST in a martial artist arena to improve their vision and imagination," Catherine replied.

The committee member responded, "They were looking for OUT OF THE BOX THINKING—yes?"

"Yes," Catherine answered.

"And how did that work out?"

"My income during those years would indicate that I performed extremely well, but a few years down the road, I got a PINK SLIP."

"Why?"

"They never said why."

"You were fired?'

"No, I was sent back out into the world, because they no longer needed my services. If you choose TO RUN WITH THE DOGS, you've got to accept DYING LIKE A DOG," Catherine replied.

"Really!?"

"BUT—NO WHIMPERING."

"I know we have gone beyond our scheduled time," the committee chair said, "but I have a question that I've been wanting to ask for some time. Why don't you use your title—Doctor—you've earned it?"

"That title seems to put a wall up between me and other people, so I don't use it. I know I'm a DOCTOR?"

"Fair enough, Ms. Sinclair. Thank you for your presentation and willingness to spend some extra time with us today—we appreciate it."

¤

The next morning the newspaper reported information from Catherine's appearance before the Prison Advisory Committee. The reporter even included the last questions that were put to Catherine and her responses. Morgan read the article while he waited to see her, and the first thing he said when he entered her office was, "What was HIS point, Catherine?"

"I'm not sure, of course, but I think he was exposing in a very public way that I have enjoyed a very privileged life, ensconced in academia until I was thirty-five, then moved on to a Wall Street financial powerhouse, which provided me with a lavish annual income without having the education nor work experience to justify it."

"Why make that point NOW?" Morgan asked.

"I think he's going after the governor, not me. The governor, as you know, is looking ahead to his next political position and some people don't want him to have it."

"I see," Morgan said. "Your job is not secure, is it?"

"No, when the governor goes, I won't be far behind him."

"Then what?"

"In a very short period of time, I will have neither a husband nor a job, which will make me very FREE to do whatever I want. The lavish income I earned on Wall Street will underwrite my next adventure."

"I have good news. Christy and I met with a wealthy gentleman yesterday who is willing to help me establish the Golf Driving Range of Loveville. By HELP I mean he's offering to provide the land and everything else to get it rolling…NO STRINGS ATTACHED!"

Catherine smiled, "Sounds too good to be true. Doesn't it?"

"It does, but what do I have to lose?"

"Get a lawyer and have him or her look over the contract," Catherine advised.

"I can't afford a lawyer, Catherine," Morgan replied.

"Can you afford to put your heart and soul into this venture and then possibly have it taken away from you with no recourse?"

"I understand what you are saying, Catherine, but we won't even have a contract. It's going to be OUR WORD and a HANDSHAKE," Morgan said, raising his eyebrows.

Catherine laughed. "Boy, what a trusting soul you've become! You weren't always this way—were you?"

"No, I wasn't, and I'm not that trusting now. It's just an offer and an opportunity that I can't pass up, and I'm in a great position because I have nothing to lose and everything to gain."

Catherine remained silent, thinking, then responded. "Suppose you work your ass off, which I know you will do, and this guy gets a great offer for his property and sells it to a big corporation which has no use for the Golf Driving Range of Loveville and plows it under. How are you going to feel about that?"

Morgan took a deep breath and sighed. "So be it, " Morgan answered. "While I don't have faith in a God who will ultimately make things right, I do have actual experiences that have taught me that I can lose everything and survive it and even benefit from the loss."

Catherine giggled, "My, my, Mr. Armstrong. I'm standing here admiring you and your strength of character. Maybe I should buy the property next to yours and establish the Loveville Tennis Academy!? I'll soon be looking for another way to earn a living."

Morgan replied, "I'll give you Ralph's contact information. He might like that idea."

"Thanks, but I'm going to have to stick with my job at the prison awhile longer. As long as the governor is in office, I think I'm safe."

□

Morgan left Catherine's office and went to the BCoolBSmartBFree set where crew members were setting up for videotaping. Bob was sitting in a chair across from a well-known stock market blogger. Both were looking at their notes while they were being wired for sound. The bank of lights overhead came on flooding them with brilliant light. The cameramen positioned and focused their cameras. When the director pointed to Bob, he introduced himself, the program, and his guest—Granville Newman.

Morgan sat down and was watching the beginning of the interview when suddenly the director stepped onto the set and told the cameraman to stop taping. Something had gone wrong with the sound. He checked the small microphones pinned to Bob's and Granville's shirts, and they seemed to be okay. When they didn't find the problem right away, Morgan looked at the shooting schedule and left the studio to check his e-mails. Later, when he returned to the set, another prisoner on the website staff, Phillip Gordon, was interviewing Dr. Justin Eden:

> Dr. Eden: I'm passionate about health and wellbeing—
> WELLNESS, and I'm angry that we have failed to educate
> children and adults about how to take care of their bodies.
> It isn't ROCKET SCIENCE. We take better care of our
> cars than we do our bodies.
> Phillip Gordon: Why is that?
> Dr. Eden: Because all of us know that if we do not take care of
> our cars, they will not perform well, will eventually break-
> down, and cost us a lot of money to get them fixed.
> Phillip Gordon: I think you are right, Dr. Eden. When I was in
> high school, I hated sitting in health class, and I couldn't
> wait to get home to work on my car—to fix it or make it
> faster, cooler.
> Dr. Eden: Yes, exactly. Unfortunately, health classes didn't and
> don't get us excited about our bodies, and our bodies don't
> come with owner manuals. Without attention, care, and
> maintenance, our bodies breakdown, and when they do,
> we don't have a manual to help us fix the problems. We
> go to doctors who prescribe drugs to fix the discomfort or
> pain we're experiencing. We take the drugs, and the symp-
> toms go away, and insurance companies cover the cost of
> the drugs. So we get rid of the discomfort and pain—the

symptoms of what's wrong—and we don't even experience the financial pain of paying for the drugs, because insurance companies pick up the cost of those drugs. All this makes us think—ALL IS WELL, WHEN IT ISN'T.

Phillip Gordon: How do we get out of the situation we're in?

Dr. Eden: When our cars breakdown, we have to pay to have them fixed, or we EDUCATE ourselves and fix them ourselves. Whether WE FIX our cars or PAY SOMEONE ELSE to fix them, our cars' problems GET FIXED. When people and doctors resort to the use of drugs to fix problems—only THE SYMPTOMS get fixed, which means the PROBLEMS are still there, and will remain there, along with the NEW DAMAGE and PROBLEMS that the drugs—toxins—create.

Phillip Gordon: What's the solution?

Dr. Eden: EDUCATION is the first thing, and I can see that our time is just about over so I don't have time to explore this further.

Phillip Gordon: Before we end this session, Dr. Eden, give us one piece of advice right now that will get us on the track to better health and wellness.

Dr. Eden: Stop eating things that contain SUGAR and WHEAT. SUGAR is poison, and WHEAT is no longer the wheat OUR PARENTS consumed. EXERCISE six days out of seven, REST one day, EAT healthy, and SLEEP seven to eight hours every night.

After the taping was over, Morgan ran into Ms. Spangler in the hallway. "I heard you were here," she said. "So I came down to see if you had brought my Revolutionary Bra back."

"I'm glad you ran into me," Morgan said. "It's in my bus."

"Good," Ms. Spangler replied. "Why don't you come over to my place for dinner? Return it then."

"I can't," he replied.

Morgan couldn't believe he was going to give up a chance to get laid. Middle age was catching up with him, he thought.

Ms. Spangler said, "Are you avoiding my overtures, because you are interested in Catherine?"

Morgan was surprised by Ms. Spangler's question. "I am attracted to Catherine, but I don't think she's interested in me."

"So why don't you take me up on my invitation—no commitment."

"Because I'm involved with another woman in Loveville."

"THAT'S good, Morgan, because I don't think you're going to get anywhere with Catherine."

"Have you and Catherine talked about this?" Morgan replied.

Ms. Spangler smiled. "No, but word is—Catherine isn't interested in men, sexually."

Morgan responded, "She's married, Ms. Spangler. SEPARATED now, which should indicate that she has been and is attracted to men."

"Maybe that's what was wrong with her marriage—her husband was of the wrong GENDER. Regardless of all that Morgan, if things don't work out with HER or in Loveville, let me know. But don't wait too long."

"Why are you interested in me?" Morgan inquired.

She winked, "Good question! Honestly, I think it's your SMELL more than your looks."

"I'm sorry that I can't take you up on your invitation, Ms. Spangler," Morgan said and realized that he didn't know her first name so he asked her. "What's your first name?"

"Natalie," she said. Then she added, "Ah, come home with me, Morgan. I just want you to know HOW GOOD IT can be— besides, I want my Revolutionary Bra back NOW—I'm not all I can be without it!"

Morgan had started walking away but he stopped and said, "I'll FedEx it back to you here, tomorrow, I promise," and then turned and started heading for the front doors.

Catherine came around the corner and saw Ms. Spangler and Morgan who was almost out of the building. She approached Ms. Spangler and said, "Are you still helping him with the IRS thing?"

Ms. Spangler replied, "No, but you know what, Catherine, I think he's very interested in you."

Catherine said, "How so?"

"Sexually!" Ms. Spangler replied. "Are you interested in him?"

Catherine paused and thought about her answer. "Maybe?"

Ms. Spangler looked at Catherine, "Now, let me be honest with you—RUMOR has it that you are not interested in men?"

"Well, Ms. Spangler, that rumor is wrong. I am interested in MEN—I was married, you know."

"I know, but you aren't now. The RUMOR MILL has it that your break up was because you weren't taking care of business at home."

Catherine cocked her head and replied, "Isn't this quite the conversation!"

"It beats PRISON TALK," Ms. Spangler replied.

Catherine asked, "Would you like to have sex with Morgan? Our prison psychiatrist told me that he was pretty good."

"Yes, I would like to have sex with Morgan. Our shrink TOLD ME that he was AWESOME."

Catherine responded, "Maybe she did characterize his performance as awesome, but I would never use the word awesome. So maybe Morgan was AWESOME, which trumps PRETTY GOOD."

Ms. Spangler smiled. "What I'm thinking is that Morgan is never going to come to my bed until YOU TELL HIM you're not interested in having sex with him."

Catherine stared silently at Ms. Spangler, who was waiting for an answer to the question that was implicit in her statement.

"I'm not ready to tell him that," Catherine replied. "The jury is still out."

□

It was Saturday morning and Catherine arrived early with muffins she had baked that morning, and Morgan and his family were enjoying the biscuits and gravy that Morgan's mother had made when Christy pulled up next to the cabin in her truck. She and her son Michael walked up the steps, knocked on the door, and entered.

Christy immediately smelled coffee and the freshly baked muffins and biscuits, and said, "Something smells scrumptious!"

Catherine stood up and went over to the counter where her muffins were sitting. "I'll put a couple of muffins that I baked this morning on paper plates for you and your son."

Christy looked at Catherine and said, "You don't have to bother. I can do it, and thanks for baking them."

Catherine put the muffins on a couple of plates and handed them to Christy. "Hope you like orange-cranberry?" Christy and her son gestured that they did.

Christy looked at Morgan and said, "Spring will be here faster than you think. What would you like around the GREEN HOUSE?"

"What do you think?" Morgan asked.

"What ideas do you have—children, Mrs. Armstrong, Catherine? It's never too early to start planning."

No one offered any ideas, so Christy said, "I've got my sketch-book, and I'll be playing with ideas today—let me know your thoughts."

Later in the day with rake in hand, Catherine walked over to Morgan and took a standing position next to him. She rested her chin on top of her hands, which were wrapped around the end of the rake handle. He was leaning on his shovel looking across the yard at the GREEN HOUSE. Without looking at Morgan, she said, "Heather's beginning to doubt the appropriateness of her decision to keep the baby."

Morgan looked at Catherine, surprised. "She's changing her mind every other day."

"Heather," Catherine said, "is thinking not only about her-self now, but also about others who will be impacted by her deci-sion—YOU, her grandmother, sister, brother, and friends. THIS is a good thing."

"She's growing up, maturing fast," Morgan said.

"Her body is changing and so is her mind, one influences the other—it's funny how we separate the two," Catherine remarked.

"What do you think, Catherine?"

Catherine lifted her chin off her hands, "All of us know that the easiest thing to do would be to give the child to someone who desperately wants a child to rear and to love."

"Here's where a belief in a God would be helpful," Morgan said as Christy arrived at his side.

"What were you saying?" Christy asked.

"I was saying that if I believed in God, things would be much easier. I could just relax knowing, believing that God would help Heather make the right decision," Morgan replied.

"I was much older than Heather—twenty-six, I think—when I had to make that decision—abort, give away, keep," Christy said. "You can see today what I chose to do. I chose to get married and raise the child. As I understand it, marriage and abortion are not options for Heather—so it's put the baby up for adoption or raise the child by herself."

"SHE WON'T BE ALONE," Morgan replied emphatically.

"When I said—BY HERSELF—I didn't mean that Heather wasn't going to have help raising the child. I meant that she wasn't going to have a HUSBAND."

"Sorry about the TONE," Morgan said as he glanced at Christy.

"My marriage hasn't worked out," Christy admitted, "but I'm thankful that I made the decision not to abort or put Michael up for adoption."

After Christy's declaration, Catherine cleared her throat and said, "Quite a few years ago I chose to abort our pregnancy, because it wasn't, in our opinion, the right time to have a child. Using HINDSIGHT now, I wish we had gone through to term. I wish that child were here today, but who knows what would have happened? I do believe in a God and that belief helps me believe that WE—me and my husband—made the right decision—a decision that PRAYER and GOD helped US make."

Christy looked at Catherine and asked, "What decision did you make?"

Catherine paused and said, "We aborted."

Later after all of the construction had concluded for the day, Christy and Michael toured the GREEN HOUSE by themselves.

When they came out of the house, Christy saw Morgan standing alone, eyeing his family's future home. She and Michael walked over to him. "Michael and I are going home now. Thanks for a great day. My son really enjoyed himself." Christy added that she wouldn't be able to see him the next day and asked when he and Ralph Tolbert were going to get back together.

"We're going to meet on the property Monday to talk about the buildings that will be needed at the driving range. Want to be there?" he asked.

After Christy told him that she did want to be there, she pulled out her phone and recorded it on her calendar. "Time?" she asked.

"TEN A.M."

Christy put the time down and looked at Morgan. "Is Catherine heading back to Richmond, or WHAT?"

The sound of WHAT? got Morgan's attention. It told him that Christy was upset, and he began wondering how best to respond.

"I don't know what time she'll be heading back to Richmond, soon, probably," he answered and kept his eyes focused on her face.

His response and inquisitive stare made Christy scrunch-up her nose and face a bit. She shrugged her shoulders. She then looked over at her son and said, "Thank Mr. Armstrong for letting us come over and help."

Her son thanked Morgan and added, "That's a really nice house. I'd like to come back next weekend and work some more."

Christy rubbed the top of her son's head and said laughing, "That's right, sonny boy! Invite yourself back."

After dinner, Catherine and Morgan left the cabin and went down to the gravel road. As they walked up the mountain, they gazed occasionally off the side of the road at the water rushing over and around the boulders.

"I'm glad you brought your mother to the cabin," Catherine said. "Having met her, I'm now interested in knowing more about your father. Did you two ever achieve a good relationship?"

"Not really. The closest we came to a good relationship was at the end—the last couple of years of his life—when he had cancer.

Maybe it was the last year when we all knew it had spread from his lungs to other parts of his body and was terminal."

"That's sad," Catherine said.

"There was one time when he was in the hospital, in bed, and I was there with him, just me, no one else was there. We had talked a little and, for us, we were probably talked out. We had little in common. But I wanted to say for the first time in my life—I love you, Dad—but I could not get those words out of my mouth, and I think he wanted to say he loved me, which would have been—THE ONLY TIME. Even with his drunken, inexcusable behavior throughout my childhood, I think I loved him at the end, and shame on me for not being able to say those words I LOVE YOU, DAD. He was on his DEATH BED. It would have been so simple, but I didn't. I never attempted to say those words again and time ran out... NO CLOSURE."

"So sorry, Morgan," Catherine said and gathered her thoughts in silence...*I was always Daddy's little girl and Mom was good with that.* "I had a conversation with your mother today, and when I found a good opening to explore a very personal chapter in your life, I took it."

"What chapter was that?" Morgan asked.

"THE FIGHT you had with your father."

"Uh huh," Morgan uttered looking down at the gravel road.

"I asked her if they—she and your father—told the truth to the Social Services people when they described what happened that evening."

"You really asked her that?"

"Yes," Catherine answered.

"What did she say?" Morgan asked.

"She admitted that they were not honest about it. She LIED and your father was silent," Catherine replied.

"I never inquired," Morgan said.

"Your mother said she told the Social Services people that you started the fight."

"That's hard to believe," Morgan said.

"I asked her why she lied, and she said she didn't want your father to get into trouble."

"So she didn't mind getting me into trouble."

"She didn't know that they would put you in juvenile detention," Catherine replied. "She was afraid that if they knew the truth, your father might go to jail and ultimately lose his job."

"That wasn't the first time, he beat her, and it wasn't the first time that I came to her defense." She never reported any of it, and it scared the hell out of me and my older sisters every time it happened," Morgan said.

I think you and your mother should talk about THIS," Catherine said as she took Morgan's hand and held it as they walked in silence. Shortly, Morgan stopped walking and looked at Catherine. "Thank you for having that conversation with my mother. I have a feeling that it was helpful TO HER."

"How?" Catherine asked.

"You gave her an opportunity to get the truth out," Morgan replied.

They started walking, again in silence for a while. Morgan was thinking about what he had just learned and how nice it was having Catherine in his life. He turned his face toward Catherine and said, "Do you want to be in my life?"

Catherine quickly responded, "I AM in your life, Morgan."

"Right now, I have YOU and CHRISTY in my life, but I don't think things can go on this way much longer."

"I have sensed that," Catherine replied.

"Do you see that SOMEONE has to go?"

"I don't see that," Catherine replied, matter-of-factly.

"You DON'T SEE THAT!?" he said, surprised.

"Other people, cultures, around the world don't have a problem with men having multiple women—wives, partners. I wouldn't have a problem sharing you with her."

"I can't see you doing that, Catherine."

"Much of what goes on in life, Morgan, happens between the ears," Catherine replied. "Change your WORDS, change your

THOUGHTS and you change your LIFE or how you EXPERIENCE your life."

"Are you telling me that you could be in my life ALONG WITH CHRISTY?"

"Yes, if that's what you desire. Do you love Christy?"

After thinking, Morgan replied, "To be honest, Catherine, I'm not sure what that word really means even though I have used it many times. I can say that I love BEING with Christy, and I love BEING with you, and the two experiences are different, but both give me joy—I could substitute the word LIKE and perhaps it would mean the same thing."

"Perhaps, it would," Catherine replied.

"What does that word mean to you, Catherine, LOVE?"

"With regards to MEN and WOMEN and RELATIONSHIPS, no matter how they are configured?"

"Yes," Morgan replied, not knowing exactly what she meant.

"You know BOOKS have been written on this subject, so giving you an answer right here and now will be quite a challenge."

"Okay."

"First let me say that there are DEGREES of LOVE that we have for other human beings. The higher the degree—the greater the love. The highest degree I believe would be POSSESSING LOVE that would predispose someone to give up their life for the sake of another. Giving up our life can be taken to mean—literally giving up LIVING for another, but it can also mean, I believe, GIVING UP what we WANT to benefit another."

"Uh huh."

"I don't know where my love for you ranks, right now, on the various levels of love, but it's high enough that it would allow me to let go of the traditional ONE-MAN–ONE-WOMAN relationship."

My relationship preference would be YOU and ME, but I could accept a THREESOME, but only if the three of us LOVE ONE ANOTHER."

"Oh!" Morgan said, excitedly. "That's a BIG IF!"

"Our lives would be wrought with acrimony if we didn't love each other," Catherine replied.

"Catherine, this is going to take some time to unravel and understand. What you have said is making me—I don't know what word can describe HOW I FEEL!?"

"Pick a word, Morgan—shocked, confused, disoriented, unsettled—"

"THRILLED!" Morgan blurted out surprising her.

"Okay, I was on the wrong track, Morgan. THRILLED is a good word and a good feeling!"

"I'm THRILLED that you want to spend your life with me, but I can't see YOU in a THREESOME!"

◻

Morgan and Christy were traveling in separate vehicles, but they arrived at Ralph Tolbert's property at the same time and found Ralph gazing over the rolling terrain. He told them that he had gotten there about an hour early, so he could mark the borders of the property that he was going to dedicate to the driving range, so they could see what they had to work with. Pointing, Ralph told Morgan and Christy to look out beyond where they were standing and pick out the orange markers that he had planted in the ground earlier approximating the perimeter of the property. Once it was obvious that they had located the orange markers, Ralph asked, "Is that area big enough to accommodate all the elements of your vision for the Golf Driving Range of Loveville?"

Morgan and Christy shook their heads, affirming that the property was big enough. Then Ralph explained, "Our perception of the size of a piece of land changes after we start putting things on it, so don't worry about realizing later that the size of this property is not adequate because, if you need more land, we can expand the borders that you are looking at now." Morgan and Christy still agreed that the size of the property Ralph had established was more than adequate but were relieved and grateful that Ralph was so thoughtful.

After ascertaining that the size of the property was adequate, Ralph asked Morgan to describe all of the physical things that he was going to need (buildings, outdoor lighting, kitchen, vehicles, earth moving) and Morgan immediately opened a folder and pulled out a business plan that contained a comprehensive list of physical things that were going to be needed, as well as other things that weren't physical. After a quick review of Morgan's business plan, Ralph told him that he would pay for all of the physical things that were going to be needed to get the driving range built, but operational expenses would belong exclusively to him. Once Morgan had accepted responsibility for operational expenses, Ralph told him that he would not have to pay rent, or any other fee, but would expect him to use some of the profits to improve the property and to operate the business in ways that would benefit the community. At the end of their meeting, Morgan and Ralph shook hands and that was it—no written contract.

After they waved goodbye to Ralph, Morgan and Christy walked over to a large boulder close to the road and sat down. Morgan had suspected for a while that Christy was wondering in a negative way about his relationship with Catherine, and thought that they needed to talk about it. Even if Christy didn't need to talk about, Morgan conceded, he needed to talk about it. Just as he was ready to get the conversation started, Christy looked at him and said, "Did Catherine stay with you last night?"

"No," Morgan responded. "She went back to Richmond."

"Did you have sex with her before she went back to Richmond?"

"No," Morgan said and cornered a smile, not because Christy's question was funny, but because he was getting annoyed. "Before you ask the next question, I'm going to answer it—NO, THERE WERE NO HUGS or KISSES." He was waiting for her to ask—*Did you hold hands?*—and while he waited, he couldn't decide how he would answer—YES or NO—but she didn't ask that question, and he didn't volunteer that they had.

"Is she special to you, Morgan?"

"Yes, she's special. She helped me in many ways while I was in prison."

"Do you love her?"

When Morgan heard that question, he started remembering his conversation with Catherine the previous evening. He replied,

"LOVE is slippery, as slippery as a small piece of wet soap. One minute you've got it, and the next minute, it squirts out of your hands, and down the drain it goes."

Christy remained quiet for a few seconds, speculating on why Morgan had avoided answering her question. "When we first met, as you know, I was separated from my husband and hadn't had sex in quite a while. You being a stranger to the area appeared to be the perfect candidate for discreet sex—stranger, older, and divorced. All the other men in the area wouldn't have made suitable sex partners. As I told you then—Loveville is a very small town and everybody is into everybody else's business. I'm sure I told you then that I was just interested in having sex, and wanted it kept secret. I was just horny."

"You did tell me that and that was just fine with me, because I was horny as well."

"Now, even though we haven't had sex—thanks to my crazy husband and an emergency medical device—I find myself LIKING you, maybe even LOVING YOU." Christy stopped there waiting to hear something back, but Morgan didn't say anything. "Now, I find myself jealous and afraid that I might not have you in my life for much longer, because there's competition."

"Catherine opened my eyes a bit wider last night when she said that she didn't see why I needed to exclude YOU or HER from my life."

"You were thinking THAT and discussing THAT with HER!?"

"Yes."

"Yippee!" Christy exclaimed. "You were talking with Catherine about possibly EXCLUDING me from your life—DUMPING ME!"

"I wasn't talking about DUMPING YOU. I was talking about being in a position where it appears that one of you has to go."

"Well, Morgan, that makes me feel much better!" Christy said sarcastically. "AND what came out of your discussion?" Christy asked.

"I still haven't totally unraveled what she said."

"She's so DAMN SMART isn't she?"

Morgan replied, "She is smart. Much smarter than I am."

"And ME!"

Morgan looked at Christy. "Do you enjoy being with me?"

"Of course, I do, Morgan," Christy answered.

"I enjoy being with you, too. And I enjoy and benefit from being with Catherine." He paused girding himself for a negative reaction from Christy. "I can see that you are jealous and feel threatened by Catherine being in the picture."

"Yes, you should, because I am," Christy replied.

"Does that mean we can't have a relationship, if Catherine remains in the picture?"

Christy looked sternly at Morgan. "You know that can't work. Two women and one man? What did Catherine say? You did ask her, didn't you?"

"She said she COULD ACCEPT a relationship that included the THREE of US," Morgan replied.

Christy jumped up and exclaimed, "HOT DAMN—I'm finally looking down the barrel of—*ménage a trois!*"

Morgan laughed.

Christy stared at Morgan. "Are you serious!? Wow, that chick had me fooled!"

"I don't think Catherine was focusing on *ménage a trois*. I think she was focusing on NO ONE BEING EXCLUDED—YOU or HER."

"Are we back to hippie days?" Christy said then pretended to be taking a hit from a reefer.

"No, I don't think so."

"She's got to be a MORMON or a MORON! Which is it?"

Morgan laughed and said, "Neither!"

"Do you think you could be happy sharing a life with—ME, MICHAEL, and CATHERINE?" Christy asked.

"Do you think YOU and MICHAEL could be happy sharing a life with me, Catherine, my mother, two daughters, a son, and a grandchild!?"

"Boy!" Christy exclaimed and started laughing. "I can hear a minister saying—Christy, do you wish to join Morgan and Catherine in UNLAWFUL WEDLOCK?"

Morgan didn't respond. He was silently telling himself that he had made a mistake and was looking for a way out of the conversation before it was too late.

"Where are we, Morgan!? A marriage between a man and a woman is hard enough. Here, we are talking about a marriage with a man with three kids (that's you), a senior citizen (that's your mother), a woman with a kid from a different union (that's me), another woman with no kids (that's Catherine), and a grand kid on the way with a teenage mother (Heather) and NO FATHER. How could a woman resist that invitation!?"

Morgan took a deep breath and looked up at Christy. "I'm sorry, Christy. You have every right to be angry. I'm trying to find a way to keep you and Catherine in my life."

"Angry, yes! I am ferociously angry, Morgan!" Christy took a breath. "THIS, THIS, WHAT IS THIS!?"

"THIS is not love, Christy. This is SELFISHNESS!" Morgan said quietly. Christy repeated Morgan's answer silently in her head. Then said, "YOURS or MINE?"

"YOURS," Morgan answered. "MINE too," he quickly added. "I WANT something and YOU WANT something."

"AND CATHERINE WANTS SOMETHING!" Christy screamed. "She's selfish too, but she's WILD OPEN—No, not WILD OPEN—she's WIDE OPEN. She'll agree to anything, it seems, JUST TO BE WITH YOU!"

"She won't agree to a THREESOME, however, if we can't LOVE ONE ANOTHER," Morgan added.

Christy jumped up and shouted, "OH, WHAT A BITCH! I just want YOU and YOUR KIDS in my life—not Catherine—and besides—I can't see myself LOVING her." Morgan stood up and touched her shoulder. Christy leaned back and took a breath then started singing a Beach Boys song about a little surfer. When she couldn't remember any more lyrics, she said with less anger, "Catherine's a West Coast chick, smart, beautiful, highly educated, and I'm a Virginia farm girl who works with her hands in dirt. How are we gonna LOVE EACH OTHER, Morgan?"

Christy wanted to say more but didn't. She walked hurriedly away from Morgan toward her truck parked in a field close to the road. A voice in his head said—*follow her, go after her, don't let her go!* but instead of moving forward, he turned his back to the road and her truck. When he heard Christy's driver's side door squeak open, he stared across the rolling terrain that would in time be the Golf Driving Range of Loveville, and waited guardedly for the collision of truck door to cab, and when it came, it sent a fierce, heavy wave of noise across the field, which caused him to tighten up and listen for the other noises that would follow. The Brawny V8 engine started with a deep-throated roar and then settled into a purr. He asked himself—*Is she waiting for me to run over to the truck and ask her not to be angry, not to leave?* Then he heard her tires spinning, hissing as they spun in the loose dirt, and he visualized the low clouds of dirt and gravel the tires were creating, as they cut wide, deep curved channels in the ground. *She's backing out onto the road,* he thought, and after that thought, Morgan turned his head and looked back and saw the truck's rear brake lights turn bright red, as the rearward motion of the truck came to a sudden stop. *Should I wave her back or run to her and say I'm sorry—I apologize—Please forgive me?* He did not hear an answer to his question. He turned his head away from the road and Christy's truck and waited for the last noises of her departure. The oversized tires squealed and laid rubber as they tore forward down the country road, and he knew without turning around that she was not looking back.

With the empty field in front of him, Morgan started imagining the buildings, signs, practice tees, putting greens, and sand traps that would soon be part of the natural landscape. The joy that usually rose within him when imagining those things was not there now. He thought about what he had said earlier—LOVE IS SLIPPERY—and then he witnessed another word finding its way into that simple sentence: Love and JOY are slippery. *At one moment, they're there, and in the next moment, they're gone.*

He looked at the VW bus, no longer in mint condition, sitting about where the main building of the golf driving range would eventually stand. His lips formed a half-smile, as he put the tips of two fingers to his throat and found evidence that his heart was still beating, and he looked at the sun that was setting behind a close range of mountains, spreading golden light everywhere, and that was enough evidence for him, that the sun would rise again in the morning, giving him another day to make things RIGHT or BETTER.

◻

It was an early spring morning. The university students and contract construction workers were already at the GREEN HOUSE and were scheduled to complete the final small things that needed to be done before the grand opening, which was just days away. Christy was there with a truck bed full of plants and flowers. So was Catherine who brought wallpaper to hang in a bath room on the second floor. Morgan's kids and Michael were helping the university students complete their projects, and Morgan's mother was baking scones and making fresh lemonade and iced tea, because the spring day was supposed to be a hot one. Ray, Ethel, and their kids were down at the river hoping to catch a lot of trout. There would be many mouths to feed at the end of the day, because many hands, old and young, were contributing to the creation of the GREEN HOUSE.

PART III

The Collapse

Ω

The completion of the GREEN HOUSE was accomplished mid-April, which left Morgan free to devote full attention to the construction of his golf driving range. As the building and grounds developed, Morgan and Ralph Tolbert, who was financing the project, thought the original name for the business—Golf Driving Range of Loveville—wasn't comprehensive nor classy enough and changed it to Central Virginia Golf Academy. Morgan's children helped with the construction on the weekends while school was in, and when school let out for summer vacation, they worked twenty to thirty hours a week earning $5.00 an hour.

Heather was heading into her last three months of pregnancy and had decided to have her baby at home with a midwife assisting with the delivery. Morgan's mother felt better and was more mobile than she was in the assisted living facility. His mother was definitely happier, Morgan thought, because she saw herself differently. At the assisted living facility, she saw herself as needy, whereas at the GREEN HOUSE, she saw herself as needed, giving her a new sense of purpose and value.

Christy had made her thoughts very clear to Morgan with regard to their relationship and Catherine. She told him, "I'm not going for *ménage a trois*. It's going to be me or her. Take your pick. If you want her, I'm gone." Christy did tolerate Catherine's presence when everyone was working on the GREEN HOUSE, and she never pressed him on a final decision. During the weeks when the final small projects were being completed on the house, Morgan was with Christy more than he was with Catherine, and Christy made sure that she and Morgan had plenty of sex. In Christy's mind, sex was her trump card, and she was very happy to play it over and over. Catherine's trump cards, as Christy saw it, were her mind, education, and something else, but she didn't know what the *something else* was. Regardless of the something else, Christy thought frequent and fantastic sex would sway Morgan to choose her as his one and only partner.

His decision this time, Morgan had decided, wouldn't be exclusively based on looks and sex, as it probably was in the past. He wanted to be more mature and deliberative now that he was looking for wife number four. When Morgan was weighing Christy's positive attributes, he saw her as a young woman, but not too young, gorgeous, bright, entrepreneurial, hardworking, passionate, highly sexual, and *freewheeling*—another trait that he could never define, but he knew Christy had it the first time he saw her jump out of her pickup truck at the convenience store in Loveville.

Catherine, by comparison, was older than Christy, and on the good side of being older, she possessed greater maturity and rationality. Along with Catherine's edge in maturity came an expansive formal education that fostered a unique and beautiful mind—a feature, surprisingly, that Morgan enjoyed and admired as much as or more than her other positive attributes such as generosity, trustworthiness, selflessness, confidence, courage, and equanimity. In the end, however, when he was comparing Catherine with Christy, he couldn't make a comparison in one very important category—sex. He and Christy had finally consummated their relationship, but he and Catherine had never come close to having intercourse. Truth be known, they had never hugged or kissed.

After recording all of the positive attributes of both women on a piece of notebook paper, Morgan became even more aware of the merits of a *ménage a trois* relationship, and the new insight had nothing to do with his being able ethically to have sexual relations with two women at the same time. Its new appeal or merit grew out of his realization that enjoying the positive attributes of TWO women would be superior to enjoying the positive attributes of just ONE woman. Its increased appeal was so great to Morgan that he chanced proposing it one more time to Christy. He worded it this way: "If I promised to be a faithful and devoted husband to you, would you give me permission to continue a close friendship with Catherine?"

Christy was caught off guard by his question, because she thought the matter had been settled. So she didn't respond immediately. She felt her heart start racing, then she began picking up on the familiar physical symptoms of anger running throughout her entire body—head to toe. Concurrent with her awareness of physical changes going on in her body, she was also experiencing a whirlwind of words and strings of words bumping around in her mind; some words were pulled into the vortex that was created by the spinning, while other words and groups of words slid off to the side and out of contention for consideration. Eventually, Christy's response to Morgan's question took shape in a form not much different from what he had proffered. She said, "If I promised to be a faithful and devoted WIFE to you would you give me permission to have a close friendship with ANOTHER MAN?"

Morgan wasn't caught off guard with Christy's response, because he had pondered what her response might be and was ready with his answer. "I'm pretty sure I could handle it."

Christy immediately replied, "Does that mean you WOULD give me permission?"

"Yes," he said. "I WOULD give you permission, if you believed that having a close relationship with another man would benefit ME and OUR relationship."

Christy mulled over what Morgan had said and replied, "And that's what you believe right now—that having a close friendship with Catherine would benefit ME and OUR relationship?"

Without hesitating, Morgan said, "Yes."

Christy smiled at him, but he wasn't sure how to take it, because he had not seen THAT SMILE before. He just waited silently not knowing what was coming.

"Okay," Christy said crisply. "I'll take a leap of faith and give you permission to continue your close friendship with Catherine, AND—I'm going to bring A GUY over tomorrow afternoon that I've been wanting you to meet."

Morgan's eyes opened wide, his jaw dropped, and his mouth hung open and remained that way until Christy could no longer hold a straight face—"Bazinga—got you, didn't I!?"

Ω

It was a very routine summer morning when it all started. Morgan was in the kitchen fixing coffee while Heather and Raquel prepared breakfast. Matt had just turned on the big flat screen TV hanging on a wall in the living area, and a close shot of the news anchor appeared on the screen. Morgan noticed right away that the man's face looked very serious, as he began to speak:

"An anonymous source at the White House has reported exclusively to CBS that the president has received an e-mail demanding that HE, all members of Congress, all Supreme Court justices, and every employee of the federal government RESIGN and STAND DOWN."

The TV anchor paused, then said, "The author or authors of the e-mail cited the following grievances that justify their demand:

1. National debt exceeding twenty trillion dollars
2. Incompetence of the U.S. Congress
3. Shameful discrepancy in family incomes and quality of life
4. Decimation of families and middle class
5. Decades of wasteful wars and destruction of other cultures
6. Influence of K Street lobbyists on Congress
7. Waste and fraud in the federal government
8. Moral decline throughout the country
9. Escalating crime and gun violence
10. Inferiority of the United States educational system
11. Greed inside and outside of government
12. Impending civil war"

The TV news anchor took his eyes off the teleprompter, paused, and then continued, "The anonymous source at the White House admitted that the president gets many strange letters and e-mails, but this one, he said, was different. The leaker said the e-mail came with a declaration of war and a threat that stated that if the STAND DOWN wasn't accomplished within three days OFFENSIVE ACTIONS would begin."

Morgan's mother had entered the kitchen during the report, and when she heard the threat, she smacked the kitchen counter with a spatula and snapped, "That's the craziest thing I've ever heard. I'm surprised CBS made that report. They just want to scare people!"

Morgan asked Matt to hand him the remote, and when he got it in his hand, he quickly switched to another channel where a reporter was just beginning to give a report. "Earlier this morning when I started interviewing people here on the sidewalk, I found that some of them knew nothing of the anonymous White House e-mail, while others had heard it, resulting in a mixture of emotional responses—fearful, disbelieving, indifferent, excited, and even GLAD—the guy who said he was glad explained his unusual response to the e-mail saying that it was about time that someone was fed-up enough with the way things were going in America to demand a STAND DOWN of our entire federal government and back it up with a declaration of war. Without exception, however, every person that I interviewed agreed that while the majority of the American public might be angry enough to be sympathetic with the person or persons behind the e-mail, they would never in a million years want our government to collapse—to STAND DOWN. The e-mail, the demand, the declaration of war—the whole thing was just ridiculous to everyone walking on this sidewalk this morning."

Another reporter in another city said many interviewees agreed with Morgan's mother—the news networks should not have dignified the anonymous message by airing it. The "on the street" consensus in that town in addition to believing it to be ridiculous was that it was a hoax created by the administration itself hoping to draw attention away from the growing list of federal government snafus—when in trouble politically, so the saying goes, START A WAR or CREATE A CRISIS.

Morgan knew he and his children had to get to the Golf Academy and get some work done, but he switched to another channel just in time to watch and listen to a panel of talking heads. The first question was—do any of you know if the White House has confirmed that they got the e-mail? No one was aware of any confirmation, but that didn't stop the panel from making comments about the demand, the list of grievances, and the declaration of war, nor from speculating on the identity of those behind the e-mail. Guesses from panelists were—a Russian kook, Chinese kooks, a group of Islamist radical terrorists, German Nazis, crazy Canadians, American Tea Party nuts, and a group of old hippies who had smoked too much grass one evening in Washington State or Colorado.

Ω

Later in the afternoon, they were eating lunch in what was going to be the lounge at the Golf Academy and watching TV when the programming was interrupted to show the White House press room. Once the press secretary got the press corps settled down, he immediately acknowledged that the White House had received the anonymous e-mail, that it was leaked, and that it had been accurately described by the news media. The press secretary also said, "It's obviously a prank, but we are taking it seriously. The president has not read the e-mail, but he has been alerted to the situation and will keep an eye on things. His golf cart and those of the Secret Service following him are equipped with the most advanced communication systems known to man. He told me to tell you—'Don't worry, the United States of America is the safest and most remarkable nation on earth. Calm down, don't worry, HAVE FUN—I am.' "

Nothing happened the second day, which made people feel better, and nothing happened the third day, so people began to relax and allowed themselves to talk about things other than THE E-MAIL. During the evening of the third day, people went to restaurants for dinner, to bars for a few drinks, and to night spots for dancing. People were celebrating in one way or another into the early morning hours of the fourth day. Many of those celebrating, when interviewed by news reporters, shook their heads and exclaimed—"What were we thinking!? Did we really think that the United States of America would STAND DOWN—never—we are a nation THAT WILL ALWAYS PARTY ON!"

At precisely 3:00 a.m. EST on the FOURTH DAY, reservoir floodgates in three different cities in three different states blew out sending walls of water into towns and city streets. The number, strength, and precise timing of the explosions actually INCREASED rather than DECREASED the number of times the word HOAX was used in the media. Two little words always preceded it—NOT A HOAX. The OFFENSIVE ACTIONS had begun as threatened in THE E-MAIL. The big questions now were—who's our enemy and where will they strike next?

In the afternoon of the FOURTH DAY, the president's press secretary met with the White House press corps and gave them this advice—"Cool down. The FBI is investigating the three bombings and all of our military forces on this continent are on high alert. The president has already promised that the people responsible for the bombings will be apprehended, tried, and if they are found guilty, will be punished. That scenario, unfortunately, might take five to six years to play out—but regardless of that—relax, be patient, and have no fear. America is the greatest nation on earth."

The attacks continued on day five. Oil refineries were bombed in Louisiana, Texas, and California. Miles of major train rails crossing the country were blown up, along with many national facilities for the distribution of agricultural products. Major meat-processing plants in the Midwest suffered significant explosions and according to spokespersons for those companies, normal shipments of meat would be disrupted for an indefinite period of time.

On day six, major power generating plants and power grids were bombed in the Northeast, Southeast, Midwest, and West Coast, knocking out power to thousands of people, businesses, manufacturing plants, docks, and airports, and if that destruction didn't severely inconvenience people, the explosions in many municipal sanitation facilities put the level of inconvenience over the top. People were experiencing levels of anger they had never reached before, and when thousands and thousands of cell towers were toppled, people really lost it—they WENT BANANAS. Some people were so infuriated when they couldn't use their cellphones they tossed them on sidewalks, against buildings, into swimming pools, and at each other. The single day on record for DIVORCE APPLICATIONS was surpassed in New York City and Los Angeles.

Mysteriously, all of these OFFENSIVE ACTIONS never resulted in a death, not one person was killed. Adding to the overall mystery was also the fact that not one person at any of the bombing sites saw a perpetrator. Law enforcement and military personnel deployed across the country told media people over and over—"It's like our enemy is INVISIBLE!"

People countrywide were angry, scared, and confused. Reporters began asking citizens if they would be in favor of the federal government of the United States of America STANDING DOWN. Many of them said YES—adding—"The terrorists seem to be NICE PEOPLE really—they aren't killing anybody."

On day seven, fifty bank buildings were bombed at night along with shopping malls, car dealerships, grocery stores, and fast food restaurants. Sports arenas were bombed but never when events were going on. According to some experts appearing on TV shows, the terrorists were attempting to win the hearts and minds of the American people. One of the most significant blows the terrorists made to the American public was knocking out social media—Facebook, Twitter, and others.

On day eight hundreds of thousands of people filled the streets of Washington, D.C., and other major cities across the country carrying signs that called for the president, members of his cabinet, members of Congress, and the Supreme Court justices to QUIT and GET OUT OF TOWN. Later that day, the president, standing next to his press secretary, announced to one member of the president's press corps that he had been notified by the Speaker of the House that all members of the House of Representatives had resigned, but the president quickly admitted that he could only guess about the status of the Senate and his guess was that the senators had left the building right after both Houses had unanimously agreed to pay themselves for the remainder of their terms. He acknowledged that he had personally received resignations from all nine justices, and by the end of the day, he said sadly, America's federal government would no longer exist. His final words were: "The oldest constitutional government on the face of the earth has come to an end. I'm sorry. I apologize. I will somehow try to make amends. Say a prayer."

Ω

Remarkably, it took only eight days from the time THE DEMAND was issued for the United States federal government to STAND DOWN. Starting on the fourth day and ending on the eighth day, citizens young and old watched big things blow up across the country, experienced confusion and fear, pondered and anticipated worse things to come, and wondered agonizingly about the identity and whereabouts of THE ENEMY—who were they and why were they destroying everything?

When Raquel saw and heard the president announce that the oldest constitutional government had come to an end, she turned and looked at her father. "What will this mean to us, Daddy?"

Morgan was asking himself that question and he, at that moment, had no idea how things would be without a federal government, but he knew he had to provide an answer that would not cause further alarm and worry for Raquel and his other two children standing in front of him. He replied, "We have the necessities of life—food, shelter and clothing—enough to keep us going until we find and destroy OUR ENEMY."

"My God," Christy said. "This can't be happening—can it, Morgan?"

Morgan replied, "Things will shake out in short order, and America will come out of this stronger and better than ever!" Even as his words left his mouth, he knew he was not expressing what he was truly thinking and feeling.

"I wish Catherine was here," Morgan's mother said from across the room. "She'd know what to make of this."

Morgan looked at his mother and shook his head, meaning that she shouldn't have made that comment.

Christy looked at Morgan and waved her hand above her shoulder, meaning that she was brushing off his mother's comment. Then she said, "Should I go to the bank and withdraw what little money I have in there?"

"Yes," Morgan replied. "Go now and beat the crowd."

Morgan's mother looked at her son and said, "I have a stack of US Savings Bonds in my cedar chest. Do you think they are any good now, son?"

Morgan shook his head. "Nope! Our federal government has left the building, but don't throw them away—you never know what might happen." After he responded to his mother's question, Morgan started wondering about his deal with Ralph Tolbert. Two questions arose in his mind: was Ralph going to be willing to go through with financing the project? and who would be interested in hitting golf balls when everything's in the toilet?

"Will we be going to school in the fall?" Matt asked from a far corner of the room. When no one responded, Matt said, "Maybe NOT, huh?" Again, no one responded. Everyone was focused on how their futures were going to be impacted by the collapse of the federal government. Matt stepped forward and out of the corner thinking that his movement might get him more attention. "To be honest about it," he said trying to make eye contact with someone. "I'll be disappointed if school doesn't open in September." Matt thought his last statement would get attention and draw a comment, because he had always complained about EVERYTHING SCHOOL, but no one made a comment. Disheartened, he said, "I LOVE YOU GUYS," and thought for certain that someone would say I LOVE YOU back. He waited, and as he scanned the room, he made eye contact with Raquel who said expressionless, "THIS is sad."

The TV screen had gone black after the president's announcement and remained black for about fifteen minutes, then the black screen turned blue and carried the following message:

> *Your president made a wise decision. Any attempt to remain in power would only have added to the destruction of your country and increased the level of fear and uncertainty in your citizenry. This is what's certain—the United States federal government has collapsed and, therefore, will no longer be able to lead the world down a path of moral decline and endless wars. With the elimination of your government, life in what once was the United States and in other developed nations will return to basics and a higher quality of life over time. DO NOT ATTEMPT TO FORM ANOTHER GOVERNMENT. Take care*

of your individual responsibilities, look after your families, get to know your neighbors, and be helpful to them. If you can't be helpful, DO NO HARM.

Everyone in the room read the message but remained silent, which made the knock on the front door jarring. The thought that went through everyone's mind except Matt's was—THAT MIGHT BE THE ENEMY! So that's why it was Matt who skipped to the entryway and opened the door.

Ethel Stewart walked in followed by her three children and her husband Ray who was carrying two rifles, a pistol, and two bags of ammunition, which he handed over to Morgan, saying, "I don't think you have any guns around here, and you might need them and more in the near future."

Morgan accepted the gifts and said to Ray, "Did you see that message that just appeared on the TV?"

Ray looked at the TV screen, and it had gone back to black. "I don't see any message, but we did see our president say GOOD-BYE to the United States of America!"

"You must have been walking up here when the message appeared. It must have been sent by OUR ENEMY and it said this—don't try to form another government, get back to basics, take care of your families, help your neighbors and if you can't be helpful—DO NO HARM."

"Well, Morgan," Ray said. "That's pretty much what I've been doing, so I'm okay with that directive."

Ethel looked at her husband and said to everyone standing in the room, "My husband got us back to BASICS long ago, and he HELPS others when he can, so he's not seeing what's coming."

Ray looked at his wife, and replied, "Naw, honey, I do see what's coming and that's why I brought THESE GIFTS to Morgan."

Morgan said, "Ray, do you think people are going to be running around up here in the mountains stealing stuff?"

"Yep," Ray replied. "And something told me you wouldn't have any guns, so I brought you some so you can protect yourself."

Matt stepped up to the guns, and Ray looked down at him, "Austin already showed you how to shoot, didn't he?"

Matt touched the shotgun and affirmed that Austin had taught him how to load, unload, and shoot the gun he was touching.

Ray smiled at Matt and said, "I'll teach you how to shoot that pistol, too." After telling Matt that he would teach him how to use the pistol, he looked at Morgan and said, "Back to your question, Morgan. When the bad guys get all they can in the cities, they're going to come out here in the country, and we better be ready for 'em."

"Should I go over to Charlottesville and get some more guns and ammo?" Morgan asked Ray.

"I'm guessing that a lot of people are at the gun stores right now—GOOD FOLKS and BAD FOLKS but, if you want to make a trip over there, I'd be happy to go with you—besides you don't know anything about guns and I do."

Morgan said he did want to go over to Charlottesville that afternoon and thanked Ray for offering to accompany him.

Ray then said, "I don't know who's behind this, but it's been coming for quite a while now. They must be real smart, and they must believe that people are basically good, but people have proven themselves both GOOD and EVIL over the centuries and that's not going to change. Now is the time to take care of your families and help your neighbors, but it's also a time to really KEEP OUR EYES ON STRANGERS."

While Ray was talking, Heather saw Catherine walking up to the front door and had walked over to the door and opened it before she knocked and welcomed her inside. Catherine acknowledged everyone as she walked over to Morgan and said quietly, "I met with the governor yesterday, and he already knew what was going to be happening in Washington today." Morgan heard what Catherine had said, but he was not responding, because he was looking for Christy who was walking toward him.

"What's going to be happening here in Virginia?" Morgan asked as Christy stepped up to his side.

Catherine smiled and said hello to Christy, then answered Morgan's question. "The governor said that no state including Virginia could last long without the federal government."

"Which means what…to you?" Morgan asked.

"It means," she said, directing it to both Morgan and Christy, "that I'll be releasing the prisoners and locking down the facility, pretty soon."

"What the heck is happening, Catherine?" Christy asked.

"Civilizations and governments come and go. This one, it seems, will not be an exception," Catherine replied.

"How long will you be sticking around at the penitentiary?" Christy asked.

"I'll be the one unlocking the cells and opening the gates, but before then I'll be doing everything I can to provide the prisoners with some money to get them through the initial weeks of living in a totally uncontrolled, LAWLESS environment."

"The penitentiary has money to give them?" Morgan asked.

"Yes, and no," Catherine replied. "The state penitentiary doesn't have money to give them, but the Parolee Relief Fund, which derived its funds from the entrepreneurial efforts of prisoners, DOES have some money and, ethically I think, the money should go to the prisoners that will soon hit the streets even though they will not technically be PAROLEES." Catherine paused and decided to change to a slightly different topic. "Anybody and everybody who has investments should be scrambling to turn everything into very liquid assets like cash. CASH WILL BE KING moving forward, but most people are, unfortunately, going to be late to the window."

"How about you, Catherine—you're going to lose your job—are you okay?"

"When things first started blowing up, I cashed out my whole portfolio of investments—mostly stocks and bonds."

"Why didn't you tell US to CASH OUT?" Morgan asked, jokingly.

Catherine looked at Morgan and answered, smiling, "With you, Morgan, I knew you didn't have anything to CASH OUT and with you, Christy, I have no excuse—I should have given you a heads up. I APOLOGIZE."

Christy replied, "No apology necessary, we're not talking about a huge amount of money."

"Depending on where you have your investments, you may still have time to turn those numbers on paper into CASH."

"What have you done with YOUR CASH?" Morgan asked. "Is it under your mattress?"

"Not hardly," she replied.

Christy smiled, "Did you buy gold and silver like I see advertised on TV?"

Catherine smiled, "Yes, I did buy gold and silver, but not from those places that you've seen on TV."

"GOLD and SILVER or gold and silver CERTIFICATES?" Christy asked.

"I bought GOLD and SILVER."

"And where did you put it?" Morgan asked with a sly smile and raised eyebrow.

"I'll draw you a map, later," Catherine replied, smiling.

Morgan asked, "Did you buy BRICKS like they have at Fort Knox?"

"No," Catherine answered. "COINS."

"This world is going to be a very CRAZY place," Morgan said, as he gestured for Christy and Catherine to accompany him over to the refrigerator. "Let's have something to drink." He opened the refrigerator door and looked in. "What will it be—orange juice, white grape juice or MILK?"

Christy smiled, "MILK, of course!"

Catherine replied, "White grape juice, thank you."

"And I'll take orange juice—my favorite," Morgan said and pulled out all three containers.

After taking a sip of the white grape juice, Catherine said, "When I open the cell doors and send them through the front gates, the prisoners will have some money from the Parolee Relief Fund and some gold and silver coins in their pockets to soften their landing into what's going to be ANARCHY."

Christy looked at Catherine. "Are you giving them YOUR gold and silver coins?"

"Yes," Catherine replied. "I have more than I need thanks to Wall Street."

Christy said, "That's very generous, Catherine."

Morgan agreed and asked, "What does your father think about THE COLLAPSE?"

"He wants me to move out of my house in Richmond and live with him," she replied.

"Why?" Morgan asked.

"He thinks, and he is probably right, that downtown Richmond will become a tinderbox. He's always looking out for my safety."

"And what did you say?" Christy asked.

"I said I would think about it, because I'm always thinking about my independence," Catherine replied and laughed at herself, because of the contrast between her father's UNSELFISH motives and her embarrassingly SELFISH motives.

"What's there to think about, Catherine? Seems like a good idea to me," Christy replied.

"Moving in with one's parent as an adult is always SOMETHING to think about."

"Yes," Christy replied sprightly. "No matter how old we might be, THEY are always OUR PARENTS!"

"It's THAT and there's something else," Catherine replied.

"What's THAT?" Morgan asked.

"The university is going to take a big hit—they're not going to get much help from the state now and in the future. They're also going to lose tuition money, because fewer students will be coming, and professors are going to drop off, because they will be working on the cheap—so I've been told that I have a job if I want it."

"So how does that influence your decision on living with your father?"

"If I take the job, a small house that belongs to the university comes with it."

"That would be real nice," Christy said. "You could walk to work. So take the job, take the house, and let your father live by himself like he's been doing forever. What's the problem?"

"I believe my father invited me to move in with him, because he's concerned about my safety, but my intuition tells me that it's more than that."

Christy cocked her head to the side and asked, "And what would that be?"

"I think he's losing it a little bit and is TOO PROUD to admit it."

Christy thought about what Catherine had said and then responded, "So why don't you ask him to move out of his house and live with you at the university—seems like a great place for him to live?"

"Besides ME, my father's life revolves around his garden and his greenhouse. Getting him out of his own little "Eden" would require Seal Team 6, and I don't have an IN with them."

Morgan had listened to Christy's and Catherine's conversation and had intentionally stayed out of it, because he wanted THEM to talk. But a question entered his mind that he felt compelled to ask lest he forget to do it later. "Catherine," he said stepping closer to Christy, "when the time comes to release all the prisoners, where's Bob going to go?"

Catherine paused, realizing that she had not given Bob's future any thought. She felt that sinking feeling that comes from embarrassment. "Gosh, Morgan, I don't know—hadn't thought about Bob."

Morgan grinned. "I hadn't thought about Bob either, until just now, but it's not like we've been sitting around twiddling our thumbs."

"No, I haven't and neither have you."

"Let me show you how generous I can be with YOUR HOUSE: move in with your father right now, and let Bob live in your house when he gets out of prison. That would be better than leaving your house vacant. Then see how things go with living with your dad, with your new job, and with the university house that you could use during the day for lunch, naps, and for planning lessons. Take the house and figure out later how best to use it."

Catherine tilted her head, "You're right, Morgan. I'll take the house now, and deal with who's going to live there later. Not having a complete plan before the *arrow leaves the bow* makes me anxious, but that's the way it will be this time. Thanks for the advice."

"Okay, now that that's been settled, what are you going to teach?" Morgan asked.

"I think they want me to develop a course—something that might prove helpful to young people heading out of academia into ANARCHY."

Ω

Weeks after the collapse of federal and state governments, Christy and Morgan rode bikes down the mountain and stopped at the convenience store to see what was available and at what price. They saw immediately that there was a good supply of milk, eggs, and bread. Cigarettes and sweets were available but expensive. So was coffee and tea. One-ply toilet tissue was available, as well as, two-ply. Molly told them that some customers were buying the one-ply and doubling it up which, in their minds, made it a better buy. Then there were other customers, Molly said, who were purchasing the two-ply and converting it into two rolls of one-ply which they then doubled up when it came time to use it. Molly admitted to Morgan and Christy that she used two-ply at full strength and always would regardless of the price. According to her, SOFTNESS was a NECESSITY not a LUXURY.

Christy turned toward Morgan and whispered after Molly had gone to wait on somebody at the cash register, "I'm glad you and Molly got that settled. My grandmother, I believe, used the Montgomery Wards or Sears Roebuck catalogs to do the cleanup."

"Mine too," Morgan replied.

After Molly finished with the customer at the checkout counter, she came back to Morgan and Christy and told them that customers were still paying for things with coins and paper money, but some were bringing in items from their homes to trade for stuff. One woman she said traded a set of earrings for a pack of Twinkies, and some guy wanted to trade a Trojan prophylactic that he must have carried in his wallet for a year for a pack of chewing tobacco, but she didn't go for it. She said things had really changed since they stopped taking credit and debit cards and personal checks.

After their visit to the convenience store, Morgan and Christy rode their bikes over to the diner to have some toast and coffee. The coffee wasn't as good as it used to be, because the proprietors were using the coffee grounds more than once. The diluted taste of the coffee didn't really matter. The main reason for them going there once a week was not for the toast and coffee. They went there to get the news and gossip. On this visit, they learned that an enterprising family was installing MAIL WINDOWS and P.O. BOXES in stores throughout the surrounding counties. They had even printed and distributed flyers listing the locations of all of them. People wanting to send letters just needed to go to one of the mail windows and get their letters or postcards literally STAMPED with a rubber stamp, pay the postage, and drop it in the MAIL BOX in that store or any store in the postal system. People who could afford to rent P.O. boxes had the advantage of picking up their mail from their P.O. boxes—rather than having it delivered directly to their homes, which took longer and required the SENDERS to spend more on postage. The enterprising couple picked up mail deposited in MAIL BOXES once a week and delivered it to P.O. boxes within a week. If they had to deliver mail to a home, it would take two weeks. Sometimes they delivered mail on bikes, and sometimes, by motorized vehicles—moped, small car, or jeep. On some days, they used horses, ponies, and even donkeys to deliver mail. Availability and cost of gasoline had an impact on mail delivery. Postage was higher or lower depending on distance and the physical challenge of the mail route. Sending mail to homes or businesses way out in the counties or on the top of mountains was costly. It made life easier for everyone concerned when people rented P.O. boxes.

When Morgan learned about the new postal service for letters and postcards, being the businessman that he had been, he immediately thought about PACKAGES and BOXES. He had missed out in his previous life—Before Collapse (BC)—on the big business of package and box delivery, but maybe this time around, he thought, he could get in on the ground floor. UPS and FedEx logos started flashing in his head. Morgan leaned closer to Christy and whispered, "Maybe I should forget about the Golf Academy until LUXURY things like GOLF pick back up ten to fifteen years from now."

Christy looked at him with a furrowed brow and replied, "And do what?"

Morgan smiled widely, "PACKAGE and BOX delivery! People still need to ship things. Maybe they'd pay a dollar or more per item."

Christy laughed, "Well, maybe...and you've got a bus—but don't paint it brown. Paint it some flashy color—like LIME—and what would you call your company?"

Morgan thought about it, and said, "Package & Box Delivery—PBD—lime background with RED letters."

"Okay, baby, go for it!"

"Seriously, Christy, who's interested in hitting golf balls right now?"

"About as many as those interested in LANDSCAPING their yards," she replied. "Maybe we can partner up like that other couple."

Ω

It was morning and Ray had walked up the road and stopped at the GREEN HOUSE to chat. "These days," he said to Morgan, "I have too much time on my hands. I'm unemployed for the first time in my adult life, and it seems like I've been working all of my life."

"You like to hunt, don't you, Ray?"

"Yep, sure do," Ray answered.

"Why don't you start killing some deer and bear around here and sell the meat? People like meat and need the protein."

As soon as Heather and Raquel heard their father's suggestion, they booed and said that it was a bad idea. Morgan told them that he was just trying to be helpful to a neighbor, which didn't persuade them to like the idea.

Ray looked at the girls and said, "That's not a bad idea, and there's no IN SEASON or OUT of SEASON NOW. Would you like to go hunting with me, Morgan?"

"No," Morgan replied.

After Morgan declined, Matt raised his hand and said excitedly, "I'd like to go hunting with you UNCLE RAY!"

Before Ray could respond to Matt, the large flat screen TV made a noise, and the black screen turned blue. In seconds, the following message appeared on the screen:

> *Your country has proven that it is incapable of creating safe and healthy communities. Under our supervision and guidance, you will make changes locally that will in time improve the lives of all human beings in your community.*
>
> *Next week, two cargo planes will land at the Charlottesville Municipal Airport—one with logistical supplies and equipment and the other will be carrying a contingent of robots. Welcome them into your community and follow their directives. Whenever possible, take advantage of the knowledge and skills they possess. There should be no barrier to effective communication; robots can speak, read, and write in all major languages and can quickly learn minor languages if they need to. It is also important to advise you that robots can always detect when human beings are not telling the truth. Don't waste their time and yours with prevarication.*
>
> *The robots' first mission is to confiscate guns. We know that is a sore subject for many of you, but it must be done. Removing all firearms from your community is a necessary first step to achieving optimal living conditions in your locality. Don't feel that we are focusing on just your community. The robots will be working in many other communities across what used to be called the United States of America.*
>
> *Adopt our axiom: Do No Harm*

When the message disappeared from the screen, Ray shook his head and said forcefully, "When I shoot someone breaking into my house, are they going to call that DOING HARM?"

Christy replied, "Yeah, when someone does something harmful to us, don't we have the right to HARM THEM BACK?"

Ray stepped out in front of the group and scanned their faces before speaking. "NOBODY's going to take my guns away and that includes ROBOTS!"

"Over your dead body, I'll bet," Christy said heartily.

Ray looked at Christy and said, "I'll have to think about that, Christy. I'm not into DEAD!"

Ω

The following week, two cargo planes landed at the Charlottesville Municipal Airport, and a large number of robots walked down the rear ramp and across the tarmac to the main terminal building. The robot leading the column stopped at the double metal doors that were chained shut and peeked inside. Seeing no one, the robot stepped back, grabbed the chain that was threaded through the door handles, and pulled. The chain snapped immediately, allowing the lead robot to open a door and walk into the building followed by the other robots in the column.

Ω

The day did come in Richmond when five hundred and ninety-eight inmates at the penitentiary were released from their cells. Every one of them took a position in a single file line that led to a table in the foyer. Catherine was sitting behind the table on a folding metal chair where she was conducting short conversations with each prisoner before handing them an envelope containing gold and silver coins and a packet of paper money. She carefully explained the value of the gold and silver coins BEFORE the COLLAPSE (BC), so they would have some idea of what they might be able to trade them for AFTER the COLLAPSE (AC) on the street. Catherine knew that the prisoners were aware of the anarchical conditions outside the prison and asked them to resist the temptation to revert to their old ways. With one exception, her last words to each of the prisoners were—*Always do what you know to be right.* Catherine's conversation and last words were not the same when Bob sat down across from her. She did not ask him WHO would be meeting him, because she knew that NO ONE would be meeting him.

"WHERE will you be staying, Bob?" she asked.

"I don't know, Warden," he responded and quickly asked, "How's Morgan?"

"He's doing okay, and we often talk about you. In fact, we were talking about you just a few days ago."

"I'm glad. I miss him," Bob said quietly.

Catherine smiled, "When I told Morgan that I would be releasing you and all of the prisoners today, he suggested that I consider offering my home to you, knowing that I would soon be moving out of my home in downtown Richmond. What do you think?"

Bob smiled and chuckled, "I think living in your house would be much superior to living on the street, but—"

Catherine interrupted him, "I am to some degree offering my house to you out of the goodness of my heart, but I am also offering it, because having you there will reduce the chances that my house will be looted, set on fire, ransacked, or illegally occupied, and eventually destroyed."

After Catherine finished explaining her motivations for offering her home to him, Bob said, "When I used the word BUT, I wasn't thinking about refusing your offer. I was heading for getting permission to have a pet—a dog—would that be okay?"

"Traditionally, that might not be a good thing for a renter to have, but in this case, it might be a very good thing for you to have—a large dog!"

"Yes, and that's the kind of dog I want—a big one," Bob said emphatically. "Another favor—do you have any guns? I would feel safer, if I had a few guns in the house?"

"Bob, to be honest, my father and I anticipated that you would do us this favor, so I have a few guns in my car, all cleaned and oiled for your use. Do I need to show you how to use them?"

"No, Warden," Bob replied and grinned. "I grew up on a farm and my best friends were horses and hounds."

Ω

After locking the gates of the penitentiary, Catherine took Bob to her house, and together, they took all of her wearable possessions and toiletries out of her house and put them in her Subaru. Everything else remained there for his use.

Ω

On the way to her father's house, Catherine composed the following course description in her head:

Rebooting America 101:

The United States of America lasted over two centuries.

Question 1: What steps were taken from its earliest days to build a nation FOR the people, BY the people, and OF the people?
Question 2: What caused the United States to collapse in eight days?
Question 3: Can nations be rebuilt once they have failed?

Catherine was aware of the WARNING issued by the people responsible for THE COLLAPSE of the United States and all developed nations around the world—DO NOT ATTEMPT TO FORM ANOTHER GOVERNMENT—so she tried to be careful with her wording.

Ω

The first thing Molly did when Morgan dropped in was to tell him that two robots had been there. She said she had heard that they had been seen in Charlottesville, but she didn't know they had arrived in Loveville. She admitted that she was scared out of her mind the whole time they were in the store. "They didn't buy anything," she said. "I mean, what would robots buy anyway—a can of three-in-one oil—or WD 40? I think they were just snooping around. I did summon enough courage to ask their names," she said, laughing. "One of them replied—I am Robot 26—and the other one said he was Robot 27. Isn't it nice how they kept themselves in chronological order, BUT you would expect that from ROBOTS, wouldn't you?"

Morgan rolled his eyes and replied, "Did they talk funny?"

Molly replied, "Not really, and I was wrong when I told you that I didn't know the robots were in Loveville. Some customer told me a week ago that they had seen some strange-looking people up on the mountain, but I didn't think they were talking about ROBOTS, but that's probably who they saw."

Morgan asked Molly if she had heard what the robots' first mission was, and she said she had. "If they ask me about guns, I'm going to play dumb and say—I ain't got NO GUNS."

Morgan smiled and replied, "You missed the part where they told us that the robots could tell when HUMAN BEINGS were lying."

"What did they look like—the robots?"

"I'd say Robots 26 and 27 were six feet two or three and had bodies like tennis players—slender and muscular—and they were wearing unbranded grey warm-up suits, running shoes, and cyclist helmets. The only uncovered body parts that I saw were their faces and hands, which were shaped like ours, but their body covering or "skin" looked like smooth, supple aluminum. No hair on their face, head, or on their hands. When they spoke, their mouths moved normal just like ours, and their voices were clear and pleasant, and they had aqua-blue eyes," Molly stopped, and paused thinking about them. Then she concluded, "They were handsome, actually, but definitely not huggable."

"Were they carrying any weapons?" Morgan asked.

"I didn't see anything that looked like a weapon. They did have a pouch on their right hip with something in it. Like an iPhone, maybe?"

Later, when Morgan was pedaling back up the mountain, he glanced over at Ray's home and saw a shiny metal wagon attached to an ATV sitting in Ray's front yard. He had a good idea who owned the wagon and decided to check things out. The front door was open so he walked in announcing himself. Ray shouted for him to come to the back of the house.

Morgan walked to the rear of the house and there they were. "Meet my friends, Morgan," Ray said, happily, "This is Robot 26 and Robot 27, and Robots, this is my friend, Morgan."

Morgan looked at them and nodded, "Nice to meet you."

"Nice to meet you, Morgan," they responded.

Ray looked at Morgan, "Robot 26 here just asked me if I had any guns, and I told him that I didn't have any guns IN my house. Ain't that right, Morgan?"

"Yes, that's right, you don't have any guns IN your house," Morgan didn't know that for sure, but he had a hunch that Ray had moved his guns out of his house. Morgan waited for alarms to go off on the robots indicating that RAY or HE or that BOTH of them had lied, but he didn't see or hear anything. Unbeknownst to Ray and Morgan, beeps were emanating from both robots' wristbands, but at a frequency that human beings would be unable to hear. The RobotMakers and therefore the robots themselves considered playing around with words like Ray and Morgan had done to mask the TRUTH was DISHONEST and thereby qualified as LYING.

Robot 27 decided he would play along with their game and asked, "Do you have guns ANYWHERE, Ray?"

Ray smiled, and shook his head, and said, "No, I DON'T have NO guns ANYWHERE." Immediately after saying that, Ray was feeling very smug, because he had never gotten a letter grade above C in any of his English classes, but somehow he had learned and had never forgotten that TWO NEGATIVES in a sentence made a POSITIVE and, therefore in Ray's mind, he had told the truth.

Robot 26 looked at Ray and said politely, "You are definitely not telling the truth, Ray. We asked you if you had any guns, just to be polite. People living down the road from you told us you had guns, and they even told us where you were hiding them. Now, give us your guns. It's for your own good."

"I don't think so," Ray replied.

"Do you mean that you are not going to surrender your guns, or do you mean that surrendering your weapons wouldn't BE FOR YOUR OWN GOOD?"

"BOTH," Ray replied.

The robots didn't reply to Ray's response. They walked out of the house followed by Ray and Morgan. The robots' eyes were trained on a small, unpainted, wooden shelter attached to the barn. They walked directly to the shelter where Robot 27 tapped its right foot on the dirt, and it made a scratchy, hollow sound. Ray moaned. The robots then removed a tiller, lawnmower, and wheelbarrow and brushed off the dirt that was covering a large trapdoor. When they raised the door, the robots saw a set of steps going down into the ground. They stepped closer and pointed their fingers at the dark space. Shafts of light shot out of their fingers and illuminated a small room filled with gun racks and guns. Ray and Morgan walked forward and watched the robots descend the steps.

Robot 26 looked up at Morgan and Ray, "A COLD CELLAR is not a good place to store guns, Ray. It's cold and damp."

"Yes, I know that Robot 26," Ray replied angrily. He was offended by the robot's comment. "I just put them there last week knowing you would be coming, and I was planning to take them out of there as soon as you got down the road."

Robot 27 looked at Ray, "We are sorry, but we have to take your guns. You appear to be a good guy, but we can't make exceptions."

Ray got madder, "Are you going to confiscate my hammers, screwdrivers, knives, and forks, too?"

The robots stared at Ray, and Robot 27 was the one who replied, "SARCASM rarely benefits those who employ it."

Ray ignored the robot's comment and said, "How about bows and arrows?"

Robot 27 replied, "Thank you for asking, Ray. We know you have them. If bows and arrows prove harmful to the common good, we'll be back to get those too."

Robot 26 went to the front yard and drove the ATV and wagon to the back yard. The two robots hauled all the guns and ammunition out of the cold cellar and placed everything in the wagon while Morgan and Ray watched.

"Are you going to pay me for my guns and ammo?"

"We were told to CONFISCATE guns and ammunition, and there was no mention of REMUNERATION," Robot 26 said.

"Who or what gives you the authority to CONFISCATE my property?" Ray asked.

"The RobotMakers," Robot 27 replied.

"Robots 26 and 27, you are taking my property without CONSENT—WE Americans call that STEALING."

Robot 26 stared at Ray as he closed the doors on the wagon. "We learned that word—STEALING—and its meaning when we were studying your culture. It describes behavior not OBSERVED, PRACTICED, or ENCOUNTERED in OUR CULTURE. If you don't know it, we are here to transform this culture into a place where people—human beings—can live an OPTIMAL QUALITY of LIFE—and an OPTIMAL QUALITY of LIFE cannot be achieved without PEACE, and PEACE can never be achieved where people are HARMING other people. At some point, IF PEOPLE WANT PEACE, they must REFUSE to harm others—no matter what."

"Oh boy, what planet are you from?" Ray asked, loudly.

The robots heard Ray, but didn't respond, because they knew that his question was rhetorical and only an expression of his frustration and anger. They got on the ATV and started moving toward the front yard and the road.

Ray's eyes followed the robots and the wagon containing his guns and ammunition, but before the robots got to the road, Ray shouted, "All of that PEACE SHIT is easy for you to say—YOU ARE NOT HUMAN BEINGS!"

The robots stopped at the edge of the road and looked back at Ray. Robot 27 shouted back, "WE guess it is PEACE EXCREMENT to YOU right now, but the RobotMakers are HUMAN BEINGS and believe you will see things differently in time."

"And where do those DICKHEADS live—in the North Pole with Santa Claus!?"

"No—Newfoundland, and they are descendants of the VIKINGS."

Ω

Two days before her class was to start at the university, Catherine had completed her lecture notes, so she decided to drive to Richmond to check out something with Bob. He opened the door after peeking through a small side window, and welcomed her inside. She looked around to see if Bob was keeping things orderly and was surprised that her house wasn't a mess. She complimented Bob on how nice things looked as she walked toward the curtains covering the patio door. When she got to the curtains, she pulled them aside and was shocked to see a dog standing close to the glass staring at her.

"You've already gotten a dog!" she said. "What is it?"

Bob went to the door and stood next to Catherine. "It's a mix of hound and something else, and I don't let him come in the house. No, that's not true. I let him in occasionally just to have company, but I never let him on the furniture."

"How did you two get together?" she asked.

"One morning he showed up at the front door, and he stayed there all day. So when I found him there, the following morning, I fed him and the rest is history."

"Nice-looking dog," Catherine replied, then looked away from the dog and explained to Bob that she was experiencing growing concerns about his safety living in an area that appeared to be getting closer and closer to advanced stages of anarchy—CHAOS. She also explained that she was worried about her father's health and wanted him to live with her at the university, but hadn't even suggested that to him, because she was pretty sure that he wouldn't agree to leaving his house to live with her. Bob asked why, and she told him about her father's greenhouse and garden. "My father," she said emphatically, "might be willing to leave his garden behind, because it's going to die naturally with the onset of winter, but he would never be able to abandon his greenhouse." After the lengthy explanation of what was going on with her and her father, Catherine just looked at him and said, "Would you consider living in my father's house, by yourself, and looking after things? I would be willing to pay you for that?"

Bob already knew about her father's interest in horticulture by way of Morgan, which prompted him to say, "I don't know anything about caring for plants, Warden."

"You don't have to, Bob. I think my dad would be very willing to teach you what you need to know up front, and I'd be willing to bring him there, let's say, once a week, so you could work together. I think you would like and enjoy working with my dad, and for the record, I'm not a warden any longer, Bob. I'm just Catherine."

After Bob nodded and cornered a brief, appreciative smile, he replied, "It would be an unusual marriage—a retired judge and a convicted murderer, Catherine?"

"I think my dad would like you. Do you want me to run this by him?"

"Can I bring my dog?" Bob asked.

"What's his name?"

"Romulus," Bob replied.

"I like that name," Catherine said and walked over to the patio door. Romulus immediately put his paw up on the glass and held it there. Catherine knelt down and put her left hand up against the glass across from his paw and left it there for a few seconds, as if they were completing a formal introduction. Then she stood up and faced Bob. "I'm pretty sure my father will be amenable to having you and Romulus living at his place. He has a fenced backyard and a nice doghouse because he used to have a dog. Can you and Romulus be ready to leave here DAY AFTER TOMORROW—I have a class to teach tomorrow?"

Bob said that he could be ready and then added, "Don't you have to see if your father is agreeable to this?"

"He will be," she said smiling.

Ω

She had nine students, and she opened with the following remarks:

"What a great opportunity you and I have right now. We are privileged to be in this classroom for a semester—to think, talk, and discuss anything and everything hoping, in just a few months, we will have a better grasp on how we can move forward—individually and collectively. I grew up in the United States of America, which doesn't exist today. We're starting over."

"If we want FREEDOM, we've got it. We have more freedom than we've ever had. YOU and I can do whatever we want now—there are NO RULES…NO RESTRICTIONS…NO LAWS…NO LIMITS. The question for WE THE PEOPLE has always been—how much freedom do we want to give up to some form of government to improve our overall quality of life?"

Catherine stopped talking and paced silently, which made the nine students squirm in their chairs. Then, suddenly, she stopped pacing and stared at them. "All nine of you have everything you need right now to live a very enriched life. You were born, I'm sure, with superior intelligence and were, most likely, reared by supportive, loving people."

"Before the United States collapsed, what did you want to do? What career did you want to pursue? And now—where are you? Have you raised or lowered your aspirations?"

All nine students responded to Catherine's questions and admitted that they were confused and scared but still aspired to achieving their full potential.

"Okay," Catherine said, "I'm confused and scared too, and we should be. Do you think the founders of this country and the signers of the Declaration of Independence were scared?"

The students didn't say anything, but they nodded their heads, indicating that they did think the founders and signers were scared.

Catherine nodded her head and said with emphasis, "You bet they were scared! From 1607 to 1776, people were coming here WITH NOTHING and carving out lives FROM NOTHING. Some came with dishes and cooking utensils; others may have brought a few pieces of furniture, and certainly there were those who brought skills and knowledge that served them well in England but was of little worth in building new lives for themselves in THE NEW WORLD."

"Here's what I want you to do for the time remaining in the class and for what other time you can donate to it before our next class. Go to the library and do some research—you may work together or independently—and determine how seventeenth century settlers from England built and sustained a settlement on the banks of a river in a very foreign world—a very primitive world FOR

THEM…it wasn't a primitive world for the people who were already settled on the banks of that river—the river they named for the King of England."

When Catherine opened the classroom door to let the students out, there were five robots sitting quietly on the benches in the hallway. All five looked her way at the same time, which shocked her. Then they stood up and walked toward her classroom. Catherine's heart started beating rapidly. "What's wrong, Ms. Sinclair?" one of the students asked, as she touched her shoulder. Catherine didn't respond. Another student peeked around her and saw the leading robot and ducked back into the classroom. "Robots," he whispered to other students standing behind him. Catherine stepped through the doorway into the hall and motioned for the robots to come into the classroom. Once all five robots were in the classroom, Catherine asked the robots and her students who were huddled in the back of the room to grab a desk and move them to the center of the room. She then drew small circles on the board in the shape of a U—"Put your desks in this configuration," she said, "so we can have a discussion." The robots didn't have any problems understanding and following her instructions.

An hour later, Catherine left her classroom filled with thoughts and emotions swirling around inside of her—disbelief, belief, joy, dismay, fear, and awe because of what she had heard and learned from the robots. She had to remind herself that she wasn't on a movie set. What she was witnessing was real—not fiction. She was excited about her class and added to that excitement was another excitement that was coming from the knowledge that she had invited her father for dinner. When she opened her front door she saw her father sitting in a chair reading, "Come with me Dad," she said. "I know I promised you dinner, but I'm so excited about my first class that I can't even think about making dinner. We'll drop into that little place on the way to Loveville and get a bite to eat."

Catherine backed out of her garage and pulled around to the front door to get her father. When he got in the car, he asked her if she was sure she had enough gas to get to Loveville and back, and when she showed that she wasn't sure, her father went over to his car and pulled out a gasoline container from the trunk, and said, "I think there's a full two gallons in here." Catherine noticed something coiled up in her father's trunk and asked what it was, and he told her that it was a siphon hose and funnel. "We aren't going to need that," he said, and walked over to Catherine's car where he removed the gas cap and poured the gas in the container into Catherine's gas tank.

"What would I do without you, Daddy? You are always prepared."

While they drove down Highway 29, Catherine told her father about the deal she had worked out with Bob. "Sounds like a good plan to me, sweetie," he said. "Good for Bob, you, and me. I think it was yesterday that I realized that living with you would be more enjoyable than living with my plants, so I'm very pleased that you took the initiative. Now, tell me about your class."

"Nine students showed up for my class and at the end of class FIVE ROBOTS were sitting outside my classroom!"

"That's very interesting," her father said. "Why were they there?"

Catherine replied, "They had read a short blurb in the course catalog about my class—Rebooting America—and wanted to determine what the contents might include."

Catherine's father looked at her. "Are they going to be telling you WHAT YOU CAN TEACH or talk about at the university?"

"I don't know, but because of THE WARNING, I was pretty careful with the course description."

"Yeah, I remember THE WARNING," he replied. "Where are they from?"

"Guess," she said.

"Russia," he answered.

"No, try again."

"China?"

"No, again, last chance."

"Her father paused, thinking. "Korea?"

"No. NEWFOUNDLAND!"

Her father replied, "No kidding. I would never have guessed NEWFOUNDLAND."

"Isn't that interesting, Dad?"

"Were ROBOTS responsible for carrying out the bombings?"

"The robots told us that they had nothing to do with the bomb-ings, but they did say WHO DID!"

"Are you putting me on, dear Daughter?"

"No, I'm not putting you on. The robots told the class that they were developed and manufactured by THE ROBOTMAKERS who are descendants of THE VIKINGS. According to them, the RobotMakers also created UNIQUE-ONES, and they carried out the bombings."

"What I remember was that no one ever saw anyone or anything at the bombing sites—the perpetrators seemed to be INVISIBLE," her father replied.

"The UNIQUE-ONES," the robots said, "were manufactured by the RobotMakers, like they were, and they're ROBOTS, but uniquely different, because the RobotMakers can make them in any configuration they want—birds, dogs, deer, rodents, or other ani-mals depending on the mission and mission site."

"Clever," her father said. "I bet they have some UNIQUE-ONES that look like GORILLAS in case they have to conduct GUERRILLA WARFARE."

"Very funny, Dad!"

"A flock of Canada Geese UNIQUE-ONES could drop out of the sky and cumulatively pack a big punch," her father said.

Catherine added, "Or a herd of UNIQUE-ONES that look like deer—would be bad news walking, grazing right into a corridor of power towers. Dad, they're going to come back to my class. Would you like to sit in when I know they're coming?"

"Absolutely." He answered. "I want to know more about the RobotMakers."

Before Catherine could say any more about the robots, she was on the narrow bridge crossing the Tye River, and when they were on the other side, she saw a sign that read Central Virginia Golf Academy with an arrow pointing right. She then remembered that they had not stopped *for a bite to eat* and immediately looked left and saw the diner. She stopped in the middle of the road, which wasn't a big deal since most people weren't driving cars or trucks because of the high prices on gasoline. She asked her father if he wanted to get something to eat at the diner but he declined saying that he wasn't hungry. They continued down the road and pulled into the parking lot and stopped. Catherine and her father walked around the main building and saw Morgan standing next to a robot, and both of them were watching another robot tee up a golf ball. Morgan saw Catherine and her father and gave them a quick wave while keeping his attention on the robot preparing to hit its first drive.

"Okay, Robot 19, do as I just demonstrated—stand back from the ball using your club and arm to determine the right distance. Now, grip the handle, left hand first then the right, and keep the grip relaxed." Morgan stepped closer to the robot and adjusted the robot's grip—"Relax, that's it, good. Now bring the club head back about a quarter swing and then bring the head back to the ball adjusting your feet as necessary. Bring the club head back two or three times to make sure you are lined up right to hit the ball squarely with the head of the club. That's right, good, breathe and relax—"

Robot 19 cut Morgan off. "Robots don't BREATHE or RELAX—we're good just the way we are."

"I wasn't thinking, Robot 19. Forget about breathing and relaxing. Go ahead and complete the full motion, as I demonstrated remembering to get your legs and hip into the swing. Try to get as close as you can to the 250-yard marker."

Robot 19 did exactly as Morgan had instructed and all five of them watched the ball fly over all of the distance markers and roll into the woods. Morgan exclaimed, "That's a perfect golf swing Robot 19. The ball must have traveled 450 yards in the air."

Robot 19 high-fived Morgan and said, "According to the distance meter in my eye, the ball went 476.7 yards in the air and rolled 60 yards up hill into the trees."

"That's good enough for me," Morgan said. "Not bad for your first drive! Now, tee up some balls with your buddy Robot 37 and hit a few balls while I say hello to my friends."

Morgan walked over to Catherine and her father. Catherine smiled, "Morgan, I came over here to tell you about robots that showed up in my class today, but I see you've already met a couple. PAYING customers, are they?"

"I haven't brought that up yet," Morgan answered. "I met two other robots the other day over at Ray's house. They were confiscating his guns—wasn't pretty!"

"Did they come to your house, too?" she asked.

"No, they didn't," he answered.

"Then you still have the guns that Ray gave you?"

"I do."

"If they come, will you give them the guns?"

"There's no getting around it—I'll hand them over without a peep."

Catherine's father looked at Morgan and asked, "What are you going to do if some hoodlums come up here and want to take what you have or want to rape your daughters?"

"Judge," Morgan responded, "that's a tough question."

"It is, it is, but it's a question that you need to have answered before it happens."

"Since we're talking about my daughters, I'd like you to come up to the GREEN HOUSE and meet Raquel and Heather, as well as my mother and son," Morgan said and paused for an awkward second, then continued, "and my girlfriend, and future wife, Christy."

As soon as Morgan finished his invitation, he looked at Catherine who was expressionless. Then she said, "You had to make a choice, Morgan, and I'm okay with the choice you made. I'm grateful that Christy gave you permission to have me as a friend."

Morgan looked at Catherine's father first, then her, "I'm feeling embarrassed."

Her father said right away, "Please don't feel embarrassed on my account. Catherine can handle it."

Catherine drove behind Morgan as they went up the mountain to the GREEN HOUSE and found everyone on the ground floor. Lights were on thanks to solar batteries. Morgan introduced Catherine's father to everyone and then took him on a tour of the house starting with the garden in the middle of the ground floor. Christy had designed and planted it, so when she saw that the judge could name every plant, she instantly liked him and took over the tour.

Later, as Christy was leading Catherine and her father back down the stairs from the third floor, she looked over the railing at the living area below and saw Heather bent over in the kitchen groaning with pain, which made her step more quickly down the stairs, leaving Catherine and her father behind. Morgan's mother was next to Heather looking up. Christy looked across the living area at Morgan, Matt, and her son Michael. Once she made eye contact with Morgan, she pointed to Heather, which made Morgan look across the room just in time to see Heather crumple to the floor.

Christy looked at Heather and the water on the floor. "She's early, Morgan. How do we reach the midwife?"

Morgan replied, "There's no way to do that now," and looked at his mother. "Do you know what to do, Mom?"

"This is weeks early, son, I don't know."

Morgan looked at Christy who shrugged her shoulders. "I was out of it when Michael dropped through. I don't know either." After the judge and Catherine made eye contact, Catherine stepped forward and said, "One of my first volunteer jobs was in a prison for women, so I have some experience along these lines. Get a bunch of towels, a couple of blankets, the biggest bowl you can find, a basket, a lamp, scissors and a stool."

Everyone took off searching for the items Catherine had listed and brought them back to her. An hour and twenty-seven minutes later, a baby girl was born and lay asleep bundled in a soft cotton blanket bathed in warm incandescent light. In the bed next to the crib that Ray had made was Heather who was also asleep. Above the headboard of the crib was a sign that said: *Welcome to the world!*

$$\Omega$$

The following morning Catherine fixed her father breakfast at her house, and headed for Richmond to get Bob. When she got to her house in Richmond she found the front door open, so she entered the house cautiously and scared. She listened for any kind of noise—footsteps, squeaking floorboards, whispering—but she didn't hear anything. She then went to the curtains and opened them. Romulus was standing there and jumped up on the glass when he saw Catherine and started barking. Catherine then went to the den and that's where she found Bob on the floor. Blood was coming out of fresh lacerations on his face. She put her ear next to Bob's mouth and determined that he was breathing. She stood up and looked throughout the house for the guns she had given him but didn't find them. When she returned to Bob, she saw a paper bag containing clothes and toiletry items leaning against a wall and picked them up. Thank God he's alive, she thought, then found herself confused as to what to do. The cellphone that she was still carrying was useless. She went outside and looked for people, neighbors, anyone but saw no one. When she started walking down the sidewalk, her fear increased and reached a level that made her reverse course. Instead of walking back to her house, she ran and when she entered the den, she found Bob's eyes open.

She went to a bathroom and got a washcloth and then walked into the kitchen where she got a bowl and filled it with warm water. The blood on his face had not dried, so it was easy to remove it. It was not so easy to get it out of his hair. After cleaning his wounds, Catherine walked him to her car, reclined the passenger seat halfway and lowered him into the seat. Then she went back in her house and got Romulus. Within an hour, she was pulling into the driveway at her father's house, and he appeared next to her car almost immediately. He peered through the car window at Bob, then looked at Catherine who was standing next to him. "You got him out of Richmond none too soon, sweetheart."

Catherine looked at her father with a guilty expression on her face and said, "I couldn't find your guns. I'm sorry."

Her father shook his head and said, "That's not a great loss. Don't worry about that. I see a dog in the back of your car."

"Yes, Dad, that's *Romulus.*"

Ω

When students walked across the campus to Catherine's classroom the next day, it was chilly, so they were wearing sweaters, jackets, and shoes, no flip flops. Catherine asked them to get their homework out and pointed to the words on the whiteboard—*After landing in 1607, English settlers…*

"All right," Catherine said, "what did the settlers do THEN and OVER THE YEARS THAT FOLLOWED? Start your answer with a verb, please." As the students provided answers, she wrote them on the board:

1. built a fort
2. scavenged for food
3. established rules
4. explored the area
5. made tools
6. started hunting and fishing
7. met native people
8. learned how to farm
9. got sick
10. died
11. gave birth

After writing *gave birth* on the board, Catherine told them that women weren't on the ships that landed in 1607, but some women started coming over as early as 1608 or 1609, so childbearing didn't happen right away. She admitted that she didn't know when the first child was born in Jamestown. Once she made that point, Catherine gestured that the students could continue providing things that the settlers did after disembarking and over the years that followed that made their lives and the Jamestown Settlement better:

1. established an apothecary
2. learned how to settle disputes
3. established a place to worship
4. started making glass objects
5. started making pottery
6. started plowing fields
7. introduced farm animals
8. provided medical care

9. started educating children
10. made paths and roads
11. made canoes
12. established work groups
13. started punishing people for bad behavior
14. elected a leader
15. started raising animals for consumption
16. formed firefighting groups/teams
17. brought in veterinarians
18. brought in medical people
19. started bartering and using money

After writing *bartering and using money* on the board, Catherine put her hand up and said, "We'll stop there for now, but we could probably think of many more things that could be added to the list. But let me point out that number 25—elected a leader—wasn't something that the settlers did. This was a BUSINESS venture—underwritten by investors in the Virginia Company and the leader was Captain John Smith who had six or seven officially appointed advisors—we might call them BOARD MEMBERS today. Elected leaders and representative government came much later—review the list for a moment."

A male student raised his hand, and said, "You said women started coming over in 1608, and I don't see anything on our list about SEX." His comment brought laughter from the other students and from Catherine. The student added—"shouldn't we find a place on our list for—*had sex?*"

"Yes, for sure" Catherine replied. "We'll make that number 31."

Once the students had stopped laughing and reviewed the list, Catherine walked over to the flipchart and flipped over the top sheet exposing a drawing of Maslow's Hierarchy of Needs that she had created earlier. "I'm sure all of you are familiar with *Maslow's Hierarchy of Needs* either from high school, here at the university, or on your own. They are, starting at the bottom of the pyramid, physical, safety, love/belonging, esteem, and self-actualization. Let's identify each level with a number 1 to 5 beginning at the bottom. So physical would be 1, safety would be 2, and so forth. Now, look at the list we just created. Starting with *BUILT A FORT*—what number would you give it? What kind of NEED was that fulfilling?"

Some students said ONE, and others said TWO.

"Physical," Catherine responded, "or Safety—which one is more accurate?"

The students looked around and agreed that Safety was more accurate.

"Let's identify all of the items on the list," Catherine said. "Number 2—scavenged for food?"

The students said ONE—Physical.

"Number 3—established rules?" Catherine called out, and the students said—ONE—Physical. Catherine replied, "Interesting,"

"Number 4—explored the area?"

Some students said TWO—Safety—and others said ONE—Physical.

Catherine continued down the list and the students called out the NEED, and once the students had identified the first thirty items, Catherine asked, "What's your observation?"

The students didn't say anything that surprised Catherine. "Come on," Catherine said. "You're top students—what observations do you have?"

One student replied, "We didn't do item 31?"

Catherine turned to face the board and remembered that they had added item 31: had sex—so she asked, "What NEED was *Had Sex* fulfilling?"

A student said—Physical.

Another student said—Safety.

When Catherine responded, "Why SAFETY?" the student replied, "The settlers were making sure that the settlement wouldn't die out—many of them were dying, getting killed, and some had probably hopped on boats and returned to England. Having SEX and HAVING BABIES was a SAFETY measure for settlement survival."

"Brilliant point!" Catherine said. "Is there another NEED that *Had Sex* was fulfilling?"

A female student replied, "Love/Belonging," and everyone agreed.

"Another?" Catherine asked, and a student replied—Esteem, and everyone agreed.

"Lastly," Catherine said, "did *Had Sex* fulfill the NEED for Self-actualization?"

The male student who had pointed out that *Had Sex* was not on the list raised his hand and said, "*Had Sex* is the realization of our NUMBER ONE and highest NEED—to GET LAID."

"Well, there you have it—THIRTY items on our list were fulfilling a Physical NEED or a Safety NEED. Item 31 *Had Sex* was fulfilling ALL FIVE NEEDS. Now, with all seriousness," Catherine asked, "What are your observations?"

A student raised her hand and Catherine gestured for her to speak. The student said, "the first thirty of those items were one or two and that's what we would expect, isn't it? A group of seventeenth century people spent four or five months crossing the Atlantic Ocean on three small ships and landed in an unknown world—the new world. First concerns would naturally be—Physical and Safety."

"Great observation," Catherine said. "Another observation?"

"The settlers must have known that their lives were going to change—drastically. They were brave. They knew they were going to have to provide two of the three necessities of life as soon as they stepped off the boat—food and shelter. They probably brought enough clothing. WE, on the other hand TODAY, aren't in the 1607 settlers' situation, we're in a WORSE SITUATION."

Catherine smiled and asked, "How so—why WORSE?"

The student replied, "All of us in this room up until recently have been living in a DIFFERENT WORLD—twenty-first century versus seventeenth century. BUT—because of our division of labor, specialization of jobs, and technological advancements in every arena, WE KNOW VERY LITTLE about how TO MAKE anything. We know how to OPERATE some things, but few of us are capable of MAKING the things we OPERATE and USE, which should make us wonder about our ADVANCED or DEVELOPED classification. Except for our planes, rockets, computers, weapons, satellites, and a long list of phoo—phoo things—how much more advanced are we, as individuals, when compared to the settlers that showed up here in 1607!?" The student paused, glanced around the room, and then continued. "Raise your hand if you can make a pot, a vase, a frying pan, a glass, a knife, a pair of shoes or boots, a saddle, a blanket, chair, telescope, microscope, calculator, radio, TV, a washing machine, dryer, telephone, computer?" No one raised a hand.

Another student raised his hand and started speaking when the other student had finished. "The English settlers came here with knowledge and skills appropriate for the mission they were on—to establish a settlement and make a new life in a new world filled with opportunities that they would never have had in their country. The PROMISE of those OPPORTUNITIES gave them the MOTIVATION and strength to face the CHALLENGES. WE, on the other hand, did not WILLINGLY get on the ship we're presently on—total collapse of advanced nations—and do not possess the skills and knowledge needed TO GET US BACK TO WHERE WE WERE. Instead of having a sense of PROMISE as the settlers had, as they hopped aboard one of the small ships, we have been THROWN ABOARD A SHIP GOING BACKWARDS and are experiencing a sense of LOSS and FORBODING."

Catherine clapped her hands and said, "Terrific observation. Well done!" Then she looked at her students and added with excitement, "Those feelings—sense of LOSS and FORBODING—can be transformed over time by EFFECTIVE LEADERSHIP and HARD WORK, which YOU and others will have the opportunity to provide." Catherine looked into the eyes of her nine students again. "Washington, Jefferson, Madison, Adams, and others stepped up when times demanded it, back in the day, and now it's time for you to step up every day to GET BACK TO THE FUTURE or to create a NEW FUTURE."

Catherine stopped talking as she walked to the board and stood next to the thirty-one things that the original settlers did and others that followed that made Jamestown the first permanent English settlement in the new world. "Like some of you today have said, right here where the American Dream started, we are having to START OVER. We have been thrown back in time, but we have a very distinct advantage over the people who came here in the seventeenth cen-

tury and every century since then—WE KNOW THE FUTURE—
we just have to find our way back to it." Catherine picked up the
marker resting on her desk and removed the cap. "Now, tell me the
TOP FIVE things we must do in this community to make life better?
Forget about rebuilding the United States of America. I called this
course *Rebooting America*, but it's really going to be about rebooting—Albemarle, Amherst, and Rockbridge counties. Let's narrow
things down—what are the FIVE MOST IMPORTANT things we
have to do?"

A student raised her hand and said, "Make sure we have the
essentials—food, water, clothing and shelter."

Another student replied, "We need to be able to communicate
quickly and over long distances—right now we're down to letter
writing and very slow delivery and smoke signals."

"How about basic laws and a system to enforce them?"

"Hospitals and doctors would be nice."

"Places to worship."

"Okay," Catherine said, raising her hand in front of her. "You
gave me more than five things, and all of them are very important.
Between now and our next class, decide as a group what the TOP
FIVE NEEDS are." Before she released her students, a member of
the administrative staff opened the door to Catherine's classroom
and walked in. He told them that people were looting stores in the
Historic District in downtown Charlottesville. The recommendation
was for students to go to their dorms or apartments and stay there.

Ω

Catherine walked to her house and was surprised to find her father
and Bob raking up leaves in her yard. Her father explained that Bob
had never been to Charlottesville and wanted to see the university
and where Catherine was living. After her father's explanation of why
they were there, she told them about the looting downtown. Without
saying anything her father took the rake that Bob was holding and
started walking and gesturing for both of them to follow him. He
placed the rakes they had been using in the storage shed and turned

to face his daughter. "I was thinking of getting my rifles out of my closet and hunkering down inside our house with the lights off," he said. "But heading for the hills might be a better idea. What do you think, Catherine?"

Catherine chose heading for the hills, and they decided to take both vehicles—his and hers—fearing that if they left one car behind, it would be stolen, striped, or burned. Her father looked at Bob and asked, "Who do you want to ride with—my daughter or me?"

"I think I'd like to hunker down right here and defend this house. Show me your guns!" Bob replied.

Once they got on Route 29, Catherine took the lead and merged into traffic. There were many cars and trucks on the road. Residents of Charlottesville and surrounding areas had the same idea—get out of town. The looters, unfortunately, had anticipated what residents might do and had stationed themselves along the highway to stop traffic and search them for things of value. After the judge saw what was going on, he passed Catherine and took the lead, and she drafted right behind him. There were places on the highway where the road had been completely blocked by barricades and piles of junk, but because vehicles had run over and through them there were gaps that made it easier and safer to get through at a high rate of speed. If vehicles had to slow way down or stop, looters jumped out and took over the vehicles stripping them of everything that might have value. The judge and Catherine were successful driving through all of the blockades that popped up every mile or two, but eventually, someone alongside the road shot and hit one of the tires on the judge's car which made him spin out, hit other cars, and land in a deep ditch. Catherine saw her father's car fall into the ditch and turned around. When she got back to his car, a mob had already surrounded it. Catherine ran through the crowd and saw her father was still behind the wheel. She ran down the embankment to the car but could not open the door and the car window was up. He was trapped inside and not moving. She turned and saw a man behind her, "Give me that gun!" she shouted, but didn't wait for him to comply. She grabbed the rifle and hit the window with the butt repeatedly. When there was an opening large enough to put her head and shoulders through, she leaned in and saw blood coming out of his nose, mouth and ears. She put two fingers on his neck just under his chin and found a pulse.

She pushed herself back out of her father's car and drove the butt of the rifle into the man's belly who was still standing behind her and told him to get her father's body out of his car and into hers. As soon as she got those words out of her mouth, she recognized the man's face. He was one of the five hundred ninety-eight prisoners she had just released from prison. "Oh no, I can't believe you're here doing this, Nate!?"

"I'm sorry, Warden!" he replied.

Catherine pointed the muzzle of the rifle at the group of people gathered behind Nate. "Tell them to get my father out of the car—carefully—and carry him face up and fully supported to my car. I'll open the back doors and drop the seat backs. There should be room for him to lie perfectly flat."

Nate and six others went down into the ditch and pulled the driver door open and started removing her father from his car. Catherine got to her car where she dropped the rifle on the ground so she could raise the hatch, but as soon as the rifle hit the ground, a man grabbed it and pointed it at her. "This is MY GUN, now," the man shouted. Catherine looked over at Nate.

"It's your gun, now," Nate shouted at the man. "But point it somewhere else. That woman is a friend of mine!"

After her father had been placed face up on the floor of the Subaru Outback, Catherine got into her car and pulled the door shut. She looked at Nate as she lowered the window. Nate bent forward and said, "You saw the blood coming out of his ears and nose. Where are you going to take him?"

"I don't know, " she replied.

"I know someone who might be able to help him, Warden. Do you want me to take you there?"

"Yes," she answered. "Get in."

Ω

Nate had Catherine drive west on 29 for a couple of miles and then he had her follow smaller roads up to Wintergreen where, he had heard, a family physician was still seeing people. What he had heard was true.

Once Catherine explained what had happened, the doctor rolled out a gurney and the three of them gently pulled her unconscious father carefully out of the car and wheeled him into an exam room in his building.

The first thing the doctor did was push the eyelids open on the judge's right eye and shine a narrow column of light directly on the eyeball. "Okay," he said quietly. Immediately, after his quiet okay, he pricked her father's left index finger and the finger quivered. At that point, the doctor looked at Catherine and Nate. "The pupillary response to the light and the response to pain are two good signs. I think he is suffering from a concussion. With your permission, I'm going to give him some medication that will lower his blood pressure, optimize the delivery of oxygen to his brain, and lower the chances of his brain swelling. After that we will wait and see. I don't think he's in a coma, but that would be worst case."

"Thank you, Doctor." Catherine said. "What should we do now?"

"You may wait here, if you wish, or you can leave and come back in an hour or two."

Catherine turned to Nate. "I've got to get you back to where you were, right?"

Nate nodded in agreement, so they left and wound their way back to 29 and headed toward Charlottesville. Catherine broke the silence saying, "Why, Nate?"

Nate thought for a few seconds before replying, "Desperation, Warden. I was afraid I'd run out of money!?"

"I can understand how you might have been feeling DESPERATE, but why would you be willing to HARM other people?"

"That's a good question, but have you ever been DESPERATE?" Nate replied.

"My honest answer is NO, so maybe I just don't understand BEING DESPERATE?"

"Warden, I'm thinking that just an hour ago you WERE DESPERATE, and you grabbed a rifle out of my hands, so you could get your father out of that car. WHAT ELSE would you have done to save your father?"

Catherine looked out her window as she considered Nate's question. "I might have SHOT someone. I might HAVE KILLED SOMEONE, depending—"

"Warden, I'm not excusing myself from being out there today. I'm probably NOT MUCH BETTER today than I was before I went to prison."

"You think you learned nothing in prison that made you a better person?"

"I learned some good stuff, I guess, Warden, but getting out the way we did—and what we found—a world without laws—made it easy for me and everybody around me to revert to past behavior."

"I'm going to get off of THIS in a minute, Nate," Catherine said, "but I really want to understand why YOU and OTHERS are willing to HARM other people, especially when those other people haven't harmed you?"

Nate remained silent for minutes, because he too wanted to know the answer. Then he replied, "Thinking about this now, as I ride safely down this road with you, I can see that I didn't have to resort to doing what you saw me doing. I still had money...watching other people looting, stealing, hurting people, destroying property sucked me in, and once I was sucked in, it was easy to do that stuff and keep doing it, because, to be honest, IT FELT GOOD."

"I believe I understand better, now, how FEELING DESPERATE can make us do things that we ordinarily wouldn't do, and I can see how that makes room for FORGIVENESS and MERCY. I also heard you say that looting, stealing, destroying property and even hurting people, once you were doing it, made you FEEL GOOD, and I'll have to think about that some more."

They rode in silence until Nate saw her father's car still resting nose down in the ditch. He said, "You can let me out right here, Warden."

Catherine pulled over and stopped on the shoulder of the road. "What now, Nate, where do you go? Do you have a place to sleep?"

"Yes, I have a place to sleep," he answered.

"I can give you more money—would that help?" Catherine said, and then added—"Don't answer that, Nate. That's a stupid question!"

"This is embarrassing," Nate replied.

Catherine replied, "You're feeling EMBARRASSED and I'm beginning to feel ASHAMED, as I anticipate leaving you on the side of this road. I can't in good conscience put you back into THAT WORLD I saw you in earlier today. WE'RE going back to the doctor's office and get my father. From there we'll head back to my house in Charlottesville, and you can stay there for a while. My father is going to need some help during his recovery. You'll help me with that, won't you?"

Nate noticed that an amber light on Catherine's gas gauge was glowing. "You need to get some gas if you want to get back to Wintergreen, and there's nothing close by. Drive over there and stop next to your father's car."

Catherine drove across the road. Nate looked inside the judge's car and saw that the keys were still in the ignition. He turned the key and the lights on the dashboard came on, and the needle on the gas gauge began to rise. "There's gas in the tank." He looked at Catherine, "Do you have any kind of container in your car?"

"No, but there should be an empty gas container in my father's trunk."

Nate opened the trunk of her father's car, reached in, and held up three things.

Catherine smiled and said, "Yep, that's MY DAD! Gas container, hose, and funnel."

Nate siphoned the gasoline out of her father's car and poured it into Catherine's tank and headed for Wintergreen where they found her father sitting up fully conscious in the doctor's office.

Catherine thanked the doctor and asked how much she owed him. The doctor pointed to the jar sitting on the reception desk and said, "Whatever you can afford to pay will be fine and appreciated. Glad I could help your father."

Ω

When Morgan closed up the main building at the Golf Academy, he rode down the road on his bicycle and stopped at the convenience store to get the latest news and gossip from Molly. There was one big news item—ROBOTS ESTABLISH BASE IN LOVEVILLE—that sent Morgan out of the store and down the road where he found the robot encampment. There were lots of tents, small, medium, and large, inside a high metal fence—two empty helipads Morgan guessed and three metal buildings—one large and two smaller ones.

Morgan pedaled down to the main gate and stopped. A robot walked over and asked if he could help him. Morgan replied, pointing around the encampment, "Last week, I was around here and none of this was here!?"

The robot smiled and replied, "Yes, you're right. We work fast compared to human beings."

Morgan looked at the robot's right earlobe and saw its ID number and asked, "Robot 41, what's the large metal building for?"

Robot 41 replied, "It's for holding human beings we apprehend for unacceptable behavior."

Morgan chuckled, "Well, I've heard that some human beings have ROBBED some businesses just up the road. Do you call that UNACCEPTABLE BEHAVIOR?"

"Yes, of course," Robot 41 replied. "At the moment we have our two helicopters and robot squads out searching for MISCREANT HUMAN BEINGS who are believed to be between here and Charlottesville."

"What were they doing?" Morgan asked.

"Stopping vehicles, assaulting people, stealing," the robot replied.

"Once you find the MISCREANT HUMAN BEINGS, will you bring them back here and put them in that building?"

"Yes."

"Then what?" Morgan asked.

Robot 41 didn't respond to Morgan's question immediately, because another robot had arrived and was standing at Morgan's side. Robot 41 said to Robot 19, "This human being is asking a lot of questions."

Robot 19 replied, "I know him, Robot 41."

When Morgan heard the robot say that it knew him, Morgan looked at its right earlobe and saw the number 19, which made Morgan and the robot smile. "Hi, Robot 19," Morgan said.

Robot 19 said hello to Morgan and then turned its attention to Robot 41. "This human being is called Morgan, and he is teaching me and Robot 37 how to hit golf balls."

Receiving that information made Robot 41 smile and say, "Nice to meet you."

Morgan replied, "It's nice to meet you."

Robot 41 looked at Morgan and said, "I will answer all of your questions. What more do you want to know?"

Morgan asked Robot 19 when he wanted to have another golf lesson, and Robot 19 replied, "We robots know that golf professionals like yourself have to MAKE A LIVING, so what do you charge for a lesson?"

Morgan was stumped for an immediate answer. He was wondering if robots were paid and, if they were paid, what was it—coins, paper, or what? And what difference would it make to him? If they paid him in their currency, what would he do with it? Morgan replied, "NO CHARGE for you robots."

Robot 19 replied, "Thank you, we do not have any money, but perhaps we can do favors for you for your kindness? I have to go now. Bye, Morgan."

After Robot 19 walked away, Morgan looked at Robot 41 and asked, "When you apprehend human beings who are misbehaving, you will put them in that largest building. Then what?"

Then we will take them over to the next building and determine what CHEMICAL IMBALANCES are present in each one of them."

"CHEMICAL IMBALANCES?" Morgan said, perplexed.

"If CERTAIN CHEMICAL IMBALANCES are present in human beings they will exhibit unacceptable behavior. So once we determine what the imbalances are, we can correct them."

What happens next?"

"We put them through TRIALS—SIMULATIONS to see if the corrected imbalances result in acceptable behavior."

"If they PASS, you release them?"

"That's correct," Robot 41 replied. "They get a second chance to live with human beings who behave."

"Suppose they don't PASS the test?" Morgan asked.

Robot 41 replied, "In our country we take them to a special place up north where they live with other human beings who FAILED—NO MORE CHANCES—because it isn't fair to other human beings who BEHAVE and CONTRIBUTE to the well-being of our communities and our country."

"That's remarkable—you take them to a SPECIAL PLACE?" Morgan asked.

Robot 41 looked at Morgan, and said, "Our procedures rarely fail. It's ALL CHEMICAL with human beings, not so with robots. No chemical imbalances with US, because there are no chemicals involved with robots—it's alignment of particles—that's what we have to look for in robots that GO OFF THE TRACKS—ALIGNMENT OF PARTICLES."

Ω

When Catherine, Nate, and her father got back to Charlottesville, they saw fires burning in the downtown Historic District, and when they arrived at her house, they saw university buildings aflame, and no one was there to extinguish the fires. When they got out of her car, Catherine told her father that she was going over to her classroom building to see if it had been set on fire. Her father told Nate to go with her, and her father went inside her house to check on Bob.

The next day, when Catherine walked to her undamaged classroom building, she was thinking that her students might not show up, so she was greatly relieved when they filed in, but she quickly found out they were not interested in talking about settlers in Jamestown in 1607. They wanted to talk about what they saw in the streets and on campus. It didn't make sense to them. The United States of America and other advanced nations had just collapsed sending everything that had been developed over centuries into free fall, and here they were on the university campus watching people destroy buildings on campus and in town—*things were hard enough*, the students were thinking, *why were people making things worse?*

About midway through the class, there was a knock on the door. Catherine turned and waited for someone to open it, but the door remained closed. When she shouted for them to come in, the door opened and the five robots that had previously attended her class were standing there. Catherine waved them in and asked them to take a seat. After they were seated, Catherine said, "My students just told me about the HEROIC ACTIONS of robots yesterday."

"Thank you, Teacher," Robot 61 replied. "We were able to stop some human beings from starting fires, but we had no equipment to put out fires once they were started. Perhaps we can learn how to use your firefighting resources and be of more help in the future. So sorry, and by the way, we don't use the word HERO to describe robots or HEROIC to describe robot ACTIONS. Robots just use the knowledge and skills they were programmed to have by the RobotMakers. One robot performs with no variation from any other robot—consequently, we have no use for the words—HERO or HEROIC—except when we interact with HUMAN BEINGS whose performance metrics vary significantly."

Catherine replied, "Thank you for your explanation Robot 61, and thank you again for doing what you could yesterday. What have you done with the looters and rioters you captured?"

"They have been confined and will be examined and treated for their UNACCEPTABLE BEHAVIOR, which is caused by CHEMICAL IMBALANCES."

Catherine replied, "That sounds interesting. I'd like to know more about that, but not now. Why are you here today?"

"We want to know more about Rebooting America," Robot 61 replied.

Catherine responded, "Since giving my course that title, I have decided that it is way too ambitious. I think we'll be focusing on what we can do in our towns and counties to restore order and a healthy lifestyle. Rebooting AMERICA is too great a task."

"Agreed," Robot 61 said. "The LESS AMBITIOUS the BETTER. The original title might have led you into attempting to RESURRECT OR CREATE A NEW GOVERNMENT, which you have been cautioned about—remember?"

Catherine cocked her head as she thought back to one of the first messages that appeared on a TV screen. "Yes, I remember that, but the course description of my class did not mention anything about GOVERNMENT."

Robot 61 replied, "WORDS can be used to REVEAL the TRUTH, DISGUISE the TRUTH, HIDE the TRUTH and OBFUSCATE the TRUTH, Teacher."

The students were very quiet. They were beginning to squirm in their seats. One student looked at the robots and wanted some clarification. "Are you saying that we shouldn't start thinking about creating another government and nation?"

Robot 62 replied. "We are here to help you START OVER but on a small scale. The RobotMakers believe that RESURRECTING your state and federal governments before establishing healthy, caring communities would lead your nation right back to where it was before THE COLLAPSE—INSANE BEHAVIOR THAT WAS LEADING TO THE EXTINCTION OF LIFE ON THIS PLANET. In fact, the RobotMakers believe—but are holding back final judgment—that HUMAN BEINGS may not be innately capable of SELF-GOVERNANCE, and a cursory review of a world history textbook sold in your university book store lends credence to the RobotMakers assessment."

The same student replied, "So, you robots, are really in this class to see if we might be thinking about doing what the RobotMakers have told us not to do, is that right?"

"Actually, Student, we are here to listen to the EXPRESSION and DISCUSSION of your thoughts and offer comments that might prove helpful."

"Are you here to SNITCH?" Another student asked.

Robot 63 replied. "Your Jamestown settlers might have known and used that word—SNITCH—and it did then and still does carry a pejorative connotation. TO SNITCH is to INFORM ON

SOMEONE with some amount of DECEIT—misrepresentation of the truth. So my answer to your question is NO, we are not here to SNITCH. Part of our job when we are sent on missions is to make accurate reports. Our ALLEGIANCE is not to THEM—the RobotMakers—or you, our ALLEGIANCE is to the TRUTH, which the RobotMakers believe leads, ultimately, to the BEST OUTCOMES and the best of all outcomes is FAIRNESS and PEACE."

Catherine had taken a seat while Robot 63 was speaking but now stood up and looked around the room at students and robots. "Hurray, for us. That was a very interesting exchange, but I think we should stop with that last thought. I want to push on right now to what we were discussing in our last class—what are the FIVE most important NEEDS that we must fulfill by ourselves and for ourselves right here in this county to improve our lives?" Catherine walked to the board and asked, "What are they?"

One student cleared her throat and said, "The other students wanted me to announce what we think are our FIVE most important NEEDS. They are:

1. Reliable food supply
2. Safe environment
3. Adequate medical/health care
4. Faster way to communicate
5. Schools to educate children"

Catherine looked at the list. "You selected RELIABLE FOOD SUPPLY as the number one NEED. I agree with you one hundred percent. What steps do we have to take to fulfill that need? I'll write them on the board as you give them to me. You may discuss this among yourselves, get consensus, then give me your answer." The students provided the following:

1. Identify land for growing crops
2. Find people who are willing and able to grow crops
3. Acquire seeds

4. Plant, maintain, and harvest crops
5. Get crops to market and sell them

A student said, "It seems to me that we really need MONEY to purchase or lease land, MONEY to buy seeds, MONEY to pay people for their work, MONEY for people to use when purchasing anything—BARTERING JUST DOESN'T WORK WELL. Isn't MONEY a significant NEED?"

The students agreed that it was a significant need, so Catherine added it to the list as Number 6.

Catherine looked at the robots. "Any comments?"

One robot said, "We don't require food, but we understand why you made FOOD your number one NEED. The other four needs are significant and the order in which they are listed is okay."

During the remaining time in the class, it was established that most people in the county no longer had jobs, so they thought there would be a large labor force to help with farming—preparing the fields, planting seeds, watering and weeding, harvesting, and distributing produce to markets. They also talked about the availability of MEAT—chicken, beef, pork, fish, and all the work that would entail. As they discussed these things, the students realized they didn't know much about farming or raising animals and turning them into food. Before the collapse, the students agreed that they knew where meat came from—GROCERY STORES and FAST FOOD places.

The more they talked, the more they started to see what a challenge it was going to be to fulfill the BASIC NEEDS of people residing in Albemarle and surrounding counties. What people were facing there and all over the country was going from life in the twenty-first century to life in the seventeenth century in a nanosecond. Most of the knowledge and skills needed after the collapse were absent in the population. The division of labor and specialization that had evolved over centuries left people ill equipped to take care of basic needs by their own efforts. A significant feature and benefit of living in an advanced nation was DEPENDENCY on other people, but after the collapse, DEPENDENCY was no longer a benefit. Being SELF-RELIANT was. The big farms of the twenty-first century were no longer possible. Even the smaller farms that operated in and around Charlottesville were not able to function, because they too used advanced technology. The petroleum-powered farm equipment couldn't be employed because fuel was not available or too expensive. Simple traditional equipment like shovels, hoes, hand ploughs, and rakes were not easy to find either.

Before class was over, Catherine's students were wondering why they were spending money and time in classes at the university that weren't going to help them make their way in the NOW. Classes in computer science, history, psychology, chemistry, biology, business management, accounting, et cetera were just about worthless. Crops that had been planted in the spring were now lying dead in the fields. Even if they knew something about farming, it wasn't the right season to be planting things. Cows, pigs, chickens, goats, and horses were still in the area but in short supply, because many of them had already been slaughtered and eaten. Milk was no longer available. Drinking water had become a problem because the water flowing in nearby rivers was becoming contaminated. People with wells were okay, but people who WANTED wells were out of luck. No one knew how to drill them.

$$\Omega$$

A week after the second wave of looting and rioting in Charlottesville, they showed up again in greater numbers. This time they went over to the university's campus and started fires inside the Rotunda and the library. They also raided the university hospital looking for drugs. For the first time, the looters went outside the city limits looking for anything of value or just anything of significance that they could destroy. Watching things burn gave them pleasure. Nate had admitted it to Catherine—destroying things made him feel good.

Just by accident, one mob found Monticello. It was closed and locked up, but that didn't prevent the mob participants from crashing through the entrance doors. Once inside, they demolished every piece of furniture, slashed every painting, not even the expeditionary items that Lewis and Clark presented to Thomas Jefferson were spared. When they were finished breaking and smashing, they set fires throughout the building, reducing all of its contents to ashes. Tragically, no one showed up to stop the destruction—not even robots. It was determined later that the robots were working in other counties and only saw the new destruction in Charlottesville after it was too late to do anything about it. The robots realized that their own invincibility wasn't enough to provide protection to property and peace-loving people. They were beginning to have doubts about the strategic value of confiscating guns from people at large and reported their concerns to headquarters in Newfoundland. It was clear that they had taken guns out of the hands of people who would use them for illicit purposes, but they had also taken guns from people who would have prevented the destruction of property and the harming of innocent people. Hardly anything had gone as planned. Even the rioters and looters who had been captured and treated for chemical imbalances were not responding to treatment as anticipated.

Shortly after the robots submitted their After Action Report, they received the following PRIORITY MESSAGE:

FIELD ORDER TO ROBOT TEAM 64

1. CONTINUE capturing and retaining human beings who demonstrate a lack of regard for community assets, human beings, and life forms. If the miscreant human beings have weapons, confiscate them.

2. DISCONTINUE examinations, corrective procedures, and confiscation of weapons in the general population.

ATTACHMENT: Schedule of Bi-weekly Extraction of Miscreant Human Beings

Epilogue

The RobotMakers had thought that bringing down the United States of America would have a domino effect on all other advanced nations, which would result in the elimination of wars, atmospheric and oceanic pollution, deforestation and egocentric disregard for other forms of life on our bountiful home—Mother Earth—and redirect the energies of human beings away from the pursuit of power and wealth, uniting all people in the building of a new and more perfect world. The PREEMPTORY ACTIONS that the RobotMakers took did immediately stop the wars, the polluting, and the deforestation; but it didn't improve the HUMAN CONDITION ON EARTH. Their actions resulted unintentionally in GREATER SUFFERING because POVERTY, HUNGER, and DISEASE increased in every nation.

Wanting to make up for the unfortunate outcomes experienced across the North American Continent and around the world, the RobotMakers ordered all robot teams to remain in place, so they and human beings could work synergistically to rebuild communities. It was the right thing to do, the spokesperson for the RobotMakers conceded. They had not lived up to their own axiom: DO NO HARM.

CPSIA information can be obtained
at www.ICGtesting.com
Printed in the USA
BVOW03s2155120717
489208BV00001B/29/P